Praise for *Hemlock Hollow*

"In this sophisticated and nuanced narrative, past and present collide to shed light on a century-old murder. With its evocative sense of place and carefully-timed revelations, reading *Hemlock Hollow* feels akin to opening a treasure chest. Highly recommended for fans of historical mysteries."

-Heather Bell Adams, author of *Maranatha Road* and *The Good Luck Stone*

"Past and present, love and loss intertwine in a magical mountain hollow. Holderfield's love of place shines in his sensitive descriptions while his story-telling enthralls the reader."

—Vicki Lane, author of *And the Crows Took Their Eyes*

"In Culley Holderfield's *Hemlock Hollow*, Caroline McAlister ponders the journal of Carson Quinn, translating what she reads, ever wanting to understand. Her haunts prompt us to remember our own heritages. A former college teacher, Caroline McAlister praises personal history, finally wearing it like a charm, researching and recalling characters she cannot let go."

—Shelby Stephenson, poet laureate of North Carolina from 2015-2018, member of the Society of Distinguished Alumni, Department of English, University of Wisconsin-Madison, author of *More and Shelby's Lady: The Hog Poems*

HEMLOCK HOLLOW

Culley Holderfield

Regal House Publishing

Published by
Regal House Publishing, LLC
Raleigh, NC 27587
All rights reserved

ISBN -13 (paperback): 9781646032860
ISBN -13 (epub): 9781646032877
Library of Congress Control Number: 2021949153

All efforts were made to determine the copyright holders and obtain their
permissions in any circumstance where copyrighted material was used.
The publisher apologizes if any errors were made during this process, or
if any omissions occurred. If noted, please contact the publisher and all
efforts will be made to incorporate permissions in future editions.

Cover images © by Natwick/Shutterstock
Cover design by C.B. Royal

Regal House Publishing, LLC
https://regalhousepublishing.com

The following is a work of fiction created by the author. All names,
individuals, characters, places, items, brands, events, etc. were either the
product of the author or were used fictitiously. Any name, place, event,
person, brand, or item, current or past, is entirely coincidental.

Printed in the United States of America

To Mom and Dad,
without whom there would be no Hemlock Hollow.

He remembered when they built the cabin. Oxen from three farms towed in hewn chestnut. Groups of four men heaved each log into place. Young boys mixed the mortar to chink the gaps, and the nimblest went atop to tamp down the tin roof. He'd been there the entire time, was there still years later, watching the cabin give way to the mountain.

Years after it was built, a young girl came round with her family. She scampered among the boulders and trees like a wild-born creature. She reminded him of the first girl, and something long since froze up inside of him thawed. He once tried to reach out to her. It's one thing for folks to be afraid of you. It's altogether another to not be believed in. That smarts for the dead and the living alike.

Time ain't nothing to the dead. But it's everything to a structure made by hand. Folks came and went, some that weren't supposed to be there, some that were. He'd watched the floorboards go soft and the windows crack and the shiny tin roof rust clean through. Were he able to wield a hammer and saw, he would sister the decayed girder and shim up the cantered stair and seal the leak in the loft. He can't though. All he can do is wait for the day when she will return, and he knows she will. A love like that can't be gotten rid of.

1

The box wasn't much to look at. Old and metal, at one point it had probably been gray. Over the years it had oxidized green. There were three clasps on the front, now corroded with grit and rust. Micah and his crew had discovered it in the attic and had carted it through the old cabin to the card table we had set up out back. Decades of dirt and dust left a trail through the loft, down the stairs, and up the hill. More crumbled onto the tarp I had laid out.

My family had owned the cabin for my entire life, and I had never seen this box before. It had been sitting in an attic I didn't know existed, waiting to be found for who knows how long.

"What do you say, Caroline?" Micah asked, wiping his brow with a bandana. He tugged at his scraggily beard. "Should we open it?"

I pondered whether to toss the box and its mystery contents into the giant waste bin out front, or to open it and take the plunge into a dark past that I had spent a lifetime trying to escape.

Down the hill, Micah's crew continued with their demolition work, their sledgehammers echoing through the hollow. Up the mountain a crow cawed.

"Well?" Micah asked. "I can get a crowbar."

I sighed, my reluctance giving way to curiosity and compulsion. "If you get me a blowtorch and a flathead screwdriver, I can open this. I am an archaeologist, after all."

"That so?" His eyes widened. He took off his Wilco hat and ran a hand through his untamed hair. "Like Indiana Jones?"

Everyone's favorite archaeologist was in no way an archaeologist, but rather than lecture my general contractor, I shook my head. "No. More interpretive than old Indy. Less running from boulders and ghosts, more thinking about the ancient stars and writing about them."

"You best watch what you say. Opening that box may release the spirit of the hollow." He chuckled, winked, and plunged down the mountain to his old pickup truck.

I laughed at his joke, but that was exactly what I was afraid of.

The summer I turned twelve, Delores Appleton and Martha Boston, my two best friends at the time, had come up from Greensboro to spend the month of July at the cabin with me. We all shared a double bed upstairs. Oh, the late-night conversations we had! Even now in middle age, I blush at the suppositions we made about sex and boys and romance.

Late one night, Delores and Martha had dozed off. I knew this because Delores snored, and Martha had the deep breathing of the truly asleep. I woke having to use the bathroom. It was so dark that I couldn't tell if I had opened my eyes or not. I pushed down the covers and tuned my senses to the night. Outside, a breeze rustled the tall hemlocks. A spray of needles and tiny cones skittered down the tin roof. Katydids, so raucous in the early evening, had quieted to a low dirge. Everyone lay fast asleep—Mom and Dad in their bedroom on the main floor, Andrew, my brother, in his bedroom across from mine upstairs, the girls in the bed with me. The only bathroom was downstairs.

As I steeled myself to climb from the bed, the old stairs creaked as if someone were coming up. I swiveled my head to better listen. Another step squeaked. Higher this time. Closer. I waited, clenching my urgent bladder. The next step let out a long and drawn-out sigh, as if the climber had sunk a heavy foot slowly. My mind ran through the possibilities. It could be my father, climbing up to check on us. I waited for his balding head to emerge in the stairwell. Another step followed, this time barely perceptible. My heart pounded. A step creaked near the top of the stairs. Maybe it was my mother.

As if on cue, everything fell silent, even the katydids outside. The air stilled. All the hair on my body stood straight. A bone-deep chill chased the covers up my neck. I was overcome with the sense that somebody was in the room with us, somebody who wasn't family and who wasn't exactly alive.

The visage of a bearded, sorrowful man in a brown suit flashed through my mind like an afterimage. Anguish seized me. I had never felt anything like that before. A twelve-year-old should never feel such despair.

He was standing at the end of the bed. Though I didn't dare look, I knew he was there. I buried my face in my pillow. He moved beside me, his breath heavy in my ear.

I shuddered at the thirty-year-old memory. I wiped my sweaty palms on my jeans and returned my attention to the box. I hadn't worked with artifacts since grad school. These days I spent a lot of time looking at the stars from sites where ancient peoples had done the same thing. But I did remember a trick or two. I began chipping away at the crust of the thing. Soon Micah returned with the blowtorch and screwdriver and handed both to me.

I lit the blowtorch, which induced a broad grin. "Nice," he said, far too enthralled at my ability to work a tool.

I held the torch just close enough that the metal on the three clasps started to expand.

"You don't by chance have any liquid nitrogen, do you?" I asked.

He scrunched his eyes. "No."

I killed the torch. Without chemicals, I'd have to apply brute force. Using the screwdriver, I worked the clasps until they gave way. I slid the lid up, moving it bit by bit until it let go and popped open.

My heart jumped. Dozens of pairs of eyes caught the light of day. They searched the world from a scattering of old photos. Nestled among the photos was a journal. It was leather-bound, stained at the edges, but cinched tight.

Seeming to understand the importance of the moment, Micah left me alone with the past. I removed my work gloves and replaced them with a pair of latex gloves from my first-aid kit.

I picked up the journal and weighed it in my hands. Made of high-quality leather, it had a rawhide tassel that held its flaps shut in a protective hug. Despite the gloves and the heat, my hands were trembling. Whose fingers had last touched this journal? Who had tied this bowknot that I was now delicately undoing?

I separated the ends of the rawhide and opened the book. The first page bore a fine penciled drawing of a boulder-strewn creek surrounded by giant, perfectly rendered hemlocks. Looking back up the hollow, I knew it was a depiction of this very place. The second page was titled *The Journal of Carson J. Quinn*.

Carson Quinn. The name echoed across the chasm of time. All the way back from my childhood. Carson Quinn. I remembered. He was the murderer.

The Journal of Carson J. Quinn

January 3, 1886—Gramps gave me this journal for Christmas this winter, and I'm just now getting down to putting something in it. I'm not much for writing, so I was not quite sure what to do with it. It's right nice, practically waterproof. I imagine Mr. Charles Darwin had something similar on his voyage on the *Beagle*. He would need as much waterproofing as possible, what with all the storms and oceans and other perils. I'm only thirteen and must content myself to wanderings I can do on foot. One day I'll set out on some fantastical voyage to yon, like Mr. Darwin, and this journal might well accompany me.

Gramps has everything Mr. Darwin has ever written in his library. He has lots of other books as well. Being a lawyer and all, he has shelves of law books, like Blackstone's commentaries and such. He also has all the ancient classics like Plato, Aristotle, Cicero, and St. Augustine. Of these I have little interest. But I've read nearly all of his natural history collection: Andre & Francois Michaux's books on oaks, flora, and sylva of North America; Von Humboldt's *Travels to the New World*; William Bartram's *Travels*; the travel accounts of John Lawson, Thomas Harriot, and Mark Catesby; and all of the books he has by Thoreau and Emerson. One day I shall travel into the great Wilderness like these men. Until then, I shall content myself with what wild bounty exists around me here in Daisy.

Reading the words sent a shiver down my spine. My mind spun backward, back to the first time I heard about Carson Quinn decades ago. As a family, we had ventured one afternoon up the state road toward the Duncan homestead. The Duncans owned the prized bottomland up the cove. Saunter Branch cut past an old two-story clapboard house in the middle of a meadow. At some point, that house had been quite the residence. But by the eighties its tin roof was rusted, its walls were porous, and the paint had been scoured away by the elements. Where corn and tobacco fields had once surrounded the home, briars and milkweed grew. We approached the fence out front.

"Hello, the house?" Daddy called from the road, mimicking how locals would greet one another from afar. "Ed, you up there?"

Old Man Duncan never did much more than rock on his front porch. If you didn't announce yourself from a distance, you were likely to inspire his other favorite pastime of blasting away with the double-barreled shotgun that always accompanied him. "For the law, should it ever come..." he'd always explain.

"Hello, the road!" came the reply. "Dan, is that you?"

"Yes, sir," Dad said.

"Come on up. Let's have ourselves a visit," the old man said, delighted to have guests. "I just opened a jar of fifty-six."

The porch moaned with our weight. The old man with creased eyes and a wayward white beard motioned us to sit. Mom cleared off some rabbit hides from a bench to give us space. "Oh...you can set them aside somewhere," Old Man

Duncan said. He handed Daddy a Mason jar, then poured it full of a pungent clear liquid.

"Try it, Dan. It ain't gonna drink itself."

Daddy took a sip. His eyes got big. He coughed and shook his head like a dog that had gotten into a yellow jacket's nest. "Whew!" he finally said in a high-pitched voice I had never heard before.

Old Man Duncan lit into a fit of knee-slapping laughter at his response. He turned to Mom. "Madeleine, you care for any of my finest?" He held out the bottle.

"No, Ed," she said. "I think Daniel prefers me without hair on my chest."

That sent the old man into another laughing spell that wound slowly down into a spate of coughing. Aside from drinking and blasting away at the law, Ed Duncan's next favorite pastime was storytelling.

"Well, well," he said, squinting at me. "Little missy." He took a breath and cocked his head as if trying to remember something.

"Caroline," Andrew blurted out before I realized that Mr. Duncan was tripping over my name. I was as shy with people as I was confident in the woods, but Andrew had never met a stranger.

He loaded his gums with a wad of tobacco. "Yes, yes, yes. Little Miss Caroline with the purty name for a purty face. What can mean ole Ed Duncan do for a sweet thing such as yourself?"

Emboldened by his kindness, I asked, "Who lived in our cabin before us?"

He worked his tobacco for a bit, then commenced. "That cabin of yours was built for Marinda Quinn," he said. "She was a young widow at the time. The Quinns lived down by the hardtop in the Grayson place. 'Course, it weren't a hardtop then."

The Graysons' place was the nicest house around. It was a white, two-story wooden house nestled by a waterfall on Saunter Branch. Out behind the house once stood a grist mill. The only evidence that remained of the mill were two huge millstones that we used to climb on and around when my parents visited with the Graysons.

"Widow?" Mom asked.

"That's right," Mr. Duncan allowed. "Her husband was slain. She finished her years in the old yella house down on the hard-top."

"Slain as in murdered?" Mom asked, frowning.

"You know of another kind?" The old man spat a string of tobacco juice into a Folger's coffee tin at his feet. It rang like a struck bell.

"I guess not," Mom said.

Old Man Duncan continued. "She was the purtiest thing ever, even as she got up in years. I ain't ashamed to tell it to the world I was smitten. We all was. But boy was she trouble."

Mr. Duncan sat back in his chair and looked up at the mountainside. He started rocking in silence, his mind searching.

"Trouble?" Dad asked.

"There were two brothers, you see. Carson and Thomas Quinn. And both was in love with her. Thomas wound up a-marrying her. Had a daughter with her. Ten years later, he winds up shot dead."

"By Carson?" Mom asked.

"Officially…no. You see, Thomas was not well liked. The list of suspects could have been put together by the census taker, and it included some extremely violent men. None was ever charged due to lack of evidence. But everybody knew Carson did it. On account of Marinda."

My young mind was struggling to keep up with it all.

"Andrew," Daddy suddenly scolded. "Put that down."

I looked over, and Andrew was in a staring contest with some creature's skull. He had picked it up and held it at eye level.

"Son," Mom said. "That's not Yorick and you're not Hamlet. Sorry, Mr. Duncan."

"That's all right, young'un," he said, already starting to chuckle at the joke he was about to make. "That there cat done learned its lesson about curiosity. I reckon we all got to some-day."

"This is a cat?" Andrew asked, turning the skull in his hand.

"Was," the old man answered.

Andrew set the skull back down, wiping his hands on his jeans.

"Where was I?" Mr. Duncan continued. "Marinda. Marinda only lived in that cabin of yours for a year or so before they moved her down to the house by the road. After that, Carson Quinn hisself lived alone there for years. 'Bout as likable as a timber rattler, but smart as all dickens. He could tell you the names of everything: plants, animals, trees, rocks. In Latin even. He had been places, seen things. Knew all sorts of languages and customs from all over the world. The burdens he carried were heavy, and he never did cotton to the Lord, so I reckon he carries them still."

Daddy took another sip of his drink. This time he was care-ful, and it didn't cause him to spew or cough. "So, he wasn't churchgoing?"

"No sirree," the old man said. "It was one thing for him to be a likely murderer. That folks might understand. But the ru-mor was he was one of them there…what do you call a person don't believe in God?"

"An atheist?" Mom tripped slightly over the words. She was a devoted churchgoer, making us attend the local church, some-times even on vacation.

Ed Duncan nodded and spat disgustedly into the can.

"So, none of these Quinns were well liked," Dad surmised.

"I reckon Marinda was, but she were Quinn by marriage alone. All goes back to the war, I suppose."

"The Civil War?" Dad asked.

Old Man Duncan narrowed his gaze. "The War of North-ern Aggression."

"How so?" Dad asked.

"The Quinns were enemies of secession," he said, as if still affronted by an event that had transpired a century before.

"They fought for the Union..." Mr. Duncan trailed off into silence.

"My understanding is that that wasn't uncommon up here," Dad said. "There were Union counties around here."

I eyed that shotgun for fear that the old man was about to fire off the final two shots of the war. He worked a bit on his tobacco, took a long pull from his jug, and finally let out a distasteful "Reckon so."

I held Carson Quinn's journal in my hand, distant past and present slamming hard together. I didn't know what I thought would be in the box, but certainly not a murderer's journal. I laid it down and turned my attention to the other contents of the box.

There were the photos. Some appeared older than the cabin itself. They crumbled in my hands, so I spread them carefully onto a flattened-out newspaper. A somber family stared back. In one photo a dashing young man gazed confidently into the distance, his pressed soldier's uniform sporting a chest full of shiny medals. There was a similar photo, but much older, of a severe-looking man who appeared to be a Union soldier from the Civil War. He seemed as stern as a Sphinx.

One photo featured a large group of people. The bride and groom at the center suggested it was a wedding. The guests were spread out across the wide stone steps of a massive white house, bigger than any residence in Hickory Nut Gap. The somber brood gazed from behind the happy couple. Another photo showed what appeared to be four generations of a family sitting on a wide porch. Not a single one of them wore a smile. Their clothes were dark. The women had dresses that covered every inch of their bodies from ankle to chin. The men all wore suits and bolo ties with slicked-down hair and various stages of beards.

My heart jumped. There, in the back row, stood a scowling young man with a dark beard. I could feel his breath on my neck. He was calling from beyond the grave. That was him, the ghost. His eyes bore into my own. When I placed the picture aside, he alone from the group of people seemed to track me. My arms bristled with goose bumps. I covered the photo and looked away into the tops of the swaying hemlocks.

2

January 8, 1886—My family consists of my parents, William and Sheila Quinn; my older sister, Sarah Anne; my brothers, Thomas and Taylor;, and the aforementioned Gramps, Aurelius Quinn. Then there is myself, Carson J. Quinn, born on Saunter Branch in Henderson County, North Carolina in 1873. The children go like this: Sarah's the oldest at seventeen, then comes Thomas, who's fifteen, then me, age thirteen, then Taylor, who's eleven. I don't know how old Ma and Pa are, but Gramps is older than the hills and just as tough. He's old enough to have fought under General Taylor in the Mexican American War. After Santa Anna took his leg, he came home to practice law. Don't ever talk to Gramps about Texas; he says we'd a been better off letting the Mexicans have it. Everybody loves Gramps. He's a hero in these parts. Not for what he did in the war, but for all that he's done after.

Pa is just the opposite. Some folks downright revile him on account of the fact he wore blue instead of gray in the war. Some folks being primarily the Duncans. It doesn't bother me. My pa just knows how to pick a winner's all. It was in New York once the war was over that Pa met Ma. She was fresh off the boat from Dublin. New York was bad then, dirty and riotous with all the soldiers. Pa told her about the rolling Blue Ridge, and they married and she came home with him, thinking it would be like bonny ole Sligo. I guess it's enough like it, because she seems happy here.

Today, I went out to the stable and fed Henry the mule. Henry is older than Taylor, so he's seen cold winters before. I knew he mighty appreciated the oats I gave him, even though he didn't indicate as much. Pa runs a hominy mill out behind the house. He also has a forge where he does blacksmithing. He's the best smith in all of Hickory Nut Gap, and people come to him to make and mend all manner of things. We had a huge snowstorm with nearly a foot of snow a couple of days ago. The cold cracked the water wheel, so Pa made Thomas and me fix it. He doesn't let a little cold or a lot of snow stop progress. With him, everything's always got to be working perfectly or he's not content. We fixed it, and then I went on a walk up the cove. So as Pa wouldn't think I was wasting time, I carried the shotgun in case I saw any game. Pa would never hunt himself. He hasn't touched a gun of any sort since the war.

There's nothing like being out after a good snow. The world rests quiet and changed. It's like being alone in a church. I crunched through the snow up the mountain. In times past, there were all manner of creatures in these mountains: panthers, wolves, even bison and elk. At least, that's what the old folks say. Nowadays, bears and bobcats are about all that's left, and you have to go far afield to find them. Every once in a while, you'll see a deer, but not often. What I like about meandering about in the snow is you can really tell what creatures abound in these parts by their tracks.

Anyhow, as I ventured up the mountain, I kept a-glancing all about in the snow, looking for signs. Some folks, well most folks I reckon, are fine without the panthers and wolves. Me, I'd love to be the one to see a big ole paw print at the edge of Saunter Branch. I'd be like Darwin finding the *Megatherium*. Except the *Megatherium*, which is a giant prehistoric sloth, was extinct when he found its fossil. The panther and the wolf aren't extinct, not yet at least.

Today, nobody was out at the Saunters' Place as I passed by. Smoke curled out of the chimney, but I heard no noises within. Then I passed by the Duncans' clapboard house as quickly as possible. Old Isaac Duncan doesn't care for us Quinns much. It has to do with the war and all. On up beyond the Duncan place is pure mountain. No people at all a-living up there. I went way up, as far as I could, all the way to where there was no more up to go. From there, I could see all the way out to Hickory Nut Gap out past Blue Rock Mountain to Round Top in the distance. Everything was pure white. It's funny how things look different in the winter and especially in the snow. Off to the west, way on down, was a patch of dark green I hadn't noticed before. It lay tucked in the fold of the mountains about where Big John Creek would be if you were to follow it up from the Mill. It was a mile or so distant from where I was, but I could tell the trees were taller than normal and still green this deep in winter. I thought they were most likely a stand of pine, but I wanted to check, so I detoured over that way on my way home.

On making my way down there, through drifts of snow nearly as deep as I am tall—and I stand nearly six feet tall—I discovered an enchanted place. It's a cove I had somehow never encountered previously in all my wanderings. The trees, mostly hemlocks, must be ancient, because they are massive. It would take two or three of me to wrap arms around the smallest one. A little creek, a tributary to Big John Creek, meandered through, and scattered all around were massive boulders as big as the smokehouse. The creek, being frozen, was silent. The only sound was a whispering wind high up in the tops of the hemlocks. Surrounding the cove on three sides was a dense laurel hell. You wouldn't be able to find this place during the summer unless you came up the creek, which I knew had some pretty steep falls on down the mountain.

Mr. Darwin might describe this place in geologic terms and talk about glaciers and Laurentian rock and sediment. But for me, it was nigh on a religious experience. The place seemed like no other I'd ever been. I had the feeling I had discovered something no one else knew about. I hereby named the place Hemlock Hollow and decided that it would be my church. My worship, as it were, consisted of silent observation. Though the temperature was well below freezing, I did not feel cold. I was enraptured.

I squatted by the creek and noted the following tracks: raccoon (*Procyon lotor*), chickadee, titmouse, bobcat (*Lynx rufus*). I don't know the proper names for the birds. The raccoon had come down from the laurel hell where it was most likely bedded down for a spell as raccoons are apt to be. The bobcat came in along the creek, picked up the coon's scent, and followed it down the creek then back up into the hell. The birds—well, I'm not good enough to track a bird in flight. Yet.

I may have been in the little hollow for an hour before I decided it was time to make my descent to the house. Getting down was tricky. There's probably a way to go straight from the hollow to the house, but you'd have to be a monkey and swing from tree to tree to do it. The mountain's too steep and the rhododendron too dense, especially in a deep snow. For a human to get out, one has to trek back up the mountain to find a sure path to the east to go back down and around. Doing so brings you back by the Duncan place, and old Isaac Duncan was outside when I passed by.

"Howdy do," I said. I figure he can be ornery all he likes, but it doesn't mean I have to be.

"Afternoon," Mr. Duncan answered. He had a bucket and a pick and he was on his way to his springhouse.

"Mighty cold," I offered.

Mr. Duncan grunted (perhaps that's his way of agreeing) and cleared his throat. "You tell your pa if his shoat gets in my corn again, I'm going to roast it on a spit, you hear?"

"Yessir," I said, seeing as how Pa always said to be the nicest to them that rile you up the most. Of course, if Isaac Duncan really didn't want pigs in his corn, he'd put up a fence like everybody else does.

I went on home. Ma was mad at me. They'd had to have dinner without me. Apparently, I was gone four hours. Since I came home empty handed, Pa clicked his teeth and sniffed real loud at how I'd wasted the day. But it wasn't wasted to me. It was a mighty fine day.

❧

I swallowed hard and took in the hollow in which the cabin sat. Some things change over a hundred and twenty-five years. Others stay the same. The hollow itself, with its broad-limbed hemlocks and sky-piercing poplars, remained the enchanted realm it had been when Carson Quinn discovered it in 1886. At some point between then and now, they built our cabin for Marinda Quinn smack dab in the midst of Carson Quinn's sanctuary. That some point was after he had killed her husband, who was his brother. Or did he? The inquisitive young nature lover in the journal didn't seem the type for fratricide.

Carson Quinn's sanctuary became my play place a century later. Up the hill a bit lay a fissured granite boulder with a nearly perfectly flat top. As a child, it was my special place. I called it Caroline's Perch. Sometimes I would go up there and lie on my belly. Peering over the rock's edge, I could look down on the hollow. Below me, water would trickle into a pool at the base of a tiny waterfall where salamanders darted around. Ferns would wave in the constant breeze from the creek. The tops of hemlocks would sway toward the tin roof of the cabin. Inside noises often echoed up the hollow. Dad's calm tenor instructing my younger brother Andrew in the proper rules for hangman or blackjack on the front porch. Mom clattering together dinner in the kitchen. No one ever knew I was there.

Now, I climbed to my old spot and took in the view of the steep Appalachian forest below. The creek still gurgled, salamanders no doubt still darting around. Ferns clustered in damp places still. But beyond the cabin, on the drive below, a double-wide had been parked where forest once stood, smack dab in the spot where Andrew's friend Dale had captured a black snake twenty-some years before. From my perch I could look down onto its roof no more than three hundred feet away.

I had no idea who owned the double-wide or when it had been installed, incongruous with the idyllic hollow above it. It no doubt lay on Duncan land, not ours. As a child I knew all of the surrounding land intimately. My favorite thing was to venture out into the forests and hills. Mom never chided me when I came back from my long hikes. In fact, she purchased an old glass-topped cabinet for displaying the treasures I brought back. While she would never have collected them on her own, she took an interest in them, and together we made up stories about the people attached to them. There was a coil of metal found up the cove a bit that we were convinced was from a wheat thrasher and a latch for a door long gone that we determined opened an outhouse.

Thinking back on it now, it seems unlikely that modern parents would allow their nine-year-old daughter to venture alone into the woods for hours at a time. But my mom did. "Just don't get lost, Caroline," she would say. I never did. I made all sorts of amazing discoveries. Folds of ancient hills hid old fences, roadbeds, and crumbling foundations hinting at what used to be. My young mind pieced together the families that had lived there, people scratching out a living by hog raising and corn growing, celebrating milestones with hoedowns in the old barn that barely remained, and returning to the earth in the overgrown cemetery down by Reedy Patch.

On rainy days, we would stay indoors. There was no television, not even a telephone, but we didn't miss those luxuries. Andrew and Daddy played games. Blackjack, battleship, and hangman were their favorites. Mom and I preferred more intellectual pursuits. I lost myself in the hundreds of *National Geographic* magazines gifted by my grandmother, a proud member of the National Geographic Society. I would lie on the daybed on the front porch learning about Zulu dances, Hungarian wedding customs, Thai cuisine, the mysteries of Easter Island.

Mom was an English teacher and aspiring writer. She would sit in a creaky rocking chair with a TV tray in front of her, piles of papers around her as she pieced together the intricacies of her novel. When taking a break from that, she would read, mostly mysteries.

"Now." Her words interrupted my interest in a twenty-year-old article about Jane Goodall and her chimps. Her sharp pencil hovered over her paper. "What did you name the settlement that was here?"

"Duncanville," I said.

"You're so literal. Why not Tinkertown?"

"Because the Duncans lived here."

"Hmm," she said, her pencil taking off again on the page.

"What are you writing?" I asked.

Her pencil paused mid-sentence. She lifted her eyes and winked at me. "Wouldn't want to spoil it for you."

My heart caught on the memory. Spoil it she did. I realized with a swallow and a tear what exactly it was that I thought I might find in that crusty old box.

I kicked at the boulder. A hickory nut husk took flight toward the double-wide, plummeting into a bank of ferns long before posing a threat to the eyesore. I took a deep breath. Part of me had wanted to be done with this place forever, let nature finish it off, but now the sound of sledgehammers and band saws testified to my decision to reclaim the cabin. Some part of me wanted this.

More memories clawed up from their buried depths. Being here riled them up. In fact, where I stood now, on Caroline's Perch, was the setting for the worst one of them all. It came rushing back now. I glanced down at the boulder, to where a seam of quartz cut through the granite, and I saw my mother there, exactly where she had been decades before.

"I know you like it up here," she had said. She was sitting beside me, holding her knees close to her chest. With a delicate move, she tucked my ever-wayward hair behind my ear, as if I were much younger, as if I weren't already driving a car, solving Odyssey of the Mind problems by myself, leading troops of Girl Scouts into the wild. I should have known from the gesture that something was up, but I was always more attuned to the natural world than to other people.

"Isn't it great?" I asked.

"There's something I need to tell you, something you aren't going to like."

My heart started racing. Delores's parents had just divorced. Surely the same couldn't happen to my parents. They were utterly devoted to each other.

"I'm sick," she said. My first thought was to be relieved that was all it was.

"Oh," I said. "You'll get better."

"No, honey. It's not the kind of sick you get better from."

"What kind is it?" My tears were already splattering onto the boulder, like the first raindrops of a bad storm.

"Cancer," she said. "Breast cancer."

The confining nature of the hollow had always felt reassuring and safe, like nature giving me a giant hug. Now it felt foreboding and oppressive. My ears started to ring, and soon I couldn't hear anything over the terrible screeching. She hugged me, and though I was nearly her same size, she rocked me like a baby until the tears stopped.

"Listen," she finally said. "I'm going to fight this as best I can. But it's advanced, and the prognosis isn't good."

"How long?"

"Six months. Maybe a year if we're lucky."

I took a deep breath that pulled in the damp must of the hollow. "Does Andrew know?"

"Your father is telling him now. I'm going to go down in a minute to be with him. You can take however long you need up here or go on one of your hikes if you'd like."

"Okay."

"I want you to know," she told me. "That no matter what happens, I will always be here for you."

"I know." I bit down hard to stanch more tears. I took in her features, her curled hair, her lithe athletic body, her nose that I had inherited. All I could think was that she wasn't in fact going to be there. She wouldn't see me accomplish any of my life goals, all of which now seemed ridiculously pointless.

She went back to the cabin, and I stayed. A breeze stirred the trees and cooled my skin, and I closed my eyes and tried to pretend that nothing had changed. But it had.

My mother died the summer before my senior year of high school. She passed away in a hospital bed on the front porch that now held Micah's circular saw.

After she passed, we never went back to the cabin. Going to the cabin had always been her doing. It was her favorite place.

Though we all loved it in our way, we came here because we were tethered to her.

"Mom?" I said aloud. Down the hill a hawk screeched. A woodpecker cackled from the ridgeline. A squirrel stirred the understory. A piece of rotten wood went crashing into the waste bin. She didn't answer, because she couldn't. She was dead. She had, after all, "cottoned to the Lord," but he had taken her from us and she was gone, and like the atheist Carson Quinn I didn't believe a lick of it. What I did believe was that I now owned this cabin and dear old Daddy had given me the opportunity to go back to the beginning. To take something rotten to its core and make it new again.

In the decades since my mother's death, I had made my mark in the world, had forged a successful career, won fellowships, published widely, gained tenure at a top university. That life now crumbled around me. My own nature had done to it what the earth's nature had done to the cabin. My marriage had failed. In the process of attending to the disintegrating marriage, I had missed out on two important fellowships, and my career stood at a pause. The relentless pursuit of that career had left me with no real friends, and now that Daddy had passed I had no family to speak of, as Andrew had his own, separate life. All that remained was what lay before me now: a cabin from my past populated by ghosts I didn't believe in.

3

January 12, 1886—Gramps says this is the coldest he can remember, and he's been around for sixty-nine winters. The old folks, meaning codgers even older than Gramps, used to talk of rivers freezing solid all winter long. I never believed it, until now. It's gone and happened. A person can walk clean across the Rocky Broad without getting wet. It's been so cold so long that I believe the mercury may have frozen in the thermometer. It never moves anymore. It has read zero Fahrenheit for days.

The others stay indoors, wrapped in blankets, huddled around either the stove or the fireplace. But I can't help myself. Sitting still doesn't suit me. I put on all my clothes and head afield. There are no new tracks. This cold has even the most equipped creatures stuck in their dens. The snow that was days ago soft and downy now lies sharp and slick, making movement difficult. But what is there to do in this world if not move?

Even I can't stay out long, maybe an hour at best, but that's long enough to conduct a full sortie of our small piece of land and its surroundings, to check the millhouse, at rest and silent for a change, the pig sty, now empty because Ma moved the sow and her young'uns into the kitchen to stay warm, Ma's garden plot, only made distinguishable by the outline of the fence in the snow, the barn where Henry the mule stands shivering despite the thick wool coat Pa gave him. Out front, Pa's forge belches smoke into the icy sky. He pulled the chickens in and lit the fire to keep them from freezing to death in their coop. Beyond that is the public road. A mile or so to the left it intersects with the Drovers Road in the little village of Daisy. Half a day's travel to the right is Hendersonville. Across the road, the Edney Inn Valley stretches wide and white, a long ways from being full of corn and melons.

This is our world. Whether buried in snow and ice or whipped by winds or licked by flame, it is ours, where everyone I have ever known resides. The mill was here long before we Quinns showed up. Built back in the old days, it was once the only place hereabouts for local folk to mill their hominy and to gather together. When the owner passed and the millstones stopped turning, time went to work on it. The story goes that Gramps accepted the land and what remained of the mill in payment for services rendered. He gave it to Pa, who restored it and more with his own hands. After the war he brought Ma back here. They were close enough to Gramps, down in Rutherfordton, to have family nearby, far enough away for privacy, and that's the way my pa liked it. He learned to smith, got the mill running, and set out to make a living and a family. Nothing's more important to Pa than being of Use, and of Use he has been. Folks turn to him when times are tough and he always knows what to do, and never turns a blind eye to neither neighbor nor foe. When Gramps closed up his office down the mountain, he moved in with us, and now we're all one happy family. Well, we're all one family. Happiness comes and goes.

ॐ

It was lung cancer that did Daddy in. He was seventy-four when he died. He'd been diagnosed a year before, so we saw it coming. My brother, Andrew, lived within a couple of miles of Daddy, and between him and hospice my father was able to stay at his home in Greensboro, where he'd lived practically all of his adult life.

Andrew called one Saturday in April. Final term papers weighed heavy on my desk, a tottering tower of inchoate sophomore thought, when the phone rang.

"Hey, sis." Andrew's hushed voice was indicative of something grave. "It's time."

He died before I could get there. I had always thought there would be more time to reconnect. But the end arrives quickly even when you see it coming. Daddy's funeral occurred on a Tuesday at the First Presbyterian Church, where he had been an elder for two decades. I hadn't been back to the church since Andrew's youngest child, Daniel, named after Daddy, was christened there six years before. Presbyterians aren't much for outward displays of emotion, so I kept my eulogy professorial and dignified. Daddy would have expected it.

I talked about him meeting Mom when he was a traveling insurance salesman making his way through Florida. About how they first met at a beach party, how she was transfixed with his height and deep blue eyes, and that despite (or perhaps because of) his ungainly attempt at volleyball she fell madly in love with him, and he with her, a svelte tennis-playing English teacher. I told of how they married within a year and how they moved to Greensboro when he got a position with Jefferson Pilot that wouldn't require travel. I glossed over her death, but remarked on how much Daddy missed her despite building a rich life through the church and Rotary Club.

After I spoke, Andrew spoke. Unlike me, he was an actual member of the congregation and, as a banker at a local bank, a pillar of the community. Standing before his people, his thinning hair unwinding in the breeze, he looked every bit his father's son. Except for his blond hair and thicker body, he was the spitting image of the man he was laying to rest. His remarks were straightforward and somber. He finished with a quote from Oscar Wilde. He said that Daddy used to love to quote Wilde, but I had never heard him quote anyone. "Death must be so beautiful. To lie in the soft brown earth, with the grasses waving above one's head, and listen to silence. To have no yesterday, and no tomorrow. To forget time, to forgive life, to be at peace."

In the end, his life cinched tight like a neat bowknot, Daniel Eugene McAlister was interred next to the love of his life, Madeleine Crest McAlister. Old friends and folks I hadn't seen since childhood swarmed me afterward. There were hugs and condolences, but few tears, since this moment had been telegraphed for months. Invariably, the conversations evolved into "catch up with Caroline," and I fielded questions about whether I would move home (not anytime soon), whether I would have kids (at forty-three, probably not), or whether I would ever publish another book (yes, in fact, *Waka Chan to Orion: An Introduction to Comparative Ethnoastronomy* was due out in August.)

I was preparing to head back to the house when a familiar voice called my name.

"Caroline," she said. It was my childhood friend, Delores. Seeing her reminded me of my own age. Her efforts against the passage of time were obvious: her formerly chestnut hair was dyed red, her face had been pulled tight like a Barbie doll's, and her skin glowed with the perfectly even tan only a UV bed can impart. She was dressed more appropriately for a funeral than I was. Her dress was the color of the southern night sky, and it fit her perfectly, accentuating only what needed to be accentuated. I, on the other hand, had limited formal wear. My dark pantsuit was more appropriate for a meeting with the Fulbright Foundation than sending a beloved into the afterlife.

"My goodness. Delores Appleton!"

"Beck," she corrected. "It's Delores Beck now."

"Beck as in Tommy Beck?"

"The one and only."

I hadn't seen Delores since my own wedding, ten years before. "What happened to Robert?"

"Roger, you mean?" she asked.

"That's him," I said, embarrassed to have forgotten her husband's name. I had never liked him; I always felt she deserved better.

"I divorced his sorry ass eight years ago. Then I married a builder named Barry, and that didn't even make it a year." She chuckled as if the joke had been on her.

"Wow." I cringed. "How did I miss all that? I'm a terrible friend."

"No. You're just Caroline. Always have been. Always will be."

For some reason that hurt worse than being a bad friend. Determined to overcome my own tendencies, I led us to a bench beneath a pungent cedar where we sat watching a Bobcat shove red-clay earth onto Daddy.

"How's Woody?" she asked.

"He's better now that we've divorced."

She didn't gasp or grope for words. She squeezed my thigh. "Sorry," she whispered.

"It's for the better," I said. "Turns out he wanted an actual wife, and all I could give him was the me I always have been and always will be."

Delores grimaced. "He was a great guy. Definitely the marrying type. But not your type."

"Oh yeah? What's my type?"

"I always thought you'd wind up with some sort of philosopher-biker-Marine type. A poet in the guise of a pirate. Like those guys you dated in college. Woody always struck me as too...normal...for you."

She was right. Woody loved his routines, exalted in the mundane joys of home life, lived a measured life. I had wanted to want that, but it turned out I didn't actually. Still, knowing that he wasn't my type and knowing that he deserved better than to settle for me, grief over the recent passing of my marriage stabbed at my already tender heart.

"So, what's next for you?"

"You remember my family's old cabin?" I asked.

"Oh yeah. You used to love it up there. Didn't your dad sell it after your mother died?"

"Apparently not. And he left it to me."

"So, what are you going to do with it?" Delores asked.

"I don't know," I said. "I'm going up tomorrow to check it out. Then we'll see."

"You would consider keeping it?" Her hand flew to her mouth, aghast. "After, well...you know?"

"That remains to be seen." I used the tone I would have employed with a student jumping to conclusions without all the facts.

"I don't think I could ever go back, if I were you."

"It's all memories now."

"Are you sure that's all?" she asked. Whether it was her new plastic face or my own imperfect ability to read others, I couldn't tell if she was frightened or concerned. "I'm in real estate now. If you want, I can arrange to have it all handled without you ever going back."

Real estate. That made sense. Her and Roger's kids would be college-aged by now. Michelle and Gary. Real estate would be a way for her get back into the workforce, and she had always had a preoccupation with status symbols.

"I need to see it," I said. "I need to go back." She placed a warm hand over mine. She'd always been touchy in ways I wasn't. "You're married to Tommy Beck now?" I asked, steering away from one uncomfortable past to another.

"Isn't that ironic?"

"Either that or karmic," I answered. Tommy Beck had given us both our first kiss. He had given half the girls in the first grade at Lindley Elementary their first kiss.

"Caroline." She stood up and smoothed her dress. "Let me know if I can help out at all."

"I will."

She clutched at her purse, offered a little Southern "Bless your heart" smile and walked away.

The next day, I packed up my Subaru wagon with enough gear to forge a life in the unknown and headed west, toward the mountains, a pioneer of my own making. As far as I knew, no one had visited the cabin since my mother died. I didn't know if it was even still standing.

Turned out it was. Barely. When I climbed from the car three hours later and took a deep breath, the must of the hollow, rich with earth and evergreen, nearly knocked me over with memories. I braced myself on the hood of the ticking Subaru. Though it was old and surely empty, the place didn't feel abandoned. My presence here felt known, as if each step I took through iridescent periwinkle blossoms was being observed and measured.

The tin roof had rusted into the color of a terrible bruise. Holes gaped beside the crumbling chimney. It perched crooked, the rear section having dropped into the mountain, dirt from log and dirt from earth indistinguishable. Nearly every window on both floors had been shattered by vandals or weather. English ivy strangled the stone foundation, shredded the screen on the front porch, and probably held the whole thing together.

I had swallowed and let my long legs follow the grown-over river-rock path to the front of the place. The steps up to the front porch bore huge cracks and crevices. Erosion had carved canyons between the stone steps. The wood slats had rotted in places, leaving holes that cast shafts of light into the crawl space below. I skirted a large fissure at the top of the stairs and dared to place my full weight onto a portion of the porch that seemed solid. It held.

"Hello!" I called inside. "Anyone here?"

No one answered.

The door hung open, as if the owner had just stepped out for a spell. But she hadn't. For I was the owner now, and it had been twenty-five years since I last passed through that portal, and I decided in that moment that I would restore the place. I owed it that.

I set up a camp behind the cabin to oversee my project. A large tarp strung up on a line between two poplars, probably the same two trees Mom had used for the clothesline decades ago, provided shelter. The camp consisted of a portable plastic table and camp chairs, a propane stove and lantern, and enough mosquito netting to protect an elephant. With some stones I marked out a fire pit, then set up my large camp tent on the softest, most level spot around. Using my trowels and shovels I dug a luxurious latrine and tacked up the few remaining un-decayed boards from the old outhouse around it for privacy. Compared to previous summers spent doing research in places like Belize, Thailand, and Zimbabwe, this would be a walk in the park.

From my camp, I could look down the hollow and see the

cabin and the work being done. Down the driveway there was a younger hemlock, its lower limbs cut away, leaving knobs that were easy handholds for six-year-old Andrew, who so desperately wanted to climb trees like his older sister. On the other side of the cabin, a bare spot remained on the hillside, caused by the rubbing of our feet as we launched ourselves airborne on the rope swing Daddy had hung. By the back door, carefully selected river stones outlined Mom's little garden. She had found the one spot in the entire hollow with enough sunlight to grow flowers. Even now, a lone rosebush bore tiny buds promising late summer yellow.

After lunch I made my way down to the creek to fill up a bag to run through my gravity-fed osmotic water filter. I found Micah there, sipping water from a gourd.

"Micah!" I admonished.

His eyes lifted to meet mine as he slurped the water. "Delicious," he said. "This may be the best water in the state."

"You haven't heard of giardia?"

He cocked his head. Arched an eyebrow. Took another sip.

"Don't do that. Let me filter it first." I scrambled down to the rocks.

"Condescension doesn't suit you, Caroline."

The water bag tumbled onto the stones below. Echoes of Woody rang in my ears, but I shook them off. Micah Turner was just a contractor, after all.

He had been the second contractor I had look at the place. The first had recommended demolition, so he didn't get the job. Micah showed up on time and carried himself with an almost cocky sense of self-assurance. He was tall and wiry, with a mane of wild hair and an ageless face. I told him about what the first contractor recommended, and he scowled. "What? This cabin isn't even old yet. My last job was a cabin out near Morganton. It was built of chestnut logs like this one, only it was 150 years old instead of seventy, and those logs were no worse for the wear. Let's get rid of all the nasty insides and see what we've got to work with."

I had hired him on the spot. Now fresh from scolding him for drinking directly from the creek and being summarily called out on one of my own worst tendencies, I gasped for words.

"Try some." He ladled some water from the cascading falls and offered the gourd.

"I'd rather not spend the next six weeks in that pit latrine," I said.

"Things you should know about me." He paused to down the rest of the water. "I'm a grown man, I've been drinking from mountain streams all my life, and I take risks."

"Fair enough," I said.

The gourd had a leather strap, and he slung it over his shoulder like a guitar as he ascended from the creek. "Anything I should know about you?"

He pulled out a bandanna and wiped his lips.

"What do you mean?" I asked. It's possible I had never met anyone quite like Micah. I was quickly coming to the conclusion that he was decidedly not like Woody. Not at all.

"I shared something. Now you share something."

"I'm not good at people," I offered.

He creased the bandanna down the diagonal perfectly, then stuffed it into his back pocket. "Fair enough." He offered a wink, then ambled back toward the cabin, leaving me alone with my water bag.

4

February 20, 1886—Pa has brought me and Thomas up to the Newton School in Asheville. I like it here fine, but the city's not anything like the Gorge. Asheville is a bustling town, all busy with construction. When I first arrived at Newton a couple of years ago, Asheville was quiet in the winter. Before, folks came in the summer for the sanatoria and the cool breezes. Now, people are around all the time. Downtown is a mess of construction. I don't get out of school much at all, but when I do, I like to wander up Main Street and watch the men work on the tall buildings going up. People from all over come here. Many speak all manner of languages and have accents such that I can't understand them at all. On the way here, we passed through Fairview, where Pa stopped and talked to a group of men in a tavern. They were talking about concerns I couldn't really understand, all about money and commodities and the like. While they were talking, I kept quiet and thumbed through the book I had with me, *Emerson's Essays*, which Gramps had in his library. Thomas went and sat on the porch throwing rocks into nearby tree branches. It seemed to me that these men could use some of what Emerson was saying. In one chapter he wrote, "There is a time in every man's education when he arrives at the conviction that envy is ignorance; that imitation is suicide; that he must take himself for better, for worse, as his portion; that though the wide universe is full of good, no kernel of nourishing corn can come to him but through his toil bestowed on that lot of ground which is given to him to till."

I'm only thirteen, but I know what it is to toil on a lot of ground. Pa has made sure of that. Gramps has made sure we have good book learning. He's always on us to read in English and Latin, and he's the reason we go to Newton. Thomas hates it. He's always getting into fights with the other boys. They think they're so much better than us just because their families have all the money in the mountains. We don't have much money, except what Gramps has stashed away. More than money, though, Gramps knows just about everybody everywhere. It seems that nearly everybody everywhere owes Gramps something or another, and he's not afraid to remind them of it. That's why we can come here. The headmaster and Gramps had been fast friends back in the day, apparently.

We study Latin, arithmetics, geography, history, and literature. My favorite is geography. I like learning about new places and people. We stay here all the time. It will be three months before we go back to Daisy. It seems like a long time to be away from the mountain. Mr. Emerson seems to think a man can get enough education from toil and knowing himself. But there are a lot of folks who are sure of themselves and plenty that are self-reliant who will never leave the Gorge because they don't know nothing of the world beyond the Rocky Broad. The world is a big, big place, and as much as I love my mountains, one day I'll leave this place. I'll climb over the mountains until there are no more mountains to climb, and I'll keep going until I've seen everything under the sun.

March 17, 1886—I must record the strange thing that happened to me recently. It started at school when the honorable Thomas L. Clingman visited us last week. Mr. Clingman is well-known. He was a congressman before the war and a general during it. I reckon he's best known for his argument with Dr. Elisha Mitchell, which wound up killing Dr. Mitchell.

Aside from being a politician, he has an interest in science. Back a few years ago, he came to the Hickory Nut Gorge to study the rumblings up on Bald Mountain. There had been some earthquakes. Ma felt them all the way up in the garden plot. Being pregnant with Taylor, she thought it was the warning signs of imminent birth. But then Pa & Gramps felt the earth a-shifting, too, so it couldn't have been Taylor. For a time afterward you could hear Bald Mountain on down the Gorge past Chimney Rock, rumbling like some massive giant was inside throwing boulders around. The general had come down to study the sounds and the smoke that would rise from fissures in the mountain. He concluded it was volcanic and about to erupt. That was mighty scary, of course, and lots of folks up and left. Turned out it was nothing but rocks collapsing in underground caves. You can still hear it on occasion. It's mighty spooky at night, especially when camping up on Blue Rock across the Gorge.

General Clingman came to Newton to talk to us about his theory of natural theology. It was a might puzzling trying to figure out what he meant and all. He seemed to be talking about science, but then he went to talking about moral accountability to a higher power as natural law and how "survival of the fittest" is no way to govern society. People, as he lectured, are biologically in need of a moral compass to properly order our relationships with each other and the world. Then, he went to talking about Charles Darwin and how Darwin made a key error in his theorizing, by not seeing God at work. Everything couldn't be all a struggle in the mud and random mutation and brute strength that works things out. It had to be governed by God.

"No, sir," I heard someone say aloud to him, before I realized the one talking was me. "No, sir," I repeated.

General Clingman was taken aback to say the least. He stopped cold and glared at me, but I kept talking. "What Mr. Darwin talks about ain't a struggle for survival by individuals. He means species. And it don't say nowhere in that book about a survival of the fittest."

"Doesn't," the general corrected. "It doesn't say anywhere in that book—"

"Sorry. It doesn't say anywhere in that book about a survival of the fittest. It's about how a species of creatures responds to a specific place, and how having certain characteristics enhance an individual's ability to survive in that specific place and therefore change the species to be more like that individual over lots of generations. And sometimes that there characteristic is cooperation amongst individuals, not competition betwixt them."

The room was quiet except for the headmaster's steps getting louder on the wood floor as he came up behind me. I felt him grab me by the ear and tug me up from the seat.

"I do apologize, Mr. Clingman. I will remove this student at once."

The general stretched out his hand toward me. "No need for that. Boy, what's your name?"

I told him, and he grunted like a sow.

"Any relation to Aurelius Quinn?"

"He's my gramps."

"He was quite the sophist in his time. Is he still with the living?"

"Yes, sir," I said. "Lives down in Daisy."

The general winced when I said that. I guess it reminded him of a time he was wrong about something since there were no volcanoes down there.

"I'll have to get down and see him sometime soon. Back to your question."

"It wasn't a question," I corrected, and my ear got tugged hard and the back of my head slapped.

"Back to your statement. What you say is actually correct. Mr. Darwin doesn't use the phrase 'survival of the fittest.' Others have described his theory in that way and not inaccurately, I assert. Tell me, young Mr. Quinn, haven't you ever known something to be the case without observation, without any outward information, but then been correct about it?"

"I suppose." I thought of Ma. She's got a gift for knowing things like that. Once she started to packing up a mess of herbs and liniments out of the blue. Pa asked her what for, and she said because Dora Ledbetter was going into labor and she needed to get down the road to help out. Old Dora had her baby the next day with Ma at her side. Ma just knew it to be so. There was also a time when I was ten that I found her crying out back in the herb garden. I asked her what was wrong, and she said her mother had passed away the night before. The thing was that her mother was all the way over in County Sligo, Ireland. I asked how she knew, and she said she just did. Three weeks later the letter come from her sister delivering the news of the death of Bridgit Conner, her mother and my grandmother.

"Well then," General Clingman said. "Why do you think that is?"

"I dunno," I said.

"That knowing is your perception of the spiritual world. Why would you be able to perceive the spiritual if it didn't exist? Darwin never speaks of this fundamental aspect of our existence. He leaves it out entirely, but humankind from time immemorial from all over the vast world has acknowledged the presence of a spiritual hand, of God's hand. I think science is tremendously important. It's bettering humanity by the minute. Why, look down the hill at the new rail line coming in from Spartanburg, at the construction of telephones and electricity and trolleys. The world will be an easier place for you to live in than it has for me, young man. All thanks to science. But, and this is a grand 'but,' you can't forget that this is all God's plan. We must obey the word of God if we want a supreme place in the world of Man."

I could see that we weren't talking about the same thing at all, so I hushed up. Besides, my head was ringing from it being slapped. After General Clingman left, Thomas come over to me and slapped me even harder in the back of the head. Since he wasn't the headmaster, I slapped him back and the next thing you know we were getting our backsides walloped in the headmaster's office. Though Thomas had been in that position many a time before, I had not. It was more embarrassing than painful. No doubt the headmaster was going to tell Pa, and Pa won't be nearly as gentle as the headmaster in his application of discipline.

March 20, 1886—The other boys here have taken to riding me

hard about General Clingman. They call me the atheist, and Thomas does nothing to help out. He just shakes his head at me, all disappointed like. As far as I know, I ain't an atheist. Charles Darwin wasn't an atheist either. Nor were the Michauxs or Asa Gray or Von Humboldt or Quaker naturalists John Lawson and the Bartrams. We go down to the Baptist church every once in a while. Gramps, now he ain't never been one for organized religion, and Pa has been arguing with God for thirty years, so they always stay home. But Ma likes to go to church to see all the other women, and she takes us young'uns along with her on occasion.

You've got the Bible, and even though it's the word of God, it was written down by men. Then you've got the world itself, as surely God's creation as anything. No man had to interpret the mountain and canyon. It's God's work direct. That is what I choose to worship. The mighty Hemlock and Chestnut are so much more perfect than the hand-hewn cross upon the spire.

I've also read the Bible, since Gramps has it in his library. Frankly, it seemed like a lot of begetting and smiting to me. I reckon that ain't all that different from how things are to-day. Every generation has a time to smite and a time to beget. Gramps went off to smite them Mexicans. He says he didn't get a one of 'em. He thinks he may have nicked Santa Anna before that cannonball got him in the leg. Pa, well, no one really knows what Pa done in the war since he won't talk to no one about it at all. I suspect there was smiting involved. And Gramps's father, that'd be my great-grandfather, fought with Andrew Jackson in the Battle of New Orleans. I wonder if me and Thomas and Taylor will have a chance to fight. I certainly hope not. It seems unlikely at the moment. North and South are finally at an exhausted peace. There's been some fighting in Europe, but it's mostly done now, and it doesn't concern us at all. I've never been one to fight, and I hope that war is over for good.

Now, as for begetting, I certainly feel differently about that. I aim to do my share of that, once I'm older, of course. Right now, I don't know many girls, except for Marinda. Marinda Fallon lives up the road from us. Her family has an apple orchard. Marinda is about my age, and she is right pretty. Her hair is the color of goldenseal, and she has eyes as deeply green as winter laurel. We used to play together as young'uns, but we don't see each other much anymore on account of me being at school and her staying at home to work on the orchard and care for her folks. They've lost every other child born to them in nearly every way possible. She's the only one left, so she alone has the work of a full brood.

There are no girls here at Newton, just boys. Since they think I'm an atheist, everyone scorns me. That's all right. I'll just study and read, and come May, I'll go back to my mountains. The mountains judge no one.

May 15, 1886—Pa came and got us from Newton yesterday. Now we're back on Saunter Branch. The first thing that had to be taken care of was the punishment for our ruckus with General Clingman and all. Thomas is almost sixteen years old and nearly as big as Pa, but he did not fight back as Pa pulled out the mule belt. Pa lined us up behind the forge and gave me three stinging lashes. Thomas got five lashes since he was older and should have known better.

We limped over to the house carrying our foot lockers. Gramps let Thomas by, then reached out and grabbed my shoulder. He had a twinkle in his eye. "Boy," he said. "Come here."

He pulled me to the far side of the porch where Pa wasn't likely to hear. He leaned toward me, laying his weight onto a wooden cane Pa made for him. He calls it his indoor cane, because it's simple, made from ash, with a rubber cap on one end to soften the noise. Gramps has a cane for every occasion. "I am so proud of you," he said.

He'd never said anything like that. I was surprised.

"You told that Thomas Clingman a thing or two, now didn't you?"

"Reckon so," I said.

"I deplore that man," Gramps said. "I have despised him for fifty years and detested him for nigh on thirty. He killed Dr. Mitchell, you know."

"It was the falls what really killed him, Gramps," I said.

"Nonsense." Gramps shuffled to his rocking chair, peg leg and cane working together to let him ease into it. "Dr. Elisha Mitchell would not have been on that mountain were it not for Thomas Clingman's ignorant claims. That man has been wrong in public more times than a man can count. I studied with Dr. Mitchell down in Chapel Hill, and he was one of the best men I ever knew. You know, he's the reason we live in these parts instead of Hillsboro or Raleigh?"

I shook my head.

"Dr. Mitchell traveled the mountains a lot and saw the type of families living out in these here hollows, how they had no access to schooling and lawyering and doctoring. I tell you, that man inspired me to come west and set out my shingle and do as much good as I could."

"Yessir," I said.

"And that fool Clingman went and killed him. So, boy, I'm mighty proud of you."

"Didn't really kill him," I said. "The general was nowhere close to Dr. Mitchell when he fell in them there falls."

"It was Clingman's pride that killed Mitchell, what led him to set out to prove something he already knew to be true," Gramps said. "Pride's a dangerous thing, boy. You keep that in mind, you hear?"

"Yes, sir," I said. We sat on the porch for a time, Gramps working his tobacco in silence, rocking back and forth, faster and faster, his mind no doubt latched on to the injustice of Mitchell's death. One thing Gramps can't abide by is injustice.

❧

Micah and his crew were making progress. They had started by pulling out everything from within the cabin. It turned out that the inside had been even worse than the outside. When I walked in the first time, a putrid odor nearly knocked me off my feet. The rotten floor was littered with old beer bottles, cigarette butts, and the odd bit of clothing. The carpet squished when I stepped on it, releasing a stench so vile I had to pull my T-shirt up to cover my face. Mouse droppings covered the kitchen counter. The ceilings bore brown stains from various leaks over the years, and the bathroom floor had caved in.

Thirty years of *National Geographic* magazines, now bloated with decay and humidity, sighed on the bookcase where we had left them. Time and mold had reduced them to a biohazard. Beside them, in equally bad shape, were my mom's books, the built-in shelves sagging with their sodden weight. Hillary Waugh's hardboiled mysteries had gone soft and gooey. Raymond Chandler, Dorothy Sayers, and Patricia Highsmith had met similar fates.

I helped out as best I could. They parked a massive waste bin out front. The carpet, books, paneling, and furniture went directly into the bin. I set up another tarp under which we set the few items in good enough shape to keep. That pile grew glacially compared to the volcanic eruption of trash.

I worked more slowly than the others, the process being an excavation of my own past. I would pause as Micah's crew carried artifacts of my childhood into the light of day. The mattress my parents had slept on for years went flying into the bin. The moth-eaten sofa on which we had created a decade's worth of annual family photos collapsed into pieces when lifted. The Hoosier cabinet, bearing equal measures of rust and mold, was hefted out like a prone corpse on a canvas sheet.

I paused when Micah and another man went by with the glass curio cabinet. Setting down the old basket of Andrew's blocks, I followed them outside. It was still in good condition, so Micah set it on the tarp.

"This is a nice piece." He peered through the glass at my childhood treasures. "A little Murphy's Oil and elbow grease, and it'll be as good as new."

"My mom picked it up in Thomasville," I said. "It was my eleventh birthday present. I collected all those pieces in there."

"Looks like you ran across a still or two." He wiped a smudge from the glass with his bandanna.

"What?"

He pointed at the copper coil. "That's from a still. As are those brass fittings. And that knob is from a pressure release valve."

I stared hard at the treasures through eyes that had scoured countless archaeological sites across multiple continents and saw that Micah was right. These were not the components of a wheat thrasher, corn hopper, and molasses extractor as my uneducated mind had deduced. They clearly came from a still. "And you would know about that, how?"

"No comment," he said with a smirk and a wink. He tugged his mask back up and plunged back into the cabin.

All the activity drew the attention of the neighbors later that day.

"You there!" I heard someone shouting with a shrill accent. "I don't believe I know you."

I came around the corner to see Micah, tall and confident, replying to a pudgy, bearded man. "I sure don't know you."

I sprinted down the hill, my hand stretched out. "Hey!" I said, eager to make a good first impression. "I'm Caroline McAlister." The young man scrunched up his face, weighing his response. "I'm the owner of this cabin," I explained.

"Since when?"

"Since my father died and left it to me," I said.

"Oh." He finally deigned to take my hand. "I'm Jesse. I live in that there trailer." He pointed to the double-wide, which until now had seemed unoccupied, the blinds always drawn, the Dodge Charger out front stilled, nothing but silence emanating from the spot.

"I used to hide behind a big boulder that sat where your living room is now," I said. "Back when we played hide and seek all over the mountainside."

Jesse stared at me as if I were some curiosity, as if playing hide and seek was the last thing a hillside would ever be good for. "I guess my pa didn't know you were trespassing. Or he would have put an end to it."

"Trespassing?"

"This here is Duncan land. Has been since the Revolutionary War."

"Duncan's your last name?"

He turned and sniffed, and when he did, I caught in his profile a resemblance to Old Man Duncan. "I'm guessing Ed Duncan was your grandpa?"

"That's right." He squinted.

"He knew where we were, didn't mind us playing or hiking on his land. In fact, he liked that we did, since he didn't really get around anymore."

"He died about twenty years ago."

It was hard to tell how old Jesse was. On first glance, he seemed young enough to have a lot yet to learn. But his thick beard bore flecks of gray, and tracks of crow's feet ventured from his eyes into a prematurely balding head of hair. "I'm sorry to hear that. He was always kind to us."

Jesse took a step back, looked from me to Micah, then back again. "I reckon I'll tell my pa what's going on down here. He ain't going to be too pleased."

"I'd like to meet him, introduce myself," I said. "Does he live close by?"

Jesse nodded into the yawning valley below that stretched into a south-facing bowl. "Up yonder."

"How long have you been living here?" I pointed at the double-wide.

"Ever since I got back."

"Got back?"

"From Iraq." His eyes darted from mine, glanced down the road, then up the mountain.

"Oh." I said reflexively, "Thank you for your service."

Immediately I regretted having said the words. He seemed to want, and probably deserved, something other than my thanks.

"Yep." He squinted, though his eyes were well shaded.

"It's been a pleasure meeting you. I'm going to get back to work."

"You betcha." He sulked back to his house across the road.

I turned to Micah, who hitched his pants up and arched an eyebrow toward the trailer as if to say keep an eye on that one.

I took a deep breath and climbed the old stone stairs onto the front porch of the cabin. One of Micah's workers brushed past with the remnants of an old rocking chair. Moldy and termite damaged now, I saw what it had once been. A chorus line of similar rocking chairs had once populated the screened-in porch. It was where my parents would sit and gab with family and guests alike. I remembered the floor slats then, freshly painted a light blue. That same paint now curled away in stalagmite flecks, exposing decaying wood.

Back, way back, when those floor slats were new, an orange ball had rolled across that porch floor. It had missed its target and bounced off a pair of black leather boots. The owner of those boots reached down and lifted me up. My parents, being new parents then, must have apologized to their guest for my rambunctious behavior. A joke must have been shared, because soon everyone was laughing. The bubbling glee I had felt in that moment dissipated as I took in the now-shattered front windows and gaping holes in the floor that Micah's crew had covered with plywood, which now replaced the floor that had held my mother's hospital bed.

"Ms. McAlister!" Micah called out. I turned. Down at the end of the drive, Jesse had returned, and with him, an older man.

I made my way past sawhorses and scrap piles down to the men. "Hi there." I didn't bother to extend my hand this time. "I'm Caroline McAlister."

"McAlister?" the older man said. He wore jeans and a button-down shirt. Clean shaven, with a severely parted hairstyle, he had the officious bearing of a bureaucrat.

"That's right. My father was Dan McAlister."

He appraised me with skeptical eyes.

I tried to make nice. "We stopped coming up after my mother died. I've inherited it from my father."

"Mmm-hmm," he said.

"And you are?" I asked.

He did not apologize for the lack of introduction. Apparently, it wasn't an oversight. "Charles Duncan." He squinted at me. "You realize, that our property line runs through your front yard." He leaned over to peer around Micah. "Nope, I guess not."

He tromped across the driveway to the front of the cabin where the massive waste bin sat. "You see." He pointed at the bin. "This is sitting mostly on Duncan land."

"Jesse," he ordered. Without looking at his son, Charles Duncan reached out his hand into which Jesse placed a mattock. The elder Duncan stabbed the tool into the ground decisively, as if laying claim. Then, with unwavering exactitude he gouged a three-inch trough diagonally across my front yard, excising a triangle that consisted mostly of English Ivy and dead dogwoods. "Property line runs right about here. I don't take kindly to trespassing, so you move this dumpster onto your own land, you hear?"

Micah's face went red. "You realize that Ms. McAlister did not invite you onto her property? You know what that means? It means you just trespassed yourself to make your point."

"Boy," Mr. Duncan said. "You best watch yourself."

"I'm just saying that a little common courtesy can go a long way. You're not using that land for anything."

This was crazy. First of all, Micah was long past being a boy. If I had to guess I would say he was at least forty. Though appalled at the Duncans, I really didn't want to get off on the wrong foot with them. They had inhabited this place all by themselves for twenty years and all of a sudden here I came out of nowhere. "That's all right." I layered on my sweetest Southern drawl. "We'll move the container over. I didn't realize where the property line was. As kind as your father was to us, I don't want to repay that with offense to you."

"My father was a good-for-nothing drunk. The world is better off without him." He turned and started to leave. Before he crossed the driveway, he said, "I'm cutting across your land now."

"Saying that doesn't make it not trespassing," Micah said. "The law requires mutual agreement to establish permission."

Clearly Micah was not the normal contractor, but I needed him to stop goading the Duncans. He would leave once the project ended. I was going to have to live with them.

Charles Duncan wheeled around. "The McAlister tract is five acres surrounded on all sides by two hundred thirty acres of Duncan land as deeded to Patrick Duncan in 1787."

"That doesn't make it any less hers." Micah was unfazed by the older man's angry, scrunched-up face.

Duncan shook his head and continued shaking it as he turned and walked off. "C'mon, Jesse." Jesse scrambled along behind his father. The older Duncan called back, "I'll be keeping an eye out on your project. That waste bin best be moved by tomorrow."

When they were gone, Micah let out a long exhale. "Friendly neighbors."

"Aren't they?"

"It's going to be a bitch to move that, and he knows it. I'm going to have to get the flatbed back out here." He fished his cell phone out of his coveralls.

"Sorry," I said. "You were really getting into him."

I was going to explain that I didn't want him goading my neighbor, when he said, "Yep. Keep being sweet like you are and let me play the heavy. That's the best way to handle Charles Duncan."

"You know him?"

Micah chuckled. "Know him? Shit, he expelled me from high school. He used to be the vice principal at Hendersonville High School. I'm sure this is more about me than you."

"I wouldn't count on that." I thought back to the journal and to the tension the Duncans had had with the rest of the world a century before.

The next morning I rose with the sun and to the chatter of unknown birds. Carson Quinn so occupied my mind that my first thought was that he would surely be able to identify the birdsong. After firing up the propane stove to brew coffee, I ventured down the road. The double-wide lay silent. Far below, the meadow where Old Man Duncan's home once stood glistened with morning dew. It had been recently mowed and sat as tidy and confined as a suburban lawn. No evidence of the old clapboard house remained. In the hovering condensate, a flock of turkeys clucked and pecked. I stood and watched them. There had never been turkey here in my youth. At least a dozen were scattered throughout the field. Two toms flashed their magnificent plumage at the ladies, who were unimpressed.

"Too bad it ain't Thanksgiving," a gravelly female voice said from behind me.

I jumped. A middle-aged woman stood watching me watch the turkeys while her golden retriever wound her up in the leash.

"Didn't mean to startle you," she said. "You must be the McAlister woman."

"Caroline." I extended my hand.

She shook it. "I'm Tilda Morrison."

"Nice to meet you," I said. "I just inherited the cabin up the hollow."

"That's what I heard," she said.

"Heard?"

"Oh, honey." She placed a warm hand on my shoulder. "Nothing happens up in here that don't everyone know about." She chuckled. "I chat with Charles Duncan's wife, Patsy, on a regular basis. She's not nearly as stuffy as Charles."

"Thank goodness," I said.

"Don't mind Charles. He's all bark, like a yippy little dog." She turned to the golden and her voice jumped at least two octaves. "Isn't that right, Buster? He's a little yippy dog." Buster wagged his tail in agreement.

"Buster and I usually take our morning walk up this way. I live in the house by the road."

In the process of conversing, we had begun to walk up the road toward the Duncan homestead. "In the old Grayson place?"

"Funny," she said. "I never thought of it that way, but I guess that's right."

"How did you wind up with it?"

"I was Tilda Grayson until I married a man I shouldn't have. All I got in the divorce was the name. My parents gave me the house, since they were too old to use it anymore."

We had followed the road around a bend only to be met by an industrial-strength gate peppered with signs: No Trespassing, No Parking, No Hunting, Caution: Firearms in Use.

"What is this?" I asked, agog.

"Charles Duncan." She offered nothing more in explanation.

"Of course," I said. "We used to walk all through those woods, following the road until it ended and became a game trail, then kept going on and up over the mountain."

"Well, this is where we turn around now."

We ambled back down the road in the direction we had just come from. "So, you're fixing up your cabin?" she asked.

"That's the plan." I didn't normally divulge such personal details, but I felt safe with her. "I just got a divorce of my own."

Tilda nodded as if she already knew that. Maybe she did. "There's something about this place and divorced women. It's protective. It don't judge."

"What do you mean?"

"There's a long history of lone women making a life in these parts. You got yourself, you got me, you got the Saunter sisters, you got the Baldwin lady up the road, and then there was Marinda Quinn. Between the divorcees and the widows this place might as well be a downright matriarchy. The men have always left for one reason or another."

"What do you know about the Quinns?" I asked.

"I knew a few of them, heard some of the stories."

"Did you ever know Carson Quinn?" I asked.

"Sure. I knew him...I guess as well as anybody did, which wasn't very much. He was as old as the mountains themselves, and never strayed far from that cabin of yours. Mean, ooohhh, so mean that even the yellow jackets steered clear of him. Only a few brave souls dared approach that place."

That meanness again. It didn't track with the journal so far. What could possibly have turned that earnest young boy into such an ornery old man, or worse, a murderer?

"Sometime I'd like to chat with you about him," I said.

"Any time you'd like," she said. "You can come on down and we'll set on the porch and swap tall tales."

We had reached the old Grayson place, now the Morrison place. "You want to come on in?"

"I don't want to impose," I said.

A pickup turned from the main road onto the graveled state road we'd been walking on.

"Howdy!" Micah hollered from the truck.

I waved to him. "I'll be up in a bit," I shouted back.

"Whatever you say, boss," he answered. "We'll see you up there."

"Sure." I turned to Tilda. "I'll come in."

I followed her past the old tin-roofed shed that had once been William Quinn's forge. I winced, knowing now that it was where the stern taskmaster had meted out a severe punishment on his young sons. We stepped onto the porch, and I imagined old Aurelius Quinn rocking away, spittoon at his feet.

"Have a seat." She pointed to a couple of rocking chairs.

We sat in silence for a minute, the only sounds the creaking of the chairs and the gurgle of the creek flowing by, the creek that had once powered the old mill.

"How did the Graysons come to own this place?" I asked.

"Bought it," she said. "My grandfather purchased it from Marinda Quinn."

"Was that after her husband was killed?"

"After Thomas was killed, Marinda went back to live with

her folk down the road. Those were rough times for folk up in these hollers. The Flood of 1916 came through and washed away the mill. In the twenties, Ma Quinn passed, left the place to Marinda. She needed money so she put the place on the market. My grandfather was up from Florida and offered cash on the spot for the house and its twenty-one acres."

"So, after that, all the Quinns owned was my cabin?"

"Nope." She perched forward, as if about to share the most scandalous secret. "Your cabin wasn't built for another eight years or so. All the Quinns owned was that holler it sits in. Hemmed in by Duncan land on all sides."

"How did Carson Quinn come to live in the cabin?"

"That, honey, I do not know. All I know is he was there when I come along, and we kids were told to steer clear of that murdering old coot."

"Do you think he did it?" My mind drifted over the gurgle of the creek and the chirping of a hummingbird and the rumble of motorcycles on the nearby highway.

"You're going to figure that out, aren't you?" Tilda asked.

I found myself nodding even before I had formulated a verbal response. "Yes," I said. "I am."

5

June 24, 1886—Pa makes us all carry our weight around here. A man's worst enemy is idleness, he says, and I reckon that's true if you're him and your idle thoughts are as troublesome as his. Me, I can sit and draw and read and write all day long if allowed. It's not allowed, so I find ways to do my part that don't involve working the mill or lugging coal for Pa. There are inns all around. In the summer months outliers come from all parts to visit. Across the way lies Glen Eden and farther down in the valley is the Edney Inn. I can make a few pence by tending to them. They like to go afield on picnics, and doing so requires a guide lest they get lost in a laurel hell or fall clear off a mountainside.

Since we don't want tourists getting lost, I lead them to the favorite spots, the waterfalls, the mountain views, the swimming holes. I've met quite a few interesting folk that way. Yesterday I took a group on an all-day excursion up to Hickory Nut Falls. The way we do it is to take the wagon most of the way, then once it gets to being steep and treacherous, we sally forward on foot. But that means I get to carry the food myself. One of them took kindly to me and offered to bear a portion of the burden.

His name was Thadeus Moore, and he was from Wilmington. I'd say he was a might younger than Pa, but old enough to have three young'uns that ran circles round us all the way up the mountain. He was right interested in us and how we lived up in these here hills. He had the impression that us locals were all dirt poor and made a life by hunting and growing corn. I said, "No, sir. Most folks do live off their land, but it's with apples and sows and tending to drovers and outliers such as yourself." I went on to say that Pa had a mill and a forge and that Gramps was an attorney back in his day.

"That so?" Mr. Moore asked. "I myself am an attorney. What is your gramps's name?"

"Aurelius Quinn," I said.

"The Aurelius Quinn?" he asked, his mouth open wide enough to catch a dozen flies.

"Only one I know of," I said.

"Your grandfather is well-regarded across the state, my boy. He was an integral member of the State Legislature during the war, and his hand is all over the Constitution. Not to mention the many benevolent acts which are attributed to him. This state wouldn't be on the path it's on without him."

"That so?" I asked.

"Indeed. You should ask him about it sometime."

That fella didn't know the danger of asking Gramps an open-ended question such as that. But it spiked my curiosity. It made me wonder if maybe there was some other Aurelius Quinn. It also made me realize how little I knew of my own flesh and blood.

We reached the falls, and the young'uns stripped down and splashed around in the pool at the bottom. I set up the victuals, and lunch was taken as we all looked out across the deep gorge. I pointed out some features, such as the homesteads of the Morgans and the Daltons and the red-tailed hawk soaring down below. I figured it wasn't often that folks from Wilmington could look down on a hawk as it flew.

When I got home this evening, I joined Gramps on the porch. It was after dinner, and he was taking his whiskey and pipe. Gramps isn't entirely right in the head these days. Sometimes what he says makes sense. But it's just as likely that he will issue forth some nonsense riddle that no one can decipher.

"I met a fella today said he knew of you, Gramps," I said.

Gramps took two puffs on his pipe. He rocked the chair back and forth as he looked off toward the road. "That right?"

"Yes, sir," I said. "He says your hand is all over the Constitution and that you're well known for all manner of benevolence."

Gramps held one hand out and turned it around, then the

other he did the same with. "Nope," he said. "It would appear both my hands are still attached. Though he may have been mistaken. It might be my foot." He knocked his peg leg on the porch. "I done lost track of where that right foot might have gotten off to."

Gramps took to laughing his high-pitched cackle till it caused a coughing fit that then led to a spitting fit. He wasn't inclined to say anything else, so I let him be.

July 17, 1886—Yesterday morning, Betsy Morgan came running down the road at a full sprint. I've never seen a girl run so fast. There isn't a third baseman alive that could have beat her to first base with a throw. She ran clear up onto the front porch, waking Gramps from a slumber. As he's apt to do, he woke with a shout, "Tally ho!"

"Mr. Quinn!" Betsy squawked.

"Why, young lady, it's Aurelius to you." Gramps fancies himself a dashing ladies' man, even now with one leg literally in the grave and the rest of him shriveled and wore out.

"Get Sheila! Quick!"

Ain't nothing quick about Gramps, so I ran in from where I was at the forge and grabbed Ma. "Come quick," I said. "Something's amiss."

She unhitched her apron and left the corn half shucked and came out.

"It's Miss Mabel," Betsy said. "She's having her baby early."

In a dash, Ma was gone with Betsy, and the Quinn residence was restored to its normal sounds: the water wheel whining as it turned out back, Thomas pounding iron in the forge, and Taylor shouting "get back!" at the chickens as they ganged up on him fetching their eggs.

Ma didn't come back until supper time. When she came back, she had blood on her skirt and her hair was all messed up. Her eyes were set on a horizon that didn't exist. Pa knew to get up and fix us our vittles while Ma went and took a long bath.

Miss Mabel, it turned out, had died. She wasn't much older

than me, maybe two years at most, and now here she is dead. Her baby survived. No one knows who the father is, but based on the baby's complexion it's apt to be a Negro. The only Negroes around are the Rolly family that live down in the valley. The father can't be Mr. Rolly, it just can't. He's old and married to Mrs. Rolly. And Pa says he's not the kind of person to do that. They have a son named Skeeter, but he's blind. Ma says being blind ain't enough to stop a person from being a man, but Pa thinks the father was likely a drover that came through on the last big drive what happened to be round about nine months ago.

Anyway, Mabel's parents have refused to care for the baby, not even enough to give it a name. The Morgans have it for now. Miss Betsy has a heart the size of Blue Rock. She has named the baby Bradshaw. He doesn't have a last name on account of not having a daddy.

❧

I closed up the journal carefully. Reading it took a lot of concentration because of the young boy's handwriting. Smudges and stains, probably acquired during his "meanderings" further obscured the text. I slid it into the Ziploc bag I had purchased specifically for the job and placed it in a plastic tub alongside all of the photos, which were now carefully sheaved in plastic protectors. Though the metal box had protected its contents for at least half a century, I thought utilizing some more up-to-date storage was in order. My students would be proud. They often made fun of my squeamishness about technology. I had no social media presence, and my cell phone couldn't launch a satellite. All it could do was make and receive phone calls.

My students. I hadn't thought about them in months. Preoccupied with my divorce and then my father's death, I hadn't arranged my typical summer research program. My graduate students were disappointed, but understanding. I had farmed them out to various colleagues. My own research had stalled as well. After the publication of my latest book, which looked at the cosmologies of the Maya and the ancient Irish in the context of their very different latitudes, I was seeking out something new, something that might translate more readily to non-anthropologists. I figured this break would do me good. But my academic research was the last thing on my mind.

My mind had always been prone to figuring things out. When I was an awkward young girl, my mind preoccupied itself with decoding the secrets of social fluidity. When that proved too challenging a task, it moved on to simpler questions, such as how a society's ability to perceive the night sky might inform its entire understanding of the meaning of life. The set of mysteries contained now in the plastic tub consumed me. Absent official research, Carson Quinn would do.

Demolition was progressing nicely on the cabin. Micah and his crew had stripped the interior down to the logs and framing. All the mildewed and damaged parts now filled the formerly trespassing bin out front. What remained was hardy lumber and those few pieces of surviving furniture that they thought could be restored. Micah brought in a weather-proof storage pod to house the furniture. He slammed shut the door, locked it with a giant padlock, and handed me the key.

"I told you," Micah said, admiring his work. "This old place has good bones."

"Look at it." I beamed. What once had seemed unredeemable now appeared stalwart and solid. It easily had centuries left in it, just as Micah had predicted.

"What's next?"

"Glad you asked." Micah led me over to his truck. He spread some plans out on the hood and explained in detail how he would start with the foundation and shore everything up, joists to rafters. He might as well have been speaking Italian. I had no idea what he was talking about, but it sounded good coming off his lips. He spoke of furring, footers, girders, trestles, facias, and soffits. When done, he arched a questioning eyebrow. "So?"

"You had me at furring." I draped my hand over his and squeezed.

"Oh," he said. "I almost forgot. Jed was cleaning up that old armoire from the front bedroom, and he came across this. It looks like another one of your father's old papers."

He handed me a stained, curled-up envelope that contained an old Hallmark card. "Thank you." I pulled the card from the envelope. In my mind, the past had become solely and completely inhabited by Carson Quinn. But this came from a later time. It was a Valentine's Day card. The cover art was a naked cupid, fluttering in the air, his bow quivering as though the arrow had just been loosed. Opening up the card revealed a giant heart with an arrow sticking out of it. "You got me!" read the text.

On the opposite side lay several lines of my father's precise handwriting.

My Dearest Madeleine,

You once told me a story of how you, as a young girl from Sarasota, boarded the train all alone and came up to summer camp in the mountains of North Carolina. I remember you telling me how enchanted you became with the hills and the rivers, the cool breezes and katydid nights. Do you remember why you told me this story? You said that the only time you had ever been as enchanted as you were with me then was as you were with the mountains as a young girl. Maddie, I love you, and on this, our first Valentine as a married couple, I want you to have both of your true loves: the mountains and me. This cabin is my gift to you, and I hope it brings you as much joy as you bring me. Love,

Your faithful and ever adoring husband

The tears that hadn't fallen for him at his funeral now came. He had lived decades without her, and it hit me hard knowing how very much he had loved her and why, after she died, he never wanted to come back here, and also why he could never let it go. It was hers in life and in death, occupied by only rodents and ghosts for decades.

"Ms. McAlister?" Micah asked. He placed a concerned hand on my arm.

"It's okay, Micah," I said. "And it's Caroline. Call me Caroline. Please."

"Sure thing, Caroline."

I slipped the card back into its envelope. Micah pulled a bandanna from his hip pocket and handed it to me. "Here."

"Thank you." I took it and wiped my tears, still gasping for air. "That was unexpected."

"It's okay," he said.

"Yes," I answered, handing back the bandanna. "I hadn't cried for my father yet. It felt good, actually."

"You need to cry, to grieve," Micah said, giving me reason number forty-seven why he wasn't the normal contractor and why I had been wise to hire him.

I climbed back up to my camp. Looking at the cabin, now a solid shell, I wondered if the ghost of my mother and the ghost of Carson Quinn had ever crossed paths. For surely both clung mightily to the hearty chestnut timbers of the cabin.

6

September 1, 1886—Yesterday the earth shook. I had gone afield as I'm apt to do. Carrying a bag of vittles and a blanket I wandered off across the Edney Inn Valley. There were some fancy folk staying at the inn, and they were out in the yard playing a funny game with long-handled hammers and balls. I wandered past. They pretended not to see me. Then I hiked the three or four miles on up the back of Blue Rock. Blue Rock is part of the mountain ridge that's home to Chimney Rock. I like to climb up there to get a view of the Gorge. Near the ridgeline is a good place to camp. As you climb up the mountain, a laurel hell gets dense and closes in on you. A normal person would turn around, but I get real low and slither through like a snake with legs. Eventually, you can climb out of the hell, and you find yourself on a steep rock, looking out over the Gap. On the other side, you can see Round Top, not more than a mile away. It feels like you can almost jump across the Gorge to the other side. But a body that tried would wind up crashing down the mountainside through the rhododendron and oaks. If you look to the right, you can see all the way past Rumbling Bald Mountain down into the farmland of Rutherford County.

The Cherokee have occupied these lands longer than anyone, and they say the Gap is home to fairies and little people. For them, it was an enchanted place. No Cherokee lived in the Gorge, though they used it as a way to get from the lowlands to the mountains. Now, we white folk have pushed the Cherokee out to the west, all except for Charlie Brightleaf. He and his wife have a farm in the valley and are more Christian than I am. Charlie's the one that showed me the campsite up on this ridge. He takes me bear hunting in the winter months sometimes, and we camp there where we can see for miles.

He tells me the Cherokee stories and teaches me about tracking and hunting. He says the Little People protect this gorge. They're a race of knee-high, immortal spirits who love to dance and drum, and they live in the bat caves which are down below Blue Rock. I never put much stock in such superstition. I've been over every inch of the Gap. If they really existed, one would think I would have seen them by now. Some say that at night, on occasion, you can hear them talking. You don't want to disturb them. Like most folk, if you let them alone, they'll let you alone, but they tend toward the mischievous. They'll lure you into getting lost or they may run off with your things. At least that's what Charlie says. Before last night, I thought it was but a fancy story. 'Round about ten o'clock that all changed.

I had lit a fire after darkness fell and was sitting by it, just listening to the wind come through the high trees, when of a sudden I got a bad feeling in the pit of my stomach. I thought it was maybe the jerky I'd eaten for dinner had gone bad, but then the ground started to shake. The whole mountain felt like it was going to fall down. Limbs from some of the trees began to fall. A noise angrier than thunder rang out from across the Gorge. It was the Rumbling Bald, General Clingman's volcano. I was scared.

I heard voices calling to me from the laurel hell. "Carson Quinn," they said. "Carson Quinn, come here." Were they the Little People? Or were they some hunters out a-hunting? Or was it just fear talking?

I doused my fire and took off into the rhododendron. Sometimes, Charlie Brightleaf will refer to the Little People as Laurel People. Seeing as how they're so short, they can live quite comfortable under the rhododendron. As I've mentioned, I am nigh on six feet tall, so I had to crawl on my hands and knees through the limbs. Since it was dark, branches kept slapping my face. I followed those voices, all the while the ground was a-shaking and rocks were rolling past me and tree limbs were slamming into the ground right and left. I reckon I may be an atheist after all, because never once did I think it was the end of the world. Later I learned that a lot of local folks thought the end times was upon them.

I never did find the source of the voices, but they led me clear on down the mountain out into the Rolly's cornfield. Since there was nothing to fall on me, I felt a might better, but the ground was still rumbling and shaking, though not nearly as badly. It took me a minute or two to gather myself out there in the cornfield. Then I set out back toward home, my legs still a little uncertain, as though I'd had some of Pa's moonshine. I've only had a sip a time or two, and I must say, one might as well drink fire.

Old man Rolly was out in his field as I approached, looking up at the top of the mountain.

"Howdy, Mr. Rolly," I called.

I guess he didn't see or hear me at first. He didn't reply to my greeting, just kept on staring up the mountain. Finally, he caught sight of me. "Carson Quinn. What in tarnation is you doin' out in all this?"

"I was camping up there," I said.

"It's a good thing you come down. God's angry with someone tonight!"

Mr. Rolly didn't budge an inch, his eyes fixed on the top of the mountain.

"Mmm-hmm," he said. "God is angry."

At the inn, it looked like all the tourists had come out to watch fireworks. They were looking up at the mountain too. You could still hear the rumbling and pounding off in the distance, but the shaking had stopped.

"You there," someone called to me.

"Yes, sir," I answered.

"Is that the Rumbling Bald?"

"Reckon so," I answered. "It's on past that there mountain we call Blue Rock."

"What great luck! We've heard of the Rumbling Bald. Now we've experienced it."

The tourists were drinking champagne, it looked like, and

giggling and chatting. That was as curious as the rumbling itself. I had never seen nothing like it.

It was nigh on midnight when I crept into the house. I set up a blanket to sleep by the fire instead of going up to my room so I wouldn't wake Thomas and Taylor. We share a bed upstairs. Ma appeared in the doorway.

"Carson, are you all right?" she asked.

She came closer and held my chin to look at my face.

"You're bleeding," she said. "Why are you all cut up, son?"

As she dabbed the scratches on my face with warm salve, I explained about running through the hell and the voices I heard calling. She's the only person I'd ever tell about hearing the voices. I said nothing about Charlie and my suspicions that they might be the Little People. Tears welled in her eyes as I relayed the event.

She hugged me tight, so tight I could barely breathe. "You are special, Carson. The Tuatha Dé are very particular about who they protect."

"The what?"

"The Tuatha Dé Danann. The Little People."

The hair on the back of my neck bristled.

"In Irish, they are known as the People of Danu, a goddess from olden times. They are an entire race of little people, like those that live in this gap."

"Like leprechauns?" I asked.

"Leprechauns are members of the same race. They're magical, and they often play spiteful games with humans. They don't particularly like humans, because humans are careless and often destroy the places most dear to the Little People."

"That's what Charlie Brightleaf says too. He says the Little People are mischievous."

"I suspect that Charlie would know the most about those that live in these parts. You should listen to him. He's a kind man."

I wasn't sure what to say to that. Ma is often surprising in this way. It's like she knew all about the Little People, but never said nothing about it to no one. It makes me wonder what else she knows but keeps to herself. One day, I shall ask her to tell me more about what she knows, but last night I was tired and soon dozed off.

The talk today is that there was a massive earthquake yesterday in Charleston. Nothing is coming or going from there. I can't imagine what it was like down there, given how tumultuous it was this far away.

September 15, 1886—Gramps and old Judge Logan often get together to shoot the breeze, play checkers, and reminisce. When Gramps goes to Logan's, he usually takes one of us young'uns for company and to drive him back in case he drinks too much. Yesterday, it was my turn. I hitched Henry the mule to our wagon, and pulled it around so Gramps wouldn't have to walk so far to get up there. He refused my help, as usual. He's had only one leg for almost forty years, so he knows how to swing it on up. He can do a lot more than you would think. I've even seen him run with his peg leg once when Taylor was little and about to fall off the porch.

Anyhow, Gramps got in and drove us the seven miles down to Logan's. The judge, that's George Washington Logan, was out on his porch when we drove up. The judge and Gramps go way back, and there's nothing they like more than to set there and gab about the old days.

"Aurelius, my old friend," the judge said, rising and coming to help Gramps up on the porch. Gramps shook him off and used his cane to lever himself up the stairs by himself. He had his black-lacquered, silver handled model that he used to carry into the courtroom. One of his canes has a sword hidden inside it. I can never remember which one it is, though.

"G.W.," Gramps said, taking his friend's hand.

"And who do you have with you this time?" The judge peered down at me with his fierce eyes.

"Why that there's Sarah." Gramps hobbled on up the steps without turning back toward me.

"My friend, I believe you may be—"

"Nonsense," Gramps interrupted.

"Gramps," I implored, "I ain't Sarah."

"Ain't Sarah? Then I expect you'll have to do her courting for her. Now, Judge Logan, where's your whippersnapper grandson off to?"

The judge laughed. Gramps, ever the court jester, feigned offense. "Now, are you telling me we Quinns aren't good enough for you and yours?"

"No, not at all, Aurelius. I do think my grandson might be more likely to be swayed by your Sarah than her proxy there, young Carson."

"What good are you, boy?" Gramps said, scowling so hard I almost believed he believed himself. Since he followed his scowl with a wink, I knew the joke was on the judge, not on me.

Gramps allowed the judge to lead him to a comfortable chair and they both sat. I hung back by the steps, close enough I could still hear them. So they wouldn't think I was listening, I pulled out my jackknife and commenced to whittling a piece of pine I found.

"Any news on Charleston, G.W.?" Gramps asked.

"Oh, it's terrible, I'm afraid. Reports are of at least a hundred deaths. Lots of buildings came down. Folks are afraid to sleep indoors now, so many have taken to sleeping in tents. We're mighty lucky here that we didn't have more damage, what with Rumbling Bald being right in my backyard."

Gramps clicked his teeth in agreement. "Speaking of. My grandson, er, young Sarah's proxy, what's his name…"

The judge laughed. "Carson, you mean to say?"

At the mention of my name, I jerked my head up, and both of the old sophists wore wry grins. The joke was on me this time, caught eavesdropping by the oldest trick in the book.

"Tell him, boy," Gramps commanded. "About your run-in with the general."

I relayed the story, best as I could, of my encounter with General Clingman. "He seemed like a nice enough fella," I said in summation. "He wasn't talking about the same thing I was is all."

"You've raised a kind young man, Aurelius."

"That'd be his mama's doing," Gramps answered. "Kindness ain't my forte."

"Let me tell you about Thomas Clingman, young man," Judge Logan said. "Back in the day, myself and the then senator were the fiercest of adversaries. We came up together in the university, him a couple of years ahead of me, and we got along fine at first, sharing a love of this state and particularly these mountains. But then came the issue of slavery, and if that Thomas Clingman wasn't the defender of the slaveholding aristocracy with their fancy dances and fine china and thinking themselves so much better than the rest of us—"

"G.W.," Gramps said, setting his hand on the judge's arm. "The education of the young isn't worth the consternation of the old. Remember, united we stand!"

The judge shook his head. "Divided we fell. Truth. Virtue. Honor. Fidelity. Justice. They weren't enough in the end, Aurelius." He sighed deeply, and smoke shot from his nostrils like flames from a dragon. "The Red String Order may have won the war, but we've lost the peace."

"I don't suppose old man Rolly'd agree with you there," Gramps said, pointing up the Gorge to where the Rollys had their farm.

"That right?" The judge shook his head. "Where are his forty acres and a mule?"

Gramps spat his tobacco at the spittoon near his feet. Old man Rolly probably has at least a dozen acres of the best farmland in Daisy. He has an ox or two, but I've never seen him with a mule, and he has nowhere near forty acres.

"He was at least able to buy his property and he gets to keep the product of his labor, don't he?"

"Things are going to get much worse for men like Mr. Rolly and for your son, Will, too. Just you wait and see."

Gramps glared at the judge.

"Ain't you a passel of daisies this morning?"

The judge grumbled. "Think about it, old friend. A man can no longer go out and carve his living out of the land. The drovers, for instance, don't come through now that the trains cross over the mountain. And your Will, he's the most talented blacksmith in four counties. But give it five years, and folks will no longer need him. Everything they have will be store-bought. And as for milling hominy, ha! You go down to the general store and you buy your grits for less than it costs to grow the corn and pay William to mill it. It's a changing world out past the walls of the Gap, and not all the changes are for the better."

Gramps nodded. "Yep, you're likely right about that. But Will's the daggone stubbernest man I've ever known. And he's my own flesh and blood. He could learn a new trade if he set his mind to it."

"Your William is a fine, fine man. After what he's been through and seen...a lesser man would have folded, would have just given into the damnation. Why, the West is full of those men."

"Even the Wild West ain't the Wild West no more."

"Right you are," the judge said. "But that son of yours, despite all appearances to the contrary, doesn't fall too far from the tree."

Gramps scowled.

"He was down here in the tavern a week ago Wednesday for the Farmers Alliance meeting. He had a lot of good ideas."

"That right?" Gramps seemed a bit surprised. Of course, he goes to bed so early, he never really knows what any of us do after supper.

"Yes, sir." The judge rocked back and forth.

Unusual for them, they were silent for a time. So, I butted in.

"What's the Red String Order?" I asked.

The judge looked right at me for the first time in the conversation. "It was a good idea, once."

I cleared my throat. "Might it have something to do with them acts of benevolence you won't say nothing about?"

"Benevolence." He spat.

He sure doesn't want me to know about his past, because he was quick to start into the politics of the day, railing on the Democrats and their small-mindedness.

It was around five hours and half a dozen games of checkers later that Gramps hollered to go. I drove back, though Henry knew the way. I just sat back and let him go. Gramps was snoring by the time we got to the Esmeralda Inn, not a quarter mile down the road.

&

In the shade of my tarp, I jotted down some notes on a legal pad. There was a lot to this boy's journal. I now added "George Washington Logan" and "The Red String Order" to the list that needed further research. By then the Civil War had been over for twenty years, but clearly it still dominated discussion. Even a hundred years later, when I was girl, it still angered Old Man Duncan. And a generation on, anger still simmered from the Duncans, whether from that "War of Northern Aggression" or some other slight, I didn't know.

Charles Duncan had taken to showing up on a four-wheeler every few days. He drove the vehicle cautiously, his eyes peeled as he puttered down the gravel road from his house "up yonder," as Jesse had described.

"I see you got that bin moved," he said, after pulling up and cutting the engine. It felt a bit incongruous to go from reading about his ancestor to interacting with him in flesh and blood. It reminded me that the figures in the journal weren't just characters in a book; they were real people. His people.

"I want to be a good neighbor."

He grunted, then slung himself off the four-wheeler, like a gunslinger dismounting from his steed. "Galvanized steel." He pointed at the stack of recently delivered roofing material.

"It seemed to make the most sense." Micah had walked me through the options for the roof, and I went with the more expensive option up front because it would last longer and require less maintenance over its life.

"Green's a good color. It'll get hot."

"It's nice and shaded here," I said.

"That it is." Charles climbed back aboard his faithful four-wheeler. "You'll remind your boys not to park down on my pasture. There were some tire ruts down there this morning."

"I'll let them know."

He fired up his engine, revved it twice, then circled out of my drive. He paused down by the double-wide. "Jesse!" he hollered. "Get your butt out here!" I heard the screen door squeal open. Despite living within earshot, I never heard a peep from Jesse. His car always sat silent in his driveway. On the rare occasions he would leave, he would roar down the gravel road at top speed, dust and dirt lingering in his wake like a specter.

"Yo!" he answered.

"You need to get down to the employment office, boy. Quit all the damn video games and get with it."

Jesse grunted. The door slammed shut and Charles rolled back up yonder.

The next day I rose and showered off in a specially rigged shower Micah had fashioned for me. My standard practice for showers in camp was to use my sun shower, which I filled with water and hung on a branch. The sun would heat it up, and in a few hours I'd have myself a pleasant, if rustic, shower. Micah had seen this set-up, gave it the once over, and shook his head. "I think we can do better."

"Better?" I had asked.

"You're not exactly private here. You got Jesse down there, and what if my boys get here early one day?"

Years of living in primitive conditions had numbed my sense of modesty, but he had a point. In no time, Micah had built a wooden platform and frame. He tacked up black plastic to the frame and ran a hose from an outdoor spigot, so that I didn't have to continually take the bag down to refill it.

"Nothing's wrong with the well," he said. "It works fine."

In no time I had quite the shower. Using it went from a chore to a delight. Micah beamed with pride when it was finished.

"Just add it to the bill."

"Yes, ma'am." He toted his hammer back to the real work of the cabin itself.

After showering I got dressed up, which meant my nicest jeans, cleanest blouse, and a pair of tanzanite earrings. I was going to make a trip into Hendersonville. The town is only thirteen miles from the cabin, and the journey along Highway 64 can take anywhere from twenty minutes to an hour depending on the number of slow-moving Floridians or farmers' tractors you encounter along the way. As I negotiated the hairpin turns over the Continental Divide and into the wide-open apple orchards of Edneyville, I couldn't help but think of Carson Quinn. This journey would have taken him the better part of a day back in the late 1880s. Before the improvement of the road and the blasting out of the roadbed from the mountainside, a traveler would have had to continually cross the Reedy Patch Creek in order to negotiate the climb up the mountain. It would have been treacherous and tedious. On this day, the Subaru zipped along unimpeded.

Though the journey itself hadn't changed much in the thirty years since my childhood, the scenery certainly had. The apple orchards were mostly still there, but smaller farms had been replaced with mobile homes and subdivisions. Some of the businesses along the road had not only changed hands, but also changed languages. What had once been Dolly's Mini Mart was now called Don Diego's Tiendita. I didn't realize that telegrams were still a thing, but there it was, Western Union, advertised in bright yellow and black.

As towns go, Hendersonville is small, charming even, though after spending a couple of weeks at the cabin, it felt garish and fast-paced with its Walmart, McDonald's, and Home Depot, a whole strip of commerce that could be anywhere in modern America. The first stop was a laundromat. During the summers of my childhood, Mom would haul everything down to the laundromat once a week—kids, clothes, and all. Coming to town was a ritual then, an opportunity to buy groceries, go to the library, and maybe see a movie. Washing several loads of laundry took what seemed like forever to Andrew and me. On several occasions our impatience got us in trouble. There was the time we turned the dirt embankment outside into our personal prominence for King of the Hill. Being the older child, I suppose I was in charge, but the lady from the high-end consignment shop next door spoke harshly to Andrew.

"You there!" she said. "Does your mother know you're playing in the dirt like little piglets?"

Andrew stared at her, his pants stained red from the clay we had been climbing.

I leapt down from the top of the hill. "Yes, ma'am," I explained. "She knows where we are."

"And where might she be?"

I pointed to the laundromat.

The lady led us to the door, pulled it open, and peered in. "That one there?" She pointed at a small, toothless woman in overalls who seemed old enough to be our grandmother.

"No, ma'am. There she is."

Mom peered at us over the edge of her book.

"Oh?" The lady took a long look at Mom, who looked every bit like the high school English teacher she was, then back to us, our clothes and skin all soiled and smudged. My hair must have looked like it needed hours of brushing to remove the kinks and sticks and ticks.

"Excuse me," the lady said to Mom. "Are these yours?" she asked, pointing at me and Andrew.

Andrew scoffed. "She's not my mother. I've never seen her before in my life." He ran up to the toothless, overalled woman. "Hey, Mama!"

The stranger broke into a wide, gummy grin and gave him a big hug.

"This one's mine," Mom said. "What has she done this time?"

"She was crawling in the dirt out back with that one." She pointed at Andrew. "She's going to wind up with worms if you don't keep a better eye on her."

"Shew," Mom said. "This is getting bad. Last week she stole the ice cream truck. Got all the way down to Fifth and Church before the police caught up. She's out on bail right now. Looks like she hasn't learned her lesson."

The lady wrinkled her nose at Mom, her face a contortion of confusion and derision.

"I can't believe she's progressed from grand theft auto to playing in the dirt. Next she'll probably turn to drugs. Might you be looking to adopt? I'm sure Bobbie Ann over there would gladly part with the boy, and then you'd have a matched set."

The lady straightened her back and huffed. "I was just trying to help."

"Thank you so much," Mom said.

The lady spun on her heel and went back to her shop. When the door shut, we all had a good laugh, Bobbie Ann included, whom my mother must have befriended while we were playing outside. Mom was friendly with everyone, especially with those whom others dismissed.

The memory fresh, I pulled into the parking lot. The laundromat was still there. Interestingly, the consignment shop was not. While nostalgia colored nearly everything these days, I felt no remorse whatsoever at its demise.

When I entered the laundromat, it was as though I had been transported not back in time, but across continents. The chattering song of Spanish twirled over the thumping of dryers and swishing of washers. Several Latina mothers were there with their children. Kids darting here and there, shouting and squealing, made the place seem more crowded than it was. I made my way to a free washing machine and loaded it up. As I did, one of the women approached me. Not having used a laundromat since grad school, I was sure I had immediately breached unwritten etiquette.

She was trying to tell me something. Her face wasn't angry, though. It wore a look of concern.

"No work," she said, pointing at my chosen machine. She shook her head. "No work."

"*¿Está roto?*" I asked in Spanish, having picked up the language on multiple research trips to Mexico.

The next thing I knew, we were in a full-bore conversation.

"My name is Isabel," she said.

"I'm Caroline. Where are you from?" I asked. I had thought I might be speaking Spanish this summer, just not in a laundromat in North Carolina.

"Oaxaca," she said.

"Why did you come here?" I asked.

"Love, of course," she answered. A silver tooth glinted in her coy smile.

"Oh?"

"My husband came north to work in the trees."

"Trees?"

"Christmas trees. I missed him so much, I brought the kids up. Now he works the apple orchards, and we live in Edneyville."

The trailer parks I had driven by flashed in my mind, along with the sting of guilt for having bemoaned them.

"That's Teresa," she said, pointing across the room to the oldest of her kids, a younger teenaged girl wearing a sequined T-shirt who was busy chasing down a toddler. That could have been me chasing Andrew some thirty-odd years before.

As the machines did the dirty work, I sat back and watched Teresa mind her brother while Isabel folded their clothes. As they left, she turned to me. Her silver-edged tooth again showed itself. "*Hasta luego.*"

"*Igualmente,*" I answered.

What a journey they must have had, crossing the desert by who-knows-how, making their way across the country to the mountains of North Carolina. These mountains, for so long, a lure for people trying to make a living from the land. I thought of Sheila Quinn, from County Sligo, Ireland. I thought of all those pioneer mothers near the Gap, who were the Isabels of their day. I thought of my own people, the McAlisters and the Crests, possessors of journeys epic in their own way. Though Isabel may have been representative of the transformation taking place here, the transformation itself was nothing new. Just ask old Charlie Brightleaf.

After the clothes were finished, I drove to the library. There was an entire special section devoted to local history. The woman staffing the section fit the very definition of librarian. In her sixties with a church lady's perm and silver eyeglasses hanging around her neck, she responded to my request with the dourest of looks.

"The red what?" she asked, pinching her nose.

"The Red String Order," I repeated. "It was an anti-secessionist movement during the Civil War."

She looked aghast. "Anti-secessionist? Here?" She pointed to a huge chest of alphabetized index cards. "You can check the catalogue. 'R' is on the lower right." Once again, the war showed itself to be source of tension even now.

There was nothing about The Red String Order in the catalogue, so I turned my attention to searching for the Quinns. There were several references, under "Q" of course.

I hadn't used microfiche since early in graduate school. The value of digitizing these old documents became evident as I rolled through countless editions of the *Hendersonville Times*, seeing the same advertisements for liniment creams and elixirs and the latest in men's fashions over and over again. The news, such as it was, focused then, as now, on the absurd: One of Delmar Fortune's bulls found its way into the First Methodist Church and rushed at the pastor when he opened it up on one Sunday morning. A collision between the trolley car and a wagon transporting lye created catastrophe on Main Street, sending men, women, and children into fits of swooning. An enraged farmer had sworn out a warrant on his neighbor's sow, who had escaped and dug up his entire potato crop. The stories made it easy to get distracted from the task at hand.

Finally, I came to it, in the August 21, 1900 edition: an article referencing the murder of Thomas Quinn. "Member of Prominent Hickory Nut Gorge Family Slain," it read.

Thomas Quinn, late of Daisy, was discovered deceased in

a waterfall behind his home. Though found submerged, it was determined that the death was not by drowning but by fearsome wounds to his upper body. Sheriff Toms promises to continue an investigation of the incident, which will require the process of elimination since there is no paucity of suspects or motivations. Mr. Quinn was a known bootlegger who had recently quarreled with federal agents and the notorious outlaw Augustus Trabor. It is also reported that on Monday of last week Mr. Quinn threatened the life of local banker T.H. Helms, and that he had a long-standing dispute with his brother, Carson Quinn. A conversation with a neighbor indicated that the brothers had competed for the affection of the deceased's wife, Marinda Quinn. Thomas Quinn left behind said former wife and a daughter, Bella Quinn, ten years of age. Also surviving are a brother, Captain Taylor Quinn, of the U.S. 7th Cavalry, sister Sarah Quinn Johnston, of Charleston, and the aforementioned brother, Carson Quinn. The deceased was the son of William Quinn and Sheila Quinn, currently of Daisy. Both his father and his grandfather, Aurelius Quinn, are known for their civic engagements, the former active in the Grange movement and the latter a prominent local attorney and key delegate to the State Constitutional Convention in 1868.

I sat transfixed by the glowing screen long after I had finished reading the piece. Here it was in black and white, family story made real by typeset and ink. I scrolled through the remainder of the year but found no other reference to the Quinns. Was the case just dropped? Maybe Thomas was such a villain as to not warrant any other action, but the article had mentioned the sheriff continuing the investigation. Having read it, I felt even more certain that Carson Quinn was no murderer. Any of the other suspects seemed much more likely to have done Thomas in than the earnest young boy I'd come to know from the journal.

All of this had been a mental exercise until now, Caroline's little game. This article brought it back to reality. In the end, Carson didn't get the girl. Thomas did. Then, Thomas had been murdered, the murder documented in print. There was a date, even, August 21, 1900. Of course, his death would have occurred sometime before that. That was the date of the article.

The mental time travel had me out of sorts. The sun blasting my eyes as I stumbled from the library back to my car didn't help. And there was a persistent beeping sound coming from the travel satchel that served as my purse. It took me a few minutes to isolate the noise, then fish out my phone. I flipped it open. There were two messages: one from Andrew and one from Delores. Since there was no cell phone reception at the cabin, there was no telling when either called.

I called Delores back first, and she picked up on the second ring.

"Delores Beck, Keller Williams," she answered professionally.

"How's business?" I asked.

"Top seller in the office two months running. If I can get this monster deal closed, it will be three months in a row."

"How's Tommy?"

"Good. You know he's in insurance? Just like your dad was."

"That right?" The sun was hot, and I was already annoyed. Comparing Tommy Beck to my father didn't help matters.

"So," she said. "The reunion. You haven't been to the tenth, fifteenth, or twentieth reunions. Don't tell me you're going to skip out on the twenty-fifth."

Stress clawed its way up my back. "That's too many reunions. Most schools torture their alumni once every ten years, not every five."

"Most schools don't have me as the class president," she said.

"Look." I decided on honesty as a tactic. "High school wasn't a good time for me, with everything that happened. I don't have many fond memories from back then."

She was quiet. "Do you have any fond memories at all?"

I was taken aback. My focus for decades had always been on whatever was next: new research, an upcoming symposium, a fellowship to apply for. Part of me was proud to never dwell on the past. Her question threw me. Were there any moments with Woody that I looked fondly back on? There might have been, but always our time together felt compromised, one of us always with some big push looming over us. We went to Scotland and Ireland for a week, but that was only because I was there doing research one summer. I showed off the sites I was using and introduced him to the cosmologists at the Royal Observatory. But I wouldn't say I looked back, fondly or otherwise, at anything…other than my childhood at the cabin in Carson Quinn's Hemlock Hollow.

"I'm sorry." Delores interrupted my mental journey. "I understand why you wouldn't want to walk down memory lane."

"Don't be. I think my fondest memories are of the cabin way back, you know when we were kids."

"You did love it up there," Delores concurred. "You seemed so at home there when we visited. All those crazy hikes you'd take us on. I can't believe your mother let us go off alone like that."

"She was good that way." I swallowed hard, tightening my grip on the phone. "I think maybe she understood exactly what you're saying, that I was different up there, more free to be myself."

"We all loved her, you know. Even those of us who had her in the ninth grade."

"That's right." I shifted the phone from my left ear to my right. "You actually had her as a teacher."

"Yep. Hardest class I had in high school. God, I hated her at the time. You sure couldn't BS your way through that class. I don't do much writing these days, but I think about her whenever I have to compose a long email. I still make each word count and form a thesis statement that all of the following sentences support. Turns out it actually works."

"I know." Even though I was never in her class, she hadn't

spared me her lessons, and my college and post-college career was the stronger for it. "Hey, Delores, once I get this thing habitable, why don't you come visit?"

"Absolutely, honey. I would love that. You say the word, and I'll be there. I could bring Martha. It would be great. But…" She paused long enough for me to hear her take a deep breath. "Is it still haunted?"

"I don't know," I said.

"Have you seen a ghost?"

"I don't know that I believe in ghosts."

"Ever the skeptic," Delores said. "I know someone that does séances, you know."

"That right?"

"Mmm-hmm. I sold a house for this gal that was an honest-to-goodness witch."

"Like Elizabeth Montgomery?" I asked.

"Different shaped nose, but she's completely normal. Very nice woman. We've since become friends."

"Okay," I said. "When the cabin is ready, we'll have you and Martha and your witch come up and do a séance. I have some questions for a dead man."

"Ooh. I can't wait!"

7

September 16, 1886—Today I went for a ramble back up above our vegetable patch. The pitch is steep, but to me, a hill isn't much of an obstacle. Ma says I'm half mountain goat on account of how nimble I am. Like a mountain goat, I tend to wander. Daniel Boone used to claim that in all his years of exploring the wilderness he had never been lost, just a tad bewildered once or twice. That's how I feel too. I've never really been lost in the woods. It's not that hard to get back to where you've come from. At times, though, I'm just not sure how to get to where I want to go.

Today was one of those days. In all my years of scouting these hills and hollers I had never gone due west out of our land, probably because the hillside is so steep that-away that it's almost like a wall. Today I climbed right on up that wall. It was more like climbing a tree than walking upright as I had to take care to find purchase amongst roots and rocks and then pull myself up with my arms like a spider monkey might do. Once it leveled out, the forest went from beeches and hemlocks to mainly chestnut, elm, and hickory. Those trees hadn't been cut in maybe forever, and they were as wide around as a—well, I don't know what. I was squatting near the base of a chestnut, looking at a puffball. It was a *Lycoperdon pulcherimum*, a kind of mushroom, but it doesn't look like a mushroom. It looks kind of like a cotton ball, and they grow in dark, damp forests such as the one I was in. You don't see too many of them around these parts.

As I was examining the fungus, I noted beside it some scat. It was feline scat, which you can tell from its shape and contents and discreet nature in which it was hid. From the size, I figured it was either a big ole bobcat or maybe a cougar. I began to track it, following the leaves it stirred up and the occasional impression in the soft, mossy ground. I envisioned it as a cougar, and it became as big as a saber-tooth cat as I followed its leavings.

It had scratched on an elm tree about two feet from the ground, then it had wandered up the mountain toward the northwest. I followed, holding my body tense and each step carefully placed, my eyes scanning the near horizon for movement of any sort. I could tell the cat had come through in a similar fashion, intent on prey of some sort. It traveled westwardly. I crept along for what was maybe an hour before I came to a pile of massive boulders. The cat must have jumped up onto them, because I lost its trail there.

This was the point at which I became a tad bewildered. I knew how to get home, just by turning around and following my own trail back down the mountain. But, you see, that's what deer do. They always come and go by the same paths, and it makes them easy prey as a result. I always prefer to loop around, to return by a different tack than the one by which I arrived at a place.

I decided I would turn a bit to the south and follow the ridge line. Eventually, it should bring me back down to the main road. It took a long time to bring me round. All the while, I was wondering how such a large expanse of woodland had remained so undiscovered so close to my home.

Eventually, I saw the light of a meadow in the distance up ahead. A meadow in these parts likely means a farm, and if I knew what farm I was at, getting home would be easy. It turned out not to be a meadow, but an apple orchard. The limbs hung heavy with fruit. Like Eve, I took the most desirable one and bit into it. It was a Jonathan apple, and I immediately knew where I was, because only one family in these parts grows Jonathan apples.

I practically skipped through the orchard on down toward the two-story, tin-roofed farmhouse that I'd been in many times before. Only I'd never approached it from above like this. Marinda saw me a-coming. She was out back hanging laundry on the line. I saw her look up at me, squint a bit, then break out into a wide smile. Marinda is the prettiest girl I know, and I told her that as I wandered up to her. Her long hair is bright as a sunflower and her green eyes are as inviting as the Bottomless Pools.

"I'm the only girl you know, Carson Quinn." She handed me a corner of white sheet and a clothespin. "Here, be of use."

Marinda is six months younger than me, but sometimes she seems so much more grown up than me.

"Still, though." I pinned the sheet to the line. "You're awfully pretty."

"What are you doing coming down through the orchard like that?"

"I was tracking a cougar."

Her eyes got wide and she glanced off toward their pig pen.

"Oh," I said. "It was most likely just a bobcat. Just wishing it was a cougar's all."

She smacked my arm. "Don't scare me like that, Carson. And you shouldn't want to have cougars around. Think of the babies and livestock."

I let go with a laugh. "Cougars are shy. They don't come after babies…unless maybe you left it all alone out in the woods. And they don't kill no more livestock than hunting dogs."

"Don't be wishing for things like that."

I nodded, but of course I still wish I could see a cougar or a wolf in these parts. It would mean there's still something wild left.

"Ain't you supposed to be at school?" Marinda asked.

"Pa's taking me back this weekend."

Marinda sighed and said the sweetest words I think I've ever heard. "It's not the same around here without you."

My face probably got as red as the apple I had eaten. I must have been feeling bold, for I said, "I surely do miss you when I'm away."

Marinda took my hand and she led me around to behind their smokehouse. I could smell the sweet tang of a slow cooking fire. I could hear the twitter of a bluebird and the clucks of chickens. I could see the deep green of Marinda's eyes. And then, then we were kissing and all thoughts of everything else were gone. There was no smokehouse, no orchard, no bluebird, and no chickens. It was just me and her and her soft, soft lips and sweet face. She was wearing a sundress that was smooth to the touch. Her hair, as bright as sunshine, hung in strands across her face. We stopped kissing and looked at each other for a time.

"Maybe that will do for you until you come back," she said.

"No, it won't," I said. "But one more would."

We kissed again, and then her name came to me as clear as a cowbell.

"MARINDA FALLON!"

Only, it wasn't inside of me like I first thought. It was in the real world. It was her ma a-yelling. "Marinda Fallon!" she said again. "You stop kissing Carson Quinn and come on back and finish your chores!"

Now Marinda's face was the one that was red.

"How do, Carson," Mourning Fallon, Marinda's mother, said.

"Afternoon." I couldn't stop smiling. I had never kissed a girl before.

"I expect you'll be running on home now. Tell your mother I'll be a-talking to her."

"Yes, ma'am," I answered.

"Bye, Marinda," I said, like nothing had happened.

She giggled a little until her mother's scolding eye silenced her. "Goodbye, Carson Quinn," she said.

I practically ran down to the road, and I could hear back up the house Mrs. Fallon saying to her daughter, "You ain't but thirteen years old!"

It matters not how old a person is. Kissing is mighty nice.

September 18, 1886—Mourning Fallon must have had that talk with Ma, because Ma came out to the mill where I was working the hopper with Pa and Thomas. It being late in the season, folks are having their excess corn and hominy milled. We're running it near all day long these days.

"Will," she said, over the steady thump of the machinery. "I'm taking Carson from you for a bit. He'll be right back."

Pa wiped his nose with the back of his hand and kept at it. Thomas, he looked up at me with scorn. He thinks he has to do all the work on account of me and my wanderings and books. Heck, he might be right about that, but this time it was Ma's doing.

She led me into her garden. If I say so, it is the nicest spot in the yard, and the nicest garden in the entire Gap. She grows a lot of herbs and flowers that can be used for healing or cooking. There are all sorts of colors and shapes back there.

"Miss Mourning came to me about your dalliance with young Marinda," she stated.

I didn't know quite what to say. My face must have gone as red as her bee balm, though.

"It's nothing to be ashamed of, son," she said. "Marinda is a pretty young girl."

"Ain't she, though?" I said.

"Was this a game you two were playing? Or was it something more?"

"A game?" I asked, thinking checkers has never been as fun as kissing.

"Sometimes young'uns are apt to want to play together in ways that they see grown folks doing. It's natural, if that's what was going on."

"Weren't no game, Ma," I said.

"Oh. Well then." She smoothed her skirts and took to fiddling with a coneflower whose time was about done. "You've grown up of a sudden."

I reckon maybe I have grown up. Wasn't long ago that I would have been repulsed by the notion of kissing a girl. "Am I to be punished?"

"For what?" she asked.

She smiled at me, and when Ma smiles I know everything is right. She sent me on my way by saying, "Best get back to your pa, then."

Back at the mill, Pa and Thomas was still hard at work. I jumped in to help Thomas. He said, "What was that about?"

"Marinda," I said without thinking.

"What about her?" he asked. He is always mean to me as I reckon older brothers are apt to be, but this time he had concern in his voice. "Is something wrong?"

So as he wouldn't get the idea that she could be his, I declared. "Nothing wrong at all. She's got the sweetest-tasting lips, though."

Next thing Pa was yelling hard at us, because Thomas had overflowed the hopper and hominy was all over the floor.

☙

On the way back from town, I had stopped at a little park where I pulled out the journal to read. At the cabin, sometimes the construction sounds made concentrating difficult. The park had a picnic table in the shade beside a little creek.

I lowered the journal to imagine this youngster smitten by the girl next door. Figuratively speaking, of course. Next door in these parts was the next hollow over. The steep wall he spoke of still existed, shrouded in dense rhododendron. Maybe in my younger days I could have scaled it, but not now. His journey to that orchard would have been at least a couple of miles, even though by the road it was only a quarter of a mile or so.

Would he have killed over her? Would any of us have killed over the first person we kissed? Tommy Beck certainly wouldn't warrant even a shoulder punch. I chuckled at the memory of Tommy and me out in the woods behind the school. Such a chaste little kiss looking back on it, but it marked a significant moment in my life. Back then Tommy Beck provided that significant moment to a number of girls, including Delores. Would she have killed for Tommy?

For about a week after my chaste kiss with Tommy I thought I was in love, and Delores and I were rivals. Then, reality set in, and my taste in boys evolved to more mature sorts. First, the young Marine before he went off to boot camp. Then the hard-partying rocker ten years my senior. Shame colored my cheeks. What had I been thinking? Delores was probably right. I had been looking for my pirate poet who would swoop in and take me away to a lifetime of adventure. Turned out I didn't need a pirate for that; I had managed it all on my own.

I still owed Andrew a return call, so after carefully replacing the journal in its plastic bag in the tub and removing the latex gloves I wore when handling it, I dialed him up.

"Hey, sis," he answered.

"Hey, bro. How's it going?"

"Fine. Fine."

"Natalie and the kids doing okay?"

"Oh yeah. They're down at Topsail right now."

"Just like Dad, aren't you? Staying back to keep the bills paid while the wife and kids get a vacation."

"Look. Speaking of which." Hesitation tinged his voice, like he had something to say that might not sit well.

"Yes?"

"So, Dad left you the cabin free and clear. It's yours to do with what you want."

"I know." Something was amiss.

"You know I'm the executor of the estate, right?"

"Uh-huh."

"As such, I'm managing the accounts he set up for you and me both." He was talking to me in his banker voice, as if I were a customer of his and not his older sister who had given him countless Indian burns and held him in neck-holds for hours on end.

"It looks like you're spending quite a bit of that money. The balance keeps dropping."

"I'm renovating the cabin." I was perturbed that he was inserting himself into my business. I didn't have to run anything by him. In fact, this whole project had been freeing in that respect. Since most of my work was grant and fellowship funded,

I had always had to be vigilant about every single expense. Now I had a vague sense of the balance in the account, and I knew what Micah's quote was and there was plenty of money to cover that and then some. Everything would be fine. I hadn't counted on the inheritance to cover anything other than renovating the cabin anyway.

"I figured as much," he said. "But there's a problem."

"Oh?"

"This is really my fault," he began. "I should have made sure that things had been set up differently, but I trusted Dad to be on top of things."

"What's wrong, Andrew?"

"So, he didn't set up a trust and he didn't put us on his major accounts or other assets."

These kinds of things were never of much interest to me, the kinds of things I left to Woody in my own life. If deeper meaning wasn't attached, I tended to ignore it.

"What does that mean?" I asked.

"It means we each owe estate tax."

"That's fair," I said. "It is a windfall after all." A lot of my work was supported by government-funded programs, so who was I to complain about taxes? "How much is it?"

"It amounts to pretty much everything left in your account."

A bluebird settled on a nearby fencepost, gave me the once over, and darted away. I continued to stare at the fencepost, my brain struggling to process this information. Did it mean that I'd have to stop everything? What kind of savings did I have personally? Could I get a loan? Again, I felt Woody's absence and wondered if he had already found someone else.

"Caroline?"

"I'm not even halfway through," I said. "I've paid Micah twenty-five percent up front. I'll owe him another twenty-five percent in thirty days. Then there are materials still to get. Mainly interior wood. I've already bought the roofing."

"Who's Micah?"

"He's the contractor."

I pushed a wayward strand of hair from my forehead, tucked it behind my ear.

"What about selling it?" he asked. "Do you know any realtors you could talk to?"

A searing pain coursed through my gut, even worse than when Woody had said he wanted out of our marriage. Sell? Charles Duncan's face appeared in my mind like a tiny devil, licking his chops at the prospect of buying me out. "Absolutely not."

"We didn't even know he still owned it. I don't know why he kept it all these years."

"Because he loved her," I said. "It was Mom's. He gave it to her. He didn't feel like it was his to get rid of. As long as he owned it, he had something of her left."

"I didn't know that." He was silent for a while. I listened to the burbling of the creek and the trill of a chickadee and the sashaying notes of the cicadas. "We have to be smart about this, though."

Something about the way he said it hurt. I had always been the smart one. Andrew was the athlete, then the popular one, then the most likely to succeed, but I had cornered the market on smarts. Now he was telling me to be smart, as if I weren't. "I'll figure something out," I said. "I'm not selling it."

"I can tell you're upset," he said. "Why don't you take some time and think about it? Call me back if you want to talk things through."

"There's no cell phone service at the cabin, Andrew," I said. "Bye."

I punched the call dead. "Goddamnitall, Dad," I yelled. The chickadee dashed away, flinging its own curses my way as it did.

8

November 13, 1886—In Latin class we've been reading Julius Caesar's account of the Gallic Wars. The headmaster loves Caesar. Caesar brought civilization to the tribal hordes of Germany and Gaul and, eventually, Britain, he says. Caesar's legacy is the reason the British now have the largest empire in the history of empires. Caesar seems like an all right fellow to me. He won by smiting like those fellows in the Bible, but he also won by gaining allegiances and building things like bridges and roads.

But it occurs to me that maybe Ma wouldn't care for that old Caesar on account of it was her people he was smiting. Of course, I don't even know if Ma knows anything about Caesar. A person can never tell with her. It's been terribly hard here these past couple of months. I miss Marinda as badly as I miss the mountain. I keep thinking about her all the time, even when I should be thinking other things like the conjugation of habeo or the rise and fall of the Roman Empire or the square root of 225. Used to be, instead of Marinda, I would think about Darwin or Humboldt or Michaux, but now they rarely occur to me. It's just Marinda, all the time Marinda. I haven't been making good marks as a result, and Gramps will have my hide for that. Pa doesn't care about my marks at all; he just cares that I mind myself and do what I'm told. Gramps, though, he's responsible for me and Thomas being here, and he expects us to represent the family well. Since Thomas ain't never made good marks, he ain't expected to make good marks. I'm the one representing the family on that front.

Speaking of Thomas, he's been mighty ornery ever since we got back to Newton. He told the other fellows about me and Marinda, and now whenever they get a chance, they start going on about me and her having a baby together. That's fine with me. Maybe we will have a baby. At least they don't call me The Atheist no more.

December 27, 1886—We came back home for Christmas celebration. We have a huge feast every year and invite everyone in the holler and beyond. Pa always slaughters the fattest pig, which he then cooks for days beforehand. Then Ma cooks up potatoes, parsnips, biscuits with gravy, turnip greens, squash, and the best apple pie a person could ever have. This year, we had the following people at our Christmas table: Ma, Pa, Gramps, me, Sarah, Thomas, Taylor, the Brightleafs, Betsy and Owen Morgan and little Bradshaw, then Mister and Misses Fallon, and across from me, Marinda. It was right nice visiting with everybody, but best of all, I got to look at Marinda all dinner long.

"I ain't no painting," she said after I had been staring at her for a good five minutes.

"I know that," I said. I really couldn't think of anything to say to her. After having kissed her, all I could think of were her lips.

"What are you studying?" she asked, and I thought she was asking me what I was staring at on her face, but finally it occurred to me she was talking about school.

"We're studying Caesar these days," I explained.

Gramps sometimes seems like he's deaf as a stone, but other times, he'll hear a thing from nigh on across the room. He had apparently heard me say I was studying Caesar, because he opened up into some Latin.

"*Fere libenter homines id quod volunt credunt,*" he said in his courtroom voice.

"What was that?" Marinda said.

I started to answer, but Charlie Brightleaf beat me to it. "Men willingly believe that which they wish."

"Right-ee-o," Gramps said, smiling at Charlie. "From Julius Caesar's account of the invasion of Gaul. That'd be France nowadays." He eyed Marinda's father. Napoleon Fallon often bore the brunt of references to France, even though he was descended from the Scots. His father had been a soldier who fought alongside General Lafayette in New Orleans, so he named him Napoleon in honor of the French. Then, Napoleon wound up growing up to be the shortest adult male in the entire Gap. Shortest, I suppose, except for the Little People. It was almost as if the name itself informed his stature.

"Why, Charlie," Ma said. "You are full of surprises, aren't you?"

"Yes, ma'am," he agreed, and he explained that they had taught him Latin at the Christian school he went to as a child. Charlie is a right interesting man. He grew up in Qualla, speaking the Cherokee language and learning the Cherokee ways, but they sent him off to a Christian school. When he came of age, he went off to Chattanooga, Tennessee, for a time. He worked for the railroad there during the war and after. He has told me stories about the battles that occurred there. Heck, Charlie Brightleaf has told me more about the war than my own pa. Anyhow, a few years after the war, he met Miss Wilma. Miss Wilma is white. Charlie brought her on down here, where her people had land, and they have farmed corn ever since.

"What do you reckon ole Caesar meant by that?" Gramps asked no one in particular.

Owen Morgan sat up real straight-like. "He meant you're prone to see what you want to see and not necessarily what is really there."

"There you go," Gramps said. "Young Owen's a thinking man in addition to being a mighty fine cider maker." Gramps raised his cup.

The room got noisy as the women started jabbering about this and that, probably so that Gramps wouldn't go on another one of his tangents. I don't really mind Gramps's tangents at all. I've learned right much from them, such as what Texas is like and the history of the Babylonians and the menace from the Spanish threat. Heck, Gramps's tangents might be why I'm so curious by nature.

After a time, dinner was finished. Pa and Owen and Napoleon all got up and wandered out to the front porch. Charlie stood, caressed his Wilma on the cheek, then reached in his pocket for his pipe and ventured onto the porch for a smoke. Thomas followed them, and since Taylor always follows Thomas everywhere, I was left as the only fellow inside. I didn't notice at first, on account of ever since kissing her, when I'm around Marinda I don't tend to notice much of anything else.

Napoleon plays the fiddle, and Thomas can pluck a tune or two on the banjo. Folks say Owen is one of the more talented harmonica players around. In fact, he's the only person I've ever heard play the harmonica. Soon their music began to filter into the house. I'm not one for music making. The tomcat that lives in the barn can sing better than me, so I typically just hang back and listen.

Sarah was the one that noticed me still sitting at the table. "Why, Carson," she said. "Have you decided to join the female persuasion today?"

I stood up in a hurry.

"Why don't you help us with the dishes then? That's what we get to do while you fellers are out on the porch with your politics and your hootin' and a hollerin'."

"Sarah, leave Carson alone," Ma said. "Can't you tell he's smitten?"

That did it. The women all laughed as I scampered to the front porch. On the porch, they were playing some Stephen Foster tune or another that reminded me of hoopskirts and hay bales. I perched myself on the railing and pretended to care. After the Stephen Foster song, they switched to a song called "Lorena," that's mighty popular these days.

Pa isn't much for music either. He'll tolerate it for a time, before he gets restless and wanders off to put himself to use somehow. When they got to a song from the war called "Tenting Tonight," Pa turned away from them and gazed off into the valley across the Reedy Patch.

"We've been fighting today on the old campground, many

are lying near," the words go. "Some are dead; some are dying, many are in tears." That must have done it, or maybe it was "Aura Lee" that they played next, but Pa took off as if he had work to do on Christmas Day.

"Hey, fellas," Napoleon said. "Let's lighten the mood. See if we can get the ladies to come out and join us." He lit into a jig that soon had the floorboards a-bouncing with our tapping feet. Almost on cue, the women came out, and Betsy, Sarah, and Marinda started to flatfoot. Then, the floorboards really were a-flying. They looked mighty good and skilled, and they should. Betsy, Sarah, and Marinda dance like that all the time. In my opinion, Marinda is the best clogger around, but other folks seem to regard Betsy as the best.

Three songs later, the three of them were a-panting like they'd just climbed up Blue Rock. Napoleon, it seemed, knew every song in the songbook. He led the musicians into "The Rose of Killarney." Ma knew the words, and began singing, "Rose, rose of Killarney, sure I love you. There was never a Colleen with heart so true…" Ma has the purest voice around. She sounds like an angel on high when she sings and is apt to make grown men cry. She made herself cry on this afternoon. As she sang, "Sometimes I see, dear, a devil in your eye, don't ever leave me Mavourneen, I would die," she trailed off, tears welling in her eyes. Then she scampered off the porch and dis-appeared around the corner of the house.

Charlie glared at Napoleon. "You're a-chasing everyone off, aren't you?"

Napoleon took a pull of whiskey and tightened a string.

"What next?" Owen asked. "How about something with some pep?"

"You got it," Napoleon said, and he lit into a reel. It got the girls up on their feet again and dancing. Betsy grabbed Gramps, who gladly hopped around on his peg leg while she do-si-doed around him. Wilma and Charlie started dancing, too, and Marinda grabbed me as if to dance. I don't know what was wrong with me. It was stupid, because Charlie and Gramps certainly couldn't dance much better than me, but I just said, "I don't dance." Thomas hopped up and handed Taylor the banjo. Amazingly Taylor joined right in, hardly missing a beat. I guess Thomas, Taylor, and Sarah all take after Ma in the music department, while I take after Pa.

Anyhow, Thomas grabbed Marinda by the waist and they tore up the porch with their moves, their fancy promenades and left star and right star and swinging one way or the other. Thomas caught me watching him and Marinda, and he cut a look at me as his hand on her back dropped lower than a gentleman's should.

I glanced Napoleon's way. She was his daughter, after all. He nodded at me as if to say, *Cut in, you fool.* What I really wanted was to push Thomas down the steps. Instead, I jumped up off the porch, and it was me who was wandering off like there was something to be done on Christmas Day.

December 29, 1886—Way on up the mountain, in the place I call Hemlock Hollow, I scampered up a boulder as large as a cabin. Several boulders of that size were spread out on the forest floor beside the creek. They were scattered as though some giant had just tossed them out. A person might believe that God had done just that, and I reckon God did do it using glaciers and such. That's the kind of sentiment I got to keep to myself or else more folks will call me the Atheist.

Atop the boulder, I could look on down the mountain, follow with my eyes the course of the stream through the laurel hell. Hemlock Hollow lay quiet. The hemlocks protected the place, and it seemed no matter how loud and unruly things got in the outside world, this place would always be tranquil. The creek would always murmur sweet nothings to the mossy banks and the trees would still the wind and the ferns would blanket the ground in emerald. A person could come here and believe that no other person had ever passed by.

I sat on the boulder and listened to the day go by, thinking about Marinda, of course, and school, and Thomas. Now, I can't blame Thomas for doing what he done. Marinda is the prettiest thing in the world. And I can't blame Marinda neither, because she asked me to dance, and I said no. Like some fool, some pure idiot, I refused to dance with the girl I can't stop thinking about. What in all hellfire is wrong with me? In a few days, I have to return to school, and then I won't get a chance to see Marinda for three months. At least Thomas won't neither.

Anyhow, Hemlock Hollow, even when I fret about such things, is there, unchanged for thousands of years. Back when Julius Caesar was writing about men believing what they wish, this hollow was as it is today. Quiet and peaceful. The creek flowed as it does today, and the trees were likely massive hemlocks such as these now.

ℒ

I had taken a chair and camp table up to Caroline's Perch to read the journal. As a child I had claimed the spot, staked it with a name, made it mine alone. It had never occurred to me that another might have done the same a century before. Here on this same spot where I now sat, young Carson Quinn sought to quell his preoccupations. While he was a teenager concerned about love, I was an adult concerned about money. I would have to talk to Micah, explain the situation, and see if he would work with me while I figured things out.

Up on the boulder, serenity was easy to find. The stream bed cut a lazy course down the mountain. Colossal boulders still hugged its banks, unchanged from Carson Quinn's youth except for the cabin and the road. You could now drive right to it in a car. Electric and phone lines coursed right up the hill that had seemed so forbidding to Carson. The impenetrable laurel hell had long since been replaced with gravel and then Jesse's double-wide. Even so, it still felt enchanted. Mist from the creek still cast rainbows in the dappled light, and the wind slithered through the tops of the tall trees.

It was not nearly so quiet now, though. The pounding of hammers and screaming of an electric saw filled the air all day long. Micah and his crew were making solid progress. Each day the place looked a little more complete. They had removed all the flooring and paneling. The rusted tin roof had been replaced with the new green steel one. The rotten and termite-riddled wood was long gone. All that remained were sturdy old logs and freshly hewn pieces that were lighter colored. Micah promised they would stain them to match.

After the day's work was done and the sun had begun its speedy plunge into the steep west hills, Micah climbed through a patch of ferns to my perch. His normal confident stride had been replaced by a halting gait. Consternation cast a troubled tinge to his face. Had one of his crew been hurt? Had he somehow found out about my financial difficulties?

"Ms. McAlister…er, Caroline?" he began.

"What's happened?" I asked.

He glanced around the hollow. "I've got some news you aren't going to like."

Now my thoughts turned to a cost overrun. This was it. This was going to be the end of my project.

"Do you know much about the hemlock woolly adelgid?"

"The what?"

He had a bough from one of the hemlocks in his hand. He turned it over and presented it. "This here," he said, pointing out a series of white clusters, like white wool adhering to the underside of the newest needles. "This is the larval stage of the hemlock woolly adelgid. It's kind of like an aphid, and it is killing the eastern hemlock all over the East Coast."

I hadn't ever heard of this creature, and though prepared for a difficult conversation about money, the news hit hard. These hemlocks, so majestic, so old, seemed almost immortal. "How do we get rid of it?" I asked.

"That's the trick. You can't really. There is a treatment if you catch it early enough, but once infected, the trees get damaged and die very quickly. The best thing in this case is to identify the infected trees and remove them. That's the only way to stop the infestation. Otherwise, it will spread and kill every single hemlock in this cove."

I looked around. Carson Quinn's young voice so assuredly proclaiming the eternal existence of these formidable beings echoed in my head. The majority of trees around the cabin were hemlock, with a few poplars, black walnuts, and hickory thrown in. "This is like the chestnut blight, isn't it?" I asked.

"It is exactly like the chestnut blight. Like the blight, this is an invasive species from Asia. It was introduced accidentally in the 1920s. It spreads slow, because the adelgids can't fly, but eventually the hemlock will go the way of the chestnut, except for in the most isolated patches."

A sadness came over me, and it was not all mine. I could feel young Carson Quinn heartbroken at the tragic tale Micah had shared. "So, what are you suggesting?"

"Let's take down the infected trees. Even if we don't cut them now, they will die within the next couple of years and fall on their own. This came from that one." He pointed the bough at a tree that loomed about twenty feet from the cabin. It wasn't difficult to see the destruction that tree would do should it fall on the cabin.

"There is some good news to this," Micah offered without smiling.

"Please share," I said.

"We need lumber for the interior of the cabin. I know a selective forester with a portable mill. He can bring it up here, cut the trees, mill and plane them, and then we've got all the wood we need to finish the project."

"So the trees wouldn't really leave the hollow?"

"Not necessarily." He cleared his throat. "Now, you will have excess timber. He'll buy that timber off you, so you're actually going to make money on this."

"How much?"

"Enough to cover the rest of my bill."

I took another glimpse around the cabin. A breeze swirled through the now silent cove, and the massive trees sang their death songs. With the breeze, the air chilled, and I wondered if it was Carson's ghost or my mother's or maybe both. I wondered if they were saying, "It's okay." It was as if the hollow itself was looking out for me, as it always had in a way.

"You're crying again," he said, holding out his bandanna.

I took it and dabbed my eyes.

"I'm sorry to have to tell you this."

"I know." I placed a grateful hand on his shoulder. "You're a good man, Micah."

When he crinkled his eyes in response, crow's feet appeared, giving away that he was older than he appeared. "It's not going to be the same without the trees."

"No," he agreed. "But it won't be as bad as you think."

I had hoped that my effort to restore the place would reclaim something of my mother, of my childhood. Despite Carson Quinn's faith in the everlasting quality of the hollow and my own reverence toward it, I was learning a hard lesson about how fickle impermanence could be.

Micah ventured back down the mountain. I sat on my perch until long after his truck had made its way down the gravel road and out of earshot and the sun had set and the katydids had opened up their nightly chorus.

The darkness settled in, and still I didn't move from my spot, from Carson's spot. Through a gap in the tree canopy Vega winked at me from the constellation Lyra. The Greeks called it Lyra because it outlined the lyre of Orpheus cast to the heavens upon his death. Music from the lyre could charm trees, streams, and rocks, and it tamed the sirens for the Argonauts. I imagined the katydids and frogs to be accompanied by the strumming of that lyre, the twinkling star keeping time with their eternal cadence, their song soothing the dying trees around me.

9

December 28, 1886—Today I wandered over to the Fallons' house. Pa had mended their clothes wringer, so I carried it with me to provide purpose to my trip. Mourning Fallon came out on the porch and took it from me.

"Oh my goodness," she exclaimed, looking at the piece of machinery. "I marvel at what your pa can do. Why, this looks good as new. Hold on a moment, Carson. Let me grab some whiskey for you."

The neighbors often pay Pa with whiskey or cider or produce on account of them not having much cash. Pa is fine with that, even though he doesn't really drink much. I reckon Gramps drinks enough for the two of them. Mrs. Fallon disappeared into the house. She was gone for a long while. And it wasn't Mrs. Fallon that brought the liquor back. It was Marinda herself.

"Were you going to go on back to that fancy school and not say goodbye to me, Carson Quinn?" she asked.

I stammered something or other. I never know what to say to her. I've said much more to her in my mind than I've ever let pass through my lips. "No," I finally blurted out. "Why do you think I'm here now?"

"To be your pa's delivery boy."

"Taylor or Thomas could be a delivery boy just as good as me. Heck, you might even prefer to see one of them up on your porch."

Marinda scowled like a bulldog. She took me by the hand and led me back to our spot behind the smokehouse. "Let me you show you who I prefer," she said, and she planted a nice, wet kiss smack dab on my lips.

When she unhitched us, I said, "From the look of your dance the other night, you wouldn't have minded it had Thomas brung over your mended wringer."

She sighed. "Thomas ain't my type. I go for the wandering soul, the redheaded wayfaring stranger type. Thomas is just a stick in the mud."

"That right?"

She nodded. I found it a might peculiar that a girl so young had already figured out her type. I reckon girls are different from boys that way. For me, my type is whatever type Marinda is. A blond-haired, green-eyed mountain girl with skinned knees from climbing trees in her summer dress and legs as long as a white-tailed deer's. If Marinda were dark-haired, short, and bookish, then that would be my type. I find it lucky that she's figured out her favorite type of boy, and I match that description.

She kissed me again. I don't think I'd ever get tired of kissing. Nothing is quite so pleasant, and we partook of that enjoyment for some time before her ma came looking for her. This time, Mrs. Fallon didn't yell at Marinda, even though she must have known what we were up to back there.

I left, toting a bottle of whiskey in each hand. When I got back to the house and placed the bottles before Pa in his forge, he assessed me for the longest time. "Boy," he said. His face was tight like a tanned hide from working alongside the fire for so long, his forearms thick and serious. "You were gone a long time for such a simple errand."

"Yes, sir," I said, because that's really all you can say to Pa.

"I need you on the squirrel cage there. Come on."

A blacksmith forge needs the proper amount of air to keep the coals the right temperature. We used to have a bellows you'd have to pump, but Pa had recently made himself what he calls a squirrel cage. It's a hand-turned blower that one of us kids has to rotate while he works away. It beats the bellows, but it's so easy that one often loses track of what's going on. I was thinking about Marinda and how it would be months before I'd see her again when I noticed Pa just staring at me.

"Slow it down," he said. "You're apt to burn through all my coal."

"Yes, sir," I said and eased off on my tempo. Thrift is one of his utmost important values, and wasting coal is akin to throwing cash money in that there fire as far as he's concerned. He kept me working until suppertime, most likely to compensate for the wasted coal.

June 25, 1887—I haven't attended much to this journal because I lost it for a time. It got put away with my school books in a trunk. And at school there is so much other writing to be done that I haven't much time for the journal. But I've sought it out so that I could record some recent goings-on. I'm back home for the summer, and Pa has worked me and Thomas harder than he works Henry the Mule. We've been helping him in the forge, milling hominy, mending the springhouse, tending to the garden patch, and handling the hogs since we've been back. Thomas really likes working in the forge. He's almost as good with iron as Pa is, and he's only sixteen. Sun-up to sun-down every day except Sunday we toil in one manner or another. It appears my days of wandering may be at an end. We're working so much because Pa has taken to going to lots of meetings around the countryside. Pa's never been one to care much for other people, so we're a tad surprised at his new interest in meeting up. Ma says it's good for him and to let him alone. It may be good for him, but it ain't too good for my back.

Today we finally got a reprieve from the work, and it's not even Sunday. The whole family loaded up and went into town for market. Usually, Ma and Sarah and maybe Gramps will go to town, but today we all went. There were the seven of us all loaded on the wagon as it bumped and rolled down the rutted road to Hendersonville. Since there were so many of us, we used two oxen instead of Henry. The oxen strained to get us up on out of the Gap and then plodded on past the apple orchards of Edneyville. We passed by the Fallon house, and I looked for her but couldn't see any trace of Marinda. We went by the Morgans' and the Dodsons' and the Barnwells'. Folks that were out all waved, and we slowed but didn't stop for fear of Gramps striking up one of his three-hour conversations.

Hendersonville isn't Asheville. There's not much hustle and bustle to be had. But it's still a right nice town that can meet a family's needs. Ma had a long list of things, and we huddled around her to split them up between us. She and Sarah would go get the fabric. Pa would go to Shepherd's to sell the milled hominy we brought and pick up some of the spices and fruits that Ma liked. Gramps would tag along with Pa so he could set himself down by the stove and gab for a spell. Thomas, Taylor, and me were to go to the apothecary and pick up some liniment for Gramps.

Ma gave us a basket to take. It was full of dried plants that included mullein (*Verbascum thapsus*), wild ginger root (*Hexastylis heterophylla*), lady slipper (*Cypripedium acaule*), and sassafras root (*Sassafras albidum*). Folks that don't have cash money often gather herbs for trade at the stores. I had gathered most of these on my wanderings. Ma knows how to put them to use healing all manner of what ails you. She grows the mullein out in her garden and gives it to Betsy Morgan all the time for her breathing troubles. The basket would be plenty for trade and to settle all of our open accounts. After Pa wandered off, Gramps hobbled over and gave us each a nickel so we could get us some candy.

It was a Saturday, and lots of folks had come to town. There was a line of folks at the apothecary. Thomas saw some fellas he knew and started to chatting with them about something or other. Thomas gets real interested in the most boring of subjects, like fasteners and bolts and tools. I really couldn't give half a care about such things, so Taylor and I left him behind. We waited in line. I'd say patiently, but Taylor's not but twelve and nothing about a twelve-year-old boy is patient. We played a game trying to count all the licorice sticks in the glass jar.

"Three thousand, two hundred, twenty-seven," Taylor announced.

"Naw," I said. "Ain't that many. I'd say six hundred forty-three."

Taylor shook his head. "At least a thousand. I ain't never seen so many licorice sticks."

"Do you even know what a thousand looks like?" I chided him. Taylor's been to the church school, but he hasn't started at Newton yet. He'll go back with me in the fall. Thomas has graduated, so now I'll be the older brother. I aim to be a better older brother to Taylor than Thomas was to me.

"I know a thousand. A thousand is like the number of stars," Taylor said.

"All right then," I said. "Do you think there are as many bits of licorice in that jar as there are stars in the sky?"

Taylor pondered this for a minute, then said, "No, I reckon not. Let's say nine hundred."

"All right, then." We got up to the counter about then, and I asked for the liniment. It's called Happy Land Liniment. Gramps uses it on his legs, and it stinks to high heavens. Whenever he puts it on, we can smell it all over the house. But he swears he needs it. Never ask him about it, though. If you ask Gramps about his liniment cream, he'll talk at you for hours about the healing effect of menthol, and then he'll get into koala bears and eucalyptus trees and Australians and the penal system of Great Britain and Gladstone's commentaries and on and on.

"Hey, mister," Taylor exclaimed when the man returned with the cream. "How many licorices are in that there jar?"

The fella squinted at us for a real long time. Then he nodded, not saying anything. Then he looked up at the ceiling for a spell. "One hundred eighty-seven," he finally said.

Taylor's mouth fell open. "Is that all?" he asked.

"Why, young man," the fella said. "That's enough licorice to rot ever one of your teeth out."

"I'll have just one then."

"And one for me too," I said.

"One hundred eighty-five," the fella said as he handed us the candy and I handed him the basket.

"Well, what have we here?" he asked, lifting them dried plants and putting them on the scale.

I told him the scientific names of all them plants, and he looked at me like I was speaking a foreign tongue. Which I reckon I was. He pulled up a big old book, slammed it on the counter, and peered through it. "Quinn, Quinn, Quinn," he said.

"That there's our name!" Taylor said.

"Don't you think I know that?" He gave a Taylor a look like a mean old bull pondering a charge. "Tell your ma she's got store credit amounting to two dollars and fifteen cents."

We turned and skedaddled from there real quick. We waited in the street for Thomas. When he finally showed up, he had a wad of something in his mouth. "What you got there?" I asked.

He spat a long stream of tobacco juice onto the boardwalk in response. "Candy's for children," he said and walked away.

We gathered up with the rest of the family back at the wagon. Pa had loaded everything up and was climbing in when Gramps cleared his throat.

"Let's go down to the Jockey Lot," he said, glancing over at us young'uns and winking.

"What's at the Jockey Lot?" Pa inquired.

"Well," Gramps explained, "Henry the Mule's getting old and tired, and I fear we'll need to replace him after a while. Let's go on down and see what might be available in the way of draft animals these days."

Pa gave one of his short, crisp nods, and we were off down the hill. Taylor and I couldn't help but yip for joy, because at the apothecary we seen the poster for the McGallagher Brothers Circus and Menagerie, which was in town for the day only. Ever since the railroad line came to Hendersonville, circuses and the like had been showing up on a sporadic basis. We had never been to a circus before.

"Pa!" my own pa exclaimed, seeing the three tents and the lines of people as we approached. "You dern old trickster." But Pa must have been in a forgiving mood since he didn't turn the rig around.

"You young'uns," Pa said, as he pulled us to a halt, "you

got two hours afore we need to head on back now. Aurelius," he said. When Pa's miffed, he calls Gramps by his given name. "You appear to be the money behind this operation, so why don't you hop on down. I'll wait right here."

"Will," Ma pleaded, "why don't you come on with us. I think you'll enjoy it."

"I've seen my share of curiosities. Besides, I'm wanting to talk to Tom and M.C. anyway." Tom and M.C. were merchants in town. As far as I know, Pa ain't got no friends, but they are awfully tight.

The six of us scrambled down to the tent and bought our tickets. They were twenty-five cents each, and Gramps didn't even blink. Once inside the ropes, we children scattered. Even Thomas, though he tried to hide it, was excited.

Inside the first tent were a variety of performers doing all manner of activities I had never even considered before. The contortionist was a skinny lady who bent and twisted her body into all kinds of shapes and twists. I had never seen so much of a lady to begin with. She was wearing nothing more than her underthings. It wasn't exciting in the way you might think, though.

The strongman was impressive. He was pert near the opposite of the contortionist in terms of musculature. The announcer, a normal-sized fellow, motioned for me and Taylor to come close to him. The strongman was named Milo the Magnificent. He was bald and had one of what they call a handlebar mustache, and he wore a tight-fitting outfit that showed off gigantic muscles.

"You boys," the announcer said to us, "come lift this weight for me." He motioned toward an anvil of sorts, basically an iron pyramid with a handle on top. It had inscribed on it *300 lbs.*

It didn't look to me like it had nearly enough mass to weigh that much, but it sure looked heavy enough anyway. Taylor and I looked at each other and shrugged. This was our day off from such chores, and this circus fellow was trying to get us to work. We played along and bent down and started to lift the weight.

Gosh darn it if it weren't heavy. The two of us managed with some heaving and hoeing to get it up to our waist level. The strongman preened for the crowd with his gleaming muscles while we grunted and struggled. The announcer finally motioned for us to put it down.

"My goodness, ladies and gentlemen!" he announced. "You grow your children strong in these parts, don't you? Most young boys can't even make this weight budge."

"We're used to it," I said, a tad sheepish.

"Our pa makes us work," Taylor announced, and the crowd laughed in approval.

"Ladies and gentlemen, Milo the Magnificent will now lift with one hand this three-hundred-pound weight that two of your strapping young men could barely budge."

Milo grinned and walked over to the anvil. He bent over and gripped the handle with but one hand. He waited for a second, his other hand braced on a knee, and preened as if da Vinci were painting him. Then, in a terrifying and sudden jerk, he launched the anvil overhead and held it, extended, like he was Hercules himself. Everybody oohed and aahed. The announcer said that for a nickel more we could see Milo lift Gertrude the elephant in the next tent in thirty minutes. I had never seen anything like an elephant, and I had to see it in person.

The Menagerie was in the second tent. The tent stank bad. It was hot, and all the caged animals were defecating and whatnot of course. It was so bad that tears stung my eyes. But I had to see what was in there, so I followed the circuit around. In the first cage was a bear. I, of course, had seen a bear before, but this one was a sad old sow. She sat there scrunched up watching us pass by. In the second cage was a little bobcat. It saw me and hissed as it had nowhere to run to. Bobcats don't much care for people. I'd a hissed at me, too.

Then there were the African animals. A leopard was curled up in a corner, asleep. The handler sitting beside it poked it with a stick when Taylor and I come up there. It opened its eyes for a second at the prodding.

"No need to wake him on our account," I told the handler. He flapped the tail of his coat and sat back down.

Then there was the lion with a mane like I never had seen. It was pacing back and forth, back and forth. It was staring at no man. Its eyes were locked on the zebra in the cage beside it. The zebra, now that could have been Gramps's mule. It made the strangest kinds of sounds, for it knew that lion was right there. Finally, we come to the elephant. It was huge, a giant beast in the largest cage I'd ever seen in my life. It was flapping its ears like it wanted to fly away, but after a few minutes of observation it was apparent it was trying to cool itself down. Taylor shook his head. He'd had enough of the smell, and he ran out of the tent. I just stood in front of Gertrude. It would have been different to have seen her in the wild. Imagine a fellow afield, wandering about as I'm apt to do, encountering such a beast. There was once such a creature in these parts, back in the Ice Age. The mastodon. It wasn't impossible that folks just like me came across creatures similar to Gertrude in these parts. It would have to be the highlight of a person's life, wouldn't it?

After leaving the animal tent and getting a much-needed breath of fresh air, I met up with the entire family gathered in front of the minstrel show, which was about to begin.

"You were in there?" Sarah asked, pointing to the animal tent. "I couldn't stand it for a second."

"You know Carson," Thomas answered for me. "He loves his wildlife."

"Ain't nothing wild about that," I said.

The minstrel show started with a band of colored folks dancing and singing up on a stage. Then they put on a play in which a Black fellow dressed up in fancy clothes and pretended to be the governor. Though he was colored, he didn't quite look like Mr. Rolly. When he turned, I noticed that he wasn't colored at all. It was a white fella with his face painted. And he had a little fella with him, his face also painted dark, who stumbled along mimicking his movements.

Thomas hollered out, "Impeach the darky!"

Gramps walloped him hard in the back of the head.

I got a tad bored, so I wandered on to see some other curiosities, like the sword swallower and the troupe of acrobats and the magician. The magician was interesting enough. He made doves fly out of a hat and he made a rabbit vanish. After a while, Sarah came running up to me in a fit.

"Is Taylor with you?" she asked.

"No. I ain't seen him since we was put to work for that Milo fella."

"We can't find him."

Taylor was always getting in trouble on account of the fact that he wasn't afraid of nothing, including Pa's belt. I shook my head. "No telling where he got to."

We commenced a search of the environs, each of us taking a direction and going thataway. I went back up to the apothecary, thinking that maybe he wanted some more licorice, but he wasn't there. Sarah didn't find him in the curiosities tent, and Thomas couldn't locate him neither. It was Ma that found him. We had all been looking for a blond-haired white little boy, but it turned out that Taylor was now dark-faced. He had been the governor's little aide in the minstrel show, and none of us had caught on to it.

His blue eyes darted nervously from Ma to Gramps to me from behind a face painted black. The paint was smudged from where he had tried to wash it off, but it wouldn't come off. Ma tried rubbing his cheek with a dampened cloth, but the paint did not budge. Gramps tapped his cane on the boardwalk and worked his gums. Thomas glared hard at Taylor.

We climbed the hill to the wagon and found Pa there chatting with several fellows, including the sheriff and the grocer, Mr. Shepherd.

"Think on that a spell," Pa finished saying to them.

He glanced up at us, and it took a second before he noticed Taylor. You could see Pa's face go stern in an instant. Instead of addressing Taylor, he turned to Gramps. "Aurelius," was all he said.

Gramps got to working his gums a bit. "Now it ain't nothing a little turpentine can't fix."

Why it is that Taylor can get away with things that I would get skinned alive for is perplexing. I wouldn't have been able to sit for a week after pulling something like that.

We started to load up the wagon, but as Taylor was climbing onto the back, Thomas stuck his foot in his chest, keeping him at bay.

"No darkies allowed," Thomas said.

Pa shot a fierce look back at his eldest son, but even quicker was Gramps with his cane. It caught Thomas on the side of the head with a crack and he went tumbling off the rig. Thomas was lucky it was the lightweight umbrella cane and not the ash one Pa made.

Thomas shot up quick, more stunned than hurt. "Old man," he growled, his hands in fists.

Pa leapt to the ground and put himself between Thomas and Gramps. "You best settle down there, boy," Pa said. The two of them faced each other like seething bulls.

"I ain't the one painted up like a nigger," Thomas said.

"Thomas!" Ma exclaimed.

"No, sir. No, sirree!" Gramps's voice was shrill with anger. "I am ashamed of you right now, young man. Even more, I am ashamed of myself for failing to impart to you one of the values that makes us Quinns who we are."

Thomas was massaging the side of his head. Gramps stood and aimed the end of his cane at Thomas. "Even if Taylor was naturally of a darker complexion, he would be more than welcome in this here cart. In fact, we would put him up front so as everyone could see that we are as welcoming to those different from us as we are of those who are the same."

"I was just joking, Gramps. No need to whack a man for it."

"Didn't whack a man," Gramps said. "I whacked a little boy. A man don't treat others the way you just did."

"That's enough, Aurelius," Pa said. "You," he turned to Thomas, "get on up here. Apologize to your brother."

Thomas looked off down the road as if contemplating walking home rather than giving in. Still rubbing his head, he nodded, then climbed up into the wagon.

"Didn't mean nothing by it, brother," he said to Taylor.

Taylor shrugged, the most unaffected of all. Ma and Sarah looked about to tear up, but they said nothing. It seemed to me that as we pulled away from town, they were looking at Thomas in a way they had never looked at him before.

None of us knew what to do, except for little Taylor, who had really been the cause of this mess. He asked all of us, "Why do you reckon that giant called himself Milo?"

"'Cause it's what his mama named him." Thomas scowled.

"I can assure you his mama didn't name him Milo," Gramps said, refusing to look at Thomas, then cleared his throat. "Milo of Croton was an ancient Olympic wrestler who was renowned for his strength. He was said to train by carrying a bull around on his shoulders." Gramps went on for a long spell all about this Milo fella and how he was a friend of Pythagoras and how elegant the Pythagorean theorem is if you really think about it. The story allowed the rest of us to doze off all the way through Edneyville.

❧

An earth-shattering boom jarred the journal from my hands. My first thought was of the Rumbling Bald seven miles away and the earthquake young Carson had described one hundred twenty years before. That thought soon dissipated into a cacophony of voices down below.

I pulled myself up from the card table I had set up under a tarp and stumbled down to Micah. An infected hemlock had been felled. It lay askew on the soft earth. Long-impeded sunlight gushed into the hollow where the tree had once blocked it out. The forester was already at work trimming the uppermost limbs.

"They don't say 'timber' anymore?" I asked as I approached him.

"Apparently the word now is 'Get the fuck out of the way,'"

Micah answered, his face suddenly reddening. "Sorry, Caroline."

"Don't worry about it." I leaned in with a whisper. "Little secret: I've heard much worse."

His mouth twisted into a smirk, and I found myself lost for a moment in the gleam of his eyes. But then the realization hit that the fallen giant's days were over, and I turned to the stump. Easily five feet in diameter, I held my palm against it, the grain still warm from the heat of the saw.

"Do we know how old it is?" I asked.

"Jimmy!" Micah called out.

The forester stopped his pruning and came over. "How old is the tree?" Micah asked.

"Well," Jimmy said, scratching his head. "Hemlock is tricky. It don't grow regular always, so, hmm…" He peered into the rings now exposed, using two fingers to measure a space, then the width of his hand, then his entire forearm. "This one has to be nearly three hundred years old. It can't be any less than 250, and it might be as many 320, 330."

The tree wouldn't have been appreciably different for Carson Quinn as a boy than it was to me as a girl. When he found this hollow, it would have been around two hundred years old. I glanced around, identifying some smaller hemlocks that were probably now two hundred years old, imagining the young boy appraising them thoughtfully.

I heard a car coming, and it was coming fast from up the mountain, from the direction of the Duncans' house. One thing about being at the cabin is that no one can sneak up on you in a car. You hear tires crunching gravel all the way down to the hard-top road. It gives you time to prepare for anyone that might show up.

Charles Duncan's pick-up truck spat gravel into the air as it tore into our driveway. It catapulted to a stop, and he jumped out, slamming the door behind him. Jesse clambered up the hill from his double-wide, joining his father in a fast march toward Micah.

"What is going on here?" the elder Duncan spat.

Micah tilted his head curiously. When he didn't answer, Charles Duncan turned to me and lifted an eyebrow.

"Is there a problem?" I asked.

Jesse pushed past his father to stand over the felled hemlock. "You liked to kill me!" he shrieked. The tree, when it fell, did fall in the direction of his trailer but it would have had to have been five hundred feet tall to have come anywhere close to the double-wide.

"What are you talking about?" Micah asked. "You were never in any danger from this tree."

"It appears to have fallen on my property," Charles said, sternly.

"We're going to remove it," Micah explained. "This tree is going to be milled into boards and stacked by the end of the day today, and none of it will be on your property by even one inch."

Charles's face went red. "Again," he said, "there is the matter of your trespassing. I was not informed that there would be trees being felled on my property. You could well have caused damage to any of my trees."

Micah, with the calm of a Zen master, replied, "Mr. Duncan, you own in excess of two hundred acres of forested mountainside. I can promise you that trees fall all the time on your property without your permission."

Jesse pushed his chest into Micah. His fierce eyes reminded me of a mistreated pit bull. "You ought to inform a fella afore you drop a tree on his head. You knocked my television off the wall. Cracked the screen wide open."

Micah nodded. "You know, you're right about that. I apologize. Since I didn't see a car in your driveway, I didn't think anyone was home."

"I'll pay to replace the TV," I offered.

"It was a brand-new LCD high-def. To the tune of six hundred dollars," he said.

Micah cocked his head again. "That right?" he asked. "Can we go take a look?"

I stepped in between them. "No," I said quickly. "No need for that. I trust Jesse to tell the truth. Let me go get my checkbook." This was not in the budget, but I was willing to part with some cash to keep the peace, especially now that the trees themselves were financial contributors to the process.

I rushed up the hill to my car, my guts twisted and my heart in my throat. The last thing I wanted was conflict with my closest neighbors.

I returned to what looked like a standoff. Micah and his crew facing down Charles and Jesse Duncan. Thoughts of the Hatfields and McCoys flashed through my mind. No one had moved since I left, probably not a single word spoken. Men and their pissing contests.

"Okay," I said. "Should I make it out to Jesse Duncan?" I asked.

"No," he said. "Make it out to cash and endorse it."

"You don't think the bank will find it strange that you aren't Caroline McAlister?" I asked, perplexed.

"Nope. Bank don't care," he said.

I wrote the check as instructed and handed it to him, then I turned to his father. "While we're on the matter of financial transactions, Charles, what would it take for me to buy my front yard from you?"

My thoughts were that he was making such a ruckus about his property so as to incite me to buy it from him. But he seemed startled by the suggestion.

"None of my property is for sale," he said. "This land has been Duncan land for over two hundred years, and I plan to keep it that way."

"But it's always going to be my front yard," I replied.

He took a long look at the cabin, at the obvious progress that had been made in so short a time. He jutted out his jaw like the prow of a ship. "We'll see about that." He turned on his heel and fled with as much commotion and gravel spinning as he had arrived. Jesse took his check and retreated to his house.

After they were gone, Micah turned to me. "I was going to

point out that those trees he was so protective of were infected and are going to fall much closer to that trailer than this one. I think I'll just let them learn that the hard way."

10

August 17, 1887—The work has not slowed a tad. Now that the harvest is starting, we're running the mill practically all the time. Folks bring us their corn, and we mill it for them into cornmeal and their hominy into grits. It's hard work, because our machinery is old and requires a lot of attention. Pa has taught us how to tend to it without putting ourselves in too much danger. Taylor, Pa, and me work the mill all day while Thomas works in the forge. He's good enough that people can hardly tell the difference between his work and Pa's. I don't know that he's the better off for it, though. That forge can be as hot as Hades in these summer months. Here at the mill I often have to get in the creek to fix the wheel, and being in the creek is pleasant enough. But at the mill, you got Pa always a-looking over your shoulder. Even when he's off in those meetings, you can feel his gaze just as strongly as if he were there. He's as quick as a timber rattler to let you know you've done something wrong, but otherwise he says nothing at all. It's awfully like trying to choose between the guillotine and the noose in my estimation.

I don't know why Sarah doesn't have to work. She gets to prance around the house pretending to be busy with cleaning and cooking and preserving. She may be the laziest person I've ever known, and that's hard to say seeing as she's my sister and all. She sometimes acts like she's too fancy for the rest of us. For example, the ladies of Hendersonville are having a ball. That's not a ball like a baseball, but a ball like a dance. Somehow, she got herself invited, so now we all have to get our Sunday finest on and go to Hendersonville next weekend. Pa hates going to town, because it takes up a whole day that could be spent working. I, on the other hand, am looking forward to a little reprieve.

One good thing that happened was that today Marinda came over. For a time, she perched in the corner of the millhouse and watched us work. Pa didn't take too kindly to her indolence, and before long she was helping to feed the hopper alongside me. Over the past year she has become womanlier in appearance. Now that she's fourteen nearing fifteen, a person can tell what she'll look like as a grown woman. And, let me tell you, it ain't bad at all. I could look at her all day long. She's a much harder worker than Sarah will ever be. She jumped right in and did exactly what Pa told her to do. I know I'm but fifteen, but I can't help but think that she'd make a mighty fine wife. It doesn't make a heck of a lot of sense to be thinking such things, as it doesn't quite square with my plans to wander. Maybe she'll go a-wandering with me.

Pa worked us till five o'clock, then shut down the operation. I walked Marinda home, promising to be back for supper in an hour. We took the long way to her house, passing all the way down to the Reedy Patch Creek. Folks use the Reedy Patch as a source for stone, but I knew a little spot at the base of a waterfall that was deep and tranquil.

We sat there, lounging in the descending sun, listening to the water caress the granite slab of mountain. "You know something, Carson J. Quinn?" Marinda said after a spell.

"Yes, I do," I boasted. "I know quite a bit."

She huffed like a mare. "If you already know it, then I won't tell you." She crossed her arms and pretended to ignore me.

"But I don't know everything," I said. "Such as I don't know what you were about to tell me."

"That's more like it. The something I was a-fixing to tell you was that I think I like you a lot."

My face probably turned as red as the raspberry patch. As smoothly as possible, I pulled out my bandanna and wiped my brow. "That's right nice of you to say, because I know I like you lots."

I leaned in and I kissed her. We're getting good at kissing. "Why is it you's always leaving me?" she asked me.

"A man needs an education," I said.

She pulled away real sudden-like. "And a woman don't?"

"That's not what I meant," I explained. "What I was going to say was that a man needs an education if he aims to take care of his wife and children. And I aim to do that."

"Ain't you the sweetest," she said. "But I don't need a man to care for me. I can manage that myself, thank you very much."

She was right. She can manage that herself based on how much she cares for her own ma and pa and how hard she worked today in the mill.

"Well," I said, again not able to construct sentences very well in her presence, "one day you'll come with me. We'll leave together. We'll go over the Blue Ridge and keep going. We'll see whatever we can see, go all the way to horizon and beyond."

She was smiling, so I must have said the right thing. "I'd like that a lot, Carson J. Quinn." We did some more kissing afore I escorted her on to her house.

August 22, 1887—Yesterday we returned from the ball in town. I have never seen such a production. Down in the Gap we have our dances ever once in a while. Usually, it's what you'd call a hoedown, and it's held in somebody's barn or the such. This ball was nothing akin to a hoedown. It was held in the fanciest house I've ever seen in my life. It wasn't in Hendersonville at all, but in Flat Rock. The house was entirely whitewashed and had a front porch large enough to hold fifty people. We young'uns, Taylor, Thomas, and myself, felt a tad out of place, but Gramps led the way. He was wearing his finest suit, the one he used for jury trials, accompanied by his silver-handled, lacquered cane. He seemed right at home with the ladies of Hendersonville, and you could see a gleam in his eye and a hop in his step. Pa didn't come with us. He said he'd prefer to kiss a dead, wet pig than to go to such an event. Ma was angry with him for saying that. "Fine, we wouldn't want you to come anyway and spoil it for everyone with your bitterness," she said. Sarah had on a dress she and Ma and Betsy Morgan had been working on for a month. It looked just as nice as any other dress there. She was smiling and chatting like I'd never seen her do before. It was as though she'd been a salamander trying to pass as a lizard when she suddenly came across a body of water and knew just what to do.

Thomas headed right for the wine as soon as we got there. Taylor and I stood by the steps, our hands stuffed in our pockets for lack of knowing what else to do. They had a fiddler playing some music like Mozart or Beethoven. His accompaniment, instead of a banjo, was a fiddle so big it had to sit on the floor. I think that's what they call a cello. At Newton we once went to a chamber music event and the music sounded like what they were playing at the ball.

All the ladies of Hendersonville were there, dressed up in enough fabric to make a bed with. The men mingled and chatted about sorghum and buckwheat and rye and cottonseed. I'd never seen a lot of the folks there. Plenty of them were folks that lived in Charleston except for the summer months.

The house had an entire room dedicated to dances such as these, called the ballroom, where there was a massive chandelier. Folks had already started dancing. And, lo and behold, if Sarah wasn't already out on the dance floor with some young man. She even looked like she knew what she was doing. They called the first dance a waltz.

Since I didn't and couldn't know how to dance that way, I wandered off as I'm apt to do. The house had three floors, and I explored them all. They kept paintings of themselves and their grandparents all over the place. The bedrooms all had four-poster beds in them. There was a library. All it had in it were novels, except for one giant atlas. I opened the atlas and looked at the world. There was the Western Hemisphere with all of Latin America down to Tierra del Fuego. I found where little old Daisy would be, and traced a line from there south, down past Florida and Cuba and Colombia and Peru. I hadn't ever realized how far east South America was compared to North America. Then I traced another line west out past Oklahoma and Colorado all the way to California.

"Are you a traveler?" someone asked from behind me.

I turned. A dark-haired fella entered carrying a glass of wine and acting like he owned the place.

"Not yet," I said. "But I aim to be."

"Robert Johnston," he said by way of introduction.

"Carson Quinn," I answered, trying to be just as perfunctory as he.

"Quinn? Aurelius must be your grandfather."

"Yes, sir," I answered, "he sure is."

"And Sarah would be your sister?"

"She would."

"You have quite the family, young man. Your sister is the belle of the party, you know."

I didn't know that at all. But I knew my sister would celebrate for days if she knew he had said that. I promised myself not to repeat it to her ever.

"You're not from around here, are you?" I asked him.

"This is my home, or at least my parents' home."

He did own the place. "Your only home?"

"We live in Charleston during the rest of the year."

I figured Robert Johnston to be at least thirty years old, but it was hard to tell really. He was trim and his hair was as black as a rat snake.

"It's a right nice house. You read all these here books?" I asked.

He laughed. "No, no. I'm a man of science and business, myself. I haven't time for books."

"I hope your home in Charleston wasn't too badly damaged in the earthquake last year." I remembered the earth trembling beneath my feet and the devastation Judge Logan said had occurred in Charleston.

"Not at all. Old Brae Barmekin is a sturdy house."

"You named your house?" I had never heard of such a thing before.

"All the old plantation homes have names. My great-grandfather built her back before the Revolutionary War. Being from

Scotland, he gave her a Scottish name. It would be Fortification Hill, or something of the sort, in English."

"Does this place have a name?"

"Indeed. We call it Raven's Nest."

"Well, don't that beat all?"

Mr. Johnston was pleasant enough and said it was a pleasure meeting me, then turned and went back to the ballroom. He seemed like a real ladies' man, as they say. I put the atlas back and went in search of Taylor. I had a suspicion he might be getting in trouble again.

Luckily, I found him with Gramps. Gramps had set up court in the parlor. He was seated in a fine chair with a glass of brandy. He'd propped his cane against the chair, and he was going on now about something or the other. A whole passel of men and women had gathered round him. I sidled up to Taylor, who was sitting cross-legged on the floor. "What's he talking about?" I asked.

"Mexico," Taylor said. Taylor loved to hear Gramps go on about his military exploits, but he had heard this story more than a time or two.

"Hell," Gramps was saying, "cannot be nearly so hot and dry as South Texas. We were camped there for a time, and the mosquitoes were as large as hummingbirds, I tell you. Malaria and yellow fever killed more men than the Mexicans. And the land we fought for wasn't fit for anything more than growing rattlesnakes. Scrub desert and dry grasses, nary a real tree in sight. We should have left it to the Mexicans. I didn't understand at the time why a right-minded person would want to fight over that land. Came to realize later that a right-minded person wouldn't have fought over it.

"Oh, I did my duty, all right. It was the Battle of Resaca de la Palma, and I was under the command of Zach Taylor. I reckon I got off three rounds. I was strategic, you see. I shot at the ones with the fanciest hats. There was one fella who looked like a peacock astride a stallion. Figuring him to be someone important, I took careful aim at him. Just as I pulled the trigger, a shell landed not twenty feet away, knocking me down. I think I nicked the fella, but in the process, I took shrapnel in my leg. Eventually lost it, as you can see."

Gramps tapped the floor with his fake leg. "Did you know that General Santa Anna also lost his leg in similar fashion? Yes, sir. In battle against the French, he was wounded by shrapnel and had to have his leg cut off too. And that's why Santa Anna wasn't captured all at once, but in pieces as it were. The Fourth Illinois captured his peg leg after Santa Anna left it behind during his cowardly retreat from General Scott's men."

Gramps paused to take a gulp of brandy, then lit into the story about his decision to move west to the mountains after studying with Dr. Elisha Mitchell at the University.

I didn't want to hear that one again in all its long-windedness. I lurked at the edge of the ballroom, and lo and behold if I didn't see that Robert Johnston fella dancing with Sarah. They were gliding around the room, smiling and chatting as if there was nobody else around. I guess he told her what he told me, that she was the belle of the party.

October 29, 1887—Taylor and I got a letter from Sarah yesterday. She said that Pa had gone out of town, and Thomas was working real hard to keep everything going in the forge and mill. He had to hire help, and since Marinda had worked in the mill before, he hired her. They have been spending lots of time together out in the millhouse. Reading that little bit lit my ire.

Pa, apparently, has gone down to Raleigh for some sort of statewide meeting. Something to do with a farmers group. Sarah's not big on such details, so your guess is as good as mine about what he's doing. I've never left these here mountains, so I'm kind of forlorn that Pa didn't take me along. Why would he, though, seeing as how Taylor and I are back at Newton?

I was looking forward to being the older brother here at Newton now that Thomas is no longer here. But Taylor took to the school like a hawk to air. He's already tight with the other boys, and here I am all alone again.

Now all I do is study. My courses this term include Greek, history, geometry, philosophy, Shakespeare, and the Old Testament. It's a lot of work. As a diversion from our studies, many of us have taken to playing football in the afternoons. The game is a bit peculiar. There's a ball shaped like a giant egg that one tosses to another. You try to go in one direction down the field of play and cross an imaginary line to score a touchdown. All the while, the other team's trying to wrestle you to the ground. Taylor, even though he's still small, is very good at the sport. Being fast is a real asset, and he's the fastest one out there. Me, I'm about as fast as Darwin's tortoises, but I'm tall. My height helps me see the field and toss the ball forward. It's a rough game. Sam Huggins broke his collarbone playing it, and now he just sits up in the dormitory a-watching us others run around in the field. The headmaster believes that physical activity promotes character and mental acuity. Seeing as how I don't really know what mental acuity is, I can't hardly argue with him.

Earlier this term, the headmaster actually let us out of class for a day. We all walked down the hill to the train depot. There were lots of people walking down to the depot. All the businessmen from downtown strolled by in their dark suits, and women tugged their children along. Women who were normally seen in smocks toting laundry baskets were out in their Sunday go-to-meeting clothes. The headmaster wouldn't tell us what was happening at the depot, but a rumor soon arose that someone famous was coming to town. I thought it might be Mark Twain or maybe Arthur Conan Doyle.

We got down there and the crowd had assembled and nothing happened for a half hour or more. You can imagine that twenty or so young fellas wouldn't sit still for that long. Soon we were off in an empty stockyard playing kick the can. Eventually, the headmaster stomped over to us telling us to re-assemble, the train was a-coming.

The train that pulled in, its brakes squealing and its engine sweating from the climb up, was bedecked in flags and ribbons. It looked almost like a circus train with all the decoration. But there were no elephants on it at all; in fact, on that train was the elephant's rival, the biggest donkey of them all. Out of the fanciest caboose I've ever seen stepped President Grover Cleveland. President Cleveland spoke for a spell about tariffs and gold. The whole time I was thinking how disappointed Pa would be if he knew what I was doing, just a-listening to him.

Pa has gone on against this man many a time. He thinks the president has made terrible decisions and impeded the progress of the country. He's friend of neither farmer nor veteran, and Pa relies on farmers and is a veteran. There he was, not fifty feet from me, looking stern and strong and powerful. I thought maybe to shout something, but old Headmaster would have torn me up had I done such a thing.

The president wasn't here long. He's on a tour of the southern states right now. After he spoke, we climbed the hill back up to Newton. The headmaster made all of us write a summary of the president's speech. Heck, I wasn't paying close enough attention, so what I wrote was something like, "President Cleveland rode in a caboose covered in ribbons. The president is a stern, fatherly man, who believes in each to his own. President Cleveland believes the government does not exist to help the people, but to protect the people. There are others who believe differently, who think that the government, consisting as it does of its own citizens, ought to do everything possible to promote the general welfare per the Constitution."

I did not mention that those "others" were really just my pa. Since I had daydreamed through half of the president's speech, I don't expect to make a good mark on it.

Oh well, there's more to life than what marks you get in school. Which brings me back to the most important thing, that being Marinda. I have been trying not to think or write about her. Whenever her beautiful form arises in my mind, I can't help but think about her and Thomas alone in that millhouse. He is not her type, being neither redheaded nor wayfaring. I have to hope she hasn't changed her mind about all that. That Thomas, I don't trust him at all.

❧

When I was growing up, going to the cabin seemed like going to the remotest place in the world. Even now, the place seemed far from modern life. The journal lay open on my work table. A pot of coffee simmered on the gas stove. Below me the cabin was still a work in progress. The portable sawmill had been set up beside it. Now stacks of freshly fallen hemlocks waited to be planed into usable lumber. For all my access to modernity I could have been in a camp in the Rockies or Siberia.

But life in Daisy must not have been too isolated for the Quinns. It seemed from the journal that they did have regular contact with the outside world, including, apparently, the President. Clearly, they were more well off than most of their neighbors.

Early morning mists still clung to the mountainsides as I walked down the road. Tilda met me near the meadow where the old Duncan homestead used to be.

"I heard about the ruckus with Charles," she said.

"Wow," I answered. "Is there some sort of hidden camera in my hollow that broadcasts to the entire county?"

"Yep…it's called Patsy Duncan, otherwise known as the Mouth of the South."

I still hadn't met Patsy, but her white sedan often crunched along the gravel road coming and going from up the mountain. "So, what's Jesse's story?" I asked.

Tilda chuckled. "Jesse is special," she said. "He was the black sheep of the family before he joined the army. Into drugs and drag racing and guns. I've heard he's got some pretty scary tattoos."

"Scary how?"

"Like swastikas and quotes from *Mein Kampf*."

"Oh."

"He's got the PTSD now after Iraq. Just sits at home and draws."

"He's an artist?" That seemed unlikely, though his soul was certainly tortured enough for it.

"No. Draws like draws disability. He lives off the government that he so fiercely hates."

"Oh," I said. "What are the chances he had a brand-new television worth $600?"

"Yep, I heard about that too. Charles was pissed at Jesse for lying to you like that. He has a nice television all right, but it never fell off the wall and it works just fine."

A sudden fury came over me. I had suspected he was lying about the quality of the TV, but not that it had actually been broken. "That lying you-know-what!"

"Yep, that about sums him up. What happened was that he was asleep and the tree falling scared him to death. Triggered his PTSD, I guess, and made him think one of them IEDs just went off. He was freaked, called his daddy, and Daddy came running."

"I'm sorry for that, but he should give me my money back."

"He don't got your money anymore. Charles took it from him. That check'll never be cashed."

"Charles should tell me that then."

"Honey," Tilda stopped walking and held my gaze intently. "That's what's happening right now. Consider the message delivered."

"Oh," I said. The entire cove seemed suddenly alive with eyes and ears. Pride layered everything with a veneer as fragile as eggshells.

"So, how should I communicate with them? We're cutting two more trees today, and I want to make sure they know. His car wasn't home. I think if it had been, the guys would have knocked on his door to let him know what was going on."

"Oh, that." Tilda shook her head. "Jesse got his license revoked the other week after his tenth speeding ticket in a year. Charles made him leave the car up at his place until his sentence has been served."

"What a piece of work."

"You know," Tilda said, "there's a reason that double-wide is where it is."

"Really? Because it seems odd to put it right below my cabin when there are two hundred and twenty-nine other acres for it to sit on."

"It's as far away from Charles and Patsy as it can be and still be on Duncan land. That ain't a coincidence, mind you."

"Oh," I said again. Since Charles didn't want his antisocial offspring to be anywhere near him, he had inflicted him on the rest of us. "That's just great."

We walked on, the sun steadily burning off the mist. It would be a bright day here in the hollow, but it didn't feel hopeful. I was going to start off by having to knock on Jesse's door and alert him to more incoming artillery fire.

11

January 17, 1888—Snow, a good two feet deep, covers everything, and Pa can't get out to take me back to Asheville. I've been here for three weeks now for Christmas break. They will have started classes without me and Taylor, but a person can't rightly get around in this weather. All of the talk this winter has been about Sarah's betrothal to that Robert Lee Johnston fella. Ma and her sit off to the side looking at dress patterns out of the magazines and catalogues we get. Apparently, a woman has to have things just so for her wedding. The only wedding I've ever been to was Owen and Betsy's. There wasn't much to it really, just a church service, a hoedown, and a chivaree. This one's going to be different, on account of the Johnston family having so much money and so many acquaintances. It will be right bizarre to have that fella as a brother-in-law. He seemed nice enough, but a tad too cocksure.

Speaking of Owen and Betsy, they were here for Christmas again along with the Fallons and Brightleafs. Baby Bradshaw's getting big. He doesn't talk, but he waddles around like a little wood duck now. He likes Gramps. Gramps will get him giggling by singing a silly song about London Bridge.

Since I've been snowbound, I've gone into Gramps's library and read again the works of Ralph Waldo Emerson. At school, we don't read much Emerson, him being a Yankee and all. Nature is neither Yankee nor Southern, so I don't see what the problem is. Today, I came across a bit about the balance of nature. Mr. Emerson says two things, and together they don't make a whole lot of sense to me. He says in the universe all things are moral, and at the same time he says nature is like a mathematical equation, that what happens on one side gets balanced out on the other. I don't see how both can rightly be true. If there's a polarity to nature, if nature's a balancing act, then it can't be moral, can it? That would mean that whenever something good happens somewhere, something bad happens somewhere else. How is that moral? If by me making good marks at school, that little Bradshaw falls down and busts his lip, heck, I don't want any part of that morality. I'll take low marks, thank you very much.

I suspect that Mr. Darwin would disagree with Emerson about nature being moral. Nature is just nature, and yes, there is a balance to it, a balance that can be seen every day right outside the front door. You chop down a stand of trees, and you'll see nature do everything in its power to replace those trees. But there's nothing moral about it. It's not like you're punished for chopping down them trees. You should be, though. There's nothing quite like a big old tree.

One thing Emerson says hits true, though, and I read it out loud to everybody as we were sitting around after Christmas dinner. The womenfolk had gone into the bedroom to chatter about dresses and patterns and whatnot. It was just the menfolk minus Thomas and Owen who I was reading to. "The farmer imagines power and place are fine things. But the president has paid dear for his White House. It has commonly cost him all his peace and the best of his manly attributes. To preserve for a short time so conspicuous an appearance before the world, he is content to eat dust before the real masters, who stand erect behind the throne."

Pa liked that real good. He said, "Ain't that the truth," after I finished. I asked Pa then what he had gone down to Raleigh for. In her letter, Sarah hadn't mentioned the what for.

He nodded and took a wad of chewing tobacco from his pouch and tucked it up under his lip. "Son, I went down to help establish the North Carolina Farmers Alliance."

Pa was fixing to leave it at that, but Taylor scrunched up his face. "But you ain't no farmer."

Pa gave him a look that could kill a muskrat. "Son, you got me there. Now your ma does have the plot out back, and you yourself tend to our pigs, and there's the back acre of corn, but I reckon we're not farmers."

Gramps chortled like a clucking chicken. Taylor crossed his arms hard across his chest. "You know what I mean, Pa."

"What about the Saunters?" Pa said. "Are they farmers?"

"They have a melon patch," Taylor said. "But no, they ain't farmers."

"What about you, Charlie?" Pa asked Charlie Brightleaf who was puffing on his after-dinner pipe. "You a farmer?"

Charlie let go dual cascades of sweet smoke that intertwined as they rose. "Yes, sir," he said.

"What about you, Nap?" he asked of Napoleon Fallon.

Napoleon nodded.

Pa turned back to Taylor. "Now, son, why is that? Why are Charlie Brightleaf and Isaac Duncan and Napoleon Fallon farmers, and your ma and the Saunters ain't?"

"'Cause, them folk make a living from what they grow. They don't just eat it."

Pa nodded and patted Taylor's head. "That's right. They make a living from growing produce and selling it at market. Let me tell you boys something. By the time you're my age, if nothing is done, you're not going to be able to make a living like what I'm able to do. You, all of you, will have to work for somebody else in some factory somewhere or hoeing someone else's line. You, and your friends, the Fallons and the Morgans and Old Man Rolly, will all wind up spending somebody else's dollar, unless something is done to change the way of government. This Farmers Alliance is a group of folks that want the government to make life a little easier for the hardworking families of the state, to make it so farmers can make a decent living from feeding everybody else. Because, what are we, as a nation, if not farmers?"

I had never heard my father say so many things all at once. "That group sounds right nice," I offered.

"Downright Jeffersonian," Gramps said. Gramps then cleared his throat, and everyone got ready for a long story, but all he said was, "You know what Thomas Jefferson said, don't you? And your Mr. Emerson would agree, I'm sure. He declared the White House was too large, fit for two emperors, one pope, and the grand lama. And that was before they rebuilt it and added to it."

A few minutes of quiet passed, then Gramps cleared his throat again. Fixing his attention on his pipe, he started up, like a big old train engine starting up. "Now Jefferson," he began, "President Thomas Jefferson was one of the most extraordinary men to grace this country. I ever tell you about the time my own father run into Jefferson up in Richmond?"

I had heard the story about that inn where his pa and Mr. Jefferson had shared a meal enough that I could tell it myself, so I excused myself and ventured out onto the porch. It was cold out, and the porch sighed under my weight. Saunter Branch stood still, its falls now icy stalactites, its banks shaped in new ways by layers of snow. The world lay silent except for the light ticking of new snow kissing the old snow.

Then I heard the rasp of a rocker and turned. It was Thomas sitting there in one chair, Marinda in the other.

"Oh," I think I said.

"Brother," Thomas said and stood. "I guess I should leave you two lovebirds alone, now shouldn't I?"

He and I never spend much time in the same place. If he weren't my own brother, I doubt we would even speak. We barely do as is.

"Merry Christmas, brother," he said as he whipped by me into the house. I didn't respond, seeing as how he didn't mean it. I took his place in the still rocking chair.

"Howdy, Marinda," I said.

She gave me a look that warmed my insides. "That was a delicious meal, weren't it?" she asked.

"Always is when Ma cooks."

"Is that what you miss most when you're at that school of yours?"

"Nope," I said.

"What is?"

"I don't rightly know," I offered.

She stopped rocking real fast. "You don't know?"

"I can't tell if it's your smile or your eyes. Or maybe it's your pretty hair."

"Aw, Carson, you are so sweet."

We sat rocking in the cold. Our breath poured from our nostrils in thick clouds, and I tried to mimic Charlie's long streams of pipe smoke.

"You've been helping out in the mill and forge?"

She nodded. "Just while your pa was away."

"Thomas don't seem to mind none," I said.

"You two ought to act more like brothers and less like sworn enemies. I don't understand you and him. It's colder twixt you two in the middle of the summer than it is out here now."

I swallowed.

"He ain't bad, you know. You're more alike than you think."

"Ain't you smitten." I couldn't look at her direct, instead keeping tabs on a wren stirring through the snowy underbrush down below.

"It ain't like that."

"What is it like then?" I asked.

"It's like it is. He needs help when your pa's away, and I help. Like I would help Owen or Betsy or Charlie."

"I reckon that's right." I turned away from the bird to look into the laurel green of her eyes.

She shuddered and crossed her arms for warmth.

"Say," I said. "What do you suppose would happen were we to kiss right here and now? Would our lips stick together forever frozen?"

"Let's find out."

And the rest of what happened is between me and her.

January 21, 1888—Pa decided enough was enough. He said as much as Gramps is paying for that school, we needed to be there getting his money's worth, snow or no snow. He went down to the Lynch place over in the valley. They trade in horses over there. He bought a black mare by the name of Nightwalker to get me and Taylor back to Asheville. It was one of the proudest moments of my life when Pa came back up to the house and gave me a talking-to. I think every other lecture Pa has delivered to me has been right uncomfortable, but this one was different.

"Carson," he said. "You're the older brother, and you know the way as good as anybody, so I want you to make sure to get Taylor and yourself back to Asheville. When you get there, take this mare down to the livery by the river and sell her for no less than seventy dollars. If you can get more than that for her, you can keep the difference. You bring back that seventy come spring."

"Yes, sir," I said. Pa don't ever pay full price for nothing. I suspect he got Nightwalker for a lot less than seventy dollars, seeing as how he's the personal farrier for the Lynches. The thing about Pa is that he never passes up an opportunity. If he can make a dollar doing something, he will.

Now, I'm not one for horses. I don't care to sit on the back of a beast when I could be walking myself. But school's twenty-five miles away and that's a long way to walk even for me. With both of us up on her back, we trotted off down toward the Drovers Road for the journey to Asheville. Ma and Sarah and Pa all waved to us from the porch, and Nightwalker took high steps to make it through the snow.

I looked back up the road. I couldn't see the Fallon house, but I could see the chimney smoke dancing up from where the house was. I knew at the bottom of that smoke trail was Marinda, curled up in front of the fire, a blanket wrapped warmly around her. Maybe she was singing, maybe her ma or pa were telling a story. The thought of her warmed me, and I didn't have to brace as hard against the cold north wind that swirled snow all around us.

The road to Asheville winds steeply to the west, up out of the Gap to the Blue Ridge and over. Then it drops down into the valley known as Fairview. Before the trains came, this turnpike was always busy as it was the way to Charlotte from Asheville and beyond. They call it the Drovers Road on account of all the livestock that folks would drive down to the big markets to sell. We still get that ever once in a while, but mostly it's quiet except for the tourists that come to see the Chimney Rock.

Taylor and I sat scrunched together on the back of Night-walker. We passed the occasional house. The only sign of life was chimney smoke. The world was all hushed like it gets under the weight of snow.

After a time, Taylor said, "You reckon Pa knows what he's talking about with the farmers and all?"

"I suspect so," I said. "He's not the kind to talk about things he don't know. Unlike Gramps."

"Gramps knows more than anybody," Taylor said.

"At least he tells folks more than anybody."

"I don't want to work for nobody," Taylor said. "Working for Pa is bad enough."

"I ain't ever going to work for no man," I declared. "When I get old enough, I'm going to leave here lickety-split."

"Where are you going?"

"I don't know," I had to confess. "Maybe west, maybe to South America like Alexander von Humboldt. Heck, maybe even Africa. Somewhere. Anywhere."

We went on in silence for a bit. Nightwalker was struggling. The way was steep now, and she was slipping and straining.

"Maybe I'll be a soldier," Taylor said.

"Soldiers have to do what they're told, brother." I shifted around to lessen the discomfort of riding.

"Oh," he said. "Maybe not then."

We had just crested the Blue Ridge when a man jumped up from beside the road. He startled Nightwalker, and she reared back. Since we were riding bareback and I was behind Taylor, I slid plumb off that horse and landed with a plop in the snow. The horse took Taylor and galloped off down the road.

At first I was worried more about Taylor than the man. He

had never really ridden a horse before. He wouldn't know how to stop Nightwalker. Pa had taught Thomas and me, but these days he thinks travel by horse is mostly done with, what with trains and all. I stood up and started to take off after them, but that man said real mean-like, "You best not run, lessen you like the taste of lead."

I looked at him for the first time. He was a rough-seeming character, with a dark, thick beard and a tattered old hat and a slicker for covering. He had a six-shooter in his hand aimed at me. I'd never had a gun pointed at me before.

"You got any money, boy?" he asked.

"No." I swallowed. Held my breath.

"Mighty fine clothes. Fancy horse. I reckon you're lying."

My legs felt as heavy as millstones, and my heart thumped like a grouse taking flight. "One thing I don't do is lie, mister," I said. "My pa never has allowed for that."

"Your pa? Who would that be?"

I suspect he was hoping my pa would be a man of wealth that would pay him money for me. I figured there was no harm in telling him the truth, seeing as how everybody knew Pa was tighter with money than with his own kin.

"William Quinn."

The fella flinched when I told him. "He wouldn't be Master Sergeant Will Quinn of the Second Mounted?"

"Might be." I took a step away from him, eyeing the thicket where I knew I could lose him. "He never told me his rank."

His gun trembled a tad. He took a deep breath, let it go in a cloud. After a second breath, he lowered the gun. "Tell him Gus Trabor says hello. Tell him I said he has a mighty brave son too."

Nightwalker with Taylor astride her crested the ridge up above us. He reined her in like he knew what he was doing. Heck, he looked like Buffalo Bill riding up to save the day.

"You there!" he shouted. "You leave my brother alone!"

He got Nightwalker to practically leap down to us and put her between me and Trabor.

"Go on, now!" he shouted.

"It's all right," I explained. "This here man knows Pa. From the war."

Trabor turned and disappeared back into the woods from where he came. Taylor lowered his arm to pull me up onto the horse, but I told him no. I'd had enough horseback riding. I'd be walking from here on, thank you very much.

My legs were still quivering, kind of like they did that night of the earthquake, only now the ground was still. It was something else that shook me. It felt good to move along, even though the snow up there was nearly two feet deep. I took deep breaths and watched them float off into the sullen sky. That man, I kept thinking, could have done me in for good. I decided not to think about the fright and focused on the more remarkable occurrence, Taylor's ease on that horse.

Pa had spent a lot of time teaching me to ride, and I had been terrible at it. He eventually gave up, saying "No matter. You'll take the train wherever you need to go anyhow."

Now here was Taylor, a young'un who'd never been taught the first thing about horses, riding like he was born to it. And I reckon he was born to it. He trotted along, and I followed down the winding road into the valley below. On account of the snow and ice and the steepness of the terrain, the horse really couldn't go any faster than a fella anyway.

I explained to Taylor what had happened with the man. He was real interested and kept asking questions I didn't know the answer to.

"What'd he call Pa?" he asked.

"Master Sergeant Quinn," I said.

"Of the Second Mounted?"

"That's what he said. You know, it could be a different Will Quinn. There are bound to be lots of them."

"No, I'm sure it was Pa. Why do you think he was so scared of him?"

"'Cause anybody that knows him is scared of him. I'm scared of him. Ain't you?"

Taylor looked down on me from way up on that horse. "I reckon I ain't really scared of nothing." He said it in a way that wasn't boastful, just kind of matter of fact.

"You ain't scared of Pa tanning your hide?" I asked, because that was the thing what scared me more than any other.

"No, not really," he said. "He's our pa. He ain't really gonna hurt you."

That thought had never occurred to me. Thinking on it, I suspect Taylor's right. Still, I'm afraid of doing something that'll let Pa down. And that Mr. Tabor knows something about Pa that neither Taylor nor me nor even Ma knows. Whatever that thing is, it ain't likely to be something cheerful at all.

Once we reached the valley below I climbed back up onto Nightwalker. Taylor urged her up to speed, and I hung on for dear life. We made it to Newton in what seemed like no time at all. Tomorrow, I'll go on down to the livery and sell Nightwalker. Taylor wants to keep her, but there's no way we can take care of her here at school. Besides, Pa would have my hide if I don't bring back his seventy dollars, and I'm not ashamed to admit that that prospect scares me more than Mr. Tabor and his six-shooter.

&

There were no more eruptions from the Duncans as Jimmy the forester removed the remaining infected trees and milled them into planks on site. Once finished, the little hollow felt entirely different, sunlit and warm in ways it had never been before. I had feared that the tree removal would permanently alter the nature of the place, and maybe it did, but it wasn't altogether for the worse. In some ways, the darkness of the hollow had always felt foreboding. Now, at least for chunks of the midday, there was enough light to cheer the place up.

My research in Hendersonville had referenced the gravesites of Marinda Fallon and some of the Quinns. I thought today I would go pay my respects to these people I was getting to know a century after their lives had been lived.

At some point, a local historian had compiled a registry of

gravesites throughout the county. At the library I had photo-
copied several pages of the registry and had obtained rough
directions to the sites from the librarian. She had conferred
with her aides who debated whether the Clear Creek in question was the one in the southern part of the county or the
northern. That led them to venture further from the subject at
hand to discuss the varying spellings of local family names, how
the Justus family was not related to the Justice family but the
Lawters and the Laughters were.

Armed with a confusing set of directions, a U.S. Geological
Survey topographical map, and my morning coffee, I loaded
up the Subaru. The directions took me down through the village of Bat Cave, then up what used to be the turnpike toward
Asheville, the Drovers Road that Carson Quinn had ventured
up astride Nightwalker.

The directions had me turn onto an old dirt road I had never noticed before, which ascended into a shaded forest. The
farther I went from the hardtop road, the rougher the road became. The road navigated through a creek rather than over it or
around it. Finally, I arrived at the juncture where the cemetery
was supposed to be and stopped. It was just forest. I looked
at the map and at the road and at the map again. This was the
place. Grabbing my camera and walking stick, I stepped from
the car.

The morning chill still lingered. The forest smelled of pine
up here, and the nearby rushing creek invigorated me. A few
feet into the woods, I found the first headstone. It was Napoleon Fallon. A crack ran through it separating the Ls, but his
dates were clear: b. March 17, 1852; d. November 20, 1911.
There was some faint wording on the stone. I knelt and wiped
off some dirt to see better. "Father of the Jonathan Crisp apple," it said. Nearby lay Mourning Sprouse Fallon. She had lived
until 1932. There were four other graves with them, clearly their
children. Jarrett Fallon was born in 1871 and died that same
year. Clarissa Fallon had been stillborn in 1872. Hiram Fallon
was born and died in 1874. Then there was Marinda herself.

The gravestone looked remarkably modern. Marinda Delia Fallon Quinn, it said. "Beloved mother, devoted daughter. Born January 27, 1875. Died October 10, 1959. May her soul find eternal and everlasting peace."

I took in the tragedies engraved so matter-of-factly. Even if I didn't know what I knew about their history, having three children in a row not make it through their first year would have been enough heartache for a century. Even so, they pushed on through an unforgiving life. In the journal, these seemed like hardy folks with big hearts. Mourning Sprouse, interred beneath my feet, had seemed like a good mother. Protective yet kind. Here she rested, her grave untended, what was once field now overtaken by forest.

There were others, with gravestones even older than those of the Fallons. With names like Morgan, Galloway, and Lynch, the gravestones perched crooked and cracked. Some were obvious, the sunken ground giving way in the exact shapes of the coffins below. The oldest part of the cemetery lay deeper in the forest, with markers so old the etching had long since faded. The earliest date I could make out was an Edney born in 1787 who died in 1815. The Edneys were some of the first people of European descent to settle this area. The name was everywhere, from the valley across from the Quinns' homestead to the nearby town of Edneyville.

Other than Marinda, there were no Quinns here. Old Man Duncan had been right. She was Quinn by marriage only, in life and in death. I took some pictures and hiked back to the car. An old man leaned up against it, clearly waiting for whoever the owner was to return from whatever illicit deed they were out here performing. He had a full head of white hair and wore a flannel shirt tucked into worn-out jeans. A border collie hung by his side.

"So, you're the one trespassin' on my land," he said in a gruff voice.

This time I really was trespassing in the traditional sense. But again, in all the years of my childhood when my folks and

I had wandered freely all over these mountains we had never once been reprimanded. Here I was for the second time in as many months being chided for this activity. I decided honesty was the best policy.

"Hi," I said. "My name is Caroline McAlister. I own Marinda Quinn's old cabin, up the hollow across the road. I'm doing some research and was looking for her grave."

He squinted at me, then gave his dog a questioning look. "Did you find it?"

"Yes, sir," I said.

"I suspect you got a picture of it on that fancy camera," he said, nodding at my digital camera.

"Yes, sir," I repeated.

"Good," he said. "Then you won't need be coming back."

He turned to walk away.

"Can I ask who you are?" I asked.

"The owner," he offered. Then he turned, clicked his tongue to gather in the border collie, and continued up the mountain.

Taking the not-so-subtle hint I climbed back into the Subaru, executed a seven-point turn, drove back through the creek and down the valley to where the road flattened, and emerged onto the hardtop. Shame and excitement chased me toward the next gravesite on my list.

By the end of the day, I had still found no Quinns. The Duncans lay together in the Baptist cemetery, properly interred with no surprises. Charlie and Wilma Brightleaf were there too. Up the Gorge a ways, I visited the final resting place of the Rollys, whom Carson had mentioned in his journal. Everywhere I went there were the same names: Barnhill, Barnwell, Morgan, Edney, Lynch, Dolan. Not a single Quinn. Maybe the only way to commune with the Quinns really would be through a séance.

12

January 23, 1888—Today Taylor and I took the horse down to the livery. I didn't tell the fella how much I wanted. Instead, I asked him how much he'd pay. That was Taylor's idea. My brother, though younger than me, is smarter in a lot of ways. The fella wound up giving us $100 for her. We both held our tongues, pretending to be like Pa with him, all serious and quiet, but once we were out of earshot we whooped and hollered our way back up to Newton. We split the proceeds, with Taylor getting fifteen dollars and me getting fifteen dollars. I've never had that much money in all of my life. I tucked the seventy dollars away. If you think I'm going to tell you where, then you must be out of your mind. There's no telling at all who might find this journal and read it.

March 7, 1888—I am in deep, deep trouble now. The headmaster has already tanned my hide and put me on isolation, where I'm not allowed to fraternize with the other boys. There's no telling what Pa will do when I get home in June. I'm of a mind to up and skedaddle. If I still had my fifteen dollars, I'd just go away. I'd never go back to the Gap and Pa's mule strap. That durn money. It's what caused all this.

You see, what happened was that Stanley McFarland found out about my money. Stanley is kind of like me. His people don't have a lot of wealth, but they have what you call prestige. When Taylor told him about us selling the horse, he got real interested. Stanley's a year older than me and about fifty pounds heavier. He's the one who broke Sam Huggins's collarbone playing football. He thought he could just come over and take the money for his own. Heck, if that outlaw couldn't get nothing from me, then no half-wit oaf is going to get my money.

"You. Quinn," he said to me, standing over me with his chest all puffed out like a rooster going courting. "You gonna give me half them greenbacks, or am I gonna have to slug you?"

I don't get riled real easy, you see. Even though I'm half Irish, it takes a lot to fire me up. It seems like the rest of them have fiery tempers. Gramps will lose it at things like the stove that won't light or a door hinge that won't oblige, and Taylor, Thomas, and Sarah all seem to take after him that way. Me, I'm more like Pa, prone to taking whatever happens in stride most of the time. But once I lose it, there ain't no getting it back.

So, I stared real hard at that Stanley McFarland. "Ain't neither gonna happen," I told him, "so you might as well just run off now."

"I heard your daddy was a Yankee soldier. You a Yankee lover?" He pushed my shoulder.

I imagined myself as a bull deciding whether or not to charge. "You can go on down to Daisy and take that up with my pa. Why don't you go bother someone else? You ain't getting one cent of any money I may or may not have."

"Fine," he said. "I'll do that."

That Stanley turned and went after Taylor then. He didn't even ask Taylor nothing. He just walked up to him and punched him in the face. Taylor's head snapped back, and the blood poured almost immediately from his nose. It was as though I really was that bull. I saw that red, and of a sudden I was angrier than I'd ever been before. Old Stanley never knew what hit him.

When I was done with him, he was laid out on the floor. A trickle of blood oozed out his ear, and a lot of blood flowed like the French Broad from his nose and he was squawking like a hen on the chopping block. Just then, the headmaster come bounding into the dormitory. What he saw was Stanley on the ground and me standing over him, my raw knuckles evidence enough to convict me.

Since Taylor had a bloody nose and that Stanley was known to be a bully, it was clear to the headmaster what had happened. But that didn't stop him from giving me a walloping with the paddle in his office. Afterward, he made me set on my raw backside while he gave me a talking-to.

"Mr. Quinn," he said, "I know Mr. McFarland brought this on himself, but, son, you went too far. The boy's going to be in the infirmary for at least a week. Do you know who his father is? It's Judge McFarland himself. When he finds out about this, I'm going to be the one held accountable. You know about accountability, don't you, Mr. Quinn?"

I nodded.

"I've been very kind to your family over the years. Your older brother, yourself, Taylor. You've been able to come here at a fraction of the cost of the other boys, you know. And I've done that as a favor to your grandfather. But it's cost me. Oh, it's cost me a lot of money. If I had taken three full-paying students instead of you three partial payers, why I'd be forty-five dollars the richer."

I nodded again.

"Now, I'm probably going to be pressured by the most powerful judge in Western North Carolina to get rid of you two Quinn boys on account of this mess. Your grandfather and I go way back, but there's only so much an old friendship is worth. Are you understanding me, Mr. Quinn?"

"Yes, sir," I said. "I'll go get you my fifteen dollars."

"I thought you were a smart lad. And a hard puncher too."

I went and dug my money out of my trunk and brought it to the headmaster. He took it and tucked it in his breast pocket. He sighed like a locomotive after it comes to a stop. "Son, you're going to be on isolation for however long young Stanley is in the infirmary. When Stanley rejoins his classmates, you shall too. In the meanwhile, don't worry about your studies."

That was right perplexing for the headmaster to say not to worry about my studies. But then I saw why. He reached around and came back with a big old Bible, which he tossed with a thud on his desk.

"You're to copy this word for word, Mr. Quinn. Except when you're eating, I want to see your pen flowing with the word of God. Maybe that will scare the Darwinism right out of you."

It didn't seem fair. I could understand him punishing me for what I'd done to Stanley. But it seemed wrong that he would steal my money and then go on to punish me, not for fighting, but for my belief in science. A lot of different things came to mind to tell the headmaster right then. Instead, I bit my tongue. I bit my tongue about the part in the Bible that talks about thou shall not steal. I bit my tongue about how many times I was a-fixing to write the words "and," "smite," and "begat." I bit my tongue about how now I could understand that Galileo fella even better now. I held back every bit of me that wanted to do to that headmaster what I'd done to Stanley McFarland.

March 10, 1888—I'm so tired of writing that I can't believe I'm actually writing in this here journal. I've made it all the way to Leviticus now. There has been a lot of begetting, of course. Since I'm copying the words, I'm noticing them better than when I read these parts before. I reckon that's what the headmaster was counting on. That said, it still makes no sense to me. Why the heck do I care about a man selling a dwelling house in a walled city? What happens if he sells a dwelling house that's in a city without walls? Heck, I've never heard of a city these days that has walls. Maybe Old Fort once had walls, but that was almost a hundred years ago since they came down. It does seem to me that God doesn't care for folks being poor. He's all about setting things right, making the poor rich, forgiving debts, keeping folks equal. That and making up some right strange rules about things. I guess all us mountain folk are going to hell, because nearly everybody keeps and eats pigs. God's very clear about not permitting the eating of swine. It also says that every seventh year is to be kept holy as the Sabbath, and neither to sow or to reap in that entire year. It's called the Jubilee, and God's supposed to take care of you that year with the fruits of the field. I reckon that means eating what's wild and not what you planted. Heck, no one I know does that. It sounds good to me, though. I can forage pretty well, digging up roots and mushrooms and finding wild grapes and berries. It says nothing about not eating squirrel or trout. That rule would be a lot easier for us mountain folk to keep than the rule about casting out bastards from the house of the Lord. Poor little Bradshaw would never get no preaching if he weren't allowed in the house of the Lord.

March 12, 1888—Stanley came back to class today, so I finally got to stop copying the Bible. Since I was out of isolation, I was able to talk to Taylor and explain what happened. He tried to give me half of his money, but I told him to keep it. Money ain't nothing but trouble.

I made it all the way to Judges 18. When I turned my pages in to the headmaster, he was right impressed with my progress.

"And?" he asked me as he examined the pages.

It seemed like he expected me to understand his question. Since I didn't, I didn't say nothing.

"What did you learn from this exercise, Mr. Quinn?"

"God's awfully partial to them Israelites, ain't he?" I said.

The headmaster scowled at me real hard, which I don't rightly understand. It says so right there in them pages I copied, that God pretty much only cared about the Israelites, what with all the smiting of the Hittites and the Perizzites and the Amorites and the such. I said as much to the headmaster.

"It's a metaphor, son. You do understand metaphor, don't you?"

"I think so," I said. "That's like when Gramps says General Clingman is as dumb as a moose in mud?"

"That's a simile."

"Oh."

"Metaphor is the use of one thing to stand in for something else. The Israelites in the Old Testament are a metaphor for all God-fearing people everywhere. Those Hittites and their ilk are those that ignore God's word."

"Like scientists?"

"I suppose. Or the Saracen or the Buddhists or the Chinamen."

"Or them folk that charge interest on loans or use two kinds of measures or cut their hair or trim their beards? 'Cause I copied that down too. Those words are right there in them pages."

As you can see, I was real angry at that headmaster for what he made me do. It's not that I don't believe in God. I have no reason not to believe. It's just that I don't base my believing on the words of some long dead fella in a faraway land.

"Son," the headmaster said. "I'm going to have to have a talk with your grandfather. I'm very concerned about your moral progress. You should take seriously the prospect of eternal damnation."

"Yes, sir. I reckon I should." I kept my eyes on the floorboards, on the grooves worn by the goings and comings of other students receiving similar talking-tos for who knows how many years.

With that, he dismissed me. I know I shouldn't have said what I did to him, but I ain't worried about Gramps. Gramps agrees with me about the Bible. What worries me is Pa. Pa, and that mule strap of his.

June 12, 1888—We're back in Daisy now. Pa at first didn't seem as angry as I suspected he'd be. Perhaps he's too distracted by the state of the economy or Sarah's wedding to give two licks about what I did to Stanley McFarland. The headmaster had written him a letter explaining what had happened. All the ride back through Fairview he was silent, whistling ever once in a while to keep the mule interested in pulling our cart.

When we crested the Blue Ridge, right around the spot where Taylor and I had encountered that Mr. Trabor, Pa spoke up. "Carson," he said. "You're the oldest now. I expect you to be a good role model for little Taylor."

"I ain't little!" Taylor shouted from the back.

"For young Taylor," Pa corrected. "What you done to that judge's boy ain't the way we Quinns handle things. You understand me?"

"Yes, sir. I don't know what happened. I don't remember it at all."

"He walloped him real good, Pa," Taylor offered.

Pa turned to me and arched an eyebrow to say, *See, I told you so*. I sat there. There was nothing to say. Truth was, I wasn't sorry for what I done. And, in case you were thinking of messing with my family, I'd do it again.

"How would you feel if somehow that boy had died?" Pa asked.

I wouldn't want to kill any one, and I said that to him.

"You just think on that. How it would feel if you were to take a life on account of losing your temper, son. That way, maybe it won't ever happen again."

He whistled at the mule and slapped the reins. It was as though maybe he knew what it was like to take a life on account of ill temper. We were over the top of the ridge. It was all downhill now, downhill with tight curves in the road as we came through the Gap.

Taylor, never one to bite his tongue, issued forth with what both he and I were thinking. "Pa, were you a master sergeant in the war? For the Mounted Infantry?"

Pa didn't answer. He kept his eyes on the road.

"Carson, what was that fella's name? That bandit?"

Pa turned, now interested in the conversation. I had no intention of telling him about that incident, but little Taylor can't bite his tongue.

I knew his name. It was stamped into my memory forever. But I acted like I couldn't recall.

"You run into a bandit, boy?" Pa asked.

"He had a six-shooter, Pa," Taylor exclaimed, the words pouring from his mouth like water over the Hickory Nut Falls. "It was on up by the ridge that he come out of the woods. Come on, Carson, what was his name? Pa, it turned out he knew you. He asked if you were Master Sergeant Will Quinn of the…the…Second Mounted. That is you, ain't it?"

Pa grunted like an angry bull.

I turned to glare real hard at Taylor, and the disappointment showed on his face.

Pa cleared his throat, and the words came real reluctant like. "Was a time," he said. "Long time past in which maybe I was that fella."

For a mile or so the only noise was the creaking of the wagon wheel, over and over again.

"We get home," Pa announced out of the blue, "I'm gonna need you to grease that wheel, you hear?" He looked at me askance.

"Yes, sir," I said.

"That bandit?" he asked.

"His name was Gus Trabor," I confessed.

Pa clicked at the mule. "Mmm-hmm," he said.

I continued, "When we were heading to Asheville in the snow, he jumped us from the woods right up at the ridge. The horse spooked and threw me off, and took off with Taylor on the back. When he found out you were my pa, he got real scared and said to tell you that you had a brave boy and to say howdy. He run off into the woods after that. Taylor was a real hero. He came back astride of Nightwalker and put her between the pistol and me."

Pa slapped the reins against the hindquarters of the mule. "That man's trouble. You see him again, let me know. I'm glad you're both fine. I guess it weren't such a good idea to send you on your own."

"We can handle ourselves, Pa," I said.

"I reckon you can."

"Why was he so scared of you?" Taylor asked.

"I don't reckon he was scared of me," Pa explained, "so much as he was of that there master sergeant he talked about."

"But, Pa," Taylor asked. "You just said that was you."

Pa hurried up Henry the mule, and we rode in silence all the way back to the house. At the house as we were unloading our trunks, I dug out that seventy dollars and gave it to Pa. "Here," I said. "From Nightwalker."

He took it and tucked it real fast into his pocket. "That all you get for her?"

"We got a hundred dollars," Taylor exclaimed.

"My, oh my," Pa said. "You can split up that thirty."

"We already did," Taylor said. "Only Carson…"

My look stopped him cold.

Pa grabbed my arm real tight. "You split that money evenly, boy. Just cause you're older don't mean you get more of it."

Taylor was shaking his head hard and started to explain, but again, I was able to shut him up with a glance.

"Yes, sir," I said. "I'll make sure he gets fifteen dollars."

"Taylor," Pa said. "You tell me if he shorts you, son."

"Yes, sir." Taylor slumped.

Pa said, "Now, get your things put away. Carson, you and I have some business to attend to in the forge when you get done."

The business would be the mule strap. Daggum it. I thought maybe all the talking was in place of the strap, but unfortunately no. Now my rear end is all red and it stings so bad. Pa did tell me, though, he was proud of me for sticking up for Taylor, and he was of a mind to not do this to me. Except then he found out that I had kept more than my share of the money, and that really disappointed him. I gritted my teeth and took it. As far as I'm concerned Pa ain't never gonna find out the truth about the money. That's between me and the headmaster.

June 14, 1888—I sure am tired of being in trouble. Gramps called me into his room this morning. The whole room stinks of his liniment. That could be punishment enough. "Boy, I got a letter from Rodney Webster."

It took a minute for me to realize he was talking about the headmaster.

"He's concerned about your afterlife."

I nodded.

"He thinks you're headed down the path of godlessness. That true, boy?"

I shrugged.

"You don't know? Do you believe in Jesus, boy?"

"I reckon so," I said.

"You reckon," Gramps said in disgust. "You reckon," he repeated as he hobbled over to his secretary and searched on the shelves for something. "You reckon," he repeated as he pulled out a book. "Here," he said. It was a slim little book that I hadn't ever noticed up there before. "Read this, then tell me whether you reckon or not. Go on now. I've got to rub in my liniment and I know you don't care for the pleasing aroma."

He pulled his indoor cane from the barrel of canes by his desk and used the rubber tip to nudge me out of his room. It was only once I was out in the light of the sitting room that I could see real good what book he gave me. It was *The Apology* of Socrates, by Plato. So far, it's all Socrates defending himself against the charge of irreverence. Gramps has a peculiar notion of punishment. At least he didn't make me read it in Greek.

❧

The journal and all of the accompanying research had become almost a full-time job for me. When I first came up to the cabin I had hoped for a reprieve, an opportunity to step back and assess my life and my career, to figure out what was next. Instead, there was this journal into which I had plunged whole hog, as Carson might say.

I spent my days driving around these same mountains that Carson had explored on foot, speeding along asphalt highways that had then been mere trails, trying to see the past in the now. I had driven back to the county courthouse to do a records search with the Register of Deeds. The clerk eyed me suspiciously when I asked for what I wanted. She peered over the reading glasses perched on the end of her nose, her hair permed and proper and her fingers dancing across a computer keyboard.

"You aren't an attorney, are you?" she asked.

I was taken aback. "Of course not."

"You know there's this thing called the internet, right?"

Defensiveness caused my back to arch. Here I was again

being chided about my technological limitations, this time by someone old enough to be my mother. "Of course," I said.

"We spent a lot of money to get all of our records online. You can get all of the tax records and even deeds back to 1980 on the internet." She was clearly perturbed that she was doing something I could have done on my own were I less ignorant. "For next time," she said.

Feeling sheepish and defensive, I said, "I don't have an internet connection right now. I'm living in an old cabin down toward Bat Cave."

"The library has computers you can use for free, darlin'," she instructed. "For next time." She printed out the tax card and handed it over to me. "Anything else?"

"No, thank you," I said as I departed.

It wasn't until I was in the parking lot that I took a proper look at the name on the tax card of the land where the Fallons lay in eternal rest. "Hiram Q. Morgan" read the name on the piece of paper. Of course. Everyone around here was a Morgan. Deflated, I began my journey back to the hollow.

As I negotiated the steep drive up to the cabin, a stunning sight came into view. Sunlight bathed the entire cabin, and it stood whole and complete. From the exterior at least, its glory had been restored. It presided over the plunging mountainside before it, waiting for visitors, waiting for me.

I practically leapt from the car, and as soon as I did, the illusion of completion was shattered. Multiple band saws competed with a hammer and a nail gun for the honor of loudest implement of progress. Pushing the door open, I was greeted by a fully framed-out hull minus all flooring, walls, and stairs. A precariously balanced ladder led up to the loft. Micah saw me, gave a nail one more tap with his hammer, and came over. He motioned for us to step outside.

"It's much quieter out here," he shouted over the whining of the saws.

"Whatever you say." I had placed a hand on his shoulder as he led me away. Now I let it drop awkwardly.

We stepped farther from the cabin to my campsite, where my tent and tarp offered a little refuge from the noise. "It looks great," I said.

"With a little imagination you can get the picture."

"From the outside it looks better than ever," I said.

He slid one hand into his back pocket while resetting his cap with the other. "We applied the first coat of stain this morning."

"Do we have an ETA on completion?" We rarely got into those kinds of details. I trusted Micah completely.

"Four weeks," he answered. "Maybe six at most."

"Wow," I said. "Moving along."

"So where do you go all day?" He softened his interrogation. "None of my business, I know. Just curious is all."

"All over," I said. "I'm doing some research on the people that used to live here."

"Here?" he asked. "Meaning this cabin or this hollow?"

"Yes." I rolled a stone around under my boot. His questioning felt welcome, because I hadn't shared it with anyone, and intrusive for the same reason. "Both."

"Huh. You said you were an archaeologist? Isn't that digging in the dirt and stuff? Wait, no, you said 'more interpretive than practical.' Right?"

"Do you remember everything verbatim?"

"Pretty much."

I examined him for a moment. "This is not work related. It's personal."

"You know who has all the answers to any question you might ever have about the people who have lived here, don't you?"

"Don't tell me Charles Duncan."

"Nope." He paused, as if for a punch line. "Patsy."

I let go with a long sigh. "I was afraid of that."

"Yep." He hoisted his hammer. "Gotta get back at it. The boss don't like me taking too many breaks."

I smacked him on the shoulder as he turned. He tightened his cap and cast a wink my way as he ducked back into the cabin.

Caroline, I thought. *Don't even think about it.*

I settled down into my camp chair under my tarp. In town I had purchased a scrapbook, and now I carefully laid out the photos. Wearing gloves to protect them, I took great care in placing them in slots in the book.

From the journal, I could somewhat tease out who was who. The stern Union Sphinx had to be Pa, William Quinn. And the dashing, clear-eyed soldier must have been Taylor. The newspaper article mentioned he was in the cavalry in the Philippines at the time of the murder. Maybe that moment astride Nightwalker had informed the course of his life.

The portrait of one woman captivated me, or perhaps I captivated her, because her eyes seemed to follow me. The striking blond wore a white dress with a tightly cinched collar that rose all the way to her chin. She would have been considered beautiful in any era. This had to be Marinda. She could have been Helen of Troy, and, in her own way, she was.

Then there was the wedding photo. A huge crowd of sharply dressed people assembled on the stone steps of a massive home. The happy couple in the center must have been Sarah and Robert Johnston, and the home Raven's Nest in Flat Rock.

The last photo I put away was the family on the porch. Holding it close to examine it, I willed the characters to life. Gramps was easy. He was the one seated, the one with the peg leg, clean shaven in an era when beards were all the rage; I could practically smell the aroma of his liniment cream. It brought back memories of my own grandfather, who lathered Ben-Gay on his aching joints. Seated beside him was a middle-aged woman, who must have been Sheila. In the photo she seemed formidable, with a jutting chin and hair piled high in Gibson-Girl style. In the back row, one hand resting on her shoulder was Carson, his face now familiar. Reading the journal, I had taken to imagining this sad man with a thick beard carrying out the antics of a young boy. In the photo, he must have been in his mid-twenties. With a start that sent the photo fluttering to the table like a crisp oak leaf in a fall breeze, I gasped. There was no other brother present. Thomas must have already been murdered. My hands shook as I stashed the photo into its place.

13

July 1, 1888—Yesterday, Sarah officially became the wife of Robert Lee Johnston, of Charleston and Flat Rock. The wedding was a fine affair, held down in Flat Rock at the Johnston family summer home named Raven's Nest. I've never seen so many fancy people. The actual ceremony took place at a stone church with an honest-to-God priest wearing a collar. That was a first for me too. All the preachers I've seen just wore normal Sunday go-to-meeting clothes. This fella wore all black except for a patch of white at his throat... kind of like a red-knobbed coot. That's a type of African bird, also known as *Fulica cristata*.

It was the happiest I've ever seen my sister. All the folk from Daisy that came were on one side of the church, and all the Charleston folk were on the other. We didn't really cross over. The best part of the day for me was after the ceremony, up at the Johnston house, I got to dance with Marinda. This time I was not a stick-in-the-mud. Though I didn't dance particularly well, nobody knew it on account of Marinda. She led me through the steps and kept time real nice.

When the Charleston folks started some sort of fancy dancing, we stopped and went out under the shade of an old white elm. Marinda surprised me by asking what I thought about having one of these myself.

"One of what?"

"A wedding. Like this."

I'm sure I blushed to about the shade of the burgundy wine they were serving. "Oh, I don't know," I said. "It seems like a lot of fuss."

As soon as I said it, I knew it would be the wrong thing to say. She was going to be upset, I thought, and I kind of cringed waiting for an onslaught of feminine distress. Instead, she said,

"Good. 'Cause I wouldn't want it. Just a preacher and family and some friends. We'll smoke a pig or two, get the fellas to play, and have us a hoedown."

"That sounds right nice," I said. "So, should I consider that a proposal?"

"No, Carson Quinn, that ain't no proposal, and we ain't going to get married unless you propose proper, like Mr. Johnston done with your sister."

I had no idea how Mr. Johnston had proposed to Sarah. All I knew was that they were getting married. Marinda must have seen on my face what I didn't know.

"It was very romantic," she said. "He took her on a picnic to the gazebo down by the riverside, and he made a big production and got down on his knee and said he'd love her till the day he died no matter what answer she give him and, of course, she had to say yes after that."

"I ain't got no gazebo, and besides, Sarah would have said yes no matter how he asked the question," I explained. But Marinda wasn't interested in explanations. She got huffy and went off to where her ma and Betsy Morgan and my ma were all chatting. Since I would be the only fella, I didn't follow her.

Instead, I went wandering.

Thomas was with a group of fellas his age near where all the wagons were parked. I didn't really know most of them well at all, except for Owen Morgan. They stood around in a circle, spitting in turn at the ground, nodding in unison, looking all seriously at the house. I sidled up to them and tried to join the group. Owen was the only one that would budge enough to allow me in. Thomas glared at me real hard.

I nodded hello to everybody.

"This here's my younger brother," Thomas said. "He's the intellectual of the family."

That there was the first time anybody ever called me an intellectual. It did not seem right apropos to be honest. Relative to Thomas, though, I reckon I am. The other fellas were a lot nicer than Thomas, and they said things like "pleased to meet you" and "congratulations to your sister" and "right nice to meet another Quinn." Then they went back to the conversation they were having before, which though it looked contemplative and of great import, was really about how many people the porch was apt to support.

Owen said, "Well, I count forty-two people on it now with no buckling, so I'm going to say one hundred."

Thomas squinted and spat. "You can see it's built right on the whitewashed stone foundation, so the weak bit is the wooden expanse. It looks like it ain't been replaced since it was built, so that wood's probably forty years old. What kind of wood you reckon it is?"

Another fella said, "It ain't pine. I'd say it's oak or chestnut."

That conversation bored me quicker than copying the Bible had, so I quietly wandered off. Nobody noticed me go. I ventured indoors. In the parlor Gramps held court. Quite literally. There were two fellas that had apparently been fighting, and Gramps had sat them down in front of him and was getting to the bottom of it all.

"Now, Mr. Ford. Titus, you don't mind if I call you Mr. Ford, do you?"

Titus shook his head.

Gramps continued, "You claim that this gentleman, Mr. McDougal, had promised you one third of the profits from the sale of the jointly owned corn hopper. That true, Frank, er, Mr. McDougal?"

He nodded. The room was full of folks watching Gramps work. Gramps had never been a judge, but he'd been a lawyer for thirty years, so he knew how such things were supposed to work.

"I take it this contract was never written down," Gramps said.

Both fellas shook their heads.

"When was it entered into?" he asked.

Mr. McDougal looked over at Mr. Ford. "Tell the man."

The first fella shuffled his feet a little. "I believe it was in '62."

"Seventy-two, you say?" Gramps said.

"No, sir. 1862."

Gramps looked around the room. "And what year is it now?"

"Eighty-eight," a man obliged.

"And, Mr. Ford, when was the last time you used said hopper?"

"I suppose it would have been maybe ten years ago."

"And, Mr. McDougal, how much did you get for said hopper?"

"One dollar."

Mr. Ford was starting to look like he was feeling a tad foolish for being so upset. "So, the bigger question at play, aside from something called a statute of limitations and the unenforceability of an oral contract in which the parties can't recall the terms agreed upon, is where is this fool who paid a full dollar for a thirty-year-old hopper?"

The room erupted into laughter, and Gramps turned his attention to his glass of wine. Just then, a servant came into the room with an announcement. "Mr. Johnston requests your presence on the veranda," he said.

We all looked at one another. The servant said, "The front porch."

Everybody nodded and made agreeable noises as we filed out to the porch. Everybody from the wedding was there, well over a hundred folks, and the porch didn't sag in the slightest. I wondered if maybe Thomas and his crowd had arranged an experiment based on their all-too-boring conversation, but that wasn't it at all.

There was a photographer who was to take a picture of us all. I had never had my photograph taken before. Gramps had a daguerreotype of him and his first wife taken, and Pa had been photographed as a soldier in the war, but the only camera the rest of us had ever even seen before was once when some fella came down to the Gap to take images of Chimney Rock.

It was quite the production to assemble all of us on the porch and its side steps. The photographer and his assistant moved people here and there based on their height and importance relative to the bride and groom. I wound up in the back on account of being so tall. Marinda was down the steps with some other young ladies. Since the photographer didn't care about anything other than the composition of the photograph, we Daisy folks were all mixed in with the Charleston folks. I stood next to a man named Archibald Greene, a tall planter from the Low Country.

After the photographer had exploded off two photographs, we mingled a little. That Mr. Greene was right nice. He asked what was it like up in the Gap in the winter, and I said how much I liked the snow, but that it didn't snow all winter long like in some places. He grows rice, and he has over a thousand acres of land. His family has lived in Charleston for over a hundred years and has been tight with the Johnstons for nearly all that time.

The affair got a little less formal after that, probably on account of all the champagne and wine and moonshine that had been drunk. People were relaxed and gabbing here and there. Napoleon Fallon's the one who brought the moonshine, and I myself snuck a glass from him. He makes the smoothest shine in all the Gap. As far as I'm concerned, it's better than that fancy wine. After a time, I became a little unsteady on my feet. Somehow, I found myself in the so-called smoking room with my new brother-in-law, Pa, Gramps, and a couple other fellas I reckon were from Charleston. My recollection isn't the best, but the conversation got a tad heated.

Robert—I'm a going to call him that since he's family now—Robert was talking about cottonseed oil. Yet another boring subject, you would think. He was going on about his plans to start up several cottonseed oil plants throughout the Upstate and down around Rutherfordton. I think he was trying to impress Pa by showing that he wasn't going to sit around on his fortune, even though he could do just that. Pa, though, didn't think much of his plans.

"A factory?" Pa said.

"Factories," Robert corrected him. "You see, why is the North so much more advanced than the South?"

"Lots of small farmers," Pa answered immediately.

"No," Robert corrected him in a way no one who knew Pa would dare do. "When I was at school at Cornell, I had the opportunity to study the local economy quite thoroughly, and the engine of economic growth is clearly the manufacturing sector, a manufacturing sector that the South lacks."

Pa grunted.

"I aim to provide that to this region."

"Provide that and make lots of money off folks that have no other future?" asked Pa.

"Without jobs, what future is there?" Robert asked, holding his whiskey aloft in emphasis.

"A man should be able to shoulder his own from the land. A man shouldn't have to work for another, if he so chooses," Pa said.

Even though Robert Johnston could buy Pa a thousand times over, Pa was talking to him like an equal.

"Mr. Quinn, well, Pa. Can I call you that?"

"Why don't you just call me Will," Pa said. "That's my name."

"Well then, Will, the time when men could forge a fortune out of the wilderness is gone. Even out West you can't do that anymore. We have to broaden our definition of what it means to be successful in America."

"And you want to say that working for another is success?"

"It's better than living a life of poverty off a patch of dirt. My family will be fine, no matter what. But what about all the sharecroppers that haven't a hope for anything better? Let's get them jobs, get them educated, make a better life for them by producing goods they can afford to purchase."

Pa was messing with his pipe. "You know, Robert, it sounds all fine and dandy when you explain it like that. But let's say that you put up two or ten of these cottonseed oil factories. What does that really mean for these small farmers you're so worried about? It means that instead of growing tomatoes and melons and potatoes and parsnips and beans and squash, they'll start growing only cotton. And then what happens when the market gets glutted? They lose money, and instead of living off the land or selling a different crop, they have to go to some merchant to get credit they can't pay back. Eventually, that merchant or, worse, the bank, gets the farm, and this here proud farmer has to go to work in your factory instead of growing his own."

Robert stared at Pa. He took a sip of his whiskey. "Will, I see your point. But it doesn't change anything. Everything you just said is going to happen. It's happening now. And if there isn't a factory that a displaced farmer can work at, how will he make a living?"

Pa sighed and stood up. Tapping on his pipe, he turned and left the room. Robert looked right offended. He didn't yet know that's just how Pa is. Robert looked around. "You Quinns are mighty proud."

Thomas, barely sober, gave a one-eyed grin. "Ain't we?"

❧

As a child, my family and I had hiked every square yard of the mountains around the cabin. We came to know the crests and the folds of hills, the hidden waterfalls, and ancient roadbeds. Whether on McAlister land or Duncan land or Grayson land made no difference. There were no boundary lines, no fences, no signs. Over the ensuing decades things had changed. Back then, there were no people around, except for Old Man Duncan out on his porch. Carson's Pa, it turned out, had been right. All the folk that had lived off the land in his time had wound up moving into towns for jobs and better opportunities. The home sites and farms gave over to forest and field, and as a family we could walk for dozens of miles without encountering another soul.

Now, signs made boundaries clear. As I approached the gate that blocked the road up to the Duncans' home, a jolt of fear ran through my spine. No Trespassing! Firearms in Use! Trained Guard Dogs! It was like entering the DMZ.

I cautiously snaked my way around the gate and started up

the old road I had walked many times before. As a child, the road had been a mere suggestion, and I had cut through forest and valley on my way up the mountain, keeping Daddy and Mom and the roadbed in sight but never truly laying foot on it. Back then, no one lived up past Old Man Duncan. It was forest in varying stages of succession, having been farm, field, or orchard back in Carson Quinn's day. We would follow the road until it petered out, then keep going, up to a hidden water-fall set in a misty, fern-filled glade. We would have lunch there and splash and play in the water before continuing on up the mountain.

We never came back the same way we went, and Mom de-lighted in getting us lost in order to see where we would find ourselves. Often it was an apple orchard or a cow pasture, and we would emerge onto one of the few gravel roads which would invariably lead us back down to the hardtop and home again.

Today I kept to the road, Charles Duncan and his .44-caliber guard dog far more menacing than his father with his shotgun. The switchbacks seemed fewer as an adult and the steep climb far less so. There were outbuildings and cleared meadows that hadn't existed before, but mostly the terrain seemed familiar, the smells evoking moments from my childhood. I came around a bend, and there it sat, Charles and Patsy Duncan's amazingly suburban plot. The house was a modern rancher surrounded by a trimmed lawn, seemingly swiped from a mid-eighties sub-division and plopped in the midst of the forest. Its vinyl siding, yawning garage, and concrete front path didn't compute with the hike I had just made from my primitive camp barely more than a stone's throw away.

I climbed the front brick stairs and pushed the doorbell button. The chime echoed through the house, setting off a furious bout of yipping from some drop-kick special. There were sounds of shuffling, then the door unlocking. It opened first slightly, then wide as Patsy Duncan emerged, holding a tiny beast that wiggled frenetically in her arms.

"Howdy there, neighbor!" she said. Despite its being

mid-morning in the middle of the week, she was properly dressed, her hair coiffed and sprayed, her face as made up as a glamour model's.

"I hope I'm not intruding." I had showered and put on fresh clothes, but I found myself flattening my jeans and straightening my shirt. This trip suddenly felt like what it was: a trip to the principal's office.

"Not at all, honey," Patsy declared. "I am just so happy to finally meet you. Tilda told me you'd be coming by. Please come in. I can't put Precious down 'cause she'll run out the door."

"Is that the guard dog?" I asked, as I stepped in and shut the door behind me.

"Oh, that stupid sign." Patsy shook her head and rolled her eyes. "Yes, Precious is it. She's so ferocious."

She put the dog on the floor. It pranced around on the tile, claws clicking like high heels. Never a small-dog person, I had no idea what breed Precious was, but she clearly had been appropriately named. I had seen guinea pigs in South America that were larger.

Patsy led me back to a deck off the kitchen, where she had just finished brewing some sun tea. "You know about sun tea?" she asked as she poured some over a glass of ice cubes.

"Brewed by the sun's rays. No boiling involved," I said. "My mother used to make it all the time."

"Yes, ma'am. Sit. I'm so excited to have another female up in these parts."

I lowered myself into the reclining deck chair beside hers. The deck, bathed in the sun's rays, looked out over a grassy lawn peppered with rose bushes and peach and pear trees. The tea refreshed me, reminding me of my mother. She always had a jar of iced tea in the fridge. As an adult, I never brewed it, not having inherited Mom's domestic prowess or time.

"Welcome to our little patch of paradise," Patsy said.

"Thank you so much," I answered.

"First off," she began, "let me apologize for Charlie. He's a bit protective, and maybe a wee bit paranoid."

Words of gratitude were difficult to articulate given the meanness of her husband and son. "Yes," I eked out. "A wee bit."

"He really is a good man at heart," she said. "He just can't bring himself to show it. I take it you knew his daddy, probably better than I ever did."

"Yes, I knew Ed when I was a child. He was gruff but kind."

"Charles never got to see the kind part, just the drunk part."

"He was an old moonshiner." My mind traveled back to his front porch where he had railed against the War of Northern Aggression and bemoaned "the law."

"Blockader, they called them back in the day," she corrected, "and bootlegger, ruffian, common criminal, and general ne'er do well. Charles's mother met him in one of his more respectable moments. He had won a couple of stock-car races in his souped-up '36 Oldsmobile, and he had just enough money and fame to sweep her off her feet."

"That right?" Old Man Duncan had never mentioned racing, and I had never even seen a car anywhere around his place.

"She was a Mabe from the Upstate, and the marriage only lasted long enough to produce our Charlie. Once ole Ed went back to his alcoholic and inveterate ways, she divorced his ass and took Charlie back to Greenville, where she remarried a more respectable type. A dentist who gave her two more children and a proper place in society."

"What's a 'maybe'?" I asked.

"That's her family's name. You'd know the name if you were from South Carolina."

"Oh," I said. Charles Duncan came into better focus now.

"Anyway," Patsy continued. "When Ed died in '90, Charlie, being his only heir, inherited the entire Duncan homestead. Where we are right now!" The cheer with which she ended her story indicated that everything turned out for the best in her mind. It also explained how Charles and I had never crossed paths until now. Ed Duncan had died the same year as my mother. Charles had taken possession of the land just as we were abandoning it.

We silently soaked in the rays of the morning sun for a moment. "What do you know about Carson Quinn?" I finally asked.

Patsy pursed her glossed lips as if she had bit into a lemon. "That's like asking what you know about Bigfoot. Nobody ever knew much about that old hermit. He tended to stay to himself, down there in your little hollow." She emphasized the "little" as if to remind me that the Duncan holdings dwarfed my own five acres.

"Did you ever know him?"

"I met him once," she said. "When I was a child. His sister did what no one else ever could and got him down off that mountain, down to Flat Rock, where she had a summer home."

"Raven's Nest," I said.

"Yes." Patsy's perfect eyebrows arched into what seemed an impossible and unnatural shape. "Somebody's been doing her homework."

"That's kind of what I do for a living. Homework." I tucked a wayward bit of hair behind my ear. My own imperfections felt glaring in the presence of someone so done up.

"Sarah—that was her name—was getting up in age by then. She must have been pushing ninety. Somehow she convinced that ole coot to come down to Raven's Nest for the wedding of her granddaughter. My parents were close with the Johnstons, so we were there. I remember how tall he was. We kids were out in the yard. Being kids, we had found the perfect climbing tree. Along comes this old man, stooped a bit, but otherwise as able-bodied as anyone at the wedding. He walked right up to that tree and placed a hand out on it and closed his eyes. I thought he was about to die of a heart attack right then and there, so I called out to him. 'Hey, mister,' or something like that."

Patsy took a sip of tea.

"Nothing was wrong with him. He looked right up at me with these fierce blue eyes. He said something in some other language; maybe it was Latin. Then he said, 'Do you know what kind of tree this is that you're a-climbing?'"

"Elm," I answered.

Patsy's jaw dropped a full inch and she pulled her head back like a turtle retreating.

"The kind of tree was an elm tree, wasn't it?"

"White elm, I believe." Curiosity crinkled Patsy's forehead.

"Do you have a tree identification book?" I asked. "I think I can tell you what he said to you in the other language."

Without saying a word, she stood, slid open the sliding door, and went inside. I had accomplished what no one in three counties would have thought possible. I had silenced the Mouth of the South.

She returned with *Trees of North America* and handed the heavy volume to me. I turned to the elm section and found what I was looking for. "*Ulmus alba*," I said.

"That's it!" Patsy said. "That is exactly what he said!"

"It's the Latin name for white elm."

"I declare!" Patsy said. "How did you ever know? This is spooky."

"Been doing my homework."

"I had always thought he was saying some sort of incantation, some Satanic something or other. Damning us kids for disturbing him."

"He was telling you the proper name of the tree you were climbing."

She shook her head. "I declare," she repeated. "We were scared of him forever after that. We created these horror stories about him, all due to a...a..."

"Misunderstanding?" I offered.

"A misunderstanding." She squinted into the yard for a spell, her mind wandering down its own memory lane. She shook it off, snapping back into the moment. "Tell me about this homework of yours."

I hesitated. Patsy Duncan would tell the entire world what I was up to if I shared it with her. But what would be the harm in that, really? Though certainly a gossip, she seemed genuinely kind. Perhaps I was inspired by her own logorrhea, but I spilled everything. I told her about the journal and my quest to discover who killed Thomas Quinn.

Patsy listened. At the end, she repeated what seemed to be her mantra. "I declare. Let me tell you something, Miss Caroline McAlister. My family has been in this county since the Revolutionary War. We were some of the first settlers west of the Blue Ridge, and I have a lot of my family history."

As she paused, I braced. It seemed she was about to channel her husband's possessive nature of the land and its history. She continued, "And I will pull out all the stops to help you."

A sigh of relief escaped my lips. "I'd really appreciate it, but I'd rather everyone not know about the journal…at least not yet."

"My lips are sealed." She mimed taking a key and locking down her bright red mouth.

"Your family? Who were they?" I asked.

"I'm surprised you don't know that, given all of your research."

"It hasn't come up yet," I said.

"Fallon," she said. "My maiden name is Fallon."

14

July 4, 1888—We had an Independence Day celebration today down at the Edney Inn. Charlie Brightleaf and Pa smoked a pig. Napoleon Fallon brought a tub of cider, and Owen Morgan and the boys played for hours. Tonight they had fireworks and everything. Lots of tourists were in the valley, and practically all the folks that live in Daisy came out.

I saw Marinda helping her pa with the cider and went over to them to offer a hand. She slid over and let me lift the big old vat of cider with her pa. Because I'm so tall, and old Napoleon is so short, the cider was nearly pouring out as we carried it across the lawn of the inn. I squatted down and old Nap stood on his tiptoes, and I don't think my help resulted in much ease for him.

Once the vat of cider was in place, I turned to Marinda. "Can we walk a spell?"

We held hands as we wandered down the road. Old Man Rolly saw us. He was working out in his fields, and he waved his hat at us. We waved back and kept a-walking on down to the Reedy Patch. Here in the valley, it's wider and slower than on up the mountain. We found us a spot under a sycamore where we could sit on a rock and dangle our feet in the water.

I'm getting better about being able to talk sense around Marinda now. It's much easier than it used to be, now that it's practically a foregone conclusion that one day she'll be my bride.

When I sat down, something in my hip pocket stabbed my rear end. I reached back and pulled out the offender, which was Mr. Plato's *Apology*.

"What you got there?" Marinda asked.

"Punishment," I explained.

"Looks like a book to me," she said. "What kind of punishment is that?"

"It's my gramps's idea of punishment. He's making me read it on account of me cutting up at school."

She took it from me and flipped through the pages. "Ain't very big. What's it about?"

"Oh, it's about this fella name of Socrates who lived way on back in Athens, Greece. He was a teacher, you see, and he was accused of corrupting the young'uns he taught because he didn't believe in religion."

"He didn't believe in Jesus?" Marinda said, aghast.

"This was before Jesus," I explained. "Like the Old Testament."

"Oh."

"He didn't believe in the gods the Greeks had, you know, like Zeus and Apollo and Poseidon."

"Oh. Them's false gods nohow," Marinda said.

I didn't know what to say about that, so I went on explaining. "He was put on trial, you see, and this here book is what he said at his trial. It's called *The Apology.*"

"He was sorry for not believing in them false gods?"

"No, he wasn't sorry at all. Apology don't mean the same thing in Greek as it does in English. It's just an explanation, really."

Marinda looked at the book, turning its pages delicately. "Carson," she asked, "will you teach me to read?"

It wasn't a surprise that she didn't know how to read. Her ma couldn't read either, and she'd only been to church school a few times. "I sure will," I said. And wouldn't you know, we started right then and there by the riverside. She knew her alphabet, so we went right into the little book. I lost track of the time. It was my belly what reminded me to head back to the inn and the roasting pig. When we got back there, Gramps and Judge Logan were standing up on the porch presiding over a ceremony. The judge was reciting the Declaration of Independence. When he got done, Gramps shuffled forward.

"Thomas Jefferson," Gramps began, "knew a thing or two about proper government." Then he went off on a long and winding speech about our inalienable rights and the superiority of American democracy to any other system of government around.

When he was done, Pastor Jamison gave a prayer, then we all went and ate. I sat down on the grassy lawn with the rest of the Quinn clan, minus Sarah, of course, who just now was probably celebrating in Charleston before she and Robert left for Florida on a month-long tour. Can you believe that Sarah of all people has ventured beyond these mountains before me, the redheaded wanderer?

"Where have you been all afternoon, Carson?" Ma asked me. "We've been looking for you."

"Down by the river with Marinda," I answered without thinking. Soon as I said it, I knew Ma suspected we were doing something more than reading Plato.

"That right?" she asked.

"Yes'm," I said.

"That Marinda's a nice girl. Pretty too."

"She sure is," I agreed.

"Don't you go and break her heart, Carson Quinn."

Ma winked at me, and I didn't know what to say, so I turned my attention to the juicy pork.

"Ma," Thomas said. "His name ain't Carson no more. It's Casanova."

"Who's Casanova?" Taylor asked.

"An Italian lover boy," Thomas said.

Ma noticed my face turning all red, but she only made it worse when she said, "Boys, leave him alone. He's smitten."

"Ain't he, though?" Thomas said. "What was you a-doing down by that river? There gonna be a little Carson coming along?"

"It ain't like that!" I popped up onto my toes. Thomas didn't take too kindly to that, and next thing I knew I was on my back with Thomas on top of me. I tossed him off using my legs, then we were rolling around wrestling. Ma was screaming. Taylor ran off. I heard people yelling about a fight. I heard folks laughing. I heard other folks, Marinda in particular, saying to stop. And I wanted to stop, but ever time I let off, Thomas came at me harder. He kept pinning me into the grass, and I kept squirming out. My brother's a lot stronger than me, but I ain't no pushover. In the back of my mind, I heard what sounded like horse hooves pounding. I thought my heart must be racing, and I knew I had to get out of his grip or else my heart was going to burst from exertion. Using every bit of strength I had, I was able to get on top of him. As soon as that happened, there were two loud cracks. The musicians had stopped playing, and it appeared that the sunny day had become dark with thunderclouds.

When I looked up, I saw that the thunderclouds were Yankee soldiers, a whole passel of them sitting astride horses, with a fella that looked like General Custer pointing a revolver in the air.

"Sorry to break up your wrestling match," the fella with the big Colt said, talking to the whole group. "We're looking for an outlaw."

Napoleon and Pa came forward then. Pa took me and Thomas by the collar and yanked us to our feet. "I'll deal with you two later," he said through gritted teeth.

Old Napoleon answered quickly, "Ain't no outlaws here, sir. Merely us revelers out to commemorate the independence of our dear country."

"I see," the soldier said. He looked over the lot of us real slow-like. For a second, his eyes settled on that vat of cider. "We're looking for an outlaw by the name of Augustus Trabor. He's been seen recently in the Gap here. Anyone know of his whereabouts?"

I stole a quick look at Taylor, fearing he would open his mouth as he's apt to do, but he was apparently bewitched at that moment by the soldiers. He was staring at them as if trying to take in every detail of what he was seeing—the boots, the sabers, the rifles in their scabbards, the canteens, the blue uniforms. Pa answered. "Can you describe him?" Odd, given that Pa knew him from the war.

"Better than that," the soldier said, holstering his piece and going into a satchel. He pulled out a piece of paper. "Here's a rendering." He handed it down to Pa. "You see him, be very careful. You should consider him armed and extremely dangerous."

"What's he wanted for?" Gramps shouted down from the porch.

"Murder of a federal official," the soldier said. "Shot a revenuer up in Madison County."

There was a murmur through the group. Nobody likes revenuers, but we like murderers even less.

"Keep an eye out. You see him, send word to me, Major James Hutchison, up at the garrison. If you have a mind to, capture him. The bounty is five hundred dollars. Proceed with caution. Gus Trabor is a dangerous man. As for the matter at hand, I'd be willing to overlook your illegal spirits here if you'd allow my boys to partake."

Gramps, ever the wise counsel, corrected the major. "That cider ain't taxable, Major," he said authoritatively, "because it isn't a distilled spirit and it's a special batch brewed especially for our personal consumption here today."

"And," Napoleon said real kindly, "you and your men are more than welcome to quench your thirst."

The soldiers swung down from their horses and went to sampling the cider. Soon enough, they were relaxed and mingling with the revelers. After all, it was a holiday. The lot of them weren't much older than me. Taylor had already pulled one soldier aside and was asking him all about his gear. Pa just up and left. I looked around and saw him way out in Mr. Rolly's field with his eyes set on the back of Blue Rock way up above. That's when I noticed another of them soldiers, a blond-haired fella with blue eyes, fix his attention on Marinda. He went over and started to chat with her. My blood went to boiling. I lickety-split went to intervene.

"Howdy there, Marinda."

I acted like I didn't see the soldier.

"Carson, this here's Corporal Nelson. He's from all the way up in Maryland. Imagine that."

"Howdy," I said. "They don't have girls where you come from?"

"Carson," Marinda said. "Be kind now."

The corporal offered his hand, and I begrudgingly shook it.

"We have women in Maryland, but one thing I've learned is that among the chief produce of the South is unmatched prettiness."

I ain't never seen a woman swoon, but my Marinda practically collapsed hearing that corporal wax poetic. Thing is, he's gone now and she'll never see him again, but it irks me to no end that she'll treasure that moment for the rest of her life. I aim to erase it from her memory with a thousand superior moments. There's no reason at all I can't say such meaningless but nice things myself.

The soldiers hung around into the evening and watched our fireworks with us. That corporal didn't leave Marinda's side, so I hung back and watched the proceedings. Pa and Napoleon and Charlie were all huddled to the side, talking something serious. Ma and Wilma and Betsy and Mourning and Alma Duncan were all sitting on some blankets watching little Bradshaw teeter and totter about. Taylor ran around with Egypt and Moses Nye, a couple of young'uns from the village. Thomas and Owen were gabbing with a group of soldiers. And Isaac Duncan and his boys were quietly seething in the corner. About all they do is seethe. Old Isaac don't get along with us Quinns nor our friends on account of the war. The war in these parts got real personal, and he probably still carries some of Gramps's buckshot in his backside. He was glaring at them soldiers, like they were trespassing on his land. I just wanted the soldiers to leave, because there was no telling what Isaac Duncan was capable of. The fireworks made everyone forget to seethe and conspire for a few minutes at least, then we all went home.

July 24, 1888—Last night I could not sleep because of the heat.

As I tend to do, I ventured outside to sit by the creek. What did I see then, but Pa coming out to the porch carrying the Sharps rifle? Now, I ain't never seen my pa with a gun. In fact, in all my years of knowing him, he has always refused to touch a firearm of any sort. Though he could fix anything, he has always declined work on guns out of personal reprehension. Seeing him carrying that Sharps, I knew something had to be brewing. He strode from the porch out to the road. I crept along the creek bed behind him. In the moonlight I spied two other figures, also carrying rifles. From their voices, I knew them to be Charlie Brightleaf and Napoleon Fallon.

They were up to something, and I aimed to find out what. I stayed in the shadows behind them as they crossed the road, went down across the Reedy Patch, and headed out across the valley. The full moon made it possible to see almost as good as in daylight, so they moved without a light. They avoided the road and tramped right through Old Mr. Rolly's cornfield. They were going to where Pa had been looking the night of the fireworks. Right up the back of Blue Rock. They moved quickly. It was hard to keep up and stay hidden. I've done my share of tracking and hunting, but they moved like ghosts through the woods.

They steered around the laurel hell, but I dove right in. It was possible for me, like a black bear, to use the thicket to hide and the sturdy rhododendrons to pull me up the steep hillside quietly. When they got to the top of Blue Rock, they found the trail down the other side. This is a steep and perilous trail, fit more for a mountain goat than a human being. I was fearful that I might lose purchase and tumble head over heels the hundreds of feet down into the gorge below. But they grew up here too. They knew the secrets of the mountain and were able to navigate down, down, down to wind up in the shadows behind the big Bat Cave. I watched how they went and followed their way carefully.

Somebody was in the cave. You could tell on account of the flickering campfire. It's said that the Cherokee used the cave as a hunting camp, and it's known for certain that during the war, deserters from both armies sequestered themselves up here. Ever since then, the only folk that bed down in the Bat Cave are those on the run. Pa positioned Napoleon and Charlie back in the shadows with their guns trained on the opening, while he hollered out and stepped forward.

"Gus!" he shouted. After all the silence, his voice echoing off the rock sounded like the voice of God coming down. "Gus Trabor! This here's Will Quinn."

"Sergeant?" Gus hollered back, poking his bearded head out of the cave.

"I ain't no sergeant no more," Pa said. "The war's over. I'm just a man now."

Gus stood up and stepped into the light. He looked like Blackbeard the pirate, as burly and bearded and hairy as he was. He had guns strapped all over him. Pistols tucked in every pocket and two bandoliers chock full of bullets crisscrossing his chest. I was scared then for Pa, for all he had was that single shot rifle. One bullet against a hundred.

Gus Tabor went for Pa, and I thought he was attacking him, but it was just a hug. Pa kind of hugged him back out of politeness, but you could tell he wasn't eager to do so. Pa ain't never hugged none of his own sons, so that kind of tells you how he feels about the gesture to begin with.

"Sergeant Quinn!" Gus said. "Good to see you. Come on into my fine abode. Can I get you anything? I've got whiskey or whiskey."

Pa entered the mouth of the cave and took a pull of the whiskey. He wiped his mouth with the back of his sleeve. Gus sat down, but Pa stood, that rifle cradled in the crook of his arm.

"You ain't here for no small talk," Gus said.

"What's this about you killing a fella up in Madison County?" Pa asked.

"Weren't no fella," Gus explained. "Just a revenuer."

"You ain't from Madison, Gus. You're from Tennessee."

"My people's from Madison on my ma's side. Been working for my cousin these past few years."

Pa don't take no dissembling from nobody. I've learned that the hard way. "Working?"

"We produce the finest spirits in these hills. Chestnut Stump White Lightning. It's all legitimate."

"Except for you shooting up that fella and ambushing my two young'uns."

Gus got real nervous. "I'm mighty sorry about your boys. It was a hard winter. I was on the run and hungry out of my mind. But that shooting weren't my fault," Gus said. "An entire company of men, led by this here revenuer raided our facility. What was I to do except return fire? That's what you and Major Kirk always preached. Stand your ground. Return fire. I did that. You would have been proud."

Pa shook his head. "War's over, Gus."

"For some." Gus wiped his mouth on his sleeve.

"You're gonna have to leave," Pa said. "This here's a peaceful part of the county. We can't have the army coming round. Get your stuff and head on."

"Where to, Sergeant?" Gus looked at Pa like Pa would actually know the answer. "Where, Will?"

"That ain't my problem."

"South Carolina? Tennessee? Georgia?"

"Pick one and head thataway."

Gus set down the whiskey. His hand fell to the butt of one of his guns. Pa rocked back and shifted the rifle. "I 'spect you ain't fool enough to come up here alone, is you?" Gus asked.

"You'll find out," Pa said, "if you don't let go of that Colt."

Gus eased his hand away from his hip real slow-like and perched on a boulder at the cave's entrance as if pondering a dilemma. I don't know what dilemma he had, though. Pa tells you to do something, you do it.

Pa whistled into the darkness, and Napoleon stepped forward without lowering his rifle. He unhitched something from his back and tossed it to Pa. It was a big poke, and it looked heavy. Pa passed it down to Gus. "This here's some vittles and blankets and such. You take 'em and be on your way."

Gus parsed through the goods. When he looked up, the light glinted in his eyes. "Youns are mighty good. Any other men would a-taken me for that there bounty."

"Don't you think I didn't consider it," Pa said. "But I reckon I owed you. We're even now. You're going to get up. We'll escort you down the mountain to the Rocky Broad. Then you're going to follow it till you're out of the Gap. Head south till you're clear of North Carolina. After that, ain't no coming back here for you. You hear?"

"Yes. I hear."

Pa waited while Gus gathered himself together, and then he led him on down the mountain to the river below. I hung back in the hell till they were out of earshot. Then I ventured on down to the cave. The fire was still burning, and I sat down beside it for a spell. It wasn't till the flames were out that my legs were solid enough to walk on. I'd figured for sure Pa was going to wind up shot. There's a lot about my pa that I don't know, but I do know this. He meant every word he said. He takes his debts serious. He'll carry one less debt from here on out, and that Gus Trabor best never show his face in these parts again.

పం

Patsy Duncan was a Fallon. Over a second glass of tea, she explained that Napoleon's father, Baxter Fallon, was one of three sons of Admiral Fallon, who had arrived in the region in the late 1700s from Pennsylvania. Admiral came to own many thousands of acres and engaged in various commercial ventures, from timber to tobacco to fruit. It was this last venture that captured Baxter's attention. Admiral carved five hundred acres of his land out for Baxter to propagate and grow apples. Baxter's brothers, Daniel and Charles, had different interests entirely. Charles Fallon went off to school in the North—Patsy wanted to say to Dartmouth—and became a highly regarded Methodist minister. It was said that his career choice was a profound disappointment to the patriarch, Admiral. There was no money to be had following the righteous path. Admiral also felt let down by Baxter. His early attempts at apple growing failed miserably, and it wasn't until long after Admiral passed on that Baxter created a variety that didn't spoil before it got to market. This was well before the train got to the region, so apples had to either become cider or survive the long drive down the mountain. His son, Napoleon, would inherit both his father's land and interest in apple growing, developing a number of varieties that did well at market.

Daniel Fallon was the favorite son. Like his father, he knew a wooden nickel when he saw it and was ruthlessly successful in business ventures that ranged from land speculation to cattle and cotton trading. His focus was to the south. He developed partnerships throughout Upstate South Carolina and owned a home in Charleston. Much to his father's pride, he became a well-respected member of the planter class. Patsy was descended from Daniel's progeny. Her great-grandfather was Daniel's only son.

Genealogy was never my strong suit, so I wasn't sure what her relationship was to Marinda Fallon Quinn, other than kin.

"I reckon that makes us cousins something or other removed," she said. "Her great-grandfather and my great-great grandfather were one and the same."

"Admiral Fallon," I said.

"Yes." She rattled the ice in her glass. "Growing up I saw her every once in a while. We would take picnics down here to Chimney Rock and Lake Lure, and we would always make a point to stop by her house down on the road and call on her. She was old and her body fragile, but boy did she have spunk. I guess being a single lady for so long made her independent and self-reliant."

"She didn't have family?"

"Well," Patsy said, "she was the last of the Fallons in this area. Her folks passed long before, and—"

"I saw their graves, all of the babies that died before she lived."

"Honey, that wasn't uncommon in those days. Life was hard up here back in the day. The only family she had were her daughter and her daughter's people."

"Her daughter…" I remembered seeing something about that in the article about Thomas's murder. He and Marinda had a daughter.

"Bella Quinn," Patsy said.

"Whatever happened to her?" I asked.

"She married a Morgan. There are still some of her descendants around."

"Hiram?" I asked.

"Hiram Quinn Morgan would be her son."

"Q for Quinn," I said.

Patsy arched an eyebrow as she quenched her thirst. "He isn't much more personable than his uncle, old Carson Quinn."

"I believe I met him. What are the chances of me being able to sit down with him, to ask some questions?"

"About the same as Clark Gable coming through my front door. That old man sticks to his mountain across the way. He'll go to church on occasion, but that's about it."

"Which church?"

"Why, Bat Cave Baptist," she said, as if that were the only possible answer.

I nodded. The fresh light of the morning had given way to a fiercely brilliant afternoon sun. Cognizant of perhaps overstaying my welcome, I stretched and stood. "I should be going," I said.

"You can't stay for lunch?" Patsy asked.

Having spent the bulk of my life in the eminently practical world of academia, I had lost touch with my sense of Southern obliqueness. Was she asking because it was part of the hostess code? Or did she actually want me to eat with her? "I don't want to impose."

"Nonsense. I've made up a huge Greek salad and it's got your name on it."

Salad sounded wonderful. Living in a camp without refrigeration prevented me from having much in the way of salads. I said as much.

Just as we sat down to eat in the dining room, Charles Duncan—not Clark Gable—came in the front door. He caught one look at me and stopped in his tracks. "Oh," he said. He glared at Patsy as he bent over to remove his boots and stash them by the door.

"Why don't you come sit down, have some lunch?" Patsy patted the placemat at the head of the table. An empty plate waited for him. She moved the giant salad bowl to his end of the table.

Charles sniffed hard. He looked at me, then he looked at her. With a sigh, he eased up to the table. "Ms. McAlister," he said.

"Hey, Charlie." I laced my greeting with as much cheer as I could muster.

He grimaced as if I'd punched him. "It's Charles. Please."

"Right."

"Salad," Charles said as he pulled a chair out and plopped down.

"Eat it, Charlie. It's good for you." His eyes bore into Patsy. A look that must have served him well with high school miscreants had no effect on his wife.

"All right." He squeezed the wooden tongs together and withdrew a dripping mound of lettuce, beets, egg salad, potatoes, and olives that landed on his plate with a splat.

"We were just talking about old Hiram Morgan," Patsy said.

Charles took a gulp of tea, then clicked his teeth. "What would anybody want with that old codger?"

"Caroline's doing some research about her place and we figured he might know a thing or two."

For the first time since entering the house Charles gave me his full attention. His hard stare bristled the hair on the back of my neck.

"Research? What for?"

"Just to find out more about the place and the people that lived in it."

"You know it's haunted, right?"

A chunk of salad slipped from my fork. I held the empty fork halfway between plate and mouth, looking for signs he was joking, a crinkle of his crow's feet or a glimmer in his eyes perhaps. But he gave nothing away. "I don't know you well, but I hadn't thought of you as someone who believed in ghosts."

"I didn't use to."

He directed his attention to finishing off his own bite of salad, then continued. "You know your father asked me to keep an eye out on the place."

"You knew my dad?" I interrupted, shock overwhelming my manners.

He nodded as he took a swig of tea. "He used to come up about once or twice a year. Just him. He'd stay for a long weekend, then go back home."

This information stunned me. Why hadn't he told anyone? Not even Andrew? "Really?"

"We had a handful of conversations. He asked if I wouldn't mind checking on the place every once in a while. He stopped coming about ten years ago, but I kept looking out. Being all hidden up in that hollow, it attracted all sorts of folks: vagrants and hippies and the sort. We don't want those type round here, and I figured you all didn't either, so I'd send them packing. A couple of times, I didn't have to chase them off. Someone—or something—did that for me. Middle of the night, you could hear the screams and the gravel flying all the way up here as they floored it away from the place. I figured it was the dope talking and didn't think anything of it."

I knew where he was going with this.

"I like to keep apprised of what's going on with my property, so I work the perimeter at various times of the day and night."

"By perimeter, Charles means property line," Patsy clarified. "One of the things he brought back from 'Nam."

"One night, there was a light up in the second-floor window. It looked like a lit candle. You could see shadows moving, like someone was in there. I got my gun, and I called out. No one answered, but the light went out. I took my flashlight and my gun and pulled open that creaky old screen door to the porch, then pushed in the front door. Back in 'Nam, I had to go into VC tunnels a time or two, but I wasn't nearly as frightened then as I was going into your cabin. I announced myself. No answer. I let whoever it was know I was armed and they should leave. Still no answer. Then I went room by room, shining the flashlight into every corner and every closet. There was no one there. But someone or something had been. The light was real."

"Are you sure you weren't just seeing things?" I asked.

He gave me that same hard glare. "I don't see things," he said, as if that was worse than believing in ghosts. "Besides, it wasn't the only time it happened. A while later I came by round about dusk, and up in that same window there was what looked like a face looking out. When I called out, it vanished. I grabbed my .45, went in, and found no one there."

I remembered the bearded man from my youth, felt his breath in my ear, his weight pressing down on the bed. My throat went dry despite all the tea, and sweat beaded on my brow despite the air conditioning. "The face," I asked, "was it a man or woman?"

"Man. Wearing a hat."

He must have seen my eyes go wide and my spine stiffen. Years of reading lying teenagers probably told him I was holding something back. But I wasn't ready to believe in ghosts, much less to confess that belief to Charles Duncan of all people.

"Charles," I asked, "are you telling me you've been trespassing on my family's land with impunity for years?"

"Like I said." He gritted his teeth. "I was doing your father a favor."

"I'm sure he appreciated it." I withheld the comment on irony that so wanted to escape my lips.

Charles clinked the ice in his glass. "Like I said. That place of yours is haunted."

"Who do you think is haunting the cabin?" I asked.

I waited for him to say Carson Quinn. Instead, he said, "I expect that hollow was haunted long before that cabin got built."

"Why do you think that?" I asked.

"Why, that hollow is where they say Thomas Quinn was murdered back in the day."

The look he gave as he took a sip of tea told me he knew what I was up to, that maybe he knew who the murderer was, and that I was never going to get any more out of him than what he'd just told me. Something else he probably learned in 'Nam.

15

Augost 1, 1888—Up in Hemlock Hollow, Marinda and I been having our reading lessons. I am convinced that no person has ever been in that hollow except me. Everything is different there. No matter how the weather is everywhere else, within that place it's always a little misty from the creek and protected by the big trees. It ain't never uncomfortable. I measured a couple of them hemlocks, and the smallest one is six feet around. The boulders are as big as the millhouse. Yesterday I took Marinda up there. When she saw it for the first time, she got real quiet.

"This is like some other world," she said. "Like a fairy world."

She's right. It is another world in that hollow. It ain't a human world, and that makes it tranquil in ways no human place can be.

So far we have only been reading from *The Apology*, the book Gramps gave me on account of the headmaster. Ain't nothing special about that book other than it's small and I can carry it real easy. We're to the part where Socrates begins his defense, which is not until about the fourth paragraph. Until then, it's just a mess of preamble. Once we got to that point, she got real interested. She had sounded out a complete sentence, then sat back and repeated it to understand it better.

"So that Socrates was accused of being an evil-doer, and a curious person, who searches into things under the earth and in heaven, and he makes the worse appear the better cause; and he teaches others to be curious, too. And they want to execute him for that?"

I nodded.

"What for?"

"Blasphemy," I said. "It means going against the scriptures, only the Greeks had different scriptures than we do."

"I know blasphemy," Marinda said. "I ain't stupid. I just don't know how to read."

"You read that, didn't you?" I said, which made her smile real big.

"I guess I did." She leaned right on past the book and kissed me smack dab on the lips. That threw me for a minute, and I forgot where I was.

"Why did your gramps make you read this, exactly? Is it 'cause you're curious too?"

"I reckon so," I said. "I ain't quite figured out why old Gramps give me this book. I'm just happy it ain't in Greek."

"In Greek? You can read Greek?"

"A tad. They teach us in school."

"You going to Greece?"

"No, I don't think so."

"Then, why do you need to read Greek?"

"'Cause, that's the language the Bible was written in," I explained.

"That there King James knew Greek?"

"He didn't write it. He just had it translated into English."

"Oh," she said, and got quiet. But she was right. Studying Greek really doesn't make sense. I'm partial to Latin on account of all the names of plants and animals being in Latin. At least it serves a real purpose.

Marinda went back to her reading. She continued, sentence by sentence, sounding out the syllables, then putting them all together into their completed sentence. I didn't have to do much except explain certain words, and explain why a "c" sometimes sounds like an "s" and other times like a "k," the answer to which takes us back to Greek and Latin again. We were reading for at least an hour.

"He's gonna win, ain't he?" she asked suddenly.

"No," I said. "Socrates lost his trial."

"But his accusers are idiots."

"According to him, they are. He made them look the fool. I reckon that could be why they didn't show him no mercy."

"He didn't want no mercy. He wanted justice."

"You're right," I said. "You ain't stupid at all."

She kissed me again.

"I like this part here, where he talks about all the fancy folks who think they know so much but don't really. While the truly wise person suspects maybe he knows something but knows for sure there's a lot he don't know. That's true today still, ain't it?"

"I reckon so," I said. "Just look at old Isaac Duncan. Ain't nothing but a planter but knows ever daggum thing under the sun. At least he thinks he does."

"Did they hang him?" She crinkled her brow in worry for a man two thousand years dead.

"No," I said. "They give him hemlock to kill him."

"That right?" She looked around at all the hemlock trees. "These kill you, you eat them?"

"No. Just make you a tad sick. Hemlock in Greece ain't the same thing as hemlock here in North Carolina. I had to look it up in the big book of flora. They had old Socrates to drink a poison made from *Conium maculatum*. That there's a Mediterranean shrub, called hemlock. It kind of looks like Queen Anne's Lace. These trees are Eastern Hemlock, *Tsuga canadensis*. Ain't no relation at all one to the other."

"Ain't you the curious one?" she said.

"I'm a downright evil-doer," I confessed.

Marinda can give the most inviting looks. Vixen could learn much from her. She gave me one of those looks right then, and the thought occurred to me that maybe that look was a lure and her lips were a trap. The thought didn't stop me from leaning in, plunging willingly into what may ensnare my soul forever.

August 12, 1888—I have made a discovery that is almost as fascinating as anything in the natural world. Yesterday, Taylor, myself, Ma, and Gramps ventured into town to take care of some business. We left Pa and Thomas at home to keep working the mill. We went to Shepherds with a package of herbs to exchange for some dry goods and what-not, and Gramps got a tad uppity with the shopkeeper. He was all out of the liniment Gramps likes to rub on his aching parts.

"I'll tell you what," Mr. Shepherd said. "That liniment comes from the Kingdom of the Happy Land."

Gramps jutted his jaw at the man. "Don't you think I know that? Says so right on the bottle."

"If it's such a dire matter, I'd suggest making a trip down to the Kingdom of the Happy Land where you can buy it direct from the manufacturer."

I was a little perplexed, for I had never realized there was a kingdom anywhere close by. But indeed, there is. It rests down the mountain near Tuxedo, smack dab on the border with South Carolina. It would have taken all day for us to ride the wagon down and back, so Gramps rented a stallion from the livery and set me and Taylor after the liniment. It was with reluctance that I climbed onto that steed, having forsworn the riding of horses altogether. But it wouldn't have been right for little Taylor to go by himself.

We followed the state road on down the mountain. There was a time when that road would have been full of livestock from drovers taking them down to market, but the railroad has changed that. Now only a few folk follow the old ways and drive livestock to market. There were a few hogs and a scattering of turkey on the road, and that was it.

The Kingdom of the Happy Land was on a former plantation. We came upon it at a gallop, and Taylor reined in the eager stallion. Lickety-split a Negro fella come out to meet us.

"Can I get your horse some water and feed?" he asked Taylor.

"Mighty obliged," I said, sliding down. The Rollys across the river are the only Negro folks I've ever known. This here Happy Land was an entire kingdom of them. I wondered if Gramps had any idea where his liniment came from. The fella that welcomed us was named Wiley. We gave him a few cents for helping with the horse, then we asked about the liniment.

"Yes, sir," he said. He seemed eager to talk to us about the liniment. "We've got plenty to sell. Ole Miss Rolla been sick. She ain't been into town in a few days, and usually she's the one keeps Mr. Shepherd stocked. Come on in."

He led us through a rusty old gate into the kingdom, telling us their story as he went. "This here place used to be Oakland plantation. My parents come here after the war. They was from a cotton plantation down in Mississippi. Father Abraham freed 'em, but freedom means you got to do for you and yours. And there weren't no doing in the state of Mississippi. Like a lot of folk, mine headed north. By the time they got here, this place was already turned into this kingdom. It was the promised land for sure. The king give them a spot to build a house and a plot of land to grow food on and money to spend when they needed it. When I come along Queen Louella made sure I got a good Christian education."

"You got a king and a queen?" Taylor asked. He was as surprised as I was.

"We always gots to have a king and a queen. When one passes, we choose another to follow. I'm a gonna introduce you to King Robert here right shortly."

"I ain't never met a king before," Taylor said.

"As they say, they's a first time for everything."

We walked by fields full of corn and melons, pumpkins and pole beans. They had tomatoes and okra and cucumbers even. Sunflowers as tall as our horse lined the edges of the place, and across the way, fields of sorghum waved in the breeze.

The king came out to meet us. He was a tall fella with a straight back and fine-looking jacket. He looked down at us like a snapping turtle eyeing your fingers. Wiley explained why we were there, and the king cleared his throat. His face relaxed a tad, like knowing our names took the edge off, and he no longer looked like a mean turtle. "Welcome to the Kingdom of the Happy Land!" He opened his arms wide.

He led us down along a fence line, pointing out the cross on the hill and a schoolhouse, and we followed. "My brother put that up," he said, waving at the cross. "He was king before I was." He asked where we were from.

"Daisy," I explained.

He squinted into the sky. "I never heard of such a place as Daisy."

"On up the mountain. In Hickory Nut Gap," I further explained.

"Oh yes. There is a man lives up in them parts who you might know, who everybody should know for his kindness and righteousness."

"Rolly?" I asked. It occurred to me that I didn't know Mr. Rolly's first name. He was always "Old Man" or Mister.

"No, not Rolly," he said. He had stopped walking completely in order to more fully work the wheels of his mind. "It's been years since he come by. He was a mighty fine fella. Would stop by on his way to Greenville. This was back in the sixties and seventies. He'd spend the night over at Miss Serepta's inn. Over yonder." He pointed to a brick house off a ways on the other side of the road.

Taylor and I looked at each other. Our eyebrows crested at the same time.

"He was more man with three limbs than most are with four. Talked about everything under the sun. His name was Aurelius. Aurelius Quinn, Esquire."

"That's our gramps!" Taylor beamed like one of the sunflowers at the king and at me. "He's the one wants your liniment so bad."

The king peered at us as if examining us for lice. "Let me get a good look at you. My eyes ain't what they used to be."

He scanned us both from head to toe. "I believe," he said after a spell, "I can see the resemblance. Your granddaddy was always a good friend of this kingdom. He drew up the papers that made it our land. We are mighty beholden to him. Mighty fine man, your granddaddy. Let me tell you something, boys. You listen to that man, you hear? You do what he says, and you'll be all right."

The king started walking again. He paused whenever he come to somebody, in order to introduce us. He made a point of saying we were the grandchildren of Aurelius Quinn, Esquire. I never knew that Gramps was an esquire. Heck, I don't even know what that means, exactly. It sure sounded respectable. We met Bessy and Tigris and Loman and Charlotte, all of whom were out working in the fields in some capacity or another. They had a smith named Josiah, pounding out horseshoes in the forge, and a spinner by the name of Walleeda, working a wheel out in front of her cabin. Everybody seemed so contented that a person might think their kingdom really was the Happy Land.

The king came to an old shed that looked like its best days were before the war. The door creaked open. Inside, jars of that liniment were stacked one on top of another almost up to the ceiling. The shed smelled to high heavens. It smelled of a thousand Grampses.

The king pulled out a wooden crate. "I'm gonna fill this crate up with the liniment."

"Our gramps only gave us the cash for two jars." I sank my hand into my pocket in search of the money.

"You ain't even gonna pay for one. Aurelius Quinn has earned as much as he desires. On the house, as they say. If Miss Rolla knew he was a customer, she'd a seen to it long ago he got this here liniment gratis."

"I'm sure he'd insist on paying you." I held out the money, but King Robert pushed my hand away.

"I know it. I know it," he said. "Of course your granddaddy would insist on paying. That's the kind of man he is. But he ain't here to fuss about it, now is he?"

"No, sir," Taylor said.

He handed us a case full of twelve liniment jars. I made Taylor carry it.

The king rested his hands on his back and gave us a squinty smile. "You boys are welcome here any time you please. And tell old Aurelius Quinn, Esquire, to come on by sometime. I assume time ain't been no kinder to him than it has been to me."

"Yes, sir," I said.

He held out his hand, made rough by toil and darkened by the sun. Taylor stared at it, as if pondering whether to take it. Neither of us had ever shook a Black man's hand, nor had we seen a white person ever even come close enough to shake hands with a Negro. I thought about Gramps and how he'd reacted to the incident at the Jockey Lot, how he threatened to make Thomas walk home for what he'd said about darkies. I took the king's hand, shook it like he was the most important person I'd ever met, because maybe he was. Taylor did the same.

"It was right nice meeting you," I allowed.

Taylor nodded. "You're the first king I ever knowed."

King Robert winked at us, and we were soon on our way. It was a bit of a chore getting that liniment back up the mountain on that stallion. After some discomfort, we got to where Taylor sat in front of me holding the box while I held the reins from behind. It wasn't until late afternoon that we got back to Hendersonville.

We found the oxcart outside of Shepherd's. Gramps was inside conferring with Mayor Ewart. He wasn't the mayor anymore, but everybody called him that even though he now represented us in the state legislature. They went way back, and if left to their own devices, they might gab for days. They weren't talking much now. It was all somber inside, like somebody died.

Turned out somebody had died. The mayor's half-sister's husband had been killed. He was a revenuer for the federal government, but everybody liked him just the same. Upon learning the news, Taylor and I looked at each other, and I could tell he was thinking the same thing I was: had that Gus Trabor killed again? It probably wasn't him at all. Plenty of folks in these parts would be inclined to shoot revenuers. But it was easy to think that old Gus could be the one.

Gramps started the process of getting up. He had his leather-wrapped shepherd's crook cane with him this time. It creaked when he planted it and pulled himself to standing. "Young'uns,"

Gramps said. "I was starting to get worried about you. Thought maybe you'd decided to skip town with my fifty cents."

Mr. Ewart chuckled.

"It ain't that close, Gramps," Taylor complained. "It was all the way down in durn South Carolina."

"Hey!" Mr. Ewart said. "Don't you say durn in respect to South Carolina."

Gramps pursed his lips at his friend. "Hamilton here is a graduate of the University of South Carolina. We don't speak ill of South Carolina in his presence. Save it for when we're out of earshot."

Mr. Ewart had a twinkle in his eye despite his recent loss. "Nonsense. If you're going to speak of South Carolina, don't sugarcoat it. Call it what it is, and just say 'damn South Carolina.'"

Gramps erupted like a volcano into a laughing spell. Taylor and I looked at each other. We must not have gotten their joke. Gramps said his goodbyes and his condolences, and we left to get Ma. She was down at Lila's, Mr. Ewart's half-sister. She was the young widow. It was a ways away, so we rode the oxcart on down there. They were out on her porch rocking in sad silence. The entire Barnwell family was there. Barnwell was her husband's name. Ma saw us, gave Lila a hug, and came on down to us.

"Gracious alive," Ma said, climbing up into the cart. "I don't know how they get folks to be revenuers these days. They're dying right and left."

I kept quiet, wondering if Pa had done the right thing by letting Gus Trabor go. If Gus had gone and killed somebody else, why, I don't know how Pa would live with himself. But he already seems to have trouble living with himself as it is.

It wasn't till we were on the road that Gramps spied that entire case of liniment. He and Taylor were in the back of the cart, propped up on feed bags, while I drove and Ma sat beside me. "Boys, I believe I'm going to be set for the remainder of my days with the supply of liniment you brought back."

"We met a king that knows you," Taylor shouted out.

"Did you now?" A sly grin lit his face.

"King Robert," Taylor said. "He give you an entire case for the price of two jars."

I was a tad surprised at how easily Taylor lied, and not at all surprised that Gramps saw it immediately for what it was.

"Boy," Gramps said, "there are lots of reasons to lie, for instance if the truth impedes a good story, or if in the process of wooing a young lady you need to augment your description of her beauty. But lying for profit is the lowest of low. We Quinns don't countenance such a sin."

Taylor dropped his head. "Yes, sir," he said.

"You can give me back my money."

I dug around in my pocket and handed the coins to Ma who handed the change back to Gramps. "We spent two pence on getting that horse watered and fed."

"That's fine. Now you should know I'd a let you keep it had you not lied about it."

"Yes, sir," Taylor said.

"It's the lying that cost you." Gramps settled back against the feed as if warming up for a telling. "Why don't I tell you about the time I met that King Robert? It was way back, right after he had become the king of the Kingdom of the Happy Land. Must have been twenty years ago now, right after I came home from the State Convention where we had worked hard to guarantee the voting rights of Negroes. President Grant had appointed me federal attorney for these parts, which required me to go down to Greenville about six times a year.

"My journey took me past the Kingdom of the Happy Land. In fact, I often stopped to overnight at the inn there, where many of the Happy Land residents were employed. It was run by a widow named Serepta." His eyes brightened like they do when he's about to light into a tale.

"It beguiled me at first, how such a kingdom might exist in our midst. Over time I got to know King Robert's brother, William. William had led the first-comers—that's what they called themselves—on a journey from way down south. He became the first king and his wife, Louella, the queen. What they had created on the grounds of that old plantation was no less than the Promised Land for many former slaves from the deep South. Mississippi, Louisiana, Alabama, even Georgia. Despite having a king and a queen, their form of government was a lot more democratic than our own even today. Everybody could vote, even the women. Before a decision was made, everybody had to come to agreement. The king and queen just carried out the will of the people. Ain't that something?"

"You mean Ma can't vote?" Taylor asked, perking up from the shame of being caught lying.

"No, son," Ma explained. "I cannot."

"That ain't right!"

"Carson," Gramps shouted, "turn this cart around. Take this boy back to Lila. We got a suffragist on board."

Ma laughed to herself, straightening her dress. Lila was known around the county for wanting to grant the franchise to women. She was kind of like Pa in that she went around and held meetings and the such.

"If your ma lived in the Kingdom of the Happy Land she could vote, and she would be educated on account of the queen making sure every child, male and female, getting at least a basic education in reading, writing, and arithmetic. This whole kit and caboodle was fascinating to me as an experiment in government. I wondered how such a thing was possible. Why hadn't they been chased off by the owner, you might wonder?"

"Because they killed them?" Taylor asked. "Or they locked them up in one of those sheds?"

"See," Gramps continued, "we are inclined to intrinsically think the worst of folk. But that's not what happened. The widow Davis couldn't operate it herself after the war ended. These former slaves knew how to run a plantation, because that's what they'd been doing all of their lives. She allowed them to live there and reap profits from the fertile soil in exchange for them supporting her. That's what you'd call a *quid pro quo*.

"I saw that everything hinged on one lady's kindness and made the suggestion that maybe kindness wasn't enough. King Robert made an offer to buy some of that land for a dollar an acre. And we formalized the deal. I recorded it, and today that kingdom is owned free and clear by its residents."

"They're mighty grateful, Gramps," I said. "King Robert suggested you come by sometime to catch up. He said time probably ain't been kinder to you than it has to him, and he'd like to catch up."

Gramps grumbled. He didn't seem to take kindly to the reference to his mortality. "That's the story of how a kingdom is alive and well right here in North Carolina in the year of our Lord eighteen hundred and eighty-eight."

"Gramps," Taylor said. "He called you Aurelius Quinn, Esquire. I never knowed you was an esquire. Does that mean you're a knight, like the Knights of the Roundtable?"

"Wouldn't that be a trick?" Gramps said. "No, I ain't a knight, but maybe I can get King Robert to do the favor."

Gramps cleared his throat. I turned and glared at Taylor, who was perched forward to hear whatever was to come out of Gramps's mouth. He's still young, and he doesn't realize the danger of asking Gramps such an open-ended question.

"Esquire is a term that has its origins in the old country, where men wore titles like soldiers wear epaulettes today as a distinction of one's rank. An esquire was a station above that of gentleman."

Gramps went on and on about esquire. He was still talking when we pulled up to the house in the dark. All he had to say, it turned out, was since he held public office he was entitled to the use of the term. Instead, now we all know the entire history of a word we will never put to use.

September 19, 1888—I've been back at Newton for quite a spell now. I've been studying hard, so I have neglected this journal until tonight, when I have a minute to set some things down I've been pondering.

First of all, right before I came back to school Gramps pulled me aside. It was a mild evening out on the porch. The katydids were singing away. I haven't a notion of where the others were. It was just me and Gramps. He propped himself back in the rocking chair to enjoy his pipe.

"Before you go back to the clutches of Rodney Webster, we need to have a discussion, boy."

"Yes, sir," I said.

He smacked his lips to savor the flavor of his pipe. "Tell me about Socrates," Gramps said. "Why do you suppose I had you read that?"

"I don't rightly know, Gramps."

"Surmise something."

I stammered. I had read the book myself, then Marinda and I had made it all the way through as I was teaching her to read. I had read it twice, and I couldn't figure out why Gramps had given it to me.

"I suspect you give me the book so I could see that believing different is dangerous, and I got to keep my thoughts to myself lest others accuse me of things that ain't true."

Gramps didn't much care for my summation.

"That, my friend, is disappointing," he said. "You've got it entirely backwards."

You see, I had been assuming that Gramps was trying to punish me by giving me that book. In fact, it was his attempt to enlighten me to the ways of the Rodney Websters of the world.

"This book ain't about religion, so to speak, at all. It's about the lengths to which the petty and small-minded will go to get to those that threaten them. Do you really think Meletus gave two cents about religion?"

"He's the fella that was Socrates's accuser?"

"That's right."

"He wasn't a priest. He was a businessman."

"Exactly. If it was about religion, then why didn't the priests press the charges against Socrates?"

"Do you suppose it had to do with Socrates going around exposing other men's deficiencies?"

"Now you've got the mule in the right row. His quiver was filled with truth. And his targets were those with the most to lose."

"That's why they came after him?"

"I've learned a thing or two in my days on this earth. One of them is that material possessions corrupt. The more you got, the more you want. Rodney Webster and I go way back. He's at heart a good man, but he has some powerful weaknesses, most notably piety and desperation. That's a potent combination."

"Yes, sir." For the first time in my life, I paid every bit of attention to what Gramps was saying.

"Religion has given old Rodney Webster a lucrative career, you see. You worry him with your questioning and idealism. He is your Meletus. That's why he focuses on you so much."

"Yes, sir," I said.

"I said I'd learned a thing or two in my days on this earth. I've not always been this old, much to your surprise, eh? Another thing I have learned is that there are fates worse than death. Old Socrates, he's got that right. 'To fear death is no other than to think oneself wise when one is not, to think one knows what one does not know.' The older I get, the less death worries me. It's like an old friend who lives just over the hill. You know he's there, and going to pay him a visit ain't the worse thing ever."

"You ain't going to die, are you?" I asked.

Gramps took a long toke on his pipe and let the smoke out real slow. "Everybody dies. Don't matter whether you're a Vanderbilt or a Quinn, death eyes you the same. That's what Socrates says too. He asks his accuser, 'Are you not ashamed of your eagerness to possess as much wealth, reputation, and honors as possible, while you do not care for nor give thought to wisdom or truth?' There are more important things to worry over than death or money. Don't you forget that! It's awfully easy to forget."

"Yes, sir," I said.

"Wickedness runs faster than death. All a man can do is to take himself into account and decide whether his actions are for good or for ill. You do your best to make them for good. I don't know where your beliefs run, and really that's between you and God. I reckon it's my fault you're so smitten with Darwin and all."

The light glinted off his spectacles.

"I'm of a mind that it don't really matter what you believe, it's how you act that matters in the end, what you do with what you got."

Gramps relit his pipe and stared off into the darkening night. The creek splashed past the house and a choir of mountain chorus frogs (*Pseudacris brachyphona*) sang out. The rich tang of his freshly lit pipe settled over us.

"I will," I said.

Gramps gave me a sidelong glance. "I reckon you will."

He started rocking. I rocked alongside him for a spell. It may have been the longest period of quiet I'd ever had with Gramps. Then, as if he couldn't stand not talking, he said, "I gave this same talking-to to your pa way back. One thing I wish I'd a told him that I'm gonna tell you, is being good don't mean you got to be serious. It's all right to let loose a little, you hear?"

"Yes, sir," I said.

"Life is too short and too hard to go through it without a little spice."

"Yes, sir."

Since being back in Newton, I've tried to live right. That headmaster so far has left me alone. He's got his hands full with Taylor right now. Taylor has taken to running with a group of youngsters that like to let loose more than just a little. They're always playing games of football and baseball and running out into the woods at night. They don't invite me, and that's all right by me.

❦

It was a Sunday morning. Absent the pounding, whirring, and

shouting that accompany construction, the place lay tranquil. A woodpecker in the distance filled the gap in construction with hammering of its own. Closer, a squirrel chucked at a crow. Morning light splintered through dew-cast specters.

Despite the peaceful setting, butterflies swarmed in my belly. I hadn't been this kind of nervous in a very long time. The nerves came in anticipation of my morning's excursion: I was going to church.

Growing up Presbyterian, I appreciated the contemplative intellectual approach of the denomination. But that approach had led me to try to make Christian theology make sense, and it didn't. I couldn't square this God's ignorance of China and Australia and America with his alleged omniscience. And despite having all the power, he was incredibly petty. I was willing to perhaps overlook these inconsistencies and many others, but then, God did the unforgivable; he cruelly and arbitrarily killed a woman who was devoted to him. He took my mother, Madeleine Crest. Other than for funerals and christenings, I hadn't been back to church since her death.

Instead, I had sought out meaning through science. I had turned my gaze to the stars and toward the lives of peoples who had lived centuries before Jesus, who had formed their mythologies long before his capricious father created the earth one Monday in the Near East six thousand years ago.

I would take my doubting self to the Baptist Church. After a warm shower in Micah's contraption, I dressed in a simple white blouse and blue ankle-length skirt. I would have been under-dressed in the First Presbyterian Church of my youth, but something told me the Baptists wouldn't mind.

At Bat Cave Baptist Church, mine was the only Subaru in a parking lot full of trucks and SUVs, but everyone welcomed me with genuine smiles and open arms. As I suspected, I was not underdressed. The congregation was composed of families who drove late-model vehicles, wore nice shirts and jeans, and proceeded into the sanctuary in an orderly way. Patsy and Tilda were there, so I sat with them. Charles, it turned out, seldom made it to church. The basic liturgy of the service was familiar: Invocation, Confession, Old and New Testament readings, the Sermon, Offering, and Benediction. As with the church of my youth, the service was peppered with opportunities to sing hymns.

The biggest difference was the sermon. Where the Presbyterian sermon was always sedate and theological, this one was fiery and relatable. It was about how there's no escaping God. He's there wherever you go, even in the unlikeliest places such as social media and the hippest hangouts. Therefore, the preacher deduced, it was the Christian's duty to reveal God wherever he was, whether that be on Facebook, on Twitter, or in bars and clubs. Since I was expecting hellfire and brimstone, maybe some snake-handling and talking in tongues, the service felt safe and refreshing. I felt foolish for those expectations. After the service, the preacher, a bearded, burly man about my age, expressed his gratitude for my attendance and said he hoped to see me again next Sunday. I nodded, said I would do my best to be there, but my attention was drawn to an older man hobbling through the parking lot.

"Excuse me." I left the preacher to the next in line. I approached the old gentleman tentatively. "Mr. Morgan?"

He turned, his scowl in direct opposition to everyone else's smiles. "Eh?" He turned, saw me, and snorted. "Oh. The trespasser."

"Mr. Morgan," I repeated. "May I have a minute of your time?"

"My time?" He cocked his face, and a wayward brow hair stirred in the breeze.

"If you don't mind." The sight of his wayward hair caused me to tuck my own behind my ear.

"Starting now. One minute." He glanced at his watch, a simple old Timex. "If you're looking for forgiveness for your trespasses, I believe that was taken care of in the service in there."

"No, though I do apologize for that. Again. My name is—"

"McAlister," he interrupted. "I got it the first time."

"Caroline, please," I said.

He made no move to escape into his pickup, easily the oldest vehicle in the lot, but well cared for, not a single blemish marking the decades-old exterior.

"I'd like to talk to you about your family history," I said.

He glanced again at his watch. His arched eyebrows indicated our minute was drawing to a close. He placed a hand on his door handle.

"As it relates to the history of my family's cabin."

His bright gray eyes seemed to betray a crack in his impervious facade. He turned and opened the door. "Take care about what you go digging into. Once a thing gets known, it never goes back to being unknown."

He slid into the car, started it up, and cranked down his window. Though old, he displayed a suppleness of both mind and body. He did not strike me as the kind to equivocate.

"You know who killed Thomas Quinn, don't you?" I asked.

"Is that what this is about?"

I gripped the open window, as if I could hold the truck in place with my own strength.

He let out a long sigh. "Why don't you follow me on up to the house? I suppose I can spare more than a minute. No more than an hour, though."

"Thank you so much," I said.

I scampered over to the Subaru, jumped in, and glanced over at Tilda and Patsy. I gave them a thumbs-up as I pulled out behind his truck. Their eyes did not share my enthusiasm, and both shook their heads in concern as I left them behind.

Hiram Morgan drove like a stock car racer. I had to floor it to keep up with him. He turned onto a dirt road that snaked up his mountain, and then turned off into his drive. We passed the spot where the cemetery lay hidden. Soon afterward the road skewed upward and I had to pay attention to where he drove so that I wouldn't get stuck in the deep ruts cutting through the middle of the passage. He did not drive much slower than he had on the hardtop, and not for the first time I was grateful for my car's all-wheel drive.

I was so attuned to the road that I lost track of time and distance, but after a while we emerged from forest onto a grassy bald at the top of the mountain, the kind of bald that would have been common during Carson Quinn's youth and earlier. Most of the old balds had long since grown over with forest. Not this one, though.

On the very top of the mountain perched a collection of antennae, surrounded by open pasture populated by a herd of sheep that eyed us warily. The sky stretched into the distance in every direction, billowy clouds sailing by like tall ships. Hiram's house was a two-story farmhouse down a bit from the summit. As we drove up, the border collie bounded up to us. Hiram didn't gush and coo like most people did upon seeing their pets. He just said, "Sallie, that'll do," and the dog immediately dropped its interest in me and fell in line behind him.

He led me onto the porch, then into his home. His living room was orderly, the furnishings simple and well cared for. He pointed to a sofa covered in an afghan for me to sit on, and he perched in an old Morris chair in front of his fireplace. A bay window looked out over a fenced-in backyard peppered with a variety of bird feeders. A hummingbird dashed past, and a couple of bluebirds splashed in a stone birdbath. By the window, a pair of binoculars sat upright atop the *Sibley Field Guide to Birds*.

He did not apologize for the state of the house as some might, and he offered nothing in the way of refreshment. He immediately got down to business. "So, you think you know who killed Thomas Quinn."

"No," I said. "I was hoping you did."

He went silent, his attention drifting to a brilliant red bird with black wings that perched on one of the feeders. He was silent for so long that I thought maybe our conversation was over as abruptly as it had begun, and that all that driving up here was for naught.

I shifted forward on the sofa to begin my departure, when he said, "*Piranga olivacea.*"

"Pardon?"

"Scarlet tanager," he translated. The colorful bird snatched a beak full of seed and leapt to a nearby dogwood branch.

"It's beautiful," I said.

"It's itinerant. Like you." He squinted to track the bird from tree to feeder. "Its mate is off in the distance."

"Like me?" I asked.

"A passerby," he clarified.

"I know what itinerant means." My back straightened, and I slid forward. "I'm a college professor. But I'm no passerby. I've grown up in these parts. My first memory is at that cabin." My mind's eye flitted back to that memory, to the bouncing orange ball and the cardboard box and the black leather boots.

"A professor?" He arched an eyebrow at the first thing I'd said to interest him. "Of what?"

I hesitated. Even among educated people, I had trouble explaining my academic interests. Sticking to my strategy of being straightforward and direct, I said, "Archaeoastronomy." Usually what followed after that statement was some version of "What the hell is that?" Not in this case.

"That so?" He ruminated a second. "In that case, I've got something for you."

He bounded up, energized. The dog popped to its feet, and Hiram stepped outside. I followed hesitantly. Soon we were crossing the pasture behind the house, the dog leading the way. He approached the fenced-off collection of antennae and passed them without regard. They bore the names of various cell phone companies and government agencies. Just beyond the array, we reached a crest that seemed like the highest point on the bald. There lay a much more ancient version of the antennae. An assemblage of rocks bore a series of etchings. The 360-degree view from here stretched off into the far distance. Immediately I knew what these rocks were and what the etchings represented. I had seen similar patterns on similar collections of stone on mountaintops in Scotland, Ireland, Mexico, Arizona, and Canada.

"What do you make of this?" He pointed his walking stick at the stones.

"It's a calendar of sorts." I dropped to a knee to get closer. The etchings were crude but fascinating. They were pre-Cherokee, probably made a couple thousand years before the Cherokee actually formed a distinct culture. "It's a representation of the grand octal." My mind immediately switched back into academic mode.

"Figured," he said.

I craned my neck back at him, perplexed that I didn't have to explain a concept that didn't occur in the curriculum until grad school.

That smirk returned. "At the vernal equinox, this stone here lines up at sunrise." With his walking stick he tapped a symbol that looked like three stars. "At the fall equinox"—he shifted to another symbol that looked sort of like an ear of corn—"this one lines up."

I pointed to another symbol. "This should be the winter solstice. Over here we've got what should be the summer solstice."

"That's right." Those gray eyes twinkled. "Any idea on age?"

"I'd say around three thousand years." I scratched at the back of my head, took in the lay of the land and the panoramic view. "Of course, it would take some further investigation and dating to say for sure, but that would my best guess."

"An educated one, though." He shifted on his feet, resting more weight on his walking stick.

"That's right."

He turned to the west where, like a sea of crashing tides, mountains folded upon mountains. To the east the waters of Lake Lure shimmered in the afternoon sun. Beyond the lake, hills flattened into piedmont. The view easily stretched fifty miles in all directions, except for the north, where the Seven Sisters of the Brown Mountains, with the highest peaks in the East, loomed. It made sense that people would use this spot for observation and calendar-keeping.

"My great-uncle," he said, "was the most misunderstood person I've ever known."

It took me a second to realize he was talking about Carson Quinn.

He sighed and turned to look at me. "He never did anything to disabuse folk of their erroneous assumptions about him. I expect he relished their suspicions. He was ornery and set in his ways and closed off to people, but he was no murderer."

"How do you know for sure?"

"Uncle Carson practically raised me. I never feared him like others did. Starting out knee high to turkey, I followed him around. I suppose Uncle Carson was as close to a father as I ever did have since I never met the real one."

"Your real father?"

"Bradshaw Morgan."

I remembered the little boy of unknown origin from the journal, whom Betsy and Owen Morgan had adopted and raised as their own. "Carson taught you the bird names?"

"He taught me a lot more than that. He knew all the scientific names of everything: birds, plants, trees, mammals, reptiles. He taught me Latin and Greek. He taught me what it means to be a man and to love a place."

I knew then that the journal was not for my eyes but for Hiram's. I was an itinerant intruder, the possessor of someone else's history. "He had you read Plato's *Apology*, didn't he?"

His eyes betrayed neither surprise nor anger. Hiram didn't turn at me agog or gasp, as Patsy had. Instead, he sighed and said, "In Greek."

I had been prepared to reveal the existence of the journal, but he didn't take my bait. It was odd that he didn't question how I knew such an obscure detail. Maybe he was so old that it was easy to lose track of such things. Yet his mind seemed sharp for someone as old as he.

Hiram used the silence as an opportunity to continue. "Uncle Carson provided my earliest and best education, better than high school, college, or engineering school."

"You're an engineer?" My eyes surely telegraphed my surprise.

He lifted his wayward eyebrows at me. "I was an electrical engineer for thirty years. All thanks to the navy, the GI Bill, and Uncle Carson."

He watched with amusement my feeble attempt to lift my jaw from the grass.

"Contrary to all appearances, I have not always been an old man on the top of this mountain."

"Of course not," I said. "So, did your uncle ever talk about the death of his brother?"

Hiram took a deep breath and kicked at a pebble on the ground. "Thomas dying really tore him up, you know. It's part of why he seldom left that holler."

"Did he know who did it?"

Hiram turned and started to head back down to his house. I trailed behind, waiting for an answer, but one never came. He stretched to his full height at the edge of his porch. "Sallie and I need to tend to some chores now. When you're finished with it why don't you bring that journal back? Take care of it in the meanwhile. It's awfully old."

16

June 16, 1889—Today was Sunday, and Pa finally relented and gave us a day off. That doesn't mean I just sat around on my behind like some banker. It means I spent the afternoon with Ma back in the herb garden. Ma knows herbs like nobody else. She grows a little bit of everything, from *Angelica atropurpurea* to *Zinnia augustifolia*. But she also goes out into the forest and gathers different plants, like ginseng, for instance. She uses most of her herbs herself to treat ailments and the such. But we also take them in to the general store where they're as good as cash. The storekeeper often tells Ma what's selling, and then we can gather it and get top dollar, so to speak, for it.

It's amazing to me what Ma knows. We were in the garden harvesting some plants when she said, "That Marinda thinks the world of you, Carson Quinn."

"And I'm mighty fond of her too." I bent low to pinch off some *Verbascum thapsus*. Most folks call it mullein. It's good for breathing troubles.

"Son, what's going to happen when you leave?" She said it real casual-like, not even looking up as she trimmed some comfrey leaves.

"Who says I'm going to leave?" I asked.

"You'll leave," she said. "Thomas is here for good, but, Carson, you're a horizon watcher. Your eyes are always on the next hill. Your mind is a wandering mind."

"Maybe I'll take her with me when I go a-wandering."

"What about her mother and father? She can't leave them behind. She's their only child."

Ma's words hurt. It was as though she was taking a dream and turning it into a nightmare. I hadn't thought about what she was saying, that Marinda's folks might need her more than I would. Weren't children meant to grow up and leave? It's what Ma did, after all.

"Be careful with her, son," she said. "Try not to hurt her."

"I've still got a year left here. Then maybe I will be like Thomas and stay. Who says I have to go down to the university?"

"No one," Ma said. "That's up to you entirely. If you can live with yourself, and your grandfather, afterward, then so be it. But people can be hurt by things such as love. It's best you take care not to wound the one you're fond of."

I didn't much like the tenor of that conversation. I tried to steer it to more comfortable waters. "What was Pa like when you met him?"

Ma rearranged the stack of comfrey leaves she was holding and took a deep breath. "The war had just ended, and he had made his way to New York City. I had worked as a nurse back in Ireland, so when I arrived, I found work in a hospital. He came to that hospital looking for someone else, and found me instead. He told me of the beauty of these mountains. They sounded so much like County Sligo to me that I followed him here as his bride. I've never regretted it for one second."

"Did you know you were leaving your family forever by coming here?"

"You're my family, Carson. You and Pa and your brothers and sister and Gramps. I'm a blessed mother."

She had a basket full of comfrey now, and she set it aside to sit down on a little rock bench. "There's nothing like New York City. I think there were more Irish in New York than Dublin when I lived there, but it was the loneliest place on earth."

"And these hills ain't?"

"These hills are each a friend to the other. There's nothing lonely about them if you see them for what they are."

"What's that?" I sat down beside her. A woodpecker rat-a-tat-tatted up the mountain, and smoke from the kitchen fire drifted past.

"Each mountain is an island connected by an emerald sea

between them. You pay attention, and they'll provide for you everything you might need, like the ginseng and the witch hazel and the chestnut. A mountain is alive and ancient."

"Don't let Pastor Jamison hear you talking that way, Ma."

She adjusted her apron strings. "Pastor Jamison's a good man, Carson. You should come to church and listen to him. I worry your pa and grandpa have ruined religion for you."

"I ain't no atheist," I said.

She reached out and touched my cheek. "Of course not."

"That's what they call me at school."

"In life people will say lots of things about you, some of it terrible and some of it wonderful. Cling to neither good nor bad, and you'll be fine."

She stood and kissed my head and went on inside to the kitchen. I was left alone in the garden, a mite befuddled by the conversation.

June 23, 1889—Wilma Brightleaf has died. Ma had been treating her with the tinctures and herbs, but that stopped working. They got a doctor to come down from Hendersonville, but there was nothing to be done. He said it was scarlet fever. Charlie is all tore up. They buried her in the plot beside the church yesterday. It was a beautiful day, a terrible day for a funeral on account of all the young'uns wanting to run around and play while the rest of us were beside ourselves in grief. The reverend gave a somber benediction as they laid her in the ground. Old Charlie sobbed quietly to himself. He and Wilma didn't have children. He told me once on a hunt that she couldn't have them, but that never stopped Charlie from loving her. Why, I don't think I've ever seen two people more in love than Charlie and Wilma. And that includes Marinda and me.

After the ceremony, folks come up to Charlie and consoled him. Ma invited him over to the house for dinner, but he declined. He said he wanted to be alone. Marinda, of course, was there. She was crying too. Life is hard in these hills. We see death all the time. She's lost every one of her siblings. But there was just something about it being Wilma that got us all. Everybody seemed affected, everybody that is, except Pa. Nothing affects him.

Ma come up to me and Marinda as we walked back to the house. "I'm worried about Charlie," she said. "I want you two to keep an eye on him for the next little bit. He's liable to go off and do something terrible."

"Yes, ma'am," I said.

Marinda and I hung back and watched as Charlie stayed by the gravesite while three men filled in the hole. "That's so beautiful," Marinda said, wiping the tears from her eyes.

"It's sad is what it is," I said.

"And beautiful. He still loves her so much."

"She was the sweetest woman around," I said, then added, "except for you, of course."

"Carson Quinn, you and I both know I ain't sweet at all."

Once they had tossed the last spadeful of dirt on the grave, Charlie turned and walked into the valley toward his clapboard farmhouse. We hurried down after him. Charlie didn't stay there for long. When he come out, he was toting his long rifle and rucksack. He made a beeline out across the valley. We struggled to keep up.

He kept a-walking till he entered the forest and went up the mountain. It looked like he was heading up to Blue Rock. I had a bad feeling. Blue Rock is steep enough that a distraught person could fling himself off and fall hundreds of feet before hitting the ground. There's a legend about such a place down west of Hendersonville called Jump-Off Rock. It's a precipice similar to Blue Rock, where it's said that a young Cherokee maiden, upon learning of the death of her lover off at war, threw herself over the edge in grief.

The last thing we wanted was for old Charlie to throw himself off Blue Rock. After all, he is Cherokee, just like that maiden. We scrambled after him. It turned out that he was headed where we thought he was. He got there, and he stepped out on the rock. Marinda and I clutched at each other as he got near the edge. I was about to shout out, when we heard him singing. It was quiet and in Cherokee. He held his arms out as if to give the wind a big old hug.

Charlie sang for a long time. Marinda and I settled down on a bed of moss in the dark shade of a white oak. We held hands. Her hands weren't soft like a woman's in one of them romance novels Sarah's always reading. They were nearly as rough as mine. That's kind of why I love her so. She's someone who knows hard work.

I have no idea what Charlie Brightleaf sang into the wind up there. I think he was telling Wilma goodbye from a spot a little closer to heaven in a way that no preacher would understand. When he finished singing, he took that long rifle and pointed it at the deep blue sky and tugged off a round. The report echoed all over and back again. And all the birds and bugs that had been singing suddenly stopped. It was silent except for the wind. Charlie stood there a long, long time. We held our breath in the shadows.

Finally, he turned and came back from the edge. He looked toward us. I was sure he couldn't see us, but then he said aloud, "Come on, young'uns. Let's go have some of your mother's dinner."

We were embarrassed and didn't say nothing at first.

"Carson and Marinda," he said. "You followed me all the way up the mountain. Why don't you follow me on down now?"

We emerged from the shadows. "We was worried about you," Marinda confessed.

"You don't need to worry about me," Charlie said. He led us off the rock into the forest.

We didn't ask him to explain what he was doing. It didn't seem right to. But he explained a little bit by saying, "This was one of our favorite spots to bring a picnic. We had many a long talk up here. You can sometimes hear voices in the wind. Maybe it's the voices of the departed or maybe it's God talking to you."

And I remembered then being up there that night of the earthquake, and hearing the voice calling my name to lead me down the mountain in the darkness. I got chilled, despite it being a warm summer day. I had long since decided that the panicked state I was in had caused some sort of hallucination. Perhaps I really had been hearing voices in the wind. Maybe it was God steering me out of harm's way.

July 12, 1889—Up the Gorge a ways, after ascending a pitch near as steep as Chimney Rock itself, lies a hidden waterfall with a pool beneath it. It's another one of those places I may be the only one knows about. So as not to inspire Pa's ire, I had collected a basketful of ginseng and dug half as much ginger root. Marinda had joined me on my outing. We brought along *The Symposium*. She had liked *The Apology* so much that she wanted to hear what else old Plato had to say. The falls poured on down beside us while we splayed ourselves out on a broad boulder in the sun. She wore a work dress and leather boots, and concentrated hard on the ancient words of the long-dead philosopher. I cut us some bread from the loaf I was toting, topped it with some cheese, and shared it with her.

"This is all about the different kinds of love there is." She turned the book over in her hand, tracing the lettering on the cover.

"Reckon that's so," I said.

"What kind of love do we have?" she asked, as if asking what was for dinner.

I cut a slice of apple and handed it to her. "In that book I believe it's Aristophanes who talks about beings that were once one person that were then cut into two individuals. I think our love is that. We are two halves of the same person. Together we are whole."

She scowled like a bulldog. "That ain't it at all, Carson. Our love is the one what says one would sacrifice one's life for another. All this other love is only for men according to Mister Plato. He says there that women are only capable of the sacrificial sort of love. That's a bunch a hogwash if you ask me, but if I had to die for you, I surely would."

"Don't say that!" I studied her face for signs of a joke, but she looked as serious as a storm.

"I would." She crunched down on that apple.

We sat for a bit while the waterfall misted rainbows into the air, and its breeze stirred the clumps of nearby nettles. I leaned in and kissed her, and she kissed back. After a time of this, I pulled back. "Marinda, this is going to be my last year at Newton. I'm bound for the university after that."

"The university?" She said it like it was three words, not one. Yoon-avers-city.

"In Chapel Hill. It's where Gramps went way back. He and Judge Logan both."

"You gonna be a lawyer too?" she asked. "Like your Gramps?"

"More of a scientist I expect."

"Oh," she said. Sadness creeped across her face like a shadow.

"I was thinking you could come with me when I go." I was thinking she was sad I'd be leaving her.

"To Chapel Hill? What's a girl going to do in Chapel Hill?"

"Study, like me. You're as smart as any boy there."

"Carson," she said. She looked into my eyes like I was little Bradshaw and had just dirtied my pants. "What good is a university going to do someone like me? I ain't no Quinn."

"What's that mean?" Family pride stiffened my spine.

"You all are different. Your gramps, well, he's like our own Thomas Jefferson, and your pa ain't just a blacksmith. You Quinns believe in ideas, while the rest of us just try to get by. How many other folks from around here you see going off to university?"

I thought hard, and there weren't many others I could name.

"Just promise you'll come back afterward." She pushed her hair from her forehead, where it had fallen from our kissing.

My mind danced over all the places I aimed to go and see, to the Western lands written about by John Muir, following Humboldt down in South America, and my heart lurched, knowing that promising Marinda might mean never going wandering. But if we were two halves of the same whole, then being with her would be worth it. "I promise," I said. "I'll come back for you."

She stood up of a sudden, her fingers fiddling with her buttons. "How cold you reckon that water is?"

I looked over at that pool. The sun was warm on the rock, and the pool looked mighty refreshing. "Maybe sixty degrees," I said. When I looked back at her, her dress was open down to her belly, and she was tugging on her underthings.

"Let's jump in." She shucked herself free of the dress.

If you think I'm going to tell you what happened next, you got me pegged wrong. I don't kiss and tell.

∽

"You asked to see me, boss?"

I looked up from the journal to see Micah looming over me. He pulled off his leather work gloves, doffed his Wilco trucker cap, and wiped his brow.

"You know, no one's ever called me 'boss' before you." I shaded my eyes from the sun behind him.

"Sorry. Caroline.'"

I slid the journal back into its plastic home. "Boss'll do just fine."

He broke into a toothy grin. The whiteness of his teeth contrasted with his tanned skin and scruffy face. "What's up, boss?"

"I wanted to let you know that I'll be out of town for a few days."

"That so?"

I sealed the plastic tub shut with a snap.

"Where you headed?"

"Chapel Hill," I said.

"What's in Chapel Hill?" He sniffed. His cheek twitched and he brushed away a gnat.

"A university. It's the first and finest public university in the country, and my alma mater."

He mashed his lips together, pinched his two middle fingers

to his thumb, and lifted his pointer finger and pinky into the familiar sign of the Wolfpack. "State fan here."

"I knew you were too good to be true." I nudged his shoulder.

"It was only a matter of time before the other shoe dropped. What could have been, eh, boss?"

"Indeed." I felt my cheeks warm.

"When will you be back?" He tucked his hands into his back pockets.

"Early next week. I'll probably stop in Greensboro to see my brother."

He scanned the hollow and the cabin. His eyes tracked back to me. He wiped his brow. "I'm ninety percent sure this will all be here when you get back."

"Better be. I'm putting you in charge. While I'm away, you can be the boss."

He snapped to attention, gave me a crappy salute and a coy wink. "Have a good trip," he said, "doing whatever it is Tar Heels do in Chapel Hill. Lord only knows." He tromped back down to the cabin, sparks from our spastic sarcasm singeing the morning mist.

There were gaps in the historical record available to me up here, gaps that could be filled by the archives in Chapel Hill. Besides, maybe I needed a break from these hills, some real food, and perhaps a night or two in a soft bed. I packed up the Subaru and hit the road.

After two months spent balancing between rustic living and a century-old journal, modern America hit me with dazzling culture shock. I navigated the tight turns of the double-lane hardtop through the folds of the mountains until the road spat me out onto the wide-open cut of I-40. The interstate was lit by unnatural color combinations of red and gold and blue and purple from the fast-food and gas establishments that clung to its right of way. The farther I got from Hemlock Hollow, the more lurid the scene became. By the time I reached Chapel Hill, I was fully enmeshed in twenty-first-century America.

Chapel Hill was not College Park. I had neither students nor a department here. What I had here was history, my own, reflected back to me in a flickering montage as I crossed the campus. There was the planetarium, where the night sky became decipherable to me for the first time, and where the course of my academic career had been set. Then there was the alumni building, where anthropology classes taught me about the peoples and cultures of the world and where I first learned how to do the research I now teach to others. Not far from where I now stood, my sophomore self had caught up with my professor of archaeology and told him that I wanted to study ancient peoples' relationships with the stars. He shook his head. "In that case, you need to do better in my class," he said and walked on. What a bold thing to do! I still cringe at my eager precociousness.

Easing into the flow of students moving across campus, I crossed the quads to the south. My feet led me directly to the granite steps of Wilson Library, a monument to the Greco-Roman sentiment of the 1920s and home to several archival collections. I climbed the steps, avoiding the spot where, as a socially awkward freshman, I had eaten lunch alone, then glanced at the corner, where as a confident senior I had made out with a baseball player whose name I can't remember. While over those four years here I became increasingly earnest in my studies, my taste in guys drifted away from the academically devout. Delores was right. I was drawn to extremists: athletes, ROTC soldiers, rock climbers, and tattoo artists. Again I cringed at my past. Shaking it off, I pulled open the massive front door.

Once inside Wilson Library, I settled myself in the North Carolina collection, where I requested everything they had that was related to the Quinn family.

They brought the papers I'd requested in state-of-the-art archival boxes, incongruous with the crumbling vestiges of times long past that were held within. By the end of the day, it was possible I knew more about his gramps from those crumbling contents than Carson Quinn ever did from life itself.

Aurelius Quinn had studied at Chapel Hill in the class of 1836. A member of the Dialectic Society, he apparently had a predilection for feistiness even then. He was hauled before the Honor Court when it came out that he'd been the author of a series of abolitionist pamphlets that had been appearing around campus. They charged him with dishonesty for using a pen name. With a deftness reminiscent of Socrates, he successfully defended himself by pointing out that the charges themselves were evidence of the need for a pseudonym in the first place. This I learned from yet another pamphlet published after the trial, this time in his own name.

An article describing the commencement ceremony of 1836 placed his hometown as Greensboro. I gasped, then looked around to apologize, but no one had noticed. Gramps, from my hometown? Carson Quinn felt closer than ever. Aurelius had been a legacy student. His father Richard Quinn graduated in the class of 1810. The directory from that year placed Richard's hometown as Plymouth, down east. The Quinns followed a westward course generation by generation it seemed, and Gramps must have been as much an outsider to the likes of the Duncans as I was to old Hiram Morgan.

That year, Aurelius was awarded first distinction, which required him to speak at commencement. His speech was called "The Obligation of the Educated Man." They didn't print the content of the speech, but I could imagine him pointing at his fellow graduates, imploring them to pursue noble truths over selfish interests in much the same way he had schooled young Carson.

He appeared on a list of UNC students who served in the war with Mexico. The record did not mention whether he'd actually nicked Santa Anna. Later, it appears he relocated to Rutherfordton, where he gained prominence as an attorney. He no longer hid his opposition to slavery or secession, willingly signing his name to letters sent to the Raleigh *Weekly Standard*.

I wondered if he did more than write letters opposing secession. His name appeared in the papers of Levi Coffin, an abolitionist, like Aurelius from Guilford County, who had relocated to the north. In 1858 he wrote a letter to Coffin. It was cryptic, nominally about linseed oil, but Coffin's home in Newport, Indiana, was known as the Grand Central Station of the Underground Railroad.

Later, both Aurelius and George Washington Logan became representatives to the state legislature during the Civil War. Though both Whigs were openly opposed to secession, they were elected to the Confederate Congress, where they represented their districts to a government they evidently wanted to topple. Logan was accused of being a member of the Heroes of America, also known as the Red String Order. It was a secret society created during the Civil War by men who lived in North Carolina but supported the Union. Their aim was to bring down the Confederacy from within. I couldn't find any record that tied Aurelius Quinn to the society, though in Carson's journal it was clear he had been a member. Gramps, apparently, could keep a secret.

After the war, Aurelius went to Raleigh to help craft the new government's state constitution. Logan became a member of the state legislature, and Aurelius Quinn became a federal attorney, charged with bringing the full effect of Reconstruction to a wide swath of the southern mountains and beyond. Way beyond, in fact. All the way down in Wilmington, there was a reference to Aurelius Quinn bringing charges against a white merchant who refused to execute a transaction to sell several acres he owned. Aurelius, as United States attorney, persuaded the court to order the land transferred to a former slave at the value agreed upon between the parties before the seller learned of the buyer's race and backed out. The case helped foment a thriving Black economy in the city. That may have been one of the acts of benevolence that he wouldn't talk to Carson about.

As Reconstruction ended and Home Rule went into effect, another secret society arose. Never having hidden their opposition to secession, Quinn and Logan also didn't hide their opposition to the Ku Klux Klan, which led to Logan's downfall. The

Klan targeted him. Composed of powerful men, the Klan managed to bring impeachment proceedings against Logan. They didn't succeed, but as a result he lost his seat to a Klansman named David Schenck. Embittered, the judge retired to run an inn at the mouth of Hickory Nut Gap. After Home Rule was enacted in 1877, the federal government withdrew from North Carolina, and Aurelius Quinn lost his federal job. He went back to private practice and eventually became the Gramps of Carson's journal. The two men, so integral to statewide politics, spent their remaining days mere miles apart, getting together weekly for gab sessions and checkers.

I pushed myself back from the table full of old periodicals, books, and papers, and took in the room. Portraits of old white men adorned the walls, many of whom would have been the enemies of these two rabble-rousers. Students slouched at tables and chairs throughout the room, their minds occupied by the buds in their ears and the computers at their fingertips. They were white and Black and Asian and Latino, beneficiaries of battles that had to be fought again and again by men and women they had never heard of and would likely never know about. I sighed too audibly for a library, but no one turned my way.

I was no closer to figuring out if Carson had indeed killed his brother, but I felt almost kin to him now, our pasts intertwining, hometown to hollow. Hillbillies they were not, though no one I had encountered either in the journal or in my research was, not even the Duncans. That Gramps had opposed the KKK gave rise to the notion that perhaps Thomas had been killed by the Klan. But why go after the one member of the family who seemed to share the Klan's racist views?

Speaking of likely suspects, there was one more individual I wanted to look up. I wasn't sure if there would be anything about Augustus Trabor in the archives. Surprisingly, there was. He showed up, of course, on the muster rolls for the NC Second Mounted Infantry, along with William Quinn. His postwar activities also drew some attention in the newspapers of the times. As noted in Carson's journal, he was a wanted man, implicated in a string of crimes that included bootlegging, highway robbery, and murder. It appeared that old Gus followed Pa's instructions to leave the state, but he didn't get far. He continued to lead his outlaw ways on the North Carolina–South Carolina line. When the government finally caught up with him in 1903, it pinned a slew of charges on him that included the murder of federal agents in both Madison and Henderson Counties.

Carson had been right; his pa had let Trabor go only to have him kill again. Could Trabor have later murdered Thomas? He was among the suspects at the time, but as far as I could tell, the authorities did not charge him with that killing. He was found guilty of the other murders, and Augustus Trabor was executed by hanging in 1905. He had the dubious distinction of being one of the last people hanged by the state of North Carolina. In 1909 the state banned it and switched to the electric chair for state-sponsored killing.

With the fruit of my research stored as digital images on my camera, I packed up and headed out. The more I learned about the Quinns, the more questions I had. First, though, it was off to Greensboro, my hometown and that of Aurelius Quinn, where I was going to reckon with my own brother.

Greensboro is an hour away from Chapel Hill, and Andrew's house is a two-story Tudor in a tree-lined neighborhood. I pulled into the drive and cut the engine. I listened to the car sighing and neighborhood kids shouting in the distance and a mockingbird singing every song it knew from the crest of the neighbor's roof. The freshly cut lawn glowed a deep green in the slanting sunlight. It was everything I had never wanted.

Andrew emerged from the front door and practically bounded over to me.

"Hey, sis!" He seemed oblivious to the way our last conversation had ended. After delving so deeply into a possible fratricide, I couldn't sustain any real anger at my brother. My ego wasn't that fragile. It was just money.

"Andrew." I climbed from the car to give him a hug.

He led me inside. The house seemed unnaturally silent. "Natalie and the kids still at the beach?"

"Yep. Just me here during the week. I'll go down to see them after work on Friday."

"Just like Dad would do when we were at the cabin all summer," I said. Andrew had followed our father's footsteps into a life of family, respectability, and work.

Andrew winced. "I've been putting his house in order." He sighed. Sadness weighed on his shoulders. "Come on in."

Inside was orderly, if not clean. He led me back to his man-cave/home office, a converted bedroom that featured one wall full of trophies, another with a big-screen television, an assortment of sports pennants, jerseys, souvenirs, and a massive desk. He sat not at the desk, but on a leather love seat in front of the television, on which a golfer pondered a putt. I sat down beside him and he flicked off the television.

"Look," he said. "I'm sorry about the tax thing. It's my fault. I'll figure it out."

"No need. It sorted itself out."

"What?"

I explained about the trees and the adelgid. How they were, in death, helping to pay for the cabin by becoming the cabin. "You can use the remaining funds in the account to pay the tax."

"What about my tree?"

"Your tree?" The leather seat crinkled when I shifted.

"The one Dad cut the limbs off so I would have handholds to be able to climb. I loved that tree."

It was a younger one down the hill from the giants that had been felled. I remembered it well, but for some reason it surprised me that Andrew remembered, and even more that he cared. This had seemed like a purely financial deal for him.

"It's fine for now. We have to treat the healthy ones with an insecticide to save them."

"Good. You know, I really am glad you're doing this. I hadn't thought about that place in ages, but I've been thinking about it ever since you started this project. Brings back the memories."

"That it does," I agreed.

He pushed himself up and strode over to a cherry sideboard that matched his desk. On it sat enough booze to keep an Irishman drunk for a lifetime.

"Gracious, Andrew!" I said. "Do I need to take you to the nearest AA meeting? Do not pass go, do not collect $200?"

He chuckled. "Blame Dad, not me. This all came from his place. Behold our inheritance." He turned and held out one hand like Bob Barker in front of "your brand-new car!"

I stood to get a closer look. I had never seen so much liquor outside of a bar. There were dozens of whiskeys, Scotches, brandies, and rum. Beside them sat an array of unlabeled crystal decanters and bottles filled with unknown liquids.

"I don't remember Dad drinking much at all." I looked up at my brother. "Did he start after I left?"

"Nope." Andrew turned a tequila bottle by the neck to square it with the others. "This is what happens when you drink a little bit of a lot of things over fifty years."

"What a collection!" I was learning so much today.

"I've got something special for you." He pulled a Mason jar from the mix. The liquid inside was clear. On a piece of masking tape affixed to the lid was written, "Ed Duncan. 1958."

I turned the jar over in my hands, examining it. History come to life again. The original mountain dew, white lightning, moonshine. Old man Duncan's cackle reverberated in my head, an echo of a time long passed.

"There are several jars. Different years. Different colors."

"Wow," was all I could say.

"I've been waiting to open one up. It didn't seem right without you."

"Pick one." I extended the jar back to him.

He tapped the lid of the jar I was holding, grabbed two tumblers, and we went out back. He and Natalie had added a brick patio with a terra-cotta chiminea since I had last visited. We sat in comfortable Adirondack chairs. On the glass-topped table between us, the jar waited to be opened. Andrew met my eyes, nodded, and cracked open the moonshine. He sniffed it.

He shook his head. Hard. "These must be 80-proof fumes."

I took a whiff. My sinuses erupted, scorched by the drink.

"Okay." Andrew poured out two servings.

"I don't think I can do this." I cringed. I hadn't had anything to drink in months.

"Do it for Dad." He lifted his tumbler. "To good old Dad, who drank just enough to leave us a lot."

"To Dad," I said through gritted teeth. That feeling you get at the top of a roller coaster roiled my insides.

"Bottoms up, sis."

I braced myself, then downed the liquor. It wasn't as bad as it smelled. There was a sweetness to it that cut the fire. But then it hit hard, took the breath out of me like a hard fall. Onto cement. From a great height.

"Whew!" Andrew exclaimed. "Wowza!"

"You can say that again."

"Whew! Wowza!"

We sat across from each other, owl-eyed and mute. Fireflies danced in the grass, and the elm tree spun above us.

"Did you know that Dad went back to the cabin a couple times each year for a while after Mom died?"

Curiosity cocked his head. "That so?"

"Yeah. I had no idea."

"Me either. He never said anything about it, never even mentioned the cabin."

It's remarkable how little we know about even those closest to us.

"More?" Andrew extended the jar my way.

"You must be kidding me."

He set the jar down.

"How did Daddy wind up with Ed Duncan's booze?" I asked.

"He didn't."

"What do you mean?"

"Mom did." He straightened his hair with his hand as if Mom had shot him one of her looks and bit his lower lip.

"Mom?"

"She used to go down to the old codger's porch and listen to his stories. She wrote them down, and he'd send her back with a new jar each time."

"How did I not know this?" I brought my feet up into the chair and backed myself into its depths.

"Probably because you were always off doing your own thing. Wandering around in the woods or whatever it was you did. I tagged along with her since you weren't around to babysit me. You know, you never babysat me."

"No one ever babysat me," I said. "Besides, it was serious archaeology I was doing, unearthing great mysteries. Turns out misidentifying parts of a still as farming implements." I lifted the tumbler to my nose, took a sniff that tickled my nose hairs, and put it back down.

"Yeah, well." He actually took another sip of the moonshine. His eyes watered like he'd bitten into a ghost pepper. "You know, I've been going through all of Dad's stuff, gotten rid of nearly everything, and there's hardly anything of Mom's. It's like he let her go entirely."

"Not entirely."

"What do you mean?"

"The cabin. It was hers. He held on to it."

He poured himself another splash of the moonshine, raised it to his lips, then grimaced. "Geez," he said. "That's too much." He set the tumbler down. "What do you say we break into the gin? I've got some tonic and lime."

"Oh yes, please!" I was grateful for something that wouldn't sear my insides like molten lava.

He mixed the gin and tonics inside and brought them out on a tray. As the day dimmed into night, lights came on automatically, illuminating the outstretched limbs of the giant elm overhead.

"I found something in the cabin," I confessed. "It's a jour-

nal." I shared with him the story of the murder of Thomas
Quinn and Carson Quinn's journal.

"Dang," he said. "That's heavy. Too bad Mom didn't find
that journal, though. That's the kind of thing she would have
loved."

"Yeah." My throat caught. "She would have loved it."

We sat through nightfall nursing our gin and tonics. A gentle
silence settled between us. Memories bubbled up and broke the
silence, like sea creatures breaching the surface of still waters
only to disappear, leaving behind the slightest ripple.

"Hey, sis," he said after a time, "I've got something for you."

"Yeah?"

He rose unsteadily from the chair, then disappeared into the
house. He returned carrying a wooden box. He held it out in
front of him like some holy relic and set it down on the table
between us.

It was clearly an heirloom. Made of mahogany, it had brass
reinforced corners and silver handles that folded into special
grooves flat against the sides. On the front, directly above the
keyhole, initials had been stamped: H.L.C. From the initials, I
knew this did not belong to my father. Those were my mother's
grandfather's initials. Harold Linus Crest.

"This is it," he said. "The only thing he had of hers in that
old house."

"You mean other than that terrible booze." My attempt at
humor masked my sudden unease.

"You're going to want to be alone when you open this."
Andrew pulled a silver skeleton key from his chest pocket and
handed it to me. "You might want to wait until you get home."

He ran his hand again through his thinning hair and gave me
the same little smirk that my father used to use. "I'm turning
in," he said. "Goodnight."

"'Night," I said. "Would you turn the lights off?"

"You bet," he said. "It's not Costa Rica, but the stars here
are pretty good."

The door squealed shut behind him and then it went dark.

I let my eyes acclimate by staring at the darkness of the box. Once the box came into better focus, I craned my neck to take in the night sky. Vega and Lyra were there as always in the summer, and I could see off to the west the constellation Aquila anchored by the bright star Altair. While Western eyes drew an eagle with the stars, the Chinese called it the cowherd star. They told the story of the goddess Zhinu who fell in love with a poor human cowherd. She descended to earth to marry him, and they had children together. When her mother, the Queen of Heaven, discovered this, she made her daughter return to the other side of the Milky Way. After the banishment, her children could only visit once a year, on the seventh day of the seventh lunar month. Magpies would form a bridge over the Milky Way so the children could cross into heaven.

I looked at the box. It sat heavy in the darkness. I had the sense that maybe it was my flock of magpies, and just maybe, it would take me to my mother.

17

August 11, 1889—I am now an uncle. It's a mighty peculiar thing, seeing as how I don't have any uncles of my own. On second thought I reckon I do, but I've met nary a one of them. Ma says she has five brothers. Two of them live somewhere here in the United States. She thinks they're probably out west somewhere. The other three live back in County Sligo, Ireland. I aim to be an uncle little Flora Lee knows and loves. In order to meet Flora, we went down to Flat Rock for a big get-together at Sarah and Robert's home.

Flora's not much to look at. She looks kind of like a piglet, if you ask me. But Ma thinks she's just adorable. I ain't held a baby before, and when they gave her over to me, Ma had to show me how to handle her. She was warm and cooed like a hen. One of the most surprising things I've seen in a long time was Pa with the baby. He picked her up and walked around with her just as natural as if he was a wet nurse. My pa continually amazes me. He's the hardest man in four counties, but handles a baby more comfortably than he handles a gun.

Gramps, I suppose that's Great-Gramps to Flora, acted the fool, of course. He leaned over her and made all manner of faces and noises. And he sang her that terrible song about a cradle and a tree and falling. Taylor didn't want to hold her. He said holding babies wasn't anything he had interest in at all. But Thomas did, and he even rocked her awhile. Marinda was there. She saw that and went over to him and looked down over his shoulder as he sat with the baby in the rocking chair. They glanced at each other over that baby's head, and it was like some sort of fancy painting, a painting that I cared not a lick for.

It was all a bit much for little Flora Lee and she got fussy, so the menfolk went out on the porch. Robert gave ever one of us, except Taylor, a cigar to smoke.

"Cuban," he said. "The finest cigars in the world."

It felt like a day of accomplishments to me. First, I became an uncle. Then, I'm considered adult enough to smoke a Cuban cigar. The cigar itself wasn't anything to write home about at first. It was like holding any old rolled-up leaf in your mouth.

Thomas said, "Cassanova, you're supposed to breathe it in. Don't just chew on it."

I glared at my brother. I took a big breath of that cigar, and the next thing I knew my lungs were on fire and my head was a-spinning. I spat into the spittoon, and Thomas erupted into laughter. If it'd been just me and him, I'd a shoved him clean over the porch railing.

"Boys," Pa said. That was enough to quiet us down. I did not take another toke of that cigar, but I kept my eye on Thomas. I could tell he was still laughing at me under his breath, and maybe it wasn't entirely about that there cigar.

Pa turned his attention to Robert. "How are your…enterprises…going?" he asked, making the word *enterprise* sound equivalent of pillaging or murdering.

"Coming along quite well, sir," Robert said. Robert is unfailingly polite. "We've got a mill scheduled for completion in about two months down in Rutherford, and a second one outside of Aiken that should be producing in six months."

Pa did the thing where he sniffs hard. Those of us who know him know it means he's displeased. Others may think he's just got a runny nose.

"We hope to have six total going in a year's time," Robert boasted.

"And every one of those plants is only going to produce cottonseed oil?" Pa pointed his cigar at Robert like a dagger.

"That's right." Robert pushed a cascade of smoke out of the side of his mouth.

"What happens if the price of cotton goes up or if the price of cottonseed oil goes down? You thought of that?"

"We're sufficiently capitalized to be able to absorb fluctuations in the marketplace."

"What the heck does that mean?" Taylor asked.

"They've got money," I answered.

"And you can get rid of some workers if you need to one year," Pa said. "Hire them back the next, right?"

Robert eyed Pa in the way you might eye a timber rattler. "Only as a last resort. Remember, Will, this is not just about turning a profit. We hope to provide employment, education, and general welfare as part of the operation. Manufacturing is the key to the South's resurrection."

Gramps piped up. "Who is this 'we' you keep talking about?"

"Me and my partners have formed a firm called John-Lor Incorporated. John-Lor is a combination of the last names of the two principals, Johnston and Baylor."

"How many of you is there?" Thomas asked.

"We're five partners total. Mr. Baylor and I have fifty-one percent ownership, and the other three make up the rest between them."

Pa sat back, took a long draw on his cigar, and gazed off at the Blue Ridge in the distance. "I reckon you got it all figured out."

"What I ain't got figured out," Taylor announced to everybody, "is what the heck you do with cottonseed oil."

Robert cleared his throat. "Why, cottonseed oil is about as versatile a product as one could be," he said. "It's superior to just about any other oil for cooking and frying. It's also highly prized as a lubricant for machines, and the more factories this country builds the higher in demand cottonseed oil will become. It's an essential ingredient in many manufactured products, from soap to medicines. Of course, we have a chemist in our employ who is testing the transferability of cottonseed oil to a variety of products. It turns out that there is no limit to what you can use the oil for. Why, you can even run machinery on it. Our plants will run entirely on their end product. If that's not efficiency, then I don't know what is. Right now, it's considered a by-product, but in time cotton will be grown specifically for its oil."

Pa clicked his teeth and shook his head and stared off at the mountains.

"Will," Robert said. "We have many high-ranking members of the Farmers Alliance that support us, you know."

Pa turned to Robert and glared at him hard. If he'd a looked at me like that, I'd have wilted like a fern in a drought. He said real stern-like, "Membership in the Alliance doesn't grant omnipotence."

Taylor, ever the interested one, piped up, "Pa, what's wrong with cottonseed oil? Sounds smart to me."

Pa cleared his throat. "Nothing's wrong with the product itself. The problem's in what it represents. Poor farmers will get in debt to grow more cotton instead of your corn, potatoes, tomatoes, melons, what have you. When the price drops, then they'll lose their farms and have to go to work for your brother-in-law here. Then, a decade or two down the line, when some other product proves more profitable than cottonseed oil, all them mills will go out of business and the workers will lose their jobs. No farm, no job, then what?"

Pa commenced to rocking. He is the most stubborn person I know. The future is coming, and it's coming fast, but he's dead set on fighting it tooth and nail.

Gramps tapped his lacquered cane twice on the wood floor. "Enough of this talk of markets and oil. Let's move on to something less contentious, like religion. Now, Robert, you are Episcopalian and Sarah is a Methodist that goes to a Baptist church. What exactly does that make young Flora? Would she be Episcobaptist? Or, perhaps Methobaptalian?"

Everyone laughed at that. If Gramps is good at anything, it's setting things right. The older I get, the wiser he seems.

October 17, 1889—Stanley McFarland and I got into it again. He's the son of the judge from up in Boone and the one who tried to steal our money last year. I was out by the tulip poplar minding my own business reading my assignment for Greek, a play by Aristophanes. written in Greek. Stanley came and sat down beside me. He's never showed much interest in me before, especially after I laid into him.

"Why don't you go play football with the others?" I suggested. "They got a game going."

"They won't let me," he said. "They say I'm too rough."

"For football?"

"That's what I said."

As surprised as I was that he chose to make friends with me, I actually wanted to do my reading. "Don't you have to read this too?"

"It's all Greek to me." His portly body jostled as he laughed at his own joke.

"Ain't that the point?"

"You're some sort of stick in the mud, ain't you?" he said. "What is it, Quinn? You too good for the rest of us?"

I hadn't ever thought about that. Of course, I'm not too good. That's kind of the point, in order to keep up with everybody else, I have to work twice as hard. That, and I need to keep my nose clean so I don't get thrown out of Newton.

"No," I answered. "I ain't too good for nobody."

"Why don't you ever play football with us, then?"

"Football don't suit me," I said. "I'm no good at it."

"You don't play baseball neither," he said. "You know what I heard about you?"

I knew then that Stanley wasn't trying to be friendly at all. I could see what was coming, and as badly as I wanted to stop it, I sat there and let it come.

"What's that, Stanley?"

"Your family's a bunch of nigger lovers. Your brother told me about that there Happy Land and how your grandfather saved it for them and how your pa was a Yankee. You Quinns ain't right."

I stared hard at my book. In reality I wasn't reading it. I was just staring at them indecipherable pages hoping that Stanley would up and go away if I ignored him.

Since I gave him no response, he shoved me.

In my mind I became Henry the mule in terms of stubbornness. He was not about to move me.

"You must not mind being a nigger lover. It must be true." I finally looked at him. I'm real proud of what I said, and I hope Pa will be proud, too, that I didn't kill that boy. "Let me get something straight," I said. "First, didn't I already put you in the infirmary once? Why would you want to go through that again? Second, what's wrong with loving another human being? Ain't you Christian? Jesus don't say nothing in there about only loving the neighbors what look like you. In fact, I believe he says something about loving everybody regardless of whether they're tax collectors or thieves. So why don't you go away and come back with something actually insulting if you really want a walloping so bad."

Just then the headmaster came around the corner. Stanley jumped up and ran off toward the football game. The headmaster stood over me. He put a stiff hand on my shoulder.

"Mr. Quinn," he said, "I believe you're on the righteous path now."

He held that hand on my shoulder for a long minute, then disappeared into the building. While I'm right pleased with the way I handled Stanley, it ain't all that pleasing to be told by the headmaster that I'm on some righteous path. I guess as long as I don't get thrown out, that will do. I only have six more months here at Newton. If I can make it through that period, I'll be free from the Rodney Websters of the world.

January 12, 1890—I've been ruminating on what Ma told me about Marinda, about her never being able to leave Daisy. Her parents aren't old or decrepit. They can handle themselves while she's away. Then she went and said she ain't no Quinn. Not yet at least. I aim to make her a Quinn.

All my life I have wondered what lies on the other side of them mountains. To see a horizon then sally toward it until another appears in its stead, this is what I've always yearned for. What if by venturing forth into the wide world I will never explore Marinda's mysteries? What if she is my horizon? Vexation grips me like a snapping turtle. It is only three months before I finish with Newton and the headmaster forever. Then I will either leave Daisy or not. I'll go down to the university or stay put in the Gap.

When I was back home this past Christmas, Marinda and I talked about this. It didn't feel like Christmas at all. The weather was so warm the jonquils got confused and started to bloom. We took a walk through her pa's apple orchard. He feared that them apple trees might start to blossom, then a freeze would hit and kill every one of them.

We climbed up through the orchard, keeping an eye out for any overeager trees, but it turned out I was the only overeager one. I offered her my hand several times, but she didn't take it. And then I went to kiss her, but something about her lips was different.

"Carson," she said, when we paused to look back over toward the creek. "Don't come back."

"Why would you say that?" I took the end of tree branch between my fingers and felt for early budding.

"After you finish with school, go on down to that university of yours. It's what you've always wanted after all. This here ain't big enough for you." She swept her arm toward the orchard, but she meant Daisy and the Gap and probably the county too.

"I reckon that's what everybody expects of me. Gramps would kill me if I didn't go. I'll come back. I promise."

"Come back. But don't come back for me."

Her words hit me harder than that Stanley when he hit Taylor. She didn't draw blood, but she might as well have. I turned to an apple tree that had started to bud out. "This one," I said. "Your pa's going to need to tend to it."

She flagged it with a piece of ribbon. "You always talk about where you're headed. You look at them mountains and want to see what's on the other side of them. I've never heard you say nothing about staying put, setting down roots, having a family."

"I reckon in time I'd want just that."

"In time." She took my hand. We continued on through the orchard, talking no more of the future. We set ribbons on a dozen or so trees. She and her pa are going to try to save them from freezing, but nature ain't so kind as to let overeagerness go unpunished.

<p style="text-align:center">&

The mystery of whether Carson had murdered Thomas seemed no closer to resolution, but the knowledge that my own mother had taken an interest in these families spurred me forward. It also left me reeling. How had I not known that about her? What else about her had I missed as a self-absorbed teenager?

The morning after our late night, I packed up the car, hugged Andrew goodbye, and drove back up the mountain. In the back of the Subaru sat her box, still unopened, in which perhaps lay some answers to the questions I was pondering. My mind kept drifting back to it, locking on to it, and a constant unease stirred in my belly. I desperately wanted to open it, yet I knew that whatever was in there might change my life forever.

Three hours later, I pulled into the gravel driveway. I emerged from my car to a peculiar sound: silence. There were no screaming saws or pounding hammers or shouts of instructions from Micah to his crew. Birds trilled in the tops of the hemlocks, and a squirrel welcomed me home with eager clucking. I had grown so used to the cacophony of progress and the state of perpetual toil that I never considered that the end might be in sight.

"Hello, the house!" I called out, thinking it empty.

"Hello, the car!" the house replied.

I climbed the rock stairs and saw it at long last: the end, as expressed by Micah sitting on a rocking chair on the porch, bottle of beer in hand.

He reached down into an ice-filled cooler at his feet. "Have one," he said, extending the dripping bottle my way.

I took it, popped it open, and plopped down in the empty rocking chair by his side.

"All done, boss." He rocked back, took a tug on his bottle, and let out a satisfied sigh.

"How did I not see this coming?" I popped the bottle cap off against the arm of the rocker, sparking a boyish grin from him.

"You've been so preoccupied with your research"—He made air quotes when he said *research*—"that you haven't noticed what my crew and I have been up to. And I haven't bothered you with the details."

I chuckled. "I guess you're right."

"The inspector left about an hour ago." He handed me a sheet of paper inscribed with a series of numbers, check marks, and cryptic verbiage. I would have better understood five-thousand-year-old hieroglyphs. I said as much to Micah. "It's your certificate of completion," he explained. "Means you can now legally occupy the dwelling."

"What's the fun in that?" I abruptly withdrew the hand I had unconsciously placed on Micah's shoulder. What was I doing again? Why did flirting come so easily around Micah?

"Now for the not-so-fun part." He pulled another sheet of paper from a notebook and placed it on a clipboard that he handed to me.

This one I understood. The final bill. But it was wrong, completely wrong. The total was a fraction of what I was expecting, even with the substantial discount for the hemlocks.

"Micah?" I asked. "What's this?"

"Well," he said, defensively, "it's what you owe me. You know, for all this." He pointed at the sparkling cabin, sitting prettier than ever.

"It's not nearly enough."

"That's the bill. I don't know what else to tell you."

"I was out of sorts at first," I said. "But I'm pretty sure you told me it was probably going to cost at least double this amount."

"I employ the Scotty principle when it comes to estimating."

"What?"

"You know, 'Beam me up, Scotty,' from *Star Trek*. Captain Kirk asks for the impossible, Scotty says it can't be done, then figures out a way to do it. He buys himself time by constantly overestimating the time needed to complete the impossible."

"Okay." My hand again found its way to his shoulder. "I'm sure that makes sense in your brain, but the rest of us in this conversation are located here on planet Earth."

He pointed the open bottle toward me. "Caroline, I can't figure you out. You're not the typical woman by any means. You seem like a chick that would get a *Star Trek* reference, being an astronomy nerd and all."

"Chick?" The hairs on the back of my neck bristled. "Likewise, you're not the typical contractor, and I would have pegged you as the evolved kind of man who would never, ever use 'chick' to describe a woman."

His face turned the color of Mars, which he hid by taking a swig of his beer. "Sorry," he said, wiping his mouth on his sleeve. "I don't know where that came from. I haven't used that term in a long, long time. It's probably the beer that brought it out."

"Take another swig and have the beer wash it back down."

He took a long pull, cutting his eyes at me like a freshly scolded toddler. I turned my attention to my beer and looked out over the hollow. Our chairs rocked slow and steady rhythms. Cackling birdsong splintered the silence.

"Now that's a pileated woodpecker," he said.

"You know," I said. "My *research*." I repeated his use of air quotes with the term.

"Mmm-hmm."

"You're going to think this is ridiculous."

"Shoot," he said.

"When I was kid...I...I encountered what most people would call a ghost in this cabin."

"I actually don't think that's ridiculous." He gave me an earnest once-over.

"You don't strike me as someone who believes in ghosts."

"I'm not inclined to dismiss anyone else's authentic experience." He swirled the bottle, as if checking the remaining level, then finished it off.

"Who are you?" An involuntary giggle surfaced and escaped. A wry grin twisted his lips. "Just Micah Turner."

"There's no *just* about it." The heat went to my cheeks. I knew I was blushing, so I switched the subject fast. "You know that metal box we pulled from the cabin?"

"Uh-huh."

"Didn't belong to my father."

"No shit."

"It belonged to a former occupant of this cabin, a man by the name of Carson Quinn. That's what my *research* has been all about."

"Carson Quinn," he repeated, savoring the syllables. "The ghost has a name."

"How many more of these are in there?" I swiveled my empty toward him.

"I didn't count." He arched an eyebrow. "Why don't we find out?"

We drank two beers each in silence, and my mind drifted back to Woody. He would have stopped drinking by now. Two was always his limit. Never one to exceed the moderation demanded by good health and clear-mindedness, he would have placed a loving hand on my shoulder and suggested we turn our attention to something other than beer. Not Micah. No, Micah knew that certain occasions such as this one required excess.

"So." He broke the silence. "You worried about spending the night inside?"

"Worried?" It hadn't occurred to me to be worried. After all, having a roof would certainly be an improvement over the tent out back.

"About the ghost?"

I found myself biting my lip, a gesture I had given up long ago. "I hadn't thought about it."

"When's the last time anyone spent the night here…that you know of?"

I thought back, my not-quite-sober mind racing uncontrollably into the past. All the way back to high school. After Mom died, we never came back. It had been nearly thirty years.

"Discounting all the unknown hippies and drifters, it's been a long time," I said. "You would have been knee high to a turkey the last time someone who was supposed to be here spent the night here."

"You turning local on me?" His loose fist playfully tapped my shoulder.

"Reckon so," I drawled, channeling the accent I imagined Carson Quinn to have, given his peculiar verbiage in the journal.

Six empties lined the front porch railing like a squadron of soldiers ready for inspection before another word was spoken. I'd had no hesitation about sleeping in the cabin until now.

"Damn you," I said.

"Me?"

"Number one." I raised my pointer finger. "You've got me thinking about the possibility of that ghost. Number two, I'm drunk."

He took a deep breath, let out a resigned sigh. "All right then, Caroline."

"All right what?"

"If you insist, I'll spend the night."

Ignoring his suggestion, I stood. "I suppose I should inspect your work before I pay you."

"Fair enough."

We went inside. I was expecting the interior to be finished, but not furnished. The rascal had gone and emptied the storage bin. The dining room table stood in the dining room alongside an old sideboard that had been recovered prior to demolition. In the living room, my curio cabinet sparkled fresh and clean in the corner. In the bedroom was a bed, assembled and made, my grandmother's old patchwork quilt covering it like the wrapping on a present.

"You planned this." I turned to him, punching his chest lightly.

His look of feigned innocence told me everything I needed to know. I found myself leaning in, my lips searching for his. In the back of my mind stirred a doubt as to whether the old bed would be up to this. It didn't matter. His kiss cleared all thoughts from my mind. Gone were any worries about the ghost or doubts about fooling around with him or anything except for his lips and his arms and his warm body.

There was no ghost that night, and I don't think we would have noticed one if it had been there, as focused as we were on each other. With the morning, sunlight streamed through the window and danced on Micah's bare chest. He caressed my back. A lightness I hadn't felt in years buoyed me.

"Caroline, I have a confession to make, and you're not going to like it."

I took a deep breath. My mind swirled in search of something, anything that would lower my opinion of Micah at this point. Nothing came to mind.

"Look." The figure eight he had been tracing on my back evaporated as he laid his palm flat. "Three months ago, when you had me come out to estimate this job, was not the first time I'd been here, to this cabin."

"What?" I pushed myself up, befuddled.

"You remember when I said Charles Duncan had expelled me from school?"

I nodded.

"It wasn't for anything I did at school. He caught me and my friends up here on that very porch."

He must have seen my jaw set and felt my back go rigid. I sat all the way up, pulling the sheet to cover my chest.

Micah retreated, bringing his hands to his lap. "I know. I should have told you. But I didn't think you'd let me do the work if I told you, and this job has been my opportunity to pay something back."

"That's why you only charged half?"

"Yes. And I know that's not enough. That bill covers the

materials and the labor for my crew. I'm not charging you a dime for my time."

My voice came out in the professorial tone honed by years in the classroom. "You could have told me. It would have saved me some stress."

He stared at me like a sophomore back from spring break. "I was a different person back then. I'd say I was mixed up in the wrong crowd, but that would be a cop-out. I was the crowd. We thought being cool meant living a hard, wild life listening to Black Sabbath and Slayer and doing all the drugs available to country boys in the early nineties. Saturday nights we would go out and find old, abandoned homes and cabins, get high, and trash them. We kept the volunteer fire departments busy. I was already on probation when Charles Duncan found me up here. That was the final straw."

He had intimated that he had a checkered past, so that part didn't surprise me so much. But his connection to this cabin, this place that was the physical representation of my father's love for my mother, hit hard. "Let me get this straight," I said.

He offered a contrite little nod.

"If it weren't for Charles Duncan chasing you off, this cabin wouldn't be standing now. Charles Duncan is the reason this place isn't just a pile of ash."

"Sort of," he said.

"How is it *sort of?* Either it is or it isn't."

He cleared his throat. "Charles Duncan is the best thing that ever happened to me. Him expelling me from school caused me to re-evaluate what was cool and subsequently turn my life around. The fact that he still hates me is a bit disappointing, but I suppose it's a small price to pay for a second chance. But he wasn't the one that kept us from destroying this place entirely. That came from a different realm entirely."

"The ghost." I pushed distance between us.

His unblinking eyes locked on mine. "I've always tried to blame it on the pot, but in the back of my mind was the knowl-edge that marijuana isn't exactly hallucinatory. Then last night you told me about your experience, and I kind of felt validated."

"Yeah, no. It wasn't the pot."

All of the lightness and joy I had felt upon waking beside him dissipated. "I can't do this," I said. "You're going to have to go."

He nodded and stood. "I'm sorry."

"I know." I softened my tone. "But understand that this isn't about what you did or didn't do twenty years ago."

"No?" He zipped up his jeans and pulled his T-shirt over his chest.

"You should have told me sooner. Instead, you let me believe Charles Duncan was even more terrible than he really is. That...that's cowardice, and it's unseemly." I heard Carson Quinn in my voice again, and I wasn't sure if I really believed what I was saying, but somehow the wisdom imparted by old Aurelius Quinn to his grandson had found its way into my outlook and speech.

"I best be going then." He patted his pockets and his chest, looked everywhere but in my eyes.

"First, hand me my purse." He pulled it from the dresser. I shook it to sift out the checkbook. I folded open the cover and made a check out in the amount of the invoice. The sound of the check being torn from the checkbook was perfunctory and professional, exactly like you'd expect from the termination of business transaction.

He took it, folded it without looking at it, and tucked it into his front shirt pocket. "This is awkward."

"Would you rather not be paid?"

"I'm sorry." He turned and left. The floorboards squealed. The screen door screeched and banged shut as he left.

18

May 25, 1890—Today should have been wondrous for I am done with the headmaster and Newton forever. Instead, it was the worst day of my life. I cannot imagine a viler day could ever strike me should I live to the age of Methuselah.

The following is nigh on impossible to put to paper, but I don't know what else to do. I fear to do anything else lest it lead to fratricide. Though the consequences of such might result in a bodily imprisonment that would appropriately accompany that of my soul. I dawdle. To wit, my brother has betrayed me. My own brother, Thomas.

When I arrived home, he had the nerve to congratulate me for my graduation. At the time, I thought little of it beyond that he was my brother and perhaps happy for me, or at least felt the compulsion of family obligation. But there was really only one person I cared to hear from. I immediately set off up the road to the Fallon home so that I could hear congratulations from the one I love.

Mrs. Fallon at first wouldn't let Marinda out to see me. She told me to go on home. I was befuddled. It made no sense. Only after I made it clear that I would not be leaving their front porch until I'd seen Marinda did she come out.

I didn't notice nothing askew at first. But when I went to hug and kiss her, I found more of her than there was when I left. Considerably more. Especially in the belly. I jumped back as if suddenly I realized I was kissing a mule instead of a girl.

Then I uttered the stupidest words ever to come out of my mouth. "What happened to you?"

She shook her head.

I saw out of the corner of my eye that both her ma and pa had come onto the porch, as if to protect her. They must not know me that well. I would never, ever harm a hair on Marinda Fallon's head. Not even now.

"Who done this to you?" I asked.

She was crying now, and I was thinking of that there corporal from Maryland and how maybe he had come back for her. Oh, how I wish now that had been the case. As soon as I had that thought, she said, "Thomas."

My head swirled. Nothing made any sense all of a sudden. "Did he attack you?"

She shook her head. "Carson, we're getting married come June."

I stumbled off the Fallon porch as if she'd shot me rather than stabbed my heart. I've never felt anything like it. I reckon I was crying, too, because I couldn't really see anything. There was this roar, like a waterfall, in my ears. Somehow, I got back to our house.

Pa was standing out between the road and the house with his hands on his hips. Taylor was kind of behind him. Ma and Gramps and Betsy Morgan were all standing on the porch. They were ready for this. They knew I'd come back from the Fallons' in this state. Boy did I make a fool of myself in front of all of them. I was spitting mad, and Thomas was nowhere around.

Pa stepped forward and placed his hands on my shoulders. I knew he was strong, but in that moment, I learned how strong. I couldn't have gone anywhere he didn't want me to go, as firm a hold as he had on me. He said, "Son."

All I could do was yell, so I did. I can't remember everything I said now. There was something in there to the effect of, "Get that lying, two-faced coward out here now." I'm sure I threatened to tear his head off his neck, among other things. I kicked and I hollered, but Thomas never showed his face. He still hasn't.

Thinking on it now, I'm sure it wasn't his idea to hide like a ninny. My brother is a traitor. He's a lying you-know-what. He ain't family to me no more. But I will give him this: he ain't no coward. I'm sure wherever he was, he was itching to fight. Let me you tell you something: it ain't over. He'll get his fight before all is said and done.

May 26, 1890—I went up to my Hemlock Hollow today. I reckon it will be the last I see of it, for I aim to set out and never come back here. The wind was stirring the tops of the trees such that they creaked and moaned. It was like the hollow itself was talking to me.

Turns out, I'm not the only one knows about this spot. I had perched myself on one of the big boulders beside the creek and was simmering like a vat of hot oil about what Thomas done to me, when I spied movement from above. The movement was bedecked in a blue summer dress. It was Ma.

She came on down to the creek and pulled herself up onto the rock beside me. "Son, we're worried about you."

"How'd you know where I was?" I asked.

"This is where I'd come if I were you." She surprised me. I ain't told no one about the hollow other than Marinda. "It's a magical place, isn't it?"

"How long have you known about it?" I asked.

"Ever since we moved into the white house. I came upon this glen once when I was out hunting ginseng. It's a special place. You can feel it, can't you?"

It was little disappointing to learn that I hadn't been the first to lay claim to this spot. But if it had to be anyone else, I'm happy it was Ma that found it before me.

"I'm so sorry for what has happened," she said.

I stared at her. Hard.

"No one knew how to tell you." She flattened her dress across her legs, her eyes tracking the creek down the mountain.

I swallowed. I had no words for her, for any of them.

"You can't see it now." She set her hand on my shoulder. "But this is for the better. Carson, you are free to see the world. You've always wanted that."

Finally, I got my tongue back. "This is all the world I need." I meant my Hemlock Hollow.

"A person could find peace here, that's for certain," Ma said. "You, my son, need more than a spot to sit. You need the earth stretched wide and inviting before you. You need to feel the wind at your back. You need to reach the last horizon. Thomas will never leave. He's not curious in the way you are."

"He don't love her like I do." Nobody could love another as I loved Marinda.

Ma touched my cheek softly. She frowned. She touched my hair, red like hers. "That's true, Carson. He doesn't love her like you do. But he does love her in his own way."

For some reason, hearing her say that kind of calmed me down a bit. It never occurred to me that maybe Thomas actually cared for Marinda. It was in my head that he had done what he done out of pure spite.

"I ain't done with him." I crossed my arms and pulled apart from her.

"For the love of your dear mother, please do not harm Thomas," she said. "He's your brother. He'll always be your brother."

"He don't act like it. Ain't never acted like it."

"He's his father's son. Sometimes his love doesn't feel particularly kind. He didn't do what he did to hurt you. Think about it, son. He's here, and so is Marinda. Who else would it be for him?"

"She was going to go away with me," I explained.

"To university?"

"They let women take courses now."

"Marinda's place is here. She's got her folks to care for. Imagine her at university. She'd be a fish in a forest in more ways than one."

"I taught her to read," I confessed.

"Is that right?"

"She read Socrates. She's as smart as anybody."

"Oh, my Carson." She wrapped her arms around me. I hugged her back. "You are something, aren't you?"

"I'll be heading out. If I aim to keep the promise I'm making to you right now not to hurt Thomas, I have to leave. Tomorrow at first light."

Ma didn't say anything. She was crying. I could tell she was tore up, so I said, "It ain't forever."

"I know," she said. "I know you'll be back. It's hard on a mother. You all have grown up so much."

We sat for a spell, listening to the wind and the trees. A redheaded woodpecker (*Melanerpes erythrocephalus*) came through squawking like they're apt to do. Then it sat on a giant poplar tree and hammered into it for a while. Ma climbed down from the boulder and left me to myself. She's uncanny about certain things, and she knew all I wanted then was to be alone. It was nigh on dark by the time I made it home.

Thomas still wasn't around. Since my belongings were still stashed away in my school trunk, I had nothing to pack. I asked Gramps and Taylor if they would drive me down to Logan's Inn where I could catch the coach eastward. I reckon I'll take it down to Salisbury, then get the train to Raleigh. We have family there. Gramps has a sister, my great-aunt Louise, who lives in the capitol. I've met her a time or two when she came up to visit. He says I can stay with her until classes start in Chapel Hill come September. Who knows how a fella can occupy himself for three months? It will be better than staying here, though. I fear I will not be able to keep my word to Ma should I ever actually see that traitor Thomas.

☙

That was it. The journal ended there. With my gloved hands, I leafed through the leather-bound relic, searching its blank pages for more. But this was where it stopped, with an entry that read like a prelude to fratricide.

My heart sank. From the census I had known that Thomas and Marinda had a child together, but I hadn't realized the timing of it. All that certainty about Carson Quinn's innocence evaporated. It made sense that everyone thought he murdered his brother given the crazed threats he had made in front of family and neighbors. But those threats had been made in 1890, and the murder didn't happen for another ten years.

I stood. Unease gripped me, both from the end of the journal and from the way things turned out with Micah. I could still feel his strong hands on my shoulders, could taste the beer on his breath. The figure-eight he had traced on my back that morning lingered still.

I became aware that I was alone in the cabin for the first time ever. Leaving the journal on the porch, I entered the old place, listening intently. It lay silent. I drifted from room to room, a ghost of my own making. Resentment clouded my mind. Resentment and disappointment in Micah and myself. I had perhaps seen in him what I wanted to see, and not what was. Which was the same old story for me when it came to relationships, and not unlike what happened to Carson.

My research project seemed at an end, for surely Carson had in fact killed Thomas. The rage described in that passage seemed real, seemed deadly, and now I had no doubt that he had the capacity to commit the worst crime imaginable.

I turned to the cabin, my sole remaining project. Though Micah and his crew had moved the few solid pieces of furniture back in, much still needed to be done. The cabin lay mostly empty. Upstairs contained no furniture. It would all have to be replaced. In a notebook, I jotted down the pieces I would need to get. One bed and dresser for upstairs, chairs for the dining room table, a sofa for the living room. Micah's unexpected gift of his time left me with more money than I had expected. That gesture caught in my mind for a second, and the resentment gave way ever so slightly. Maybe I had been too harsh.

I trawled through the cabin, admiring the fine finish-work, the stair rails wrought from rhododendron, the carefully laid-out patterns in the tongue-and-groove flooring, the perfectly stained walls. I appreciated the plumbing that worked, the old wood stove that had been cleaned up and re-attached to the chimney, the refurbished built-in bookcase. In the kitchen, he had installed a new range and refrigerator as part of the renovation. I would be able to cook, though I would have to use my camping implements for now, since the cabin contained no kitchen supplies.

In the living room I came to the curio cabinet. After unloading the car, I had placed my mother's box on top of it. Circumstances being what they were, I hadn't thought about it since. It had become like a dream forgotten. But there it sat, real as rain, as Mom would say. The cabin creaked as a breeze cut through the hollow.

I fished the key from my purse then moved toward the box, as if in a trance. I picked it up and carried it out to the front porch, where the light was better. All it would take would be a twist of the wrist, and the box would open. I took two deep breaths and looked around. The freshly painted porch, newly screened in, stood sturdy beneath me. The orange ball of my first memory had bounced across this very spot, the same spot where on a shady afternoon the summer before my senior year of high school, my mother had passed away. All things came from and led to this spot.

I had forged a path into an academic discipline where few women had tread before. I had ventured into jungles and climbed mountains and faced down malaria. But nothing in my life felt nearly as daring as turning that key.

The lock clicked, and the lid gave way.

The box was full of pages in my mother's precise handwriting. Poking from the midst of the splayed papers lay my mother's novel, as written in her own hand in a composition book.

My knees gave way. I collapsed into a squat against the sturdy wall of the cabin.

"Mom?" I asked aloud. No one answered. The refrigerator kicked on. A freshly made cube of ice clanged in the kitchen. A breeze whistled through the screen. I swallowed hard and opened the composition book.

The first page was a table of contents revealing a series of stories. The titles were:

"Caroline and The Crooked Chimney"

"Caroline Solves the Mystery of the Icelandic Wedding"
"Caroline Discovers the Door to Nowhere"
"Caroline and Blackbeard's Bounty"
"Caroline Saves a Bootlegger"
"Caroline in the Yucatan"
"Caroline Goes to Africa"

My hands quaked as I turned to the first page of text, which began:

> In the small mountain village of Duncanville lived a young girl named Caroline. She ventured into the uncharted unknown, facing great peril (and sometimes pirates, bootleggers, and thieves) to solve unsolvable mysteries, to wrestle priceless treasures from the clutches of forgotten time, and to discover what only she could, for she was the greatest explorer in all the land. These are her stories, and they are all decidedly, absolutely, unequivocally, completely, 100 percent true...

A heat more searing than Old Man Duncan's moonshine tore through my chest and belly. The porch went dark as a deluge of tears cascaded down my face. I gasped, unable to take a full breath. Putting the book back down to preserve it and to contain myself, I fell once again against the wall. I howled a full-throated shriek that echoed through the remaining hemlocks. I couldn't place the emotion I was feeling. It overwhelmed. It hurt more than anything had ever hurt before. It was as though my heart was being torn from my body. But at the same time, it was like something long dead was being revived inside me. And it was the best feeling I'd ever felt.

She didn't live to see me grow up, but by writing those stories, she had lived a life in full for me. I turned to "Caroline in the Yucatan." Where I had actually spent a significant amount of time, exploring, trying to solve mysteries. Mom had written it long before it really happened. I turned to Africa, where the Caroline that Mom wrote about lived in the jungle with gorillas, like Jane Goodall. I allowed a wholehearted cry to overcome me, gave into it entirely, and bawled until there were no tears left.

After all the tears and wailing, I lay spent on the porch floor unable to move. I didn't know whether minutes or hours had passed when I heard a voice calling out.

"Honey?"

The voice dripped Southern. "Mom?"

"Caroline?"

I pulled myself up. At the top of the stone stairs, a jar of sun tea in one arm, a portfolio in the other, and motherly concern on her face, Patsy Duncan peered through the screen door.

"Oh." I wiped my eyes and scrambled to my feet. "Patsy."

After adjusting my shirt, I opened the door for her, and she slid in. "Is everything okay?"

"Yes," I lied. "Come on in."

"Doesn't look like it," she said. Her eyes swept the porch, paused at the open box and at the journal which lay on the table where I'd left it, then darted back to me. "I heard you were back. I heard the renovation was finished. Just wanted to bring this tea by. You'd said how much you missed it."

She extended the jar of freshly brewed sun tea. I took it. Out of sorts still, I stood looking at her.

"Maybe," she said. "We should have a glass."

"I have ice now."

I took the jar into kitchen, doled out ice into two plastic cups, and poured the tea.

"Have a seat." I motioned toward the rocking chairs.

We sat side by side, rocking. Patsy, for once, seemed at a loss for words.

"I've finished the journal," I announced. "I think he did it."

She stopped rocking. "Really?"

I told her about the final entry in the journal, about how he vowed getting even with his brother, and how there was no more after that.

"Lordy," she said.

"I guess that's that."

"I have something else for you." She held out the portfolio.

I took it into my hands. It was an old black-leather portfolio, the kind an attorney would bring into a courtroom. I wondered why Patsy Duncan of all people would have such a thing.

"That belonged to Charles," she explained, "back when he was a school principal."

"Ahhh," I said. "Makes sense."

"Open it."

I pulled it open. Inside lay a thick bundle of old, yellowed envelopes. I thumbed through them. They bore a colorful collection of stamps and postmarks: Chapel Hill, Wilmington, Hawaii, Guam, Panama, San Francisco. The dates, some barely visible, ranged from the 1890 to the 1900. The earliest letters were all addressed the same way: Marinda Fallon Quinn, in care of Charlie Brightleaf, Edney Inn Road, Bat Cave, NC. My heart skipped.

"You got me going all through our attic looking for these," Patsy said. "I told you I would pull out all the stops, and that attic is sweltering in the summer. Turned out they weren't even in the attic. They were in an old secretary desk in our guest bedroom."

"How did you get them?"

"My mother helped Bella out after Marinda passed."

"Bella wouldn't have wanted them?"

"Lordy no. These were illicit letters from the man who murdered her father. Knowing my mother, she probably found them and took them to spare Bella the pain of knowing about them."

I looked back down at the bundle. A sliver of hope cut through my grief. Maybe I would solve this mystery yet.

"I don't need them," she said. "They're yours." She beamed with generosity.

I nodded.

"As long as you promise to tell me what you find out."

"Deal," I said.

She again looked past me to the box on the floor. She flattened her oh-so-red lips and blinked her long eyelashes at me.

"I was just going through something of my own mother's,"
I explained. "She died when I was seventeen."

She placed her hand on my arm. "You know, it doesn't matter how or when they go. It's never easy when mothers pass."

I placed my own hand on top of hers. Her words gave me
comfort.

She took a breath and stood. "I should let you be."

"One second," I said.

I went into the kitchen and pulled a jar of my own out of
the box I'd unloaded from the back of the car. This wasn't the
use I had planned for it, but it would do, perhaps even better.

"Here." I held out a jar of a clear liquid, labeled *Ed Duncan,
1962*.

"Lordy," she exclaimed, giggling. "Doesn't this beat all!"

"I know Charles doesn't care much for his father. But maybe
he'll like what his father made."

Patsy leaned forward and gave me a hug. "I can't wait to
share this with him."

Mom's voice echoed over the decades, and I heard her dis-
tinctly saying, "Dan prefers me without hair on my chest." Old
Ed Duncan's cackle merged with the cawing of crows in the
hemlocks.

"Be seeing you." I watched the prim back of Patsy's head
bob down the steps into the hollow.

19

September 24, 1890
Chapel Hill, NC

My Dearest Marinda,

I hope you know you still have a hold on my heart. For some reason, I can't bring myself to hate you the way I hate Thomas. Every thought of you inspires the bitterest sweetness possible. I think of you often, despite the fact that by now, you will have become the mother of his child.

Things are different down here. There are no mountains to hide the horizon. If you climb any of the local hills, such as the one called Piney Prospect, you can see mile upon mile of flatlands, with no mountain to end it all. I think it is for the best that you didn't come with me. There are a smattering of women around who sometimes sit in on the more advanced classes, but they are not considered full students. None are your equal. I daresay that we would see each other only a little more than we already do now, which is not at all. To be honest, my lovely Marinda, I am not so sure this place is for me either. While I love my classes, natural philosophy being my favorite, the other fellas here are not kind to me. They have taken to calling me everything but my proper name. I am the Loping Loo-Loo (on account of how I walk) and the Mountain Stork and the Orang-utan Man (on account of my red hair). There are traditions here I know nothing of, such as what they call "freshing." I messed up real big with that. Apparently, if you don't allow the older fellas to degrade you, you are outcast forever.

I put a fella in the infirmary when he and his friends tried to pour hot tar on me. This boy has a last name attached to more influence than mine. Now I am on some sort of probation, wherein should I mess up again, I will be expelled from this place. There are moments when anger takes ahold of me, and

I have no control. My pa warned about this. I reckon he has it too. I struggle mightily against it.

I take long walks by myself. There is much here to explore, as there are plenty of forests and streams close by. One fella I get along particularly well with is Uncle Jerry. He's a colored fella that works on campus. I have run into him out fishing, and he tells me all the secrets of campus. It is because of him that I was able to find a pleasant spot south of campus called the Fairy Vale. President Battle is said to have cut the trail to that spot himself. It reminds me a tad of my Hemlock Hollow. I go there when I need to find quiet. Uncle Jerry often comes around to sell us fresh food, such as fish and eggs and vegetables. Some of the other boys are quite mean to him on account of his complexion. I reckon that could be why we get along so well together. He reminds me some of Old Man Rolly.

The fella I share a room with is also interesting. His name is Shadrock Williams. It's a puzzling name, ain't it? He's from down in Wilmington. His family used to own the biggest bank in town, but they no longer do. They lost it in the war. He's a nice enough fella, only he spends a lot of time trying figure out how to get out of doing his schoolwork. If he were to put as much effort into doing the work as he does in trying to get out of it, he would vastly improve his standing.

Oh, my dearest Marinda, life seems so gloomy without you. I know we shall never have the future I had dreamed of. But I can't forsake my feelings for you. My deepest hope is that you find happiness even if I never do.

With a Heavy Heart,

Carson

December 1, 1890

My Dearest Marinda,

I regret to inform you that I shall not be coming home this Christmas. I could offer the excuse that it is too far to travel for so short a break, but the truth is that I could not stand to see my brother. I fear what might transpire should our paths cross.

I shall go to Wilmington with my roommate for the break. His father is gone and all he has is his mother and sister, who run a boarding house. Besides, I have never seen the ocean, and I aim to go out to Wrightsville while there, to see what a horizon really looks like.

My classes have gone well this term. I expect to make high marks in all subjects, including algebra, geology, and Latin. All I do is study, so it would be greatly disappointing to perform poorly. I suppose my favorite course this term was natural philosophy. I have learned all about the teachings of Sir Isaac Newton in that class and considered things I had never before considered.

I must express my utmost gratitude for your last letter. It fills my heart to read your words of encouragement and adoration. While I despise my brother, you shouldn't suffer due to his lack of income. Enclosed you will find a dollar bill. It is not much. I earned it from work I did in the campus forge. Though I'm no match for Pa or even Thomas with a hammer and anvil, I can hold my own.

I keep my eye on Shadrock. Though he means well, he has demonstrated a lack of moral character that no child of Pa would dare evince. He has been reprimanded twice now for attempted cheating. He would much rather concoct an elaborate means of acquiring good marks than to take the simpler course of just doing the work required of him. I can but watch and admonish. My admonishment is met only with scorn in return.

Your true love,
Carson

March 27, 1891

My Dearest Marinda,

Things are well here in Chapel Hill. My classes this term consist of natural history, applied mathematics, philosophy, English, and history of the ancient world. They are not so challenging as last term's classes were. I am pleased to say that I have had no further trouble with any of the other boys here.

They let me alone, and I let them alone. There are two debating societies that pretty much run this place, the Philanthropic Society and the Dialectic Society. Anybody who is anybody is a member of one or the other. My gramps was a Di, and he insists that I should become one too. But, as no one has nominated me for membership, I remain just me, which suits me fine. Perhaps I shall skip the Di and Phi and go straight to the Elisha Mitchell Scientific Society. Though it's only for faculty or alumni of the science and math departments, I have managed to become acquainted with a professor of biology here, a man by the name of Dr. Henry Van Peters Wilson. I have not yet taken his class, but he is quite impressed with my notebooks and sketches. He seems to think I have a place in the society sooner rather than later.

The story of how we met is worth retelling. Miles of forests surround the campus. I often wander alone into their depths. I had decided to follow this creek for a ways. I saw signs of raccoon and bobcat and fox. The trees down thataway consist largely of oaks and hickory. I had meandered for a good hour along this creek, the topography of which reminded me greatly of home, when I came across this fella squatting beside a little plant. He had a book with him and was trying to identify it. I called out to him so as not to startle him, and he looked up unfazed, as though he knew I was about to come around the bend.

"This is not in the book." His tone was laced with a combination of annoyance and intrigue.

I bent down to better see the plant. "That there's *Thermposis fraxinifolia*. It's not supposed to live in these parts. It lives mainly up in the mountains."

Only then did he really take a good look at me. "Are you one of our botany students? I don't recognize you."

He was a mite surprised to learn that I had never taken a botany class in my entire life. We introduced ourselves and got to chatting. He said the reason he needed the book to make identifications was because his specialty was zoology, specifically zoology of sponges. Ever since that meeting, we have maintained regular conversation, and I have shown him some of my notebooks and drawings. He thinks I have a future in science. This is the first time a person has found my obsession worthwhile, and it is quite encouraging. It is amazing to me, though, how I get along much better with all of the professors than with my fellow students. I don't try to be a stick-in-the-mud, but it seems to come natural to me.

On another note, Taylor informed me of his desire to attend West Point. I'm sure our pa won't approve of that, seeing as how he's so averse to anything to do with war anymore. Taylor would probably get along much better here in Chapel Hill than I do. There are more athletics than a person can know what to do with. There is a gymnasium and a tennis court and even a cinder track on which to run. They used to have football, but it was banned this past year due to some shenanigans that happened during the contests. There's talk of bringing it back. Besides baseball, it is the most desired sport to play. As you know, I am not one to play many sports. I did pitch in a baseball game last fall, but that was it for me. I get distracted too easily to be real good at it. When I was pitching, a flock of *Branta canadensis* flew by and I lost track of what I was doing. (That's the Canadian goose.)

Enclosed is another two dollars for your safekeeping. I received your last missive, and I'm heartened to hear that little Bella is growing so fast. I'm certain you are the best mother in the Gorge. I look forward to the day when I will gaze once again into the flecked emerald green of your eyes. Close your eyes and ask Thomas what color they are. I wager he will have no idea, but I see them still.

With Earnest Love,
Carson

There were dozens of letters over the next ten years, tracing the course of Carson's self-imposed exile. At no point during that time was there any indication that he returned to Daisy. In 1892, the letters came from Wilmington instead of Chapel Hill.

He had been expelled for cheating. Apparently, he got caught up in a scheme of his roommate, Shadrock Williams. He was in Wilmington for at least a year before the letters began to flow in from overseas. He got work on a series of freighters that allowed him to circumnavigate South America and the Pacific. By 1895, he was in San Francisco. He continued to mention the inclusion of money in the letters, even as he crisscrossed the West, referencing Yosemite, the Sonora desert, the Rockies, and the Great Plains. He found work as a stevedore, a cowboy, a farmhand, and a teacher, staying in a place no more than a few months at a time.

Then, in 1900, ten years after leaving, came the letter that would lead to his brother's death.

July 20, 1900

My Dearest Marinda,

The answer is Yes, a Yes bigger than Chimney Rock itself, a Yes for all time and all place. My heart has yearned for this request from you for nigh on a decade, across continents and deserts and all the in between. I have seen the extraordinary, ridden roiling seas, and climbed rocky peaks that put our mountains to shame, but all the while what I wanted most was to come home to you. I will be there in a month's time and will send word to Charlie Brightleaf to let you know when and where we shall meet. While my brother's infidelity is not a surprise, I am ashamed on behalf of my family for the hurt he has caused you. I pledge to you all steadfast love and adoration. Know that I have enough money saved now for us to go live anywhere we want. Think upon a place, and I will take you there.

Your True Love,

Carson

The letters had offered me hope that maybe, just maybe, young Carson Quinn, lover of this hollow and Marinda Fallon, had somehow not come to murder his brother. No longer. This letter from July 1900 put him coming home right before the murder of Thomas Quinn. Motive: check. Proximity: check. No alibi: check.

I stashed the letters away with the journal and put my attention on the cabin. It occurred to me that I didn't have to try to furnish the cabin by myself. Delores was an expert shopper and knew how to find the best deals. Besides, maybe I wanted help from her friend who could talk to ghosts.

The following weekend, Delores came up to the cabin, towing along with her Martha Boston and the person she had called her witch, a dowdy-looking woman named Adele. Delores took one look at the cabin and broke into a wide smile that she covered reflexively. "Oh, honey!" she exclaimed upon jumping from her car. "It's better than ever!"

I hadn't seen Martha since high school. She couldn't make it to the funeral. For Delores, Martha was an old friend, but for me she might as well have been a stranger. Other than for old times' sake, I wasn't sure why Delores had brought her. Like Delores, Martha still lived in Greensboro. She had gone to Guilford College, married an artist, and divorced the artist, and now was on marriage number two, this time to a businessman. "Second time's the charm!" she exclaimed, still in love with the man who owned a franchise of car washes.

After a day of furniture shopping that resulted in new bedding, dining room chairs, and kitchen implements, we shared a bottle of wine while rocking on the front porch. Adele did not look the part of psychic, medium, or witch. Middle aged with a wholesome, middle-America presentation, she came across as grounded and practical. She discussed what would happen during the ritual.

"Don't tell me what your experiences have been," Adele said. "I don't want to know. I should be neutral, a conduit of sorts."

"Look," I said. "I'm a scientist. Even though some things have happened here to multiple people, I'm still not sure I believe in ghosts."

"What?" Delores's eyes went wide. "After what we experienced that night? How can you not believe in ghosts?"

"You're reacting to what I experienced," I said. "You never actually saw or heard the ghost, did you?"

Delores took a sip of wine and searched her memory.

Martha's rocker stopped with a squeak. She took a deep breath. She let it out slowly, her head shaking side to side. "No, she didn't. But I did."

I lurched forward in my chair. "What? You never said anything about it."

"When I was nine, I was in the room when my grandmother died. Ever since then, I've been particularly sensitive to... well...certain things."

Adele cleared her throat. "You're clairvoyant." She said it matter-of-factly, as if describing left-handedness.

"Yes." Martha held no pride in it. It seemed to her an affliction rather than a gift.

Now I understood why Delores had invited her. "Did you see the ghost when you were here before? When we were kids?"

Martha nodded mutely.

I turned to Adele. "Are my doubts about this whole thing going to affect what you're doing, Adele?"

"Doubts are good," she said. "I'm not sure I exactly believe in ghosts, either. You know, I don't make my living from this or anything. I don't know what these phenomena are, whether they are lost souls or some warped energy or just projections of our own psychology, but I do know how to ripen the conditions to make what I see apparent to others."

She shot a knowing look at Martha, who had grown increasingly withdrawn and timid the moment she entered the cabin.

"What?" Delores asked, excitedly looking from one to the other. "Is the ghost here now?"

Adele and Martha stared at each other for a long pause, then both turned their heads to a corner of the front porch. There was nothing remarkable about that corner as far as I could tell.

"Martha?" Adele asked. "Do you want to tell them what's there by the wall?"

Martha closed her eyes. She craned her head over her neck

toward the corner, opened them, and then flinched, as if seeing a snake.

"Wait!" I said, my inner scientist awakening. "Don't say anything." I ran inside and grabbed a notebook and two pens. Tearing out two sheets of paper, I gave each a piece of paper and a pen. "Write it down separately."

"Ooh." Delores rubbed her hands together. "This is like *Ghostbusters*. I like it."

Once they were finished, they handed me their descriptions. Holding them in my hands, I hesitated. All of a sudden, the last thing I wanted was evidence that my fears were justified. All this time, like Micah, I had created a narrative that there had to be a rational explanation for my experiences. These two sheets of paper could dispel that possibility.

I read the first one aloud: "A sad, bearded man wearing a brown suit." I calmed myself, placed it aside, took a deep breath, and read the second: "A man with a beard and a brown hat."

"Oh, I forgot the hat," Martha said. "He's definitely wearing an old, beat-up hat."

Delores jumped and screamed, her wine sloshing out of its glass. "I just got chills!"

Mere chills would have been nice compared to the foreboding that weighed on my shoulders and back. The man I had seen, whom Charles Duncan had seen, who was now lurking in the corner, was no figment of my imagination.

Delores's scream was still echoing through the hollow when Adele said, "We should do this now."

We went upstairs. I offered Carson's journal, and Adele set the candles around it. We formed ourselves into a circle around the candles. Adele spoke some words about the elements and directions. She told us to let go of all thought and expectation and to bring our focus entirely into this room. Then she invited any others present to join our circle. We sat while the candles hissed and the katydids broke into a chorus outside. Adele had us inhale together, then exhale together.

Martha broke the silence. "He's here."

I didn't see anything.

"Where?" Delores looked around into the darkening corners.

"Top of the stairs." Adele welcomed him warmly. "Think kind thoughts."

I still didn't see or sense the presence, but I thought of that peculiar voice from the journal, at the end, his heart broken. Always an outsider, even with his own family. His sadness, the despair that had soaked from him into this place, made all the sense in the world. In my mind, I formulated the question, "Carson, did you kill Thomas?"

There was no answer forthcoming. In fact, I was beginning to wonder if Martha and Adele hadn't gotten together beforehand to conspire a ghost into being. After all, I had actually perceived the ghost as a child. Now, as far as I could tell, there was nothing. Had a lifetime of scientific inquiry closed me off from such things? Or was it all a hoax, a joke played on Caroline, because she, like Carson, had never quite fit in?

"We can ask questions," Adele explained. "Ask them aloud."

I swallowed. "Carson Quinn," I said. "Did you kill your brother? Thomas?"

Three loud explosions tore through the night. We all jumped. One of the candles toppled, spilling wax all over the floor. I stomped on the swimming flame, extinguishing it as two more explosions echoed through the hollow, followed by a rowdy "Yeeehaww!"

My heart pounded. Delores and Martha turned questioning looks my way. I crawled over to the window and cautiously peered over the sill. Down the hill, on the porch extending from his double-wide, Jesse Duncan stood bathed in the floodlight on his deck, a bottle in one hand and a pistol in the other. Lifting the gun, he took not-so-careful aim and squeezed off two more rounds in the general direction of the mountainside. He took a swig from the bottle and let loose an indecipherable scream.

"What is it?" Delores asked.

"The neighbor." I sighed.

Martha flinched when an eighth shot tore through the night.

"I'm going to call his father." I scrambled down the stairs and grabbed the phone, hastily dialing the number Patsy had provided. She answered on the third ring.

"Patsy," I said. "It's Caroline."

"Hey, honey." Her drawl laced the words with a sweetness primed to gossip.

"You need to get Charles down here pronto," I said, forgoing niceties. "Jesse's out on his deck with a bottle and a gun." Another gunshot slapped a period on the end of my sentence.

Her answer wasn't aimed at me. "Charlie!" she shouted into the depths of her rancher. "Charlie! Get down to the trailer. Your son's shooting up the mountain."

In the background I heard Charles grumble, "That boy's gonna be the death of me."

Then Patsy spoke into the phone. "He's coming now," she said. "You and your friends stay put."

My friends? I started to ask how she knew I had visitors but stopped myself. The cove had eyes and ears that the NSA would be jealous of. "We will," I answered and hung up.

Immediately the phone rang. It was Patsy. "Charlie wants to know how many shots there've been."

"Nine," I said.

"That's good," she answered. "Charlie only gave him ten bullets."

She hung up, and I couldn't help but shake my head. He gave a man receiving disability for PTSD a gun and ten bullets, and that's a good thing?

I went back upstairs where the three ladies were crouched by the window, more frightened by the crazy with the gun than the ghost. "I suppose the commotion scared the ghost away," I offered.

"Probably not." Adele did not take her eyes off the man on his porch. He had now taken his shirt off. The floodlight illuminated a huge tattoo coloring his back. It was large enough for us to see from nearly a hundred feet away the rippling of the Stars and Bars, the Confederate Battle Flag. The war that hadn't ended in 1890 still hadn't ended over a century later. "The ghost doesn't leave, but our ability to perceive it wavers. Our minds are not going to pick up on something as indeterminate as a spirit when there's a very real bodily threat at hand."

"He's only got one more bullet."

The others squished their brows together and turned to me.

"How do you know that?" Delores asked.

"They only gave him ten." I held up all ten fingers.

"You've been counting the shots?" Incredulity contorted Martha's face at my counting as mine probably had at her clair-voyance.

"You see ghosts. I count things."

Charles's car roared up to the double-wide, slinging dust into floodlit night. He left the headlights on and climbed out. "Jesse! It's your dad! Hold your fire!"

Charles climbed the stairs to the deck. His son glared at him, his grip hard on both the empty bottle and the pistol.

"Son." Charles held out his hand, motioning with his finger-tips. "Give me the gun."

"It's not a gun. It's a weapon."

"You're right," Charles said. "It's a weapon. Hand me the weapon."

"Without my weapon I am useless," Jesse said. "I will not surrender it. I will master the enemy."

"Where's the enemy, son? The enemy isn't here now."

"The enemy is there." Jesse lifted the pistol and pointed it at his father's chest. Charles lifted his hands. "The enemy is here." Jesse then pointed the pistol at his own head.

Both Delores and Martha flinched and ducked away from the window, not wanting to see a suicide. But that's not what happened. Charles covered the distance between himself and his son in a flash. His left arm pushed the gun away. The final bullet ripped into the night while his right arm wrapped his son in a tight bear hug. The bottle shattered on the deck.

Adele and I sighed in relief, while Delores and Martha peered over the windowsill. We watched Charles Duncan gather his son, load him into his car, and drive away.

"Okay," I said. "I have a bottle of red. I'm going to go open it and we're going to get silly. No more ghosts. No more guns. Just us girls." And that's what we did, staying up late until the adrenaline subsided and sleep overcame us.

20

E ven before they built the cabin in it, the holler was special. Tucked away where nary a soul would find it, flush with hemlocks and poplars, it let in only the sparest bit of light even at the height of noon. The creek poured fresh and clear from a spring not far up the mountain. To get there a fella had to either squirm snake-like up through the hells or take his life in his hands and climb hand over hand down a rock ledge from above. It was about as ideal a spot as could be found for a still.

Despite it being so remote and despite the fact he'd taken every precaution, some fool had found it. The fella kicked at the coals under the boiler and shook the thumper, swishing the tails inside. He liked to bend the lyne arm when he took ahold of it. Thomas was certain the fella was a revenuer.

"You there!" he shouted.

The fella didn't turn, so Thomas lifted his shotgun and aimed it squarely at the man's back. "Show yer face," he yelled. "So's I don't have to shoot you in the back."

The fella turned real slow. His red hair splaying out from the edges of his hat and his stooped, holier-than-thou posture gave him away. It was Carson, back from who knows where after all these years.

"What's this?" Carson's first words were angry, seething even. He pointed to the still, idle now, but soon to be cranking out a fresh batch of Quinn's Finest.

"It's good to see you, too, brother." Thomas propped the shotgun against a tree and approached.

"What's this?" Carson repeated, angrier still. Time had not quieted his unrest. Last time he'd seen his brother, he was hoppin' around in the road, fuming like some riled-up hen. Watching from the upstairs window, Thomas had heard the

crazed frothing, seen the stomping back and forth. He'd wanted nothing more than to come out and finish it right then and
there. But Ma made him promise he wouldn't harm his brother.
Then the coward left.

Now, ten years later, Carson had come back. Maybe he'd
come to collect on his revenge. Maybe for some other reason.
He had on fine attire: new black britches and a starched shirt,
a vest and a bolo tie and shiny black boots. He was dressed for
something fancier than sneaking up on a man's still.

"That there is the source of Quinn's Finest, the smoothest
moonshine you're likely to ever have. Can I interest you in a
taste?"

"What's it doing here?" Carson set his jaw. "What are you
doing here?"

Who was he to question him? A coward who cared more
about words on a page and high-mindedness than his own
kin, who'd rather than fight for what he wanted, lit out to who
knows where, tail tucked between his legs like some beat-down
cur.

"Don't that beat all," Thomas said. "Mr. Fancy Pants with
his head in a book and not a care for another wants to question
how I provide for my family? Maybe you need remindin' what
a family is."

"Don't talk to me about family." Carson took a step forward.
His knuckles went white, so tight were the fists by his side.

As much as he wanted to whup his brother, Thomas held
back. A promise made would be a promise kept.

"This hollow." Carson looked around at them big trees and
boulders. "Deserves better."

Thomas laughed. "The holler deserves better? It ain't no
person. It don't deserve nothin'."

Carson flinched as if the first punch had landed.

"You know who deserves better?" he said to Carson. "My
daughter, that is, your niece, your own kin, deserves better. I
can make a livin' with this here. Can't make no livin' no other
way. That there abomination you're staring at puts clothes on

her back, gives her good schoolin', makes it so she don't have a care in the world."

"Ain't got no right," Carson said.

"I got ever right in the world. Why don't you take a look at the deed and see whose name is on it? It sure as hell ain't yours."

"I'm sure the name on it says Duncan." Carson's face went as red as his hair.

He wondered if maybe he could make it even redder. "And you know what else I got the right to do?"

"Pray tell what?"

"These are mighty fine trees. This stand is gonna fetch a pretty penny one day. I bet we got a hundred thousand board feet of timber up in here. This holler's mine. Bought it fair and square from Isaac Duncan. These trees will make sure Bella is set for life."

Low and behold if his face didn't go redder still. He spat out a series of indecipherable phrases before he settled with, "And where would you hide your goddamn still then?"

"A man's always got more than one hideaway."

"Another still's not all you got hid away, I hear."

"What you gettin' at?"

"Esmeralda Dotson?"

"What of her?"

Carson screwed up his face. "You don't care for Marinda. You never did."

"'Course I do. But I'm a man, Carson. You ought to try it sometime."

"That's it." Carson stormed toward him.

He readied himself for the fight, tugged up his sleeves, and perched forward on the balls of his feet. He'd been looking forward to this for ten years. But the coward blew by him like he wasn't there at all.

"I'm gonna talk to Ma about this." He ducked into the laurel hell and was gone. Just like that.

Thomas shrugged off the disappointment. The fight would eventually happen. It had been brewing for decades, like a boiler with no pressure valve, the fire of their differences heating it all the while. What was to come was inevitable.

He turned his attention to the still. First thing was to light a real fire. Too bad you couldn't cook mash using the heat between brothers. He sparked flame to tinder, added to it from the pile of kindling he kept, and watched it go, wicking at the base of the mash pot.

"Carson?" a familiar voice called. "Carson, is that you?" The eagerness in her voice was disquieting. When he turned to his wife, Marinda's face told him everything he needed to know, told him why Carson had been here in the first place, why he'd been wearing them fancy duds.

"Sorry to disappoint you," he said. "Sorry I'm not him. Sorry I've never been him."

She stumbled, confusion writ large across her face. "What are you doing here?"

He closed the distance to her, the fight he'd been holding back all these years for his brother swimming to the surface. If Carson wouldn't fight, then she would surely do. Traitorous woman. She'd always loved Carson. That it was obvious and had been from day one racked his insides and lit his rage.

"Thomas!" She backed away. He'd never seen her this afraid before. It made him feel strong. Made him feel invincible. "Thomas! Stop."

She tripped over a root, fell back onto the soft earth, her new dress fell back, showing off fancy bloomers. From behind her, his brother emerged from the twisted limbs of the hell like Satan himself. Carson, in his fancy duds and high falutin' ideas, was gonna get what he deserved now.

But Carson stopped, his eyes wide and scared. His hand flew up and he shouted out. "Marinda! No!"

Thomas turned and found the twin barrels of his own gun pointed at him, Marinda with the crazed eyes of a wild creature.

"Ain't no woman gonna point my gun at me!" He lurched forward to wrench the shotgun from her grasp.

The holler thundered. It was like he was hit with forked

lightning, like he was gored by the horns of an angry bull. He found himself falling backward. The fall seemed to never end, even after the soft moss caught him. He struggled to rise, yet continued to fall. The mountain had him. It was pulling him into itself. Each breath came harder than the one before. Up above, the tallest hemlocks poked at a blue sky with limbs as emerald green as Marinda's eyes.

His fall softened. Then he was floating up, up toward those highest limbs and the sky above. The trees welcomed him, and peace came over him. A man could do worse than to die in a place like this.

He heard Carson yelling. "Marinda! What have you done?"

"I wasn't gonna kill him. He did it. He tugged on it, and it went off. He's kilt, Carson."

"No, no, no," Carson cried.

"It's for the better. We can be together now." Her voice was plaintive, practical. Damn woman.

"No, we can't," he said. "We can't ever be together now. I'll leave. Tell them I killed him. I killed him and ran off."

"I'll do no such thing."

"Think of Bella. Think of your daughter."

Two thuds woke me. A pileated woodpecker was tearing up a tree outside while a towhee implored me to drink my tea. The smell of bacon and coffee pulled me from the bed. The dream had been so real. It was as if I'd been there, as if I'd been Thomas. I crawled out of the bed and opened the door.

"Breakfast, sleepyhead!" Delores lifted a plate of eggs, bacon, and toast.

"You're never going to guess the dream I had," I said.

"Wait until you hear Martha's dream," Delores answered. "She saw the murder happen. You're never going to guess who killed him in her dream."

"His wife?"

Her eyes went wide, and I caught the plate of food before it hit the floor. "Oh my lord!" she exclaimed.

Over breakfast, both Martha and I wrote down our dreams. They turned out mostly identical. This hollow. The still. The shotgun. Marinda killing Thomas. Afterward, we sat on the porch sipping coffee. Nothing about the weekend had gone according to plan, but two of us had experienced the same dream as if in answer to the question posed.

"Dreams are powerful," Adele said. "They really are our brains trying to make sense of all the data we take in both consciously and unconsciously while awake. In the moment, we can't attend to all of the information our brain takes in. Only when it's shut down by REM sleep does the brain process everything, and we experience the processing as dreams."

I wrapped my hand in full around my warm mug, lifted it and let the coffee fumes waft into my face, pondering what she'd said. "You're saying that somehow Martha and I took in the same information and our brains made sense of it in the exact same way?"

"We probably all did," Adele said. "But you two are the only ones who remembered your dreams."

"What kind of medium are you?" Martha chuckled nervously.

"I'm not exactly a medium. I'm clairvoyant. My day job is social work."

"Just because we dreamed it doesn't mean it happened," I said.

Martha shook her head. "Mine wasn't just a dream. It was so real, like I was him."

My scientific mind wasn't willing to let go of reason. "That wasn't just any night last night either. How many times have you had a séance interrupted by a crazy man with a gun? Then we had all that wine."

"All I know," Martha said, "is you asked the question, then you and I had the exact same dream, a clear answer to the question you asked, and today that ghost isn't here."

Delores and I turned to Adele. Her empty palms weighed the air. "I haven't seen it this morning either."

"I got goose pimples again!" Delores said.

"Adele." I washed down my fear and skepticism with a hit of coffee. "Was he the only ghost here? There wasn't another?"

Adele grew quiet, as if knowing why I was asking. Delores must have told her about my mother. She took a deep breath, closed her eyes, and nodded. "There was only the one."

I searched for a second opinion by turning to Martha, who squished her lips into a no. I slid back into the rocker. I let the rhythmic back and forth soothe me as the morning sounds washed over me, the birds bickering, the creek shushing, the hollow itself breathing, same as always. Was it disappointment I felt? Or something else?

We spent the rest of the day out and about, searching for more furnishings. I wound up checking towels, linens, curtains, and a side table off the list. They left mid-afternoon and I returned to the cabin, for the first time ever with a sense of foreboding.

21

On a Tuesday morning, I placed the journal and photos carefully in the metal box, in which they had resided for decades, loaded it up in the Subaru, and drove down the hardtop. I didn't worry that he wouldn't be there. According to everyone who knew him, Hiram Morgan was always on his mountain.

I pulled up to his house as he was descending from his high pasture, Sallie at his heel.

"The professor returns," he said by way of greeting.

"I brought something for you." I pried the box from the back seat.

"That you have." He arched an eyebrow. "C'mon up. I expect you got more of those questions of yours. I'll be right back."

He ventured inside, returning with two tall glasses of cool spring water.

We sat on his porch, the box resting between us. "I haven't seen that box in a long, long time."

"How long?"

"I brought that box back from Thomasville, Georgia. Bought it at an army/navy surplus joint just off the highway. Uncle Carson was getting on in years, wouldn't never leave his, well...your, cabin. He had some items that needed a place for safekeeping. So, I got him that metal box. You see..." Hiram squinted at the horizon. A breeze stirred the butterfly bush by the front porch. "Storm's coming." He took a deep breath. "All folks die." He turned to me, glancing down at the box before casting his fierce blue eyes into mine. "But words can live forever."

Truer words had never been spoken. I thought of the journal and my mother's stories.

"Carson Quinn is as alive in that box as anywhere."

I cleared my throat. "Speaking of which, Mr. Morgan, do you believe in ghosts?"

He picked a burr from his corduroy pants and tossed it into the yard. "Depends on what you mean by ghost, I reckon. You can't rightly live in these parts without being aware of the specters that abound. Lives that overlap…places that settle into your soul a little…views that change in reality, but not in your mind's eye."

"Would you believe that my cabin is haunted?"

"Yes, ma'am. In fact, it is."

My face must have articulated the question I was too stunned to express verbally.

"Any place that's been loved is forever haunted by those that loved it."

I opened the box and pulled out the scrapbook containing the photos. I opened it to the family on the porch and handed it to him. His eyes widened as he examined the photo.

"I haven't seen this in years," he said.

From over his shoulder, I pointed out Carson. "Three different people have seen this man, Carson, in the cabin. Myself included."

"Makes sense." He craned his neck to get the right angle to see through his old eyes. "Only that ain't Carson."

I gasped.

"That's Thomas," he said, his icy blue eyes searching the photo intently. "Uncle Carson ain't in this photo. Must have been taken when he was away. Let's see if I can find him somewhere."

He parsed through the photos one by one until he got to the wedding photo. I knew where Carson would be in the photo. In the back, next to a tall planter from the Low Country. I should have gone back to that photo after reading the passage, but I didn't.

"Here he is," Hiram said, pointing to a face in the back row. "You can't tell in the photo, but his hair was near as red as a cardinal's feathers."

I gazed down at the face. Despite having spent hours with the journal and researching him, there was no familiarity. He stood slightly stooped, and clearly would have towered over most people of his generation. All this time, the man in my mind's eye had been Thomas.

"Did Marinda Quinn kill Thomas Quinn in that hollow?"

He winced. "No one knows who killed Thomas or where. His body was found in the waterfall behind his house. That's more than a mile from that hollow."

"But the same creek that flows through the hollow winds up behind the house. Bodies float."

He sighed. "Down that crooked creek? A body's apt to snag on a log or boulder between the two places."

He took a sip of water. I held his gaze in silence.

"It's perplexing to me that you arrived at the conclusion that she done the killing and not Uncle Carson," he continued. "My uncle was a mean, mean man who hated his brother."

"No, he wasn't," I answered. "You've read that journal, and what's more, you knew the man, probably better than any other person."

"Love is a bewildering thing." Thunder boomed overhead, rattling the windows of the old house. "I've never loved anyone like Uncle Carson loved my grandmother. I was always too selfish, and that's likely why my wife left me. By the time I was a young man about to head off to the navy, I had figured out that Uncle Carson wasn't nearly so ornery and irascible as he liked to act. He wouldn't hurt a copperhead, and I figured that a man what wouldn't dispatch a poisonous snake wouldn't kill his own brother."

"A copperhead never stole the love of his life."

"You got me there." He scratched at his neck and his eyes followed a flock of goldfinches across the yard. "I didn't think that one through when I was eighteen. They were both alive then. She lived down on the hardtop, and he lived a little more than a mile away up the mountain. Oh, they would see each other now and again in town or the store, and nary a word would pass between them. I pressed him about the murder of his brother. Like you, I didn't want to believe he done it. He didn't admit to it, but you could tell he wanted you to think it was him."

"I tried to find what happened with the sheriff's investigation, but there was nothing in the papers about it," I said.

"My understanding is that Thomas had gotten into some trouble with a local outlaw named Gus Trabor. Thomas was also on the run from revenuers and in deep debt to some other ne'er-do-wells. Sometime after the murder, marshals arrested Trabor and charged him with the murder of two federal officials. But the sheriff did not charge him with the murder of Thomas Quinn. Everybody knew that if Trabor had done the killing, the body never would have been found. His enemies were the disappearing sort. Folks always assumed it was Uncle Carson on account of my grandmother."

"It wasn't."

"She died in 1959," he said. "After that Uncle Carson softened a bit, but folks were accustomed to steering clear of him so that's what they did."

"Except for you."

"Yes, ma'am, except for me." Fresh rain peppered the tin roof now, an introductory cadence to the oncoming storm.

"And?"

Tears had gathered in his eyes now, just as I imagined they had in old Carson's eyes when he offered the confession to his nephew decades ago. "He loved her so much that he chose to take the blame for something he couldn't ever forgive her for."

The sky opened up. Lightning flashed, and the thunder rumbled through seconds later. "He couldn't forgive her for killing Thomas?"

"Never did."

"But he loved her?"

"Always."

"Why couldn't he forgive her for that? Thomas despised Carson."

"Brothers are brothers, even when they don't see eye to eye. Especially up here. I learned a lot from my uncle. I owe him so much. But one thing I learned that I wish I could unlearn has to do with resentment. It'll harden you, if you let it."

"When did he die?" I asked.

"At the age of ninety-four in 1967."

"So he lived for sixty-seven years after Thomas's death?"

"Your math is excellent, professor."

"That whole time spent festering over a single incident."

"Nope. Not a single incident. Remember, before Marinda killed Thomas, she betrayed Carson by having Thomas's child. And even though Marinda pulled the trigger, Uncle Carson blamed himself. He was the one that came back, after all. He always thought that if he hadn't been so selfish as to come back, his brother would have lived. Blamed himself as much as he blamed her."

We sat watching the storm. High winds tore at the grass and trees. The rain fell in slanting sheets. Lightning popped all around. Like the rest of the house, the porch was orderly. A small, upended crate served as a table where our glasses of water trembled with each roll of thunder. An old butter churn by the door held a collection of gnarly old walking stick and canes. At its base rested a pair of old leather boots. My heart skipped a beat at the sight of them.

"Those boots," I said. I couldn't take my eyes off them. Creases hinged the aged leather like lifelines on a hand. I had seen them before. An orange ball bounced through my mind's eye. The warmth of kind hands lifting me from the front porch of the cabin filled me. My first memory. "How long have you owned them?"

"I'm sure longer than you've been alive, young lady." He scratched his neck and peered at the slatted porch ceiling, ciphering out the number. "Those are U.S. Navy-issue combat boots that I got before I set sail on the USS *Rochester* in 1950. They told me at the time that if I took good care of them, they would last a lifetime. I suppose they were right."

I tore my gaze from them to stare into Hiram's eyes. They were as blue as the sea. He cocked his head. "You remember that day you caught me trespassing?"

"Sure do."

"That wasn't the first time you met me, was it?"

He shook his head. "Your folks were as curious about the former owners of the cabin as you are. Right after buying the place, they sought me out. I came over to the place, sat on that front porch of yours, and told them all about Uncle Carson. I expect that toddling little girl with the scratched-up knees and sundress would be you."

"That was me. I actually remember that."

His old eyes seemed to twinkle. "So do I," he said.

"You knew my parents," I said.

He nodded. My mind swirled. Storms lashed both inside and out. My own history had now tethered itself to the history of the hollow, to Carson Quinn and his descendants. "My mother died my senior year of high school."

"I'm sorry to hear that. She was a kind lady. You know the reason that journal was in your cabin, don't you?"

"I figured Carson left it there."

"No," Hiram said. He took a sip of water. "She was doing exactly what you're doing now."

"What?"

"She was interested in the prior occupants of that cabin for whatever reason, so I lent her the journal and the photos so as she could learn about old Carson and his family. She had started down the same road you're on now."

Something jolted inside me, like a fault line rejoining after millennia spent askew. I didn't know what to say. Hiram pulled a handkerchief from his back pocket. He offered no condolences and didn't seem uncomfortable with my emotion, just handed over the handkerchief. I dabbed my eyes and gazed off into mountains folding upon mountains.

We sat in silence while the storm swirled around us. In half an hour, it had passed. The clouds began to clear, and sunlight searched out the earth in long golden strands. "Professor." He placed his hands on his knees. "I've got some sheep to tend to."

He stood. His hand rested on his belly, and his face wore a peculiar expression. I realized that he simply wasn't scowling anymore.

"All right then," he said. "I reckon you've earned this."

He went inside for a moment and returned with a manila envelope that he handed to me. "Uncle Carson and I corresponded over the years, back in the days when such things were done with paper and pen rather than ones and zeroes. This was one of the last letters he ever wrote me, after years of solitude and loss had softened his heart."

"Earned it?" I was perplexed.

"You can keep that. It's a photocopy."

"Mr. Morgan?"

His eyes twinkled and he shook me off as if knowing what I was going to say.

"Thank you." I said it anyway.

The screen door squealed closed behind him.

22

August 12, 1965—These might well be the last senti-
ments I ever put to paper, and I want to get them
down before I lose my faculties. My head is full of
facts acquired over a long life, and at times the best way to make
sense of it all is by pulling out that which ties it all together and
putting it down in ink. A fella can learn all the knowledge there
is to be learned. He can know the names of every plant, bird,
and animal in four different languages. He can be able to recite
everything every philosopher ever wrote, and he can know the
vast eras of geology. All that doesn't amount to much at all
when it comes to living life.

Wisest man I ever knew couldn't have told you where
Krakatoa was, but he knew what it meant to love, and by loving,
to forgive. I remember as a young fella watching old Charlie
Brightleaf send a round skyward in honor of his departed wife,
Wilma. He said that the spot where he honored her was a place
they loved dearly, and where they loved each other deeply. I've
been all the way around this Earth, and I've seen lots of beauty
and lots of devastation, seen the way folks live and die and
everything in between. One thing I think I may have learned
along the way is that every person has a place, or at least should
have a place. A place where he belongs, where he can sit and be
free of judgment.

I hearken back to King Robert, whose people wandered
the South after the war in search of a place to call their own.
It gives me no small amount of pride to know that my gramps
was able to help them secure that place once it was found. A
sad fact of life that I have learned in conjunction with this
is that a place isn't necessarily forever. That Kingdom of the
Happy Land was lost to debts incurred by one of the king's

descendants in a trial. Nowadays there's no kingdom, at least not an earthly one.

I'm fairly certain that should any folks care to think about me and my life, they will likely deduce that this hollow is the place where I belong. And I reckon they would be right. But it ain't on account of it being free of judgment. No sir, this hollow judges me mightily, judges me every single day I reside in it. You see, it was spite that led me to have them build this cabin here. It was Marinda's land after all, but I had in mind that she could spend the rest of her life in the spot where she ended my brother's. Nearly as soon as it was done, I knew it was all wrong. It may not have been me that pulled the trigger, but I was the one that killed him. I killed him by coming back just as surely as I knew I would.

Marinda lived in this cabin for no more than a year. She had herself a place built down on the road on account of it being too cold up in the hollow. It wasn't the cold though. It was that my spite had conjured up the memory of my brother, and the memory was too much for a person to bear. She claimed this hollow was haunted by him. I reckon she's right. At times I think I may see him lurking about, dressed as he was on that day. Ma was right. Thomas never did love her like I did, but he loved her just the same.

If there is one thing a person should know about me, it is that I loved your grandmother, Marinda Fallon Quinn, all the day long and the night too. And I was a man who made his bed and lay in it all the days of his life. We could have had the future we had talked of so long ago, made possible by the earthly departure of a man who never expressed a single heartfelt sentiment toward me, his own kin. Yet for reasons beyond logic, we lived out separate lives merely a mile apart for the remainder of her life. I might as well have been in China as far as she was concerned. A heart is a funny thing. It can get all froze up like a waterfall in winter. And spring can be a long time coming.

I wonder if most people know the best thing they've ever done in their life. I reckon my gramps probably knew the best thing he done was to help the folks in the Kingdom of the Happy Land. He might disagree about that, because he did a lot for a lot of people, most of which he never talked about, despite having so much to say. Me, I'm lucky enough to know both the best thing I've done, and the worst. The best was teaching your grandmother to read and write. Once she started, she kept going, and I got at least one letter a month from her for the rest of her life, even when we lived a mile apart and never spoke a single word to each other. I am and have been an old fool for a very long time. The worst thing, well, you and I both know what that was.

∂

My heart thundered. It nearly drowned out the forest symphony of birdsong, katydid choruses, and trilling creek fall. Sitting on the front porch of the cabin, I was surrounded by monuments of great love: the letters from Patsy, the cabin itself a testament of my father's love to my mother, and its new condition the product of the caring and competent hand of a man intent on making amends.

The words that came to me were an echo nearly fifty years old: I was a fool, and I had been for a very long time. My own lonely life stared up at me from that letter. Like a still pool of water, Carson Quinn's life reflected my own foibles back to me.

There were several beers left from Micah's celebratory stash. I fished one out of the refrigerator. My mind lingered on its inability to forgive, its tendency to accrue high expectations and to shun all who can't meet them. No one could, of course. Not Woody. Not my father. Not my students. Not Micah. Especially not myself.

As if summoned by thought, the forest symphony was disrupted by tires on gravel. As the vehicle approached, a noise resembling music emanated from inside. Whoever it was had their stereo turned on full blast, so loud that I could hear the screaming harmonics of a heavy metal song all the way up on the porch. My first thought was that Jesse was back and driving again, but the vehicle blasted past his double-wide. The pickup thumped into the drive. It was Micah. His music, if you could call it that, was full of screeching and whining and dissonant guitar riffs.

When he shut the engine off, the music stopped, and though I had been exposed to it for only a few minutes, the silence was a relief. Micah opened his door and stepped out, a cassette tape held high like a truce flag. I thought I was a technophobe, but even I had done away with cassettes years ago.

"Hello, the porch!" he hollered.

"Hello, the truck," I answered.

"You armed?" he asked.

"C'mon up. Just don't expect me to listen to that crap."

He approached the rock steps. Only when he laid the cassette tape down did I notice in his left hand the same blowtorch that had started all this months ago. He looked up at me with a face as earnest and apologetic as any I had ever seen. After lighting the torch, he blazed away at the tape. In seconds the plastic exploded into an acrid ball of blue flame. Done with this bizarre ritual of penance, he climbed the stairs.

"Want a beer?" I asked.

"Sure," he said.

I went and grabbed one from the refrigerator.

"How did we not finish these last time?"

"An oversight on our part," I said.

"Indeed." He popped the lid.

"What was that about?" I asked, looking down at the charred remains of some musician's livelihood.

"That was Slayer," he explained. "The song that was playing was the anthem of my messed-up youth."

"That was a song?"

"You know…" He cleared his throat. "Some folks consider that high art."

"Hmm."

"I wanted to show you that I've moved on from that stage of my life." He looked up at me with pleading eyes, his hair, as always, unkempt and wild, his long, lithe body wrenched into a penitent crouch.

"I know."

"We're cool?"

"We're cool."

A sigh of relief escaped his lips. We sat slowly rocking, the sounds of the hollow gradually returning after the cacophonous intrusion of Micah's entrance.

We finished off the remaining beers. Then Micah asked, "So, I guess you're headed back to Maryland soon."

"Nope."

"No? What about your students? Don't you have to jump back into the publish-or-perish treadmill?"

"Yes," I said. "But I have research. It's up the Gorge. You ever heard of the grand octal?"

"Sounds like a magician."

"No." I shook my head. "The grand octal is the series of solar milestones that occur annually as the earth orbits the Sun."

"Like the solstices and equinoxes?"

"And the Cross Quarters," I explained. "People around the world have long devised architecture that marks those moments each year."

"Like Stonehenge?"

"Precisely," I said. "There's one up on Hiram Morgan's land that I think needs some serious study."

Micah reclined in his rocker and arched his eyebrow. He turned to me, his lips twisted in a sly grin. "Sounds like an awfully good excuse to me."

"Excuse?"

He leaned toward me, the bad boy who loved Slayer showing up in his sly grin. "You just can't get enough, can you?"

I let my eyes lock with his. "That's the story of my life, Micah."

I sat back in the rocking chair and looked out over the hollow, lit differently now without the hemlocks, yet still somehow the same, ever haunted by the spirits of those who loved it and left it and returned.

ACKNOWLEDGMENTS

This is a work of fiction, but readers should note that some minor characters are actual historical figures, including Thomas Clingman, George Washington Logan, Hamilton Ewart, Lila Barnwell, and Robert Montgomery. All other characters are entirely made up. Credit is due to those who lived lives large and small in the Hickory Nut Gap and who inspired a young explorer to imagine the world they lived in.

Countless hours were spent in the Southern Historical Collection and the North Carolina Collection at the University of North Carolina at Chapel Hill, the Henderson County Courthouse, the Henderson County Heritage Museum, the Henderson County Library, and the North Carolina Room of the Asheville Public Library (now called Buncombe County Special Collections). Apologies to the untold number of landowners whose land may or may not have been trespassed upon in the researching of *Hemlock Hollow*.

This book was a long time in the making. It wouldn't have made it into the world without the encouragement and guidance of many. I'm indebted to readers who took the time to read and comment on various portions and iterations of the manuscript, including Francesca Talenti, Betsy Martin, Michelle Roseman, Lucy Hayhurst, Howard Anderson, John Yewell, Lorena Holderfield (aka Mom), and Allie Coker.

Special thanks go to Mimi Herman, whose keen insights and editorial prowess helped turn a messy manuscript into a novel, and who invited me into the Writeaways fold, a literary home like no other.

Jaynie Royal and Pam Van Dyk do great work at Regal House, not only in bringing fine books to life, but also in their engagement with the broader community. I'll be ever grateful that they took a chance on me.

Words cannot express the gratitude I feel for Jodi Lasseter, whose love and devotion helped me believe that not only was it possible to write this book, but that it was necessary.